MW01069089

IGNITED PASSIONS

"What do you think you're doing?" Amanda demanded furiously when Luke Cameron pulled her out of the moonlight's glow and into the shadows.

"I'm about to teach you some good manners, Miss High-And-Mighty," he said, his blue eyes glinting down at her.

Luke still gripped Amanda's wrist, then encircled her waist with his arms. She felt as if she were surrounded by bands of iron, and she increased her frantic struggles to escape him.

"Let go of me!" she shrieked, ceasing to care now whether she acted like a proper lady or not.

Luke stared down into her stormy, luminous eyes for a brief moment, then brought his hard, demanding lips down upon her own, searing her with the brutal intensity of the action. She continued to struggle wildly against him, but was suddenly halted by peculiar, unfamiliar sensations.

As Luke's lips moved sensuously upon her own, she felt a flame rise—and continue to build . . .

MORE CAPTIVATING HISTORICAL ROMANCES!

SURRENDER TO DESIRE (1503, $3.75)
by Catherine Creel

Raven-haired Marianna came to the Alaskan frontier expecting adventure and fortune and was outraged to learn she was to marry a stranger. But once handsome Donovan clasped her to his hard frame and she felt his enticing kisses, she found herself saying things she didn't mean, making promises she couldn't keep.

TEXAS FLAME (1530, $3.50)
by Catherine Creel

Amanda's journey west through an uncivilized haven of outlaws and Indians leads her to handsome Luke Cameron, as wild and untamed as the land itself, whose burning passion would consume her own!

TEXAS BRIDE (1050, $3.50)
by Catherine Creel

Ravishing Sarah, alone in Wildcat City and unsafe without a man's protection, has no choice but to wed Adam MacShane—in name only. Then Adam, who gave his word of honor not to touch his Yankee wife, swears an oath of passion to claim his TEXAS BRIDE.

SAVAGE ABANDON (1505, $3.95)
by Rochelle Wayne

Chestnut-haired Shelaine, saved by the handsome savage from certain death in the raging river, knew but one way to show her thanks. Though she'd never before known the embrace of a man, one glance at the Indian's rippling muscles made her shiver with a primitive longing, with wild SAVAGE ABANDON.

SURRENDER TO ECSTASY (1307, $3.95)
by Rochelle Wayne

From the moment the soft-voiced stranger entered Amelia's bed all she could think about was the ecstasy of his ardent kisses and the tenderness of his caress. Longing to see his face and learn his name, she had no idea that he hid his identity because the truth could destroy their love!

Available wherever paperbacks are sold, or order direct from the Publisher. Send cover price plus 50¢ per copy for mailing and handling to Zebra Books, 475 Park Avenue South, New York, N.Y. 10016. DO NOT SEND CASH.

TEXAS FLAME

BY CATHERINE CREEL

ZEBRA BOOKS

KENSINGTON PUBLISHING CORP.

ZEBRA BOOKS

are published by

KENSINGTON PUBLISHING CORP.
475 Park Avenue South
New York, N.Y. 10016

Copyright © 1981 by Catherine Creel

All rights reserved. No part of this book may be reproduced
in any form or by any means without the prior written
consent of the Publisher, excepting brief quotes used in
reviews.

Fourth printing: January 1985

Printed in the United States of America

To Gene and Shirley Crow,
who gave me life, and love

One

"I simply refuse to carry out his wishes. I will not go to Texas," Amanda Lawrence interrupted with calm defiance. She fought down the rising waves of bitterness and resentment as she listened to her aunt read the offending letter.

Her father, if one could call him by that honored title, finally wished to make the acquaintance of his only child. After all these years of neglect, the man now decided it was time for the two of them to meet. I will not do it, Amanda declared silently as she dwelt upon thoughts of her father. Nothing whatsoever can force me to travel the distance to that godforsaken place to visit a complete stranger, the man who abandoned me as a child.

"Amanda, my dear, please allow me to finish the reading of your father's letter," her Aunt Martha's high-pitched voice relentlessly continued. "Yes, well, he says that you are to begin the journey no later than the end of this week. The end of this week!" she suddenly exclaimed, her usual composure shaken. "Why, the man must be daft! How can we possibly prepare you for such an extended trip in that unreasonably short time?".

"Aunt Martha, it is really of no concern to me

precisely when he wishes me to come, for I do not intend to go, and that is final. I have no wish to meet him and there is nothing you can say to convince me. You, of all people, should understand my feelings in this matter. To me, my father is a stranger, a man I cannot and do not wish to remember. He obviously hasn't cared about me for all these past years, so why should I now undertake such a journey to meet him?" Amanda said with an apparent tightening of her beautiful features. Care? she thought. Dear Lord, of course he does not care! I cared for nearly nineteen years, but to no avail, so why should I now go to him? Her aunt's voice again broke in on her silent reflections.

"My dear, please listen to me for a few moments. I assure you that I do understand your feelings, but you must also try and understand your father's feelings. Why, we've been over it so many times before. You know the entire story by now. He is, after all, your sire, and it is time you discovered what sort of person is responsible for your existence. Well, halfway responsible, that is," she amended thoughtfully. "You will never forgive yourself if you refuse this opportunity to visit him. I do not know why he chose this particular time to write to you, nor why he waited so very long, but that is beside the point. Now, Amanda, please do not make me ashamed of you. You can at least consider the matter carefully before you give me your answer." Aunt Martha noticed that her niece was getting that obstinate expression in her eyes again.

I don't know why he wrote, either, Amanda told

herself. I have dreamt of and hoped for some word from him for the majority of my life, but it never came. She glanced speculatively over at her silver-haired aunt, sitting so proudly erect. Yes, Aunt Martha, you are simply trying to do your duty by persuading me to go. As much as I care for you and Uncle David, I have long realized just how important such things as honor, duty, and social decorum are to you both.

"Aunt, may we please refrain from any further conversation about this particular issue? I must think over all you have said, but that does not mean that I will change my mind. To please you, however, I will at least consider my alternatives. Now," she suggested, anxious to turn her aunt's thoughts to different channels, "Violet and Mary are probably becoming quite impatient by now. Shouldn't you perhaps go upstairs and help them with their fittings? I know they prefer your opinion over any other when it comes to their attire. I shall remain here in the parlor and quietly consider the letter."

"Yes, of course. Well, those dear girls do depend on me to assist them, especially when they are choosing new ballgowns. Thank you, my dear, for promising to contemplate the matter. Remember, Amanda, you do have a certain duty to your father, no matter what he has done, no matter how shamefully he has neglected you in the past. He is a Lawrence, and he is your father. Please keep that in mind. You must certainly conduct yourself as befits your high station in life. I know I may depend on you to make the right decision. I shall see you later." With that last bit of persuasion, the dainty, graceful figure of her aunt glided smoothly from the room.

Duty. There was that word again. Amanda grimly surveyed the contents of the letter her aunt had placed upon the polished oak table beside the blue velvet-upholstered settee. All of my life, I've been reminded of you, she silently directed toward the letter as she scanned her father's words. Where were you when I needed a parent, one loving adult to hold me, to comfort me, and tell me that I was loved and wanted? Where were you when I grew up observing my friends and their fathers strolling in the park together, laughing simultaneously at some shared secret? Without a mother, I at least could have had a father, couldn't I? Wasn't that my right?

Not that Aunt Martha and Uncle David hadn't been good to her. They had provided her with security and some degree of reserved affection, but it wasn't the same. She was constantly reminded by her two cousins that she was but a guest in their household. Violet and Mary were several years older than she, and they were jealous of her auburn-haired beauty. With their plain and often disagreeable countenances, they had plenty of which to be jealous.

Amanda Lawrence possessed a good deal of spirit, intelligence, and beauty. Her hair was softly highlighted by lighter streaks of gold through its coppery tresses. Her eyes were the deep green color of a pond reflecting its grassy surroundings. Her complexion was flawless, as was her full-breasted, small-waisted figure. Her hips were rounded, her slender legs were long and graceful. Oh yes, her cousins were extremely jealous of their beautiful relative. Here they were, both past twenty-three, forever losing their eligible admirers to the sparkling Amanda.

Amanda's face became pensive, her eyes beginning to brim with unshed tears. She recalled once again the circumstances surrounding her entry into this world. Her handsome, spoiled father and her beautiful, equally cherished mother. The two of them had first met at the theater one evening more than twenty years ago. Her father, at that time, was a young man of twenty-one home from school for the holidays; her mother, at seventeen, was a very popular new addition to Boston society.

In a matter of two weeks, the two of them had publicly declared their love for one another. They became inseparable, their parents well pleased with the match, as they were both wealthy and respectable members of Boston society.

Samuel and Emily shared a special love. For one gloriously happy and passionate year, they were never parted. Then, Emily discovered, to their mutual delight, that she was to bear a child. The forthcoming event was viewed all around with joyful anticipation.

However, something occurred which clouded their happiness and forever intruded into their own special world. Emily's pregnancy was too much of a strain for her. She, who had always been of a healthy and active disposition, now found herself prone to severe headaches, unending nausea, and frequent fainting spells. When she was well into her seventh month, she was finally ordered to bed by her doctor.

Amanda believed that her parents must have sensed what was to follow, must have experienced some feeling of impending doom. People who love as intensely and passionately as they seem to develop a special sense about one another. Amanda was born nearly a month prematurely, and Emily never recovered. Within a few hours of her daughter's birth, she slipped away from this world and out of her husband's desperate grasp.

Samuel refused to acknowledge his tiny daughter's existence, somehow blaming the child for the mother's untimely death. He refused to eat or sleep, remaining in his darkened room for days at a time before allowing his servants entrance. After three weeks of such self-inflicted torture, he made a fateful decision. In his grief, his judgment must have surely been impaired, Amanda told herself tearfully.

Her father strode into the nursery, first laying eyes on his infant daughter, picked up the tiny bundle of humanity, and carried her swiftly across town to the house of his late wife's older sister and her husband. He entered the house without waiting for an answer to the furiously rung bell and strode into the entrance foyer to await the arrival of his sister-in-law.

Martha Jordan swiftly descended the stairs, took in her brother-in-law's haggard appearance, and called for her husband to come immediately. Without further preamble, Samuel thrust his daughter into Martha's surprised and rather unwilling hands and instructed her to take care of the child. He then declared that they would hear from him soon, after which he nearly ran from the house and down the street. That was the last time anyone in Boston had seen Samuel Lawrence.

Over the years, Samuel had erratically sent money and tersely worded messages to Martha, never once asking after his daughter or revealing much of his lifestyle, merely stating that he wished to help carry the financial burden of his child whenever he was able. Not that the Jordans needed his help, as David had also come from a prosperous New England family.

Amanda sat in silent contemplation now, wondering again why her father had unexpectedly, and quite suddenly, written to ask, no, command was a better description, his daughter to come to him out west. Perhaps he regretted his years of neglect, perhaps he was merely curious to see what sort of young woman she had grown to be. Whatever the reason, Amanda vehemently reminded herself, she would not go!

She arose from her seat and shook out her silk skirts. Proceeding into the entrance foyer, she took her bonnet from one of the hall tree's pegs and securely tied it in place upon her curls. She opened the door and stepped outside into the comfortably warm September sunshine. She directed her hurried footsteps toward the park in the center of the town's square, where she had earlier made plans to meet Peter Norman.

She and Peter had been casually courting for the

past six months, but had not yet made the final decision to make a public announcement of their engagement. Amanda smiled as she briskly approached the park's greenery. Poor Peter! Marriage and its subsequent responsibilities appeared to frighten him somewhat, although he had declared to Amanda on several occasions that they would eventually marry. She was in no hurry. She still savored her freedom too much to settle down as a proper young matron just yet. Besides, she was still unsure of her feelings for Peter. She was unable to fathom the extent of those feelings.

"Amanda, dear, over here!" she heard a voice call as she stood searching the grounds for Peter.

"Oh, Peter, there you are. I'm terribly sorry to be so late, but something came up, and I simply could not avoid the delay. Have you been waiting very long?" she inquired apologetically as he rose from the bench, which was situated in a secluded area of the park.

"No, I was a few moments late myself, my dear," he replied, then surprised her as he suddenly drew her into his arms and pulled her closely against him.

"Oh, Peter, not here!" she laughingly protested as she brought her hands up to rest upon his chest, her face becomingly flushed. Secretly, she was delighted with his masterful, romantic actions. Indeed, she had of late been hoping that their rather proper relationship would perhaps become a bit more daring. She had recently found herself dreaming of what it would be like to have Peter kiss her with passionate abandon, to mold her body sensuously against his. But, she would always scold herself most severely at such times, telling herself that she was only being wicked in her thoughts. Now, as Peter stood gazing down into her upturned, expectant features, she bestowed upon him an innocently provocative smile, which served to further embolden him.

Peter brought his lips down upon her own, kissing her with a controlled intensity, but not with the passion she had been hoping for. His warm lips moved gently on hers, and she found herself pressing even closer against him, returning his kiss with a fervor as she experienced a growing fire with his embrace. However, the fire was very faint, not at all the earth-shattering rapture of which she had dreamt. Peter's kisses were very pleasant, even enjoyable, but not the sort she really yearned for in the deepest recesses of her heart. She silently chided herself for being foolish, telling herself that Peter was everything a young lady could possibly want, that she was dreaming of an unknown something which in all likelihood did not even exist, or which only existed in the minds of silly old maids!

As soon as he had released her, Peter smiled and remarked, "Here, sit down and tell me what it was that delayed you, Amanda. I must say, it does appear as if your eyes reflect some inner turmoil," he teased lightly. She raised her face to his and observed his smiling countenance.

Dear Peter, she thought. His light brown hair waved across his aristocratic forehead, his brown eyes small yet impressive. Not exactly a handsome face, but an attractive one. He was of medium height and slender build, but he still managed to top her by several inches. She was nearly five feet, four inches tall.

"Peter, I do have a rather pressing problem. Sit down, please, while I tell you about it. My father has written to my aunt, and he wishes me to visit him."

"Is that all that has you looking so concerned? Amanda, isn't this exactly what you've always wanted—to meet your father? Why, this appears to be the perfect opportunity. When will you be leaving?"

Amanda gazed at his smiling face in surprise.

"Peter, not you, too! I do not wish to go and visit my father! Can't you understand? I've told you the whole story. He abandoned me, he hasn't cared anything about me for the past nineteen years, so why should I visit him? If he wanted to see me all that badly, he could have come here to Boston, couldn't he?" she insisted.

"My dear Amanda, why are you behaving this way? Come, come, my dear, it can't be all that dreadful. You merely visit him for a short while, then return here and into my loving embrace. I can manage to live without you for a few weeks if I have to!" he admonished her cheerfully.

"Oh, you! I do not want to go, Peter, and I cannot conceive why you are being as stuffy as my aunt about this matter! I would have liked it very much if you had lent me your support in this. Perhaps if you tell Aunt Martha that you do not wish for me to go, then she will reconsider. I hate to disappoint her, you know. She and Uncle David have been so good to me. Besides, I haven't even told you where my father is," she finished with a challenging lift of her upturned little nose.

"Very well, if you believe it will make that much difference, where is he?" Peter demanded, becoming annoyed with her behavior.

"He is in Texas! It is bad enough that he commands me to visit him, but he wants me to travel all the way to that savage wilderness! Peter, won't you please help me persuade Aunt Martha that I shouldn't go? She insists that it is my duty."

"She is perfectly right, you know," he stated, almost pompously. "You cannot very well ignore a summons from your own father. After all, he is a Lawrence. Even though all of the Lawrences moved away from Boston before you were born, you do owe them a certain allegiance, don't you see? Make me proud of you, Amanda dear, and go to see your father," he coaxed.

Amanda stared at him with growing resentment and a sense of betrayal. Her eyes widened at his traitorous words and she wondered, for the first time, how she could have become involved with such a pompous young man. It wasn't as if she hadn't always had a myriad of admirers. No, it was just that she had always felt comfortable around Peter. And he used to be so amusing.

"Peter, do you actually agree with Aunt Martha? You actually believe that I owe any loyalty at all to a man who deserted me, who abandoned his only child, who has never seen fit to visit or even write to me? I suppose I should have expected such from

17

you, Peter Norman! How could you!" she stormed at him, keeping her voice low and furious.

"I cannot understand why you are behaving so childishly, Amanda," he reproved her. "I know you have been taught better manners than this! Why, you must know in your heart that it is only proper for you to do as your father wishes. I would most certainly never disobey my parents!" he insisted.

"Well, I am most certainly relieved that I found out precisely how much backbone you possess now, Mr. Norman! I take that to mean that you would also not go against any of your parents' wishes as far as I am concerned?" she stonily inquired, rising swiftly to her feet beside him.

"Amanda, that isn't fair, and you know it! My parents wholeheartedly approve of our relationship, and they will welcome you into the family with open arms, when the time comes. Now, will you quit behaving so abominably, and sit down? You are beginning to attract attention," he whispered angrily.

"I do not care!" she hissed as she stood once more, shaking off his restraining hand upon her arm. "You have opened my eyes, Peter, and I am very glad indeed! Now, I will say goodbye to you, sir!" She whirled away from him and marched back the way she had come earlier.

Oh, Peter, she lamented silently. Just when I needed you to be supportive and understanding, you become like all the rest. So proper and dutiful. So very respectable and inflexible. She realized that she had never really known Peter at all. They

18

had never participated in any soul-searching discussions between themselves, but she still felt betrayed. I don't know you at all, Peter. And you don't know me.

I've never truly fit in, she told herself. I've never quite lived up to my family's expectations, have I? Oh, I've allowed myself to be dressed and educated properly, I've behaved politely, but there must be something deep within my very being which prevents me from believing everything my aunt has endeavored to instill in me. If I only knew more about my parents, I could possibly ascertain from which one I received certain inner characteristics. However, that was a subject which Aunt Martha and Uncle David refused to discuss. I've learned very little about Samuel and Emily Lawrence, she thought with a sigh.

Compose yourself, she commanded herself inwardly. You must send round a note to Peter in the morning, apologizing for your rash behavior, but letting him know, nonetheless, that you think it best he does not come to call on you for a while.

He doesn't really care for me at all, she thought. How could he care and completely refuse to see my side of this situation? Perhaps he hopes that I will go out to Texas, that maybe I will decide to stay and live with my father. Oh, stop it, she ordered herself sternly as she reached her aunt and uncle's brownstone house. I can't think about it all now. I must have time.

She entered the house and quickly climbed the stairs to her bedroom, locking the door behind her. She removed her bonnet and approached the full-

19

length mirror of her tall wardrobe.

She slowly appraised her appearance, noting her heightened color and creased forehead. Aunt Martha says not to frown, that it will cause premature wrinkles, she suddenly remembered. Oh, who cares? she thought rebelliously.

Amanda suddenly wondered if she favored her father at all. Aunt Martha had once revealed that her father also had red hair and green eyes. Her mother had been a petite brunette. Well, I may have his hair and eyes, she reflected, but I wonder if there is anything else about us that is similar.

She undressed and began her preparations for dinner. Dinner was always a formal affair. Violet and Mary would question her about her father's letter, she was sure, since she knew that her aunt would have informed them of its arrival and contents. They would certainly press her to go. And, Uncle David would also state his unoriginal opinion, which she knew would predictably parallel his wife's. It seemed that everyone would wish for her to go. Everyone except herself, she wryly amended.

Heaving a rather desperate little sigh, she opened her door and began descending the stairs for dinner. Violet and Mary were also going down for dinner at that moment, and the two of them turned and waited for her at the foot of the stairs.

"Amanda, it seems that we are going to be denied your presence around here for a while," Violet teased in her perpetually whining voice.

"Yes, Mama says that you will be going to Texas, of all places," chimed in Mary.

Amanda noted their pleased expressions: Violet, with frazzled blonde hair piled atop a too-thin head, and Mary with dark curls dangling on either side of her plump face.

"Oh, I can see that you know about the letter, then. Well, I haven't quite made up my mind just yet," she informed them politely, secretly wishing she could somehow erase the knowing smirks from their faces.

"Mama insists that you will go, dear cousin. I know that you will want to please dear Mama, after all she has done for you," Violet insisted.

Amanda refrained from issuing an adequate rejoinder to their insinuations and proceeded into the dining room, where her aunt and uncle were patiently awaiting their arrival.

"Amanda dear, your aunt tells me that you will be leaving us soon, to pay a visit to your father. In Texas, did you say, Martha, dear?" he asked, turning to his wife.

"Yes, dear, in Texas. Amanda, I knew you would want the entire family to know about the letter and your father's invitation. You have seriously considered your answer, haven't you, dear?" she probed.

"Aunt Martha," she began, knowing it was hopeless for her to argue.

"Yes, well, we have an awful lot to do before the end of the week, haven't we, Amanda? Now, come and sit down for dinner, then we'll go upstairs and begin planning what you will take with you afterwards. Was there anything you wished to say?" she inquired coolly as she allowed her husband to pull the chair out for her to be seated at the long table.

Amanda realized that it was useless for her to try and prevent what was happening. It seemed that everyone was in complete accordance. Uncle David would never dream of overruling his wife's wishes, her cousins could barely contain their happiness at her impending departure, and even Peter wanted her to go. She felt even more bitterness toward the culprit of the whole affair, her father.

Very well, she told herself as she faced her aunt's expectant face. I have no desire to remain here when it is clear that I am no longer wanted on the premises. She fought down the rising tears and managed to excuse herself from the table, declaring that she felt a headache coming on. She fled from the room and hurriedly climbed the steps to the sanctuary of her room, where she flung herself face-down upon the bed and sobbed out her torment into her unresisting pillow.

Two

"Amanda, please make sure that you conduct yourself with poise and dignity during your journey. And, dear, absolutely do not speak to any strangers, particularly men!" her aunt cautioned her again.

"Don't worry, Aunt Martha, I'll follow your many instructions. Goodbye, Uncle David. Goodbye, cousins. Goodbye, Aunt Martha!" she dutifully repeated. She was speaking to them through the open window of the train coach. The train was due to leave any moment, and she realized that she would not see her relatives, Peter, or Boston again for at least two months. She suddenly experienced a wave of longing and homesickness.

Peter had not come down to the station to see her off, and she was unexpectedly hurt by his absence. She had sent round a note the morning following their disagreement, but had received a reply from his mother that he would be away for the remainder of the week. She thought that she had ceased to care about him, but she was nevertheless hurt when he did not arrive at the station. He couldn't even wait to see if I were truly going, she thought resentfully.

"Goodbye, dear. Say hello to your father for us. Tell him that he is always welcome at our house, should he decide to return with you for a visit!" her aunt called out as the train began slowly edging out of the station.

"Yes, I will. Goodbye!" she answered above the noise.

She had packed ample clothing for the journey, taking along both winter and lighter clothing, not knowing anything at all about the weather in Texas. Her father had not thought to include any information in his letter about what she was to bring with her, so she and her aunt had feverishly collected and packed her various things the few days before her departure.

Amanda leaned back against the straight-backed seat and gazed out the window, watching as the green hills and trees rolled slowly past. The clickety-clack of the train's wheels as they made contact with iron rails below had a soothing effect upon her nerves.

She had said her reluctant goodbyes to her friends yesterday, promising to write the closest among them. She had informed them that she planned to be gone only a short time, the two months which her father had specifically requested that she stay with him. At least it will give me time to review my confused feelings for Peter, she told herself staunchly. Maybe a little absence will help both our hearts grow a bit fonder.

Not that she was madly in love with him, either. No, she knew she was unable to comprehend exactly what the word meant. Love was seldom mentioned in her aunt's household. A young woman's duty was to marry and raise children, to take her place in society, not to fall in love. The only reason Violet and Mary were not yet married was because of their sour dispositions, although they did so like to blame their lack of suitors on their cousin. However, with their breeding and fortune, Amanda was quite sure that her resourceful aunt would eventually find them husbands.

She would be remaining aboard the train until it reached a city by the name of Fort Worth, where she would then transfer to the stagecoach line. Her father had sent specific instructions as to her travel, which Uncle David had then arranged. She would be living on the train for a period of several days, and she viewed such a prospect with displeasure. Once she boarded the stage, it would still take another two or three days, providing there was fair weather.

Here it is 1878, and I am forced to travel under primitive conditions once I reach this remote state of Texas. Texas. She had heard it described as an uncivilized haven for outlaws and Indians. She had heard tales of the brutality of the untamed land. Tales of wild men, wild Indians, and wild animals. And, the name of the town where her father would meet the stage: Big Prairie. Even the name sounds wild, she silently complained.

She gave herself up to thoughts of her father and the wilderness to which she was now unwillingly traveling. Just living in Texas wasn't enough for Samuel Lawrence; oh no, he had to choose west Texas, a land of cowboys and sagebrush.

"Miss, may I see your ticket please?" the conductor politely asked her.

"Yes, of course," she replied, handing him the ticket.

"Thank you, Miss Lawrence. Your uncle instructed me to look after you. I hope you have a pleasant journey, and if there is anything you require, anything at all, please do no hesitate to ask me or one of the stewards."

"Yes, thank you." That's just like Uncle David, she thought with a small degree of amusement. Always using his importance.

She picked up a book that she had included in her traveling bag as an afterthought and opened its pages. *Jane Eyre* the cover read. She had read it several times before, yet she never wearied of its romantic story. If only life could be so, she sighed.

Five days later, she finally viewed the city of Fort Worth as the train pulled into the busy station. She was weary of being confined to the small area on the train, and she gratefully stepped down from the steps as soon as it came to a complete halt.

She felt dusty and tired, yet she was anxious to contact the stagecoach line and make the arrangements to be on her way. She instructed the porter to store her luggage inside the station for the time being, then set off in the direction he had indicated.

So, this is Texas, she thought, thoroughly disappointed. She hadn't seen much of it from the train, as they had gone through most of the state during the night. She viewed the unpaved streets, the wooden buildings, and hoped that all of Texas was not represented here in this one ramshackle place.

Pausing for a moment, she smoothed her heavy silk traveling suit. Its blue folds had become quite creased and dusty. She straightened her matching bonnet and wiggled her hips slightly to shake out her fashionable bustle. Her high-topped shoes had already become soiled along the dirty streets and she found herself fervently wishing for a hot bath.

Suddenly, her thoughts were interrupted by what sounded like a man's whistle. She whirled about to observe several men standing across the street, unabashedly appraising her figure as she swept past. She straightened her back, lifted her chin a bit higher, then stiffly continued upon her way.

Uncouth savages, she silently raged. No man had ever dared treat her as those men had just done. She dismissed them from her mind, telling herself that they were certainly not worth the effort of any extra thought.

As she strolled along the street toward the stage office, she became aware of many curious and admiring stares as she walked. She didn't see many other women, and the ones she had observed were dressed in anything but the latest fashion. Most of them wore what appeared to be homespun dresses and heavy boots. The men, she noted, wore equally drab attire. Dirty felt hats, flannel shirts that were stained and dirty, and some sort of peculiar, baggy trousers. Their boots were pointed slightly at the ends. Along the streets, she noticed that there were a few signs, and hitching posts to which were tied many horses impatiently pawing at the ground.

Well, she thought, most of the people here in this strange place appear to be much more in need of a bath than I could ever be!

It was getting rather late in the afternoon and she quickened her steps, finally arriving at her destination, the stage office. She stepped inside and inquired of the clerk behind the tall counter when the next stage would be leaving for Big Prairie.

"Well, now, ma'am, that won't be till tomorrow morning, at seven o'clock sharp. You'd best get yourself a room for the night and rest up a bit for the trip," he replied. She observed that he was absorbed in curiously eyeing her bonnet and dress.

"Tomorrow morning? Oh, very well. My name is Amanda Lawrence, and I believe my uncle has already booked passage for me, for an approximate date, of course. Could you please recommend a good hotel for me?" She didn't approve of the way the man was staring at her. She could feel herself blushing, but pulled herself even more rigidly erect.

"Uh, excuse me, ma'am," the clerk said, "I didn't mean to be impolite or nothing. It's just that that there dress and hat you're wearing ain't exactly what I'd recommend for riding the stage. You better get something a bit more practical, ma'am. I seen several women come out here wearing fancy duds like yours, but they don't last long. Pretty soon, they're wearing what every other woman hereabouts is wearing. I recommend

Swenson's store just down the street there," he suggested helpfully, pointing north. "And, as for a hotel, well, let me see—I'd say that the Bentley is about the nicest in town."

Amanda's green eyes flashed at his words concerning her attire, but she decided not to chastise him for his impudence. After all, she told herself, I must behave like the lady I am.

"Thank you, my good man," she informed him icily. She turned and gracefully left the office. Her aunt was right; she'd certainly have to keep to herself out here. The people appeared to have no sense of propriety.

Reaching the hotel the man had recommended, she strolled inside to register. Approaching the unpolished front desk, she observed that the hotel was far from luxurious; in fact, it was barely passable at all. She rang the bell on the counter.

"Yes, ma'am. What may I do for you?" the man behind the desk inquired as he eyed her curiously.

"I'd like a room for the night, please. I also would like a hot bath, and I need someone sent over to the train station for my luggage."

"Certainly, ma'am. Just one night? Yes, well, sign here, ma'am. I'll send a boy over for your bags right away. One moment, please," he told her politely. His hotel rarely received such beautiful and quality clientele.

As Amanda stood patiently waiting at the desk, a tall young man suddenly approached her and tapped her on the shoulder. She turned and glared at the man's insolent gesture.

"Pardon me, little lady, but you staying here all

by yourself? You see, me and my buddies are here for a few days on some business for our boss, and well, I figured you looked like you might like some company," he stated with supreme self-confidence.

"How dare you! It appears that you are sadly mistaken in your judge of character, sir! I neither require, nor wish for, any of your companionship! Now, if you will not cease to accost me this very moment, I shall call for someone to throw you out of this establishment!" she nearly shouted at him, her composure very nearly shaken. The nerve of the young man!

"Sorry, ma'am. You sure don't know what you're missing, though," he said, comically sorrowful at her words. At that precise moment, his companions spotted him and rushed over to lay hands upon the hapless fellow.

"Was he bothering you, young lady?" one of the other men asked her, concern written all over his kindly features.

"Sorry, ma'am, but old Tom has had a few too many this evening. I'm right sorry if he bothered you, ma'am. We'll take care of him, don't you worry," another one said. He and his companions ushered the offender away none too gently, berating him all the way for daring to talk to a real, genuine lady at all. In Texas, women were generally regarded as supreme goddesses, whose place was upon a much-worshipped pedestal. However, occasionally, a few of the inhabitants of the state failed to see eye to eye with this general description of sacred womanhood.

Amanda turned back to face the man behind the

desk, who was now speaking to her.

"Ma'am, let's see," he paused, noting her signature on the register. "Miss Lawrence, you're in room 29, just to the left at the top of the stairs. I'll have your bags sent in to you as soon as the boy gets back with them. Oh, and the bathroom is at the end of the hall."

"Yes, thank you," she replied absently. She took the key he handed her and wearily climbed the stairs to her room.

She had never been approached by a man before, certainly not as boldly and offensively as the young man downstairs had done. What sort of strange place was this Texas? Back in Boston, no man would have dared consider approaching her before a formal introduction had been made.

The next morning, she awoke shortly after dawn and slowly stretched her tired, aching muscles. She dressed, choosing a plainer dress than the one she had worn yesterday on the train. She also donned a less extravagant bonnet, although it was equally fashionable as the other. She surveyed herself in the single mirror at the dressing table. Strange, she mused, I didn't see any women yesterday wearing bustles. Oh well, perhaps the fashion hasn't reached here yet. After all, this was out in the middle of nowhere!

She packed her bags once again and proceeded downstairs where she instructed the porter to bring her bags to the lobby. Then, she entered the restaurant adjoining the hotel and sat down to have breakfast.

After a leisurely meal, she left the hotel and

headed for the stage office, arriving nearly fifteen minutes before the stagecoach was due to depart.

"Miss Lawrence, good morning. You all ready to go?" the clerk asked her.

"Yes, I am ready. That is, if you'll send someone to the hotel for my luggage. How soon will we be leaving?"

"Well, they're getting set to go right now. Should be another ten minutes or so, though. I'll hurry over to the hotel and get your bags myself. You just sit right down there and make yourself comfortable," he said as he left the office.

Nearly thirty minutes later, the stage was finally ready to leave. Amanda was helped up by the clerk and settled herself as comfortably as possible inside the cramped space of the coach. She was to be the only passenger, it seemed.

The day was clear and a bit warm. She removed her small cape and took off her bonnet. The stagecoach was very dusty and breezy, and she could not get situated in a comfortable position as it rocked and jolted along. She finally gave up and endeavored to adjust her body and her bustle to the coach's movements. She rolled down the flaps on the doors in order to shut out some of the sun's rays and the shadow of dust.

At the end of the first bone-wearying day, the stagecoach halted at a way station some ninety miles from Fort Worth, where they were to spend the night. Amanda required assistance in stepping down from the coach, she was so bruised and exhausted. She wanted nothing more than some hot food and then sleep. She hadn't even been able to view much of the countryside, since she had kept the flaps down throughout most of the day's journey.

She trudged inside the station and was immediately greeted by the caretaker and his friendly, robust wife.

"Howdy there, child," the woman said. "You just sit yourself down right there and I'll fetch you some vittles." She bustled back into the kitchen, only to return a few moments later with a stew and some boiling hot coffee.

Amanda was much too tired to notice what she ate or drank. She finished her meal as quickly as possible and then was led to a back room, where she would spend the night sleeping on a hard, narrow cot. However, she ceased to care what sort of accommodations she had been offered as soon as her head hit the hard, unrelenting pillow.

The next morning, she was awakened by the aroma of frying bacon and brewing coffee. She achingly rose and managed to dress, then tidied her unruly hair and washed her face and hands at the bowl and pitcher she had been provided. She then approached the kitchen and inquired of the caretaker's wife where she might find the "convenience."

"The 'convenience'? Why, honey, you must mean the privy! Why, that's right out back there. Just follow the path. You sure can't miss it!" she said with an amused chuckle.

Amanda blushed and followed the woman's directions. When she returned inside, she ate her hearty breakfast with the stagecoach drivers and then gathered her things once more. She thanked the woman courteously for the meals and boarded the coach.

This time, she left the flaps rolled up for the majority of the trip. She was able to observe the rolling hills and the disappearing trees. She noted that the countryside was rapidly changing from a green, hilly land, to a dusty, flatter, sparsely relieved landscape. There were seas of high grass waving in the strong breeze. So, this is west Texas, she thought.

Surprisingly enough, she had come all this way and hadn't yet seen an Indian, nor much of cowboys or the wild animals she had so frequently heard about. She was becoming more and more curious about this unusual state. What on earth could have persuaded her father to settle way out here?

Later that evening, they again stopped for the night. The routine of the first night was followed, and Amanda knew that the next day would see her in Big Prairie, where she would finally come face to face with her father. The trip had seemed almost endless at times, but she had in truth suffered litle hardship. Except for the stagecoach ride, her trip had been almost pleasant.

Her muscles still ached in a million places and she felt as if most of the dirt from miles around had attached itself to her person. She climbed onto her cot that night and was soon sleeping the dreamless sleep of sheer exhaustion.

When the stage actually pulled into Big Prairie the following afternoon, Amanda could barely contain her growing anxiety. As the stage slowed to a halt, she flung open the door and stepped down without waiting for assistance. She shook out her skirts and tied her bonnet back in place on her head. She glanced about at the town.

There was apparently only one main street, she reflected, since there didn't seem to be any other streets at all! There was a livery stable, a dry goods store, a hotel, and other buildings she couldn't quite identify at this distance. There were several wooden buildings with faded signs which she was unable to read. There were no sidewalks whatsoever, and there were the eternal hitching posts in front of nearly every establishment. Not very impressive, she thought. Not very impressive at all. Oh Aunt Martha, why did you insist upon my coming? Why did I listen to any of you at all?

A deep, resonant voice abruptly cut in upon her thoughts.

"Amanda Lawrence?"

She turned slowly to face the owner of the voice, catching her breath in anticipation and dread. The man who now stood before her was well over six feet tall, but he looked even more gigantic with his tall felt hat on as well. He had bright red hair, a reddish moustache to match, and hazel eyes. He appeared to be somewhere in the vicinity of forty-five years of age. Amanda knew with a certainty that she at long last faced her father.

"Are you Amanda?" he repeated, waiting almost impatiently for her answer.

"Yes, I am Amanda Lawrence," she replied as she recovered her voice and composure.

"Well, I'm your father, Samuel Lawrence," he stated simply, as if it were the most natural thing in the world for her to be standing in this wilderness, facing an absolute stranger who was calmly stating that he was her father!

"Yes, I surmised who you were, sir. I knew that you were expecting me," she declared, somewhat stiffly.

Samuel Lawrence took in his daughter's appearance in a glance. She was a beauty, her proud bearing very much like her mother's. Damn her! Why did she have to remind him of Emily?

"Well, I'll gather up your bags. You go on over there to that wagon and I'll be along in a moment," he told her, not waiting for a reply, but merely striding over to the stagecoach and catching the bags as the driver threw them down.

Amanda decided to do as he bid and slowly crossed the street, noting as she did so that there were not very many people about. Without waiting for her father to follow, she climbed up on to the wagon with some difficulty, finally settling herself upon the hard wooden seat.

He doesn't appear very pleased to see me, she thought with no small degree of annoyance. It isn't as if I made this trip without his knowledge or consent! Perhaps he has by now realized that this whole thing is a dreadful mistake, that I should not have been asked to come.

She straightened her back and stared proudly ahead as her father approached with her bags. He tossed them into the wagon bed, then deftly climbed up beside her on the seat. At a gentle flick of the reins, the horses moved forward, causing the wagon to jolt abruptly. Amanda was forced to clutch the sides of the wagon seat in order to keep from falling backwards into the wagon bed.

Oh, what foolish thing have I done in coming here? she silently lamented.

Three

Amanda and her father rode along in uncomfortable silence. She was frequently forced to clutch the sides of the wagon seat for support as the wooden wheels bounced in and out of the myriad ruts and cracks in the dirt road. After enduring several miles without speaking, Amanda finally attempted to break through her father's reserve.

"Pardon me, sir," she began tentatively, yet confidently, "but, how far is it to the ranch?"

"Oh, I'd say another five miles from here," he replied, glancing at the surrounding countryside. "We ought to reach it well before nightfall. And, Amanda," he then said, turning a displeased countenance in her direction for the fraction of a second, "I am, after all, your father. That is a fact that neither of us can change. I would deem it a great 'honor' if you would either call me Sam or Samuel, since it appears that you cannot muster the correct term." With this terse command delivered, he once more turned his full attention to driving the creaking, jolting wagon.

"Very well, Samuel," she countered frostily. So far, there had been no trace of warmth or even civility in her father's demeanor, and she regretted anew her acquiescence in coming.

Samuel experienced a small twinge of guilt for his attitude toward this daughter he had not seen in so many years. Why does she have to resemble Emily so much? he asked himself painfully, the old grief returning to wash over him once more. Damn it, this isn't easy for me. It's been all I could do to try and live with Emily's death all these years, to try and forget the torment and void her passing caused. But, Amanda would understand none of these things. Judging from what he had already observed, she appeared to possess none of her mother's warmth or spirit. Maybe I'm being too quick to form that opinion just yet, he reminded himself. Regardless of anything else, though, this is going to be a hell of an ordeal, he thought grimly.

He could at least speak to me, Amanda seethed inwardly. He could say how glad he was that I've come all this way to visit him, that we've finally met. He could say that I've grown up to be quite a lady, or something like that. Why in heaven's name did he ask me to come if he didn't want to see me?

Amanda took a deep breath and once more bravely attempted conversation, vowing to herself that she would at least discover something about this strange territory.

"The town certainly did not appear to be very large. How many people live there?"

"Well, there's very nearly three hundred people round and about here now. And, for your information, young lady, Big Prairie is one of the few real towns for miles around, so you'll eventually come to appreciate it a bit more. I know it doesn't look like much to you, seeing as how you're used to the luxury of a big city like Boston, but it suits folks around here just fine. We have nothing to be ashamed of, that's for sure," he replied, almost defensively. You can certainly tell she's been raised by Martha, he reflected dourly. Martha's a good woman at heart, but she's got uppity ideas and notions. Seems that Amanda is going to behave just like her.

Amanda bit back an angry retort at her father's slightly condemning words and once again lapsed into thoughtful, unhappy silence. Neither of them attempted to speak again, and they finally reached the ranch.

"This is it, Amanda. We call it the Circle L Ranch."

Amanda climbed slowly down from the wagon, assisted by her father's firm hand upon her elbow. She stood gazing at the unfamiliar surroundings, the setting sun casting a rosy glow over the ranch's various buildings.

"That over there is the corral, the bunkhouse, and the barn, but I'll show you all that tomorrow. Come on, we'll go on into the house now." He took her by the arm and led her to the steps of a two-story frame house, which looked surprisingly attractive to Amanda's eyes. She noted that there were several men peering curiously at her as she was escorted inside. They must work for my father, she surmised as she stole a glance at their faces across the distance of the front yard. Turning back to the house, she decided that all it needed to look very grand was a new coat of paint.

Once inside the house, Amanda nearly gasped aloud at the unexpected finery. There were several brightly patterned rugs scattered about the fine, polished wooden floors. The furniture she spied looked well worn, but expensive and stylish. There were beautiful paintings adorning the richly panelled walls. Her father ushered her into a brightly lit room and motioned for her to be seated upon a cushiony blue sofa.

She gratefully sank down into its soft depths and gazed about the room, still in awe at the furnishings of the "simple ranch house."

"I can see that you're somewhat surprised at my house, Amanda," Samuel remarked with a small twitch of amusement tugging at the corners of his mouth. "You see, we are not all the savages you probably thought us to be. Actually, this particular type of house is rather uncommon for this part of the country, but I suppose I still wanted to be reminded of my childhood, at least somewhat. I collected most of the furnishings while on my various journeys to different parts of the world. I had a hell of a time getting most of it out here, but I worked at it for quite a while. What you see before you is the result of several years of work and a lot of patience. I'm sure you never expected anything like this, did you? No, I'm quite sure your Aunt Martha prepared you for nothing other than a simple cowhand."

"On the contrary," broke in Amanda, just as he had finished speaking, "she never prepared me for

41

anything about you at all. Why, I know very little about you. I know very little about my mother, either, for that matter."

At her words, Samuel suppressed an involuntary grimace of pain. It seemed that every time she was to speak of Emily, he would experience the same pain. Amanda observed his tightened pose and wondered what she could have said to cause such a reaction.

"My housekeeper will show you to your room," Samuel said, changing the subject and effectively cutting off any communication that might have developed between them at that time.

He strode to the doorway and called for the housekeeper, who shortly appeared and approached Amanda with a welcoming smile, the first show of warmth Amanda had seen since arriving in Texas.

She noted that the woman appeared to be middle-aged, her dark brown hair streaked with gray. She was tall and rather plump, but her features were kind and warm.

"You must be Amanda. Me and my John's been waiting out in the kitchen till your pa called for us. John's gone to fetch some more firewood for the stove, but he'll be back by the time you come down for supper. I've been mighty anxious to meet you, honey," she declared, enveloping the slightly reserved Amanda in a comforting hug.

"You come on along with me, now. I'll fix you up with a room. Oh, I plumb forgot to tell you my name. I'm Mrs. Chambers, and my John, my husband, that is, is your pa's foreman, so to speak.

Come on along, child." This amazing woman led Amanda out of the room and up the curving staircase. They stopped before an elegant closed door, which the housekeeper proceeded to throw open with a flourish.

"Well, this is it, Amanda. I hope you don't mind me calling you by your given name, do you, honey? Well, there's the pitcher and bowl over there. I'll leave you to freshen up while I get dinner on the table, all right?" Without waiting for an answer, the friendly woman left the room, leaving Amanda alone to survey the room and to ponder her father's unexpected lifestyle.

Walking over to the open window of the room, Amanda peered downward and observed several of her father's ranchhands about the yard. She wondered if she would be forced to endure the presence of so many strangers at dinner. She turned away and washed her face in the tepid water she poured from the heavy porcelain pitcher. Then, straightening her windblown curls and giving a last pat to her wrinkled dress, she opened the door and went downstairs for the evening meal.

She found her father still in the room where she had left him. He immediately rose from his seat and came out into the hallway to take her arm and escort her into the dining room.

Here again was unexpected luxury. The long, gleaming table was of polished oak, the high-backed chairs were elaborately carved and cushioned with red velvet. Mrs. Chambers entered through an open door, carrying a large dish of steaming hot soup.

"I thought we'd do it up kind of fancy on your first night here, Amanda, honey. Of course, we didn't right know exactly when you'd finally get here, so I been cooking real good for your pa all week long! Mr. Lawrence, you two go ahead and sit down. You don't want any of this good food getting cold, now, do you?"

Dinner was also a silent affair. Mrs. Chambers served them the various courses of vegetable soup, fried steaks, boiled potatoes, snap beans, and hot coffee and apple cake for dessert. Amanda thanked her quite sincerely afterward, while her father absently murmured his approval, obviously thinking of something other than the delicious meal. He and Amanda returned to the parlor.

"Amanda, I know that life here will seem rather strange to you at first. Tomorrow morning, I'll take you on a tour of the ranch, then we'll ride out to the range and I'll show you around a bit out there. You do know how to ride, don't you?" he challenged her.

"Of course I know how to ride, sir," she retorted proudly.

"You will call me by my given name, Amanda," he calmly reminded her.

"Yes, of course, Samuel," she replied with surface politeness. He's treating me like a child, she thought fiercely. I'll show him that I am also a Lawrence, and quite grown up!

"Yes, well, I'll also introduce you to the hands after the ride tomorrow. They won't be back here till lunchtime, anyway. You may go on up to bed now. You will need to rest up after the long trip you've had. I'm sure you're quite exhausted."

"Thank you for your concern. Good night." She gracefully exited the room and climbed the stairs to her room, wishing she had possessed the courage to ask her father why he had invited her to visit him, why he had then behaved as if he was sorry he had.

As she undressed for bed, she reflected upon her ill fortune in possessing a father who not only had abandoned his daughter as a child, but who now appeared to find it exceedingly difficult to endure her very presence. She slipped the white lawn nightgown over her head and turned out the lamp beside the bed. She then climbed up into the large four-poster bed and quickly drifted off into a troubled sleep.

Shortly after dawn, she was awakened by the sound of male voices and whinnying, snorting horses. She jumped out of bed and hurried barefoot over to the window. She looked down on the flurry of activity below.

There were about a dozen men, most of them young, saddling and mounting their horses. She observed them as they joked and laughed with one another, then mounted and applied their spurs to the beautiful, spirited animals. She left the window and hastily struggled into her clothes, anxious to ask Mrs. Chambers about the scene she had just witnessed. Yes, she thought with amusement, Mrs. Chambers probably knows about everything that occurs around here.

She found the robust housekeeper in the dining

room, as well as a hot, hearty breakfast waiting on the table.

"Amanda, glad to see you're finally up. I thought it best to let you sleep in a little longer this first morning. Sit down and eat your breakfast before it gets cold, child."

"Mrs. Chambers, I am not a child, you know," she coolly informed the woman.

"Oh, I know that," she replied, refusing to take offense at Amanda's words, "but it's just that I always wished I could have had a daughter of my own, and I almost feel that I know you. Why, your pa has spoken of you quite a bit. Oh, that reminds me. He said to tell you that he'll be back shortly and then he'll see about that tour and ride he promised you."

"You mean he's already up and gone somewhere?" Amanda replied conversationally, already regretting her rather harsh words to this kind woman.

"He and the hands were going on out to round up a few head of cattle for some branding. There's always something going on around here, you'll soon find out. If it isn't cattle, it's them horses. And, if it ain't either of them, why, it's something else. Here now, have some of these eggs and biscuits. We got to put a little meat on your bones, honey," she said good-naturedly. Yes, she said to herself, it's just like her pa said. She's certainly been raised by a prissy aunt. But, all she needs is a little time and love, and I know she'll respond. She just ain't got it in her to be like that aunt of hers. I know she ain't.

"Mrs. Chambers," Amanda managed to say between bites, conscious of the housekeeper's scrutiny, "how long have you and your husband worked for my father?"

"Well, let's see now. I guess it's been nigh on to ten years now. Your pa's a right good man, Amanda. I've always thought it was a shame you two didn't get the chance to know one another. I'm glad he finally decided to write and invite you to come."

"Why did he invite me? He doesn't seem to enjoy my company," Amanda couldn't refrain from responding.

"Well, it's going to take some time for you two to get used to one another, that's all. Why, Amanda, your pa's wondered about you for a long time, wondered about what sort of young woman you grew up to be. I guess he finally figured it was time to find out. I can't rightly answer for him, but you can sure enough ask him yourself."

"No, I do not feel that I can do that. You see, I really know so very little about him. I don't suppose it matters, though. I won't be staying here very long."

Mrs. Chambers didn't reply, preferring to let the matter ride and allow Amanda time to adjust to her father's ways.

Finishing her breakfast, Amanda returned upstairs and donned her riding habit. Facing her reflection in the tall, beveled mirror, she smiled with approval at her neat appearance. The long, black silk skirt, the creamy white blouse, the soft leather boots, the tall, matching black hat. Yes, perhaps Samuel will at least find no fault with my appearance, she thought with satisfaction.

"Amanda!" she heard him calling. She smoothly descended the stairs, halting at the foot of the staircase to await his response.

"Are you ready, Amanda?" he started to ask, then stopped to stare at her.

"Yes, I'm ready."

"What in blue blazes are you so dressed up for, will you please tell me?" he demanded.

"I am wearing a riding habit. You know very well that ladies wear riding habits when they ride," she calmly explained.

"Not out here, they don't," he protested gruffly.

"Well, then," she inquired politely, "what do they wear when they go riding?"

"Hell, I don't know! I suppose they wear an old skirt or something. I do know that they don't wear such fancy outfits as that one you've got on now!"

"Very well, would you like for me to change?" she suggested, refraining from entering into an argument with him. She did not intend to start off their first complete day together with a silly disagreement!

"Never mind. I'll have Mrs. Chambers help you select something a bit more suitable after today. Come on, you might as well wear it now that you've got it on." He turned on his booted heel and stomped out the front door. She gathered up her heavy skirts and followed at a more sedate pace.

"I told you that I'd take you on a tour of the ranch. Well, that's the cookshack and bunkhouse. That's where all the hands eat and sleep. A home away from home, you might say," he said as he opened the door to allow her to peer inside. Then, leading her onward, he gestured toward a larger building.

"That's the barn, as I'm sure you could guess."

"Yes, they do have barns in the country outside of Boston," she couldn't resist commenting. Samuel ignored her and strode on ahead.

"And, over here," he said, pointing to a four-sided structure of crisscrossing rough wooden posts, "is the corral. As you can see, we have several smaller enclosures, also. Now, that's just about it, I reckon. Let's see about getting you a horse saddled."

He selected one of the gentler, older mares and led her out of the corral. Amanda viewed the horse with disdain.

"Samuel, I am really quite an accomplished horsewoman, you know. I'm sure you have something more suitable for me to ride than this tame old nag," she told him defiantly.

"I'm not taking any chances on your first day here, Amanda. I'll have to see just how good a seat you have before I can judge which horse to let you ride. For now, you'll have to settle for old Jessie here." Amanda bit back an angry retort at his authoritative tone and approached the horse to mount.

"Need any help?" her father inquired, eyeing her cumbersome attire with an unexpected twinkle.

"No, thank you, I am quite accustomed to mounting without assistance," she declined politely. She grasped the saddle horn, placed her foot in the stirrup, then swung her body lithely up into the saddle.

"It's a good thing I have that old sidesaddle. A friend of mine bought it for his wife a few years back, but she refused to use it, saying that she preferred to ride the 'regular' way her brothers had taught her. Anyway, if you're all set, we'll head on out."

Amanda nodded briskly in agreement and administered a small slap to the horse's rump with her riding quirt. That's something else about my father that seems a bit strange, she mused. His manner of speaking. One moment he speaks in the manner of a well-educated Boston gentleman; the next, his speech is a curious mixture of East and West. Some of the terminology he had used was very confusing to her ears, but she did not want to ask him to explain everything he said. Besides, Aunt Martha had always cautioned her never to show her ignorance concerning a person's speech. After all, her aunt had reminded her, she had been trained to become familiar with foreign languages. Well, I suppose Texas speech could be considered a foreign language, she reflected with a small chuckle.

Riding at a moderate pace for the space of several miles, Amanda reveled in the freedom of the open land. There were vast stretches of unfenced range, high grass waving gracefully in the breeze, red dirt available everywhere to blow and mingle with the warm morning air. She began to notice several animals now entering her line of vision, and recognized them as some strange breed of cattle.

"Samuel, what sort of cattle are those?"

"Why, those are longhorns. They're the only kind we raise. You know, this is a profitable business for anyone willing to take the trouble to fool with their ornery stubbornness. They aren't exactly tame animals, you see. I suppose we have nearly a thousand head around here right now. Most of them were driven to Kansas for sale last spring."

"You mean those ugly, multicolored animals are worth a good deal of money?" she asked incredulously, noting the long horns on their heads.

"They most certainly are. Why, we're getting better than twenty-five dollars a head for them up in Kansas. As you saw earlier, we also raise horses. There isn't any way in the world that a man could exist out here without good horses."

"But, Samuel," she questioned with renewed interest, "I heard tales of creatures called buffalo, of wild Indians, of vicious outlaws. Were those mere fabrications?"

"Hell, no, Amanda," he answered with an amused grin. "They are decidedly not mere fabrications. There aren't too many head of buffalo remaining in this particular area. Too many of them have been killed off by buffalo hunters and Indians. Why, I was a hunter myself for a little while before I settled down to ranching. As for the Indians, they've been on the reservations for nearly three years now. Except for a few wild

51

renegades that escape now and then. And, outlaws, well, there are dishonest men everywhere. They're just a bit more notorious in Texas, perhaps, but I refuse to believe that this state possesses any more of these men than any other state in the U.S."

Amanda noted once again how defensive her father seemed to become whenever his adopted state or its peculiar ways were mentioned. Today, for some unknown reason, he had been almost companionable. He had actually volunteered information to her willing ears, and he was behaving much more agreeably than he had yesterday. She suddenly realized that she didn't want him to withdraw from her again, that she wanted him to talk to her and share a part of his world with her, at least for the remainder of her visit. Not that she felt anything akin to love for her father. No, she told herself, I've simply undergone a small transformation. She was simply beginning to like her father.

"Amanda, are you listening?" Samuel's voice suddenly roused her from her thoughts.

"Oh, yes, I'm terribly sorry. I was just thinking over some of the amazing things I'm learning. I didn't know you had ever hunted buffalo, Samuel. As I have already stated, Aunt Martha has revealed very little about you. What precisely have you been doing with your life since you left Boston?"

"Well, now, that would take some talking. I'll tell you all about it some other time," he replied. Again, he was reminded by this daughter of his of things he would sooner forget. He was forcibly reminded of his reason for departing Boston, of his reason for abandoning his baby daughter. Shaking off such thoughts, he then said, "Come on, I'll show you a bit more of the countryside and the cattle. Maybe I can show you some of the other animals that live out here." He reined his horse away from hers and spurred it into a gallop. She had no choice but to urge Jessie onward and attempt to keep pace.

"Samuel," she raised her voice above the noise of the horses' hooves striking the dry ground, "isn't that a fence over there? I thought you said that this was all open range."

He slowed his horse to a walk and then swore under his breath.

"It was meant to be open land, damn it! That's not only a fence, Amanda, that's a barbed wire fence. We've been fighting it for a long while now, but our methods don't appear to be entirely effective. That particular stretch of land wasn't fenced last week."

"What does it all mean? I don't understand what is so horrible about a fence."

"I'm afraid you wouldn't understand the full implications of it even if I told you. You see, a man starts fencing and he cuts off the other ranchers' water supply and grazing land in a lot of cases. It simply isn't right for anyone to attempt to fence in the open range. That barbed wire is cruel and inhumane. If I had my way, I'd drive such thieving bastards out of Texas!" he declared vehemently.

Amanda was surprised at his violent outburst. She sought to question her father about the matter a bit further, but she now spied another horseman approaching them from the south.

"Samuel, it appears that someone else is riding this way," she told him as she watched the rider top the horizon.

Her father turned his head in the direction she had indicated and swore under his breath once again, then said, "That's Luke Cameron, Amanda. He's the dang fool idiot that's been fencing this land. We've done everything we can think of to 'dissuade' Mr. Cameron, but he hasn't given it up yet. You just sit there and remain quiet. I'm going to show young Cameron that he's not the only person around here that's good with fences!" He unhooked the length of rope from his saddle and proceeded to make a loop. Then, he twirled it over his head and threw it deftly toward one of the fence posts, encircling the top portion of the post. Securing the rope tightly, he spurred his horse gently forward.

"Samuel, what you are doing? Mr. Cameron isn't going to allow you to destroy his fence!"

"I don't give a damn what Mr. Cameron will or will not allow! Somebody's got to show him that he can't get away with this!" The post suddenly popped out of the ground, pulling several yards of wire and three other posts along with it as her father continued forward with the rope. At that moment, Luke Cameron finally reached them. He flung himself off his horse and quickly approached Samuel's horse. He then yanked Samuel out of the saddle and wrestled him to the ground, catching him completely off-guard.

"Sam Lawrence, what the hell do you think you're doing? I thought you had more sense than to do something like this, at least in plain view of me!" he shouted in furious tones.

Amanda's attention was now drawn to the stranger. He appeared to be in his mid-twenties, his skin was tanned and glowing with health, his blond hair was sun-streaked. His intense blue eyes, which were now blazing with fury, were fringed by black lashes. He was nearly as tall as her father, with a muscular build to match. His face was ruggedly masculine, noticeably attractive. She became aware that her father had now stumbled to his feet.

"Damn you, Luke Cameron! Now you're going to get what's coming to you!" Samuel lunged toward the younger man, but Luke anticipated his move and moved aside precisely at that moment, causing Samuel to stumble once more. He dragged himself upright, effectively regained his balance, then threw himself at Luke. Luke caught him, but was not quick enough to dodge a well-placed blow at his left jaw. He shook his head to clear it, then warned his opponent, "Sam, I don't want to have to hurt you. I don't want to fight with an old friend of my father's, but I'm telling you now, if you don't stop this nonsense right away, you're going to be mighty sorry!"

"And I say to hell with your warning!" replied Samuel in rising anger. He couldn't let this young fool best him, especially not in front of his own daughter. He attempted to plant another fist in the younger man's face, but Luke once more dodged his blow and brought his own right fist up into Samuel's midsection, knocking the breath out of his lungs and forcing him to double over in pain.

"Damn it, I told you I didn't want to have to fight you, man!" declared Luke, attempting to help Samuel to his horse.

Amanda, however, misinterpreted his move and thought he was about to wrestle her father to the ground once more. She could not sit idly by and watch as her father was beaten by the younger, more agile man. She quickly dismounted and reached for the rifle on her father's saddle.

She knew nothing whatsoever about guns, but she knew enough to know which end to point at Luke Cameron. She lifted the gun and took a determined stance.

"Get away from him! You will leave him alone now, Mr. Cameron! How dare you take advantage of him when he is so obviously wounded!" she accused him.

Luke, who knew that she was accusing him unjustly, released his hold upon her father and turned a furious, steely-eyed face to the unknown young woman.

"Ma'am, I don't know who the hell you are, but you better not go pointing any gun at me! Now, you just put that thing down right now. Because, if you don't, you're going to be mighty sorry!" he threatened her with a tone that would brook no resistance.

"I do not know you, sir, and I do not have to do

anything you say. Now, you will please get away from my father and be on your way. Move!" she ordered him with as much bravado as she could muster with the unfamiliar object weighing heavy in her hands.

"So, you're Sam Lawrence's daughter. I might have known! All right, I'll be on my way. But, rest assured, I won't forget any of this. You tell your father that I'm not ever going to allow him to get away with pulling down my fences, whether he was one of my father's friends or not. And, Miss Lawrence," he said mockingly as he mounted his horse and began to rein it away, "I don't believe for one moment that you even know how to use that gun. You tell your father that he'd better teach you a little better manners till you learn." With that, he galloped away.

Amanda stood watching until he was out of sight, then she lowered the gun and ran to help her father.

"Samuel, are you all right?" she asked with concern.

"Hell, yes, I'm all right. I think I can get up now. He just winded me, that's all." He slowly stood upright once more, still rubbing his midsection, but managing to comment, "Amanda, I'm real proud of the way you handled that. Not that I needed any help, you understand, but I can see that you do have some of your old father in you, after all. However, next time, you stay out of men's business, you understand?" he sternly insisted. "You could have been hurt. Besides that," he

57

wryly admitted, "it certainly doesn't look too good for a man to have his daughter defending him!"

Amanda laughed at his sheepish expression and waited until she saw that he could mount, then followed suit. They rode slowly back toward the ranch.

Four

Samuel and Amanda arrived back at the ranch several minutes before lunch was due to be served. Neither of them had mentioned the preceding events of the morning, Amanda having correctly sensed that her father preferred not to speak of the matter just yet. When they had both dismounted, Samuel called together his ranchhands in order to introduce them to his daughter, the daughter he was slowly learning to like and admire.

"Amanda," he said as he gestured toward the assembled group of men, "these are the men who work my ranch. Starting at the left there, that's John Chambers."

"Howdy, Miss Amanda. Sure am glad to meet you at long last. My Sally ain't talked of nothing else but you since you came yesterday," responded the slightly angular, gray-haired man with the friendly smile. Amanda could not refrain from answering that smile with one of her own.

"And these are the cowpokes he's in charge of." Samuel went on to introduce each of the eight men in turn. Amanda concentrated her attention on their names and features, seeking to find something about their appearance or manner that would help her to remember them.

There was Frank Thompson, a tall, thin fellow with an unruly thatch of wheat-colored hair and a moustache to match; Steve Watkins, a few years older than Amanda, who was rather short and stocky with ragged brown hair; Jim Boyer, nearer to her father's age, wearing the largest hat she had ever seen, his eyes small and squinty; Roy Crowley, approximately thirty years of age, his black hair gleaming in the sunlight, his clothes looking as if he had worn them for at least a week without washing them; Slim Franklin, younger than Roy, grinning sheepishly as Amanda smiled at him, his square-jawed face turning a bright red beneath her gaze; Buck Jones, about twenty-seven, his face pock-marked but attractive, his eyes seeming to assess her as she glanced at him; Clyde Adams, big and brawny, silent and grim-looking; and lastly, Tommy Evans, nearer Amanda's age, his head topped by red hair even brighter than her father's, with freckles to match. He eyed Amanda shyly and worshipfully.

"I'm very pleased to meet all of you," Amanda politely told the eight men. They all proceeded to murmur polite rejoinders, then began to slowly drift away toward the cookshack for the noon meal. Soon, only Tommy Evans remained standing before her.

"Miss Amanda, ma'am," he began tentatively, hesitantly, "uh, that is, well, we're all right proud to meet you, ma'am. If there's ever anything you need any help with, anything at all, you just feel free to call on me."

"Thank you, Mr. Evans. Please tell all of your fellow employees that I am equally proud to meet them," she replied graciously. "Please excuse me now, I see my father waiting rather impatiently on the porch for me. Good day." She turned and approached Samuel, his face stern and disapproving.

"Amanda, I don't want you becoming too friendly with any of the hands," he told her.

"I'm afraid I do not understand. They do work for you, don't they? Surely you would not employ anyone unsuitable, would you, Samuel?" she challenged him with a lift of her eyebrow.

"Amanda, don't you use that tone of voice with me. It's simply that they are all fiercely independent, each of them quite different from any other man I'm sure you've ever before met. Now," he said, dismissing the subject, "I think it's time for us to go on in for lunch. Mrs. Chambers is probably waiting for us."

Amanda swallowed the angry retort which had risen to her lips for the third time since she had met her father just yesterday afternoon. My goodness, she told herself rebelliously, my father is an extremely difficult person to understand!

They sat down for lunch and Amanda searched through her mind for a topic that would not cause any further disagreement between herself and her father. She knew this was not an easy task, finding something to talk about that Samuel Lawrence would approve of. She picked at her lunch, which consisted of potatoes, fried chicken, biscuits, and gravy, then decided to ask about the bold, brash, handsome young man her father had tangled with earlier that day, not caring whether her father disapproved of that particular topic or not.

"Samuel, do you and Luke Cameron always behave that way toward one another? I mean, surely he had done nothing that warrants such hostility? I simply fail to see why you would openly attempt to destroy another man's property."

"I'm sure you wouldn't understand," he commented, his tone sounding condescending to Amanda's ears, "but, no, Luke and I have not always clashed the way we do now. Luke's father was one of the closest friends I've ever had, but he's dead now. He and Luke's mother, a very gracious and cultured woman, were both killed by Comanches nearly six years ago now. Luke, the oldest of their three sons, took over the running of the ranch, an even larger operation than mine. Since that time, though, he has refused to listen to reason, refused to heed the sound advice of his father's friends. A more bullheaded, stubborn, hot-tempered young fool I've never met!"

"Well, I do not see why the matter of a fence would cause such a conflict," she remarked thoughtfully.

"Because, as I've already told you, this land wasn't meant to be fenced! But he went ahead and did it. He put up that damn barbed wire, saying that all of us around here would be using it eventually, no matter how hard we tried to keep progress away. Progress, my eye! We were getting along just fine without that fence, and we'll get along fine without it in the future!" he exclaimed angrily.

"Is he the only rancher who has fenced his land?"

"No, but he's the only one whose land borders mine and some of my other friends'. We've done a lot to try and force him to see things our way, but he hasn't paid enough attention to the methods we've used so far. We won't give up, though. However," he said, changing the subject once again, as appeared to be his custom, "enough about that for now, Amanda. Why don't you come outside with me after we finish lunch and watch some of the hands do some breaking?"

"Breaking? What on earth is that?"

"Horses. You know, taming them, getting them used to having a saddle on their backs."

"Yes, I suppose that would be quite interesting to watch." And later, perhaps I can get him to speak of his reasons for asking me to come here, she planned hopefully. She wanted some answers to a great many questions, questions she had stored in the back of her mind for the majority of her life.

Meanwhile, the ranchhands were discussing the beautiful daughter of their boss out in the cookshack.

"I think Mr. Lawrence is plumb crazy to have that little gal of his come out here. That type of lady is nothing but a hothouse flower; purty to look at, but not made for this country. She won't last out the month, you mark my words. She'll go running back East long before then," Roy was prophesying to the others.

"Yeah, she sure is a high-born lady, ain't she? By heaven, I ain't never seen such a good-looking woman in all my born days. I feel dirty just looking at her," put in Steve, remembering the young lady's bright hair and curvaceous figure.

"Stop it, all of you!" insisted Tommy, unusually outspoken. "You shouldn't speak about Miss Amanda that way, and you all damn well know it! The cookshack ain't no place to talk about any lady."

"Well, seems that the beautiful Miss Lawrence has acquired a new champion, don't it, boys?" teased Buck lazily.

"You shut your mouth, Buck!" commanded Tommy, his anger building by the moment.

"I got just as much right as anyone to say whatever I please about the lady, boy. Yes sir, I'd like to get to know Miss Amanda Lawrence quite a bit better during her stay here," he continued taunting. In all actuality, he meant what he said. He found the haughty Miss Lawrence quite intriguing. Someone needs to take her down a peg or two, he told himself. Yeah, maybe I'll be the one who does the taming of that little filly.

"You go to hell! Miss Lawrence is a fine, pure, real lady and nobody, especially you, can say different, you hear?" Tommy shouted, his fists now clenched tightly in his fury.

"Take it easy, boy," ordered Jim Boyer, the oldest of the bunch. "You, too, Buck. Tommy's right. This ain't no place to be talking about no ladies. Come on now, let the matter drop. We all got work to do."

Buck smiled a slow, calculating smile and turned his back on the furious young Tommy. They filed out of the cookshack and into the hot sunshine of the bright September day.

Amanda watched in fascination that afternoon as the hands roped the horses and managed to place a saddle upon their backs. She watched as they then attempted to ride the wildly bucking creatures, trying to refrain from laughter when one of the men was thrown roughly to the ground and then comically dusted the seat of his pants with his hat as he limped from the corral. She knew that what they were doing could be considered dangerous in some circles, yet these men made it appear almost enjoyable, almost as if it were some sort of sporting challenge between man and beast.

That evening, she was disappointed when she discovered that she would not have the opportunity to speak with her father privately until the next day. He and most of the hands rode out after supper, Samuel merely telling her that they had some important business to attend to, and for her to go on to bed and not wait up for him. She took his advice and climbed the steps to her bedroom, suddenly realizing that she was to some degree more tired than usual after her first full day on the ranch.

After breakfast the next morning, Mrs. Chambers invited her to ride into town to pick up a few needed provisions at the general store.

"Why, thank you, Mrs. Chambers. I'd love to

accompany you," Amanda told her, pleased that she would have another opportunity to view the town. Samuel gave his permission and the two women drove away from the ranch in the flatbed wagon.

"My John would usually take me into town, but I told him that you and me needed a chance for some private woman talk. He only agreed to let us come alone if I brought along this here rifle," she told Amanda, showing her the gun which was concealed beneath the wagon seat.

"Why, is it dangerous for us to go into town alone?" Amanda asked.

"Not really. This here gun's for just in case."

"Mrs. Chambers," Amanda said as she clutched the sides of the wagon seat for support, "my father told me that I would need to wear something other than my riding habit whenever I ride with him. I thought, that is, if it is convenient, that you might possibly assist me in designing a riding skirt of some sort."

"Why, honey, I'd love to! You know, I myself don't do much horseback riding, but I think that, between the two of us, we can come up with something that's just right for you."

Later, nearing the town, Amanda questioned her companion about her life, wondering why a voluble, friendly woman such as she would be content to isolate herself out on a ranch in west Texas, a ranch inhabited almost exclusively by males.

"Well, me and my John weren't born in Texas. No, I was from Alabama, and John came from

66

Tennessee. But, we've both been out here so long now that we consider ourselves natives. We came out here right after we got married, back in '52. We settled in San Antonio for a spell, then just sort of drifted west. Anyhow, we ended up meeting your pa and going to work for him some ten years back. He needed us, so here we are."

"Did you ever have any children?"

"No, we weren't blessed with children of our own. By the way," she commented teasingly, "seems to me that it's about time you was married and had a family of your own."

"Oh, that's not true," insisted Amanda. "I am certainly not prepared to bend my will to that of any man just yet, if I ever will be. No, I'm not ready to give up my rights—my freedom—just yet. Besides, I don't know if I will ever meet the man with whom I would care to share the rest of my life. There was a young man back in Boston, but we parted before I came out here."

"Why, I can't understand why you didn't have hordes of men after you, you're so pretty and all! But, honey, you'll feel differently about giving up your freedom and all. Because, you see, you don't really give up anything at all. Yes sir, once you fall in love, you don't think about nothing else but that man," the older woman assured her confidently.

"Fall in love? Why, I honestly don't know if I believe in that. I thought that two people just developed a fondness for each other over the years. The majority of people, anyway. That's what my Aunt Martha always taught me. She said that a woman's duty is to marry for convenience, for her place in society and to bear children. I'm not at all certain that I agree with all of that, but I don't know about love, either."

"Not believe in love? That's plumb ridiculous! I don't mean to be speaking against your aunt or nothing, but it seems to me that since she may not have had a marriage for love, she might think that all of them are the same. Well, I'm telling you right here and now that they're not! No sir, me and my John married because we loved one another, and we still love one another. Maybe even more than we ever have. You listen to me, Amanda, there really will come a time when you'll fall in love. You'll think back on what you're saying to me now and you'll laugh at your own foolishness."

"Well, I'm afraid that you may be mistaken. I thought that I had experienced something similar to love with the young man in Boston, but now I realize that I was simply being childish." Yes, she thought with an inward sigh, she knew that she had never truly experienced this emotion known as love. She had felt a certain stirring of her senses, a slight awakening of her passion and deepest yearnings that day when Peter had kissed her in the park, but she realized that it had never been love. She recalled that she had felt there was something wrong with her, something she could not truly name, but which seemed to leave a void.

"Well, then it's plain to see that you didn't love him. Honey, you're old enough to do your own thinking now. Use your heart to tell you what's right, not just your head."

Amanda lapsed into silence, contemplating the housekeeper's interesting words, but she was even more confused than before. She knew that her parents had been in love, but she wasn't sure that she wanted to experience such an overwhelming emotion. An emotion that caused such pain and torment and unhappiness did not sound as if it was the sort of thing she wanted for herself.

They arrived at Big Prairie and Mrs. Chambers guided the wagon over to one side of the main street, gradually pulling the horses to a halt before the general store.

"Do you want to come on inside with me? Or do you want to go on over across the street there and start looking at some materials?" she asked Amanda.

"If it is all right with you, I believe that I'll go across the street and look at the fabric," she replied. She climbed down from the wagon, careful to hold the full skirts of her sprigged muslin dress up out of the red dirt. She glanced about the town as she crossed the street, noting that there were several other people walking in and out of the various buildings of the town. She approached the doorway of a building which displayed a weathered sign advertising that it carried ladies' fine fabrics inside. She straightened her hat and entered.

"Yes, ma'am. Is there something I can get for you?" the short, older man wearing spectacles asked her as she neared the counter.

"Oh, I would like to see some dress goods,

please. I wish to purchase something rather heavy, something more practical than pretty," she told him decisively.

She finally settled on a heavy cotton for warm weather and a wool for whenever the weather became cooler. Of course, she mused, I may not be here when the weather becomes cooler. She waited while the man carefully wrapped the fabrics in brown paper and tied up the packages with white string. He handed them to her with a smile and she left the shop, happy with her purchases, pleased that she had chosen them herself.

She had toyed with the idea of buying something for Mrs. Chambers, but decided against it. After all, she hardly knew the woman, and she had already sensed that the people out here were proud about accepting charity from anyone, especially a newcomer.

"Amanda!" she heard Mrs. Chambers calling from across the street. "Oh, I see you already got the materials. Well, I've got just a few more things to buy, so I'll meet you back here at the wagon in about five minutes." Amanda nodded in agreement as the woman entered another store.

Well, I suppose I may as well look about the town, she told herself with a sigh. She strolled along the street, peering into each store or business she passed, curious to see precisely what a small town such as this had to offer a person who possessed a head for commerce. Coming to the end of the row of buildings on one side of the street, she began to cross the street to complete her survey of the town on the other side.

Suddenly, the heel of one of her dainty, high-topped shoes caught in a small, deep crack in the parched earth near the edge of the road. Amanda stumbled forward, her packages flying to land in the dust below. She quickly recovered her poise and attempted to pull her foot gracefully out of the rut.

She looked down to see that the heel of her shoe had loosened when she caught it in the crack. Of course, she thought unfairly, nothing like this would ever have happened in Boston! She glanced about in exasperation, then bent down to see if she could temporarily repair the shoe, so that she could at least walk gracefully across the street to the wagon.

At that moment, someone yelled loudly, "Runaway! Watch out, there's a runaway team and wagon!"

Amanda glanced quickly up to see a bolting pair of horses pulling a bouncing, careening, driverless wagon behind it. What was more, she frantically experienced an overwhelming sensation of fear as she realized that the horses and wagon were coming straight toward her.

"Get out of the way, you little idiot!" she heard a man's deep, resonant voice shout at her. Then, before she was aware of what was happening, the owner of the voice, whom she could not see at the moment, lunged at her, grabbing her securely about her waist and knocking her squarely to the hard ground below, mere inches out of the path of the dangerous hooves and wheels.

She lay pinned upon the ground, somewhat

dizzy and stunned by what had just occurred. When she finally realized that someone was still holding tightly on to her, his body still pressing closely against hers, she began to struggle.

"Will you please allow me to breathe, sir?" she demanded coldly, then raised her face to his, which was a mere three inches from her own at the moment. She uttered an involuntary gasp and was rendered momentarily speechless by her surprise.

"Miss Lawrence," Luke Cameron remarked mockingly, obviously enjoying her apparent dismay upon discovering the identity of her rescuer.

"Mr. Cameron! Sir," she commanded haughtily, "remove your hands from my person this very instant!"

He slowly did as she had ordered, taking more time than was actually necessary as his hands slid from her body. He then stood up to his full height, gazing down at her where she still sat upon the ground, her hair falling down out of its pins, her bonnet knocked askew, her skirts in utter disarray.

"Do you need any assistance in rising, ma'am?" he inquired maddeningly, his twinkling blue eyes taking in her bedraggled appearance and outraged expression.

"How dare you treat me in such a manner! I cannot believe that such abusive physical action was absolutely necessary!" she informed him furiously. She attempted to rise without his assistance, but her knees gave way beneath her and she was forced to lean upon his strong arms for support.

"Why didn't you get out of the way when you

were warned, you little fool?'' he demanded sternly, all humor now disappearing from his eyes.

"For your information, Mr. Cameron," she informed him icily, "the heel of my shoe caught and loosened and I was unable to walk at the time. However, that did not give you a right to treat me in such an ungentlemanly fashion, and it does not now give you the right to berate me in front of all these people," she said furiously, glancing about in embarrassment at the crowd that had formed around them. She knew that she should, in all fairness, thank him for saving her from a possible disaster, yet she could not bring herself to speak to him of gratitude.

"I was merely getting you out of danger the fastest way I knew how," he told her coldly, his blue eyes now appearing steely.

"Well, I must say, sir, that I might have expected such behavior from you," she replied, ignoring his rational explanation. She shook off his arm and drew herself rigidly erect.

"Yes, I can see that you don't need anyone to help you," he commented dryly. He stalked away, refusing to look back to see if she was indeed completely recovered. She glared at his retreating back, fighting down a sudden, most unladylike urge to scream at him. I won't lower myself to hurl insults at that odious man, she told herself. She once more became aware of the curious and amused faces of the people around her as she attempted to straighten her clothing and maintain her dignity.

Mrs. Chambers returned to the wagon in time to see Amanda speaking with Luke, and then as he apparently left her in a rage. She watched as Amanda hurried across the street, limping because of her broken shoe heel.

"Oh, Mrs. Chambers, the most dreadful thing just occurred. I was very nearly run down by a runaway wagon! Surely someone caused such an accident through sheer negligence. I must speak to my father about this matter," she told the older woman breathlessly, her tone reflecting her bruised pride.

"Amanda! So that's what all the commotion was about. Are you sure you're all right now? Do you hurt anywhere, honey?" she asked Amanda solicitously, her face mirroring her genuine concern.

"Oh, I suppose I'm nearly recovered now. It's just that Luke Cameron succeeded in humiliating me in front of all those people, my dress appears to be ruined, my bonnet is certainly beyond repair, and I feel bruised all over! Oh, that man!" she raged.

"Now, now, child. I'm sure he didn't mean to embarrass you or nothing. Just what did he do to get you so riled up?"

"Well, he pushed me quite roughly to the ground! He manhandled me in a most shocking way, too!" she complained.

"You mean that he pushed you out of the way of the runaway wagon? If that's so, then why are you so angry at him?" Mrs. Chambers asked in confusion.

"The manner in which he rescued me was quite unnecessary, I can assure you. He informed me yesterday that I would regret aiming a gun at him. This was simply his way of getting his revenge!"

"I can't believe that, Amanda. Don't you worry about it now, though. We'll see what we can do about your dress. As for the bruises, well, I'll see to it that you get a nice, hot bath as soon as we get you back to the ranch. Here now, let's get going." She helped Amanda climb on the wagon, then hurried around to the other side and took her own place, gently flicking the reins as she settled herself on the seat.

"Amanda, it appears to me that you didn't thank Luke Cameron properly for saving you from a certain accident. It seems to me that you've taken him in dislike for some reason. Mind my asking you why?"

"Well, I met him yesterday, you see, when I was out riding with my father. He and Samuel became involved in a disagreement, and came to blows and I simply used my father's gun in order to force Mr. Cameron to desist from hurting Samuel anymore, that's all. However, that is not the entire reason for my utter dislike of the man! He is rude, entirely too bold and insolent, overbearing, arrogant, and I don't know what all else! He is most certainly not a gentleman, of that I am certain!" No, he is a veritable scoundrel! she silently added to herself in anger. But, she could not refrain from suddenly wondering what it would be like to be kissed by such a man, to be held within the strong boundaries of his muscular arms, to have him gaze deeply into her eyes as he slowly and purposefully brought his handsome face downward toward hers . . . No! she furiously commanded herself, ashamed for even allowing herself to think of such indecent things. She did not even truly know the man, certainly did not wish to know him! Why had she suddenly pictured herself with him in such an intimate manner, what on earth was the matter with her?

"Now, Amanda," she heard Mrs. Chambers saying as she was brought back to the present, "I'm going to tell you something right now. First off, you don't know how to handle a gun, do you?" She paused as Amanda reluctantly nodded, then continued, "That's what I thought. Well, let me tell you, honey, that Luke Cameron also knew you wasn't too knowing about guns, since I'm sure it was plain for anyone to see. Why, he could have taken that gun from you with no problem at all. Furthermore, I think I need to set the record straight about something else. Your pa and Luke used to get along just fine. They just have different ideas about ranching, that's all. But, I won't get into all that just now. I just want to say that Luke Cameron is a mighty fine young man. Yes, it's true. He's got a good head on his shoulders, that young man does. He's taken over the running of that ranch as if he's got twenty years more experience that he really does. He's taken care of his two younger brothers better than anyone else could have. Luke's well liked in these parts. And, if it weren't for the matter of the fencing, there most likely wouldn't ever have been any trouble between him and your pa, or between him and anyone else, for that matter. It's true that he's a mite stubborn, and sometimes he's overbearing, and he tends to be a bit hot-tempered at times, but all in all he's a good, fine young man."

Amanda listened to this speech without comment, resenting Mrs. Chambers's defense of the insufferable Luke Cameron. I don't care whether she thinks he's absolutely wonderful, she thought stubbornly, her defiance surfacing at the mere thought of the man, I think he's rude and unbearably offensive!

Five

Before she and Mrs. Chambers reached the ranch, Amanda had reconsidered mentioning any of the details of the near disaster and Luke Cameron. She realized that such information would only serve to further inflame her father toward Mr. Cameron and she did not want to be the cause of any additional trouble.

Her life on the ranch finally settled into a busy, time-filled routine. She observed as the ranch-hands branded cattle, broke horses, repaired fences, and various other endless tasks. She had also experienced a growing friendship with the youngest of the hands, Tommy Evans, who was always near at hand to offer any explanation she required or to assist with any problem.

Amanda decided one day that she would learn to shoot. Recalling that particular day more than two weeks ago when she had aimed a rifle at Luke Cameron, she vowed to become adept with a gun.

She approached Tommy on the subject because she knew he would keep her secret. She wished to surprise her father with her newly acquired skills and knowledge.

"Tommy, would you please teach me to shoot?

You see, it seems that everyone out here knows how, even the women. Will you consent to teach me? I promise that I will be a willing and apt pupil," she coaxed him one afternoon when the two of them were standing near the corral, several yards out of earshot of her father and the other hands.

"Well, I don't see that it would do any harm for you to learn how to handle a gun, Miss Amanda. There might come a time when you need to know how. Yes, ma'am, I'll be right proud to be your teacher," the young man responded seriously. He'd do anything for Miss Amanda, anything at all.

The very next morning, shortly after dawn, Amanda rose from the comfort of her bed, quickly dressed, and crept quietly downstairs. She was wearing the new skirt Mrs. Chambers had helped her design. It was conveniently split in the middle and would afford her more ease in riding. She had even toyed with the idea of learning to ride astride in the near future. She stifled an amused giggle at the thought of Aunt Martha's reaction to a woman riding in such an indecent manner!

Tommy was patiently waiting for her, the horses already saddled. The two of them rode quietly away from the ranch and out toward the open range.

"I hope I am not the cause of any difficulty for you because of this, Tommy," she told him apologetically, having recalled her father's warning about her association with any of his employees. She knew that he would probably disapprove of her riding out alone with one of the hands.

"Well, the others ain't up just yet. I hope to be back before anyone really notices that I'm gone. Anyhow, I guess we're far enough from the ranch now. We don't want them all to hear any shooting. Come on, Miss Amanda, I'll see about teaching you to shoot." He helped her dismount, his face becoming slightly reddened as his hands circled her waist and easily lifted her down from the saddle.

"Thank you, Tommy. Now, where do we begin?" she asked, anxious to get started.

"All right, here's the rifle. You put the end of it against your shoulder like this," he informed her as he positioned the gun in her arms, then stood closely behind her to guide her actions.

"Now, hold it up tight against you. I know it kind of feels heavy to you right now, but you'll get used to it. Now, I'm going to help you pull the trigger, and you better be ready to feel a little kick against your shoulder. Just hold it tight against you like I said and it won't hurt none."

He reached around and placed his hand over hers on the trigger of the rifle. Then, he gently pressed against her finger, which in turn pressed upon the trigger, causing the gun to fire.

Amanda involuntarily winced as the sharp report of the firing sounded in her ears. She opened her eyes and lowered the rifle, rubbing her shoulder.

"I suppose I didn't keep it in the correct position, Tommy. My shoulder feels bruised," she complained as she continued rubbing the sore area.

"You did real good for the first time, though, ma'am. Now, you've got the feel of the gun. Here, put it back in place and try it on your own."

She did as he instructed and held the rifle upright once more. She tightly shut her eyes in anticipation as she squeezed the trigger.

"I did it! It didn't hurt nearly as much that time, either!" she exclaimed in excitement.

"That's real good, Miss Amanda. Now, I'll show you how to take aim."

Tommy tried to concentrate all of his attention on showing Amanda how to shoot, yet his thoughts kept straying to the memory of the feel of her softly curved body against his own. Damn, he reflected silently, I can hardly keep my mind on what we're doing. I don't know if this was such a bright idea after all. Oh, Amanda, he entreated silently, his head within inches of hers as she took aim, you don't know what your very presence does to me. He gritted his teeth and continued with his instruction.

They returned to the ranch some thirty minutes later, Tommy judging it wise not to overdo the very first lesson. He led the horses away as Amanda started for the house, anxious to sneak back up to her bedroom unobserved. However, she halted suddenly as she became aware of someone's presence at the side of the house.

"Well, now, howdy, Miss Amanda. Nice morning for a ride, ain't it?" mocked Buck Jones, who was leaning negligently against the house, his eyes sliding from Amanda toward the barn where

Tommy had just disappeared with the horses.

"Mr. Jones," she inclined her head stiffly toward him.

"Seems to me like your pa wasn't supposed to know about your little ride with young Evans, was he? Now, don't you worry your little head, Miss Amanda. I won't let your secret out. Yes sir, you can trust good old Buck here."

"Why, that's very courteous of you, I'm sure," Amanda responded haughtily, wanting nothing more than to escape from the uncomfortable situation and flee inside the house. She did not know precisely why she disliked this man standing so insolently before her, but she sensed that he was different from the other hands, that there was something evil about him.

"Maybe you and me could go out for a little ride sometime. I can promise you that I'll show you some better sights than that young puppy," he commented lazily, his eyes rudely appraising her figure beneath the white blouse and printed skirt.

"No, thank you. Now, I really must go inside at once." She whirled away from him and hurried up the steps of the front porch, wrenching open the door and then softly closing it behind her. She picked up her skirts and ran lightly up the stairs to the sanctuary of her bedroom, glancing about repeatedly to assure herself that no one had seen her.

She entered her bedroom, shut the door, then literally plopped down upon the downy softness of the bed. Her thoughts unwillingly returned to her brief, unpleasant encounter with Buck. She wondered if her father was aware that he had employed such an insolent fellow. She'd be certain to avoid the man as much as possible from now on.

Her reflections then strayed to Luke Cameron. Just you wait, Mr. Cameron, she thought defiantly, just you wait. The next time you observe me with a gun, I will most assuredly demonstrate that I do know how to use it. She could just see herself now: Luke Cameron standing near the fence as he had been that day, arguing with her father, and herself aiming the gun expertly at the arrogant man, showing him that she was perfectly able to use it if need be. She smiled with satisfaction at such a scene, then climbed down from the bed and began to remove her riding outfit. She quickly crossed the room to wash her face and hands, to remove any telltale signs of her secret morning ride.

That same evening, Amanda was finally presented with the opportunity to ask her father why he had invited her to visit him. She preceded him into the parlor after dinner and took a seat on the sofa. She waited patiently as her father stretched out in the wing chair a few feet away.

"Samuel," she began, taking a deep breath beforehand, "there is something I wish to ask you."

"Yes, Amanda, what is it?"

"Well, I've been wondering about this particular question for some time now. It is very simple, really. I want to know why you invited me to come."

Samuel shifted restlessly in his chair, his eyes

glancing away from Amanda's and peering down at the polished leather boots he wore. He cleared his throat loudly, then stood abruptly and walked over to the fireplace, where he remained standing, his back to Amanda.

"Amanda, this isn't easy for me. Please understand. I realize that you are not to blame for what has happened in my life. I used to blame you, but I no longer do," he muttered softly, then cleared his throat once more and continued.

"I invited you to come because I wanted to become acquainted with my only child, because I finally realized that I needed to know someone who was a part of me. I loved your mother more than life itself, yet I could not join her when she passed away. At first, in the very beginning, I blamed you, the innocent babe, for your mother's death. I believed that she would have lived much longer if it hadn't been for bearing you. I've come to realize that I could not have kept her with me, that she would have left me even if it had not been for her pregnancy. I realized that God meant for her to die, that He must have meant for us to be parted, though I cannot understand why. I cannot understand why the very essence of my being was taken away from me!"

Amanda sat perfectly motionless, her green eyes filling with unshed tears at this evidence of her father's pain and loss.

"After I left you with your Aunt Martha, I left behind all that I had held dear. I left behind the memory of you and your mother. I tried desperately to forget, Amanda. That's why I had to leave you. I had to try and erase the tormented memory from my mind. I'm not saying that what I did was right, but I only know that I had to do it. I knew that they would give you a good home, you see. I sent money fairly regularly, but I could not bring myself to visit you. I received word from your aunt about you once or twice, whenever her letters managed to reach me. I felt an overwhelming guilt at what I had done, for abandoning you, but I could not reverse what had already been done. So, I traveled a great deal, searching for the peace of mind and soul I had lost with your mother's death." He paused here, slowly turned and seated himself once more in the chair, facing his daughter now as he spoke.

"I went to Europe, then returned to the States. I wandered throughout different parts of the country. I also squandered a good deal of money, although I did have enough foresight to purchase much of what you now see in this house. I only bought the furnishings because I hoped to settle down again some day, although I knew not when that day would ever come. I suppose I had to have something to give my life stability. I finally came to Texas shortly before the war. As I told you before, I hunted buffalo for a time. I signed on for cattle drives. I fought Indians, and I worked at various occupations, also for brief periods of time. I had a force within me that drove me from one adventure to another, you see. Anyway, when the war was already going strong, I signed up to fight for the Confederacy. I wanted to fight against my past, I suppose. I was injured before the end came, and returned here to Texas. I began investing some of my remaining money in land and in rounding up wild longhorns and horses to begin a ranch. It was difficult at first, but I managed to make the place pay. I loved this particular area of Texas best, I suppose, because it was free and untamed. Its wild spirit seemed to beckon to my own wandering one. Now, it is home."

"Oh, Samuel," Amanda murmured softly through her tears. She realized that she was not only crying for the lonely man sitting opposite her, but also for her own lonely childhood, for her own unfulfilled need for someone to whom she could belong and call her own.

"Yes, so there you have it, my dear. I cannot undo what has been done. I had to invite you here because I had to try and free my mind of the terrible guilt that has been hanging over my head throughout all these years. I don't know exactly why I chose this particular time. I suppose I was finally prepared in some way for you. It pained me a great deal when I first laid eyes on you. You remind me so much of your beautiful mother."

"I see. I knew that you had some difficulty when I first arrived. I knew that you were not happy to see me," she replied sadly.

"Amanda," he said, crossing the space between them, sitting beside his daughter and gently taking her hands in his larger, firmer grasp, "I can't promise that things will ever be completely resolved between us. I know they cannot, for I've done you a great injustice. I've hurt you deeply for many years. For the first time since your mother's

86

death, I want to face it and then try and resolve it in my own mind, in my own heart. I know it won't be easy, Amanda, but I want us to come to know one another. Perhaps we will even come to love one another, although I realize that this would be asking too much of you. Please give me a chance to try and make up for the past, for the years of neglect. I can't change overnight, though," he cautioned her, "but I am already growing fonder of you each day. Amanda," he demanded, the old authoritative tone returning to his deep voice, "look at me."

She slowly turned her tearful gaze to his face and swallowed, then told him hesitantly, "Samuel, I don't know if I can ever truly forgive you for all those years of neglect, for all those years when I needed your love and comfort and security. However, I can promise you this: I will try. I am also beginning to care for you, you see. You are not at all the ogre I first believed you to be. Please, though, give me time. Let's take things slowly, Samuel. Let's allow things to proceed as they will. I will endeavor to allow you to know me, my true self, if you will only do the same."

Samuel smiled suddenly, a bright, illuminating smile that reflected his deep relief that this daughter of his was willing to let him make amends of some sort. He cleared his throat once again and then rose to his feet, drawing Amanda up beside him.

"Well, that's enough of that for now! I think it's about time you were in bed, young lady!" he commanded with a twinkle in his hazel eyes.

87

"Samuel, I am not a child! However, I must confess that I am rather tired. Good night," she told him, laughing silently at his words.

"Good night, Amanda," he responded softly, displaying more warmth than she had previously seen. She slowly climbed the stairs, her heart considerably lightened by what had transpired between herself and her father.

The next morning, she again rose early and hurried stealthily outside for her shooting lesson. She suddenly remembered that Tommy would be unable to instruct her that day, as he had mentioned that he and the other hands would be riding out earlier than usual. They were to round up some cattle several miles away from the ranch.

Oh, drat! she exclaimed inwardly. She was angry at herself for having forgotten. She strolled over to the barn, where she saw that the hands' horses and saddles were indeed all missing. So, they've already gone, she thought, then had a sudden idea. I can ride out by myself and do some practicing before anyone knows that I am gone. I can be back well before breakfast, so Samuel won't even know I'm out of bed yet, she schemed.

She hurried to her horse, musing that she was certainly glad she had been taught how to saddle a horse without assistance. She remembered that she had no rifle to practice with. There's one in the hallway, she recalled. She ran back inside the house and took a rifle from inside the gun cabinet in the hallway, then quickly ran to the barn once more. She mounted the waiting horse and kicked it lightly into a canter, riding away undetected.

She rode for several minutes, not knowing precisely how far she had wandered from the ranch. She had always been a poor judge of distance. She realized that she wasn't too accurate when it came to directions, either. She had no idea which way she was going, knowing only that the horse was taking her out to the open range. She experienced a small twinge of doubt as to the wisdom of riding out alone, away from the familiar surroundings of the ranch. Don't be silly, she ordered herself sternly, you want to surprise Samuel and learn to shoot, don't you?

She finally slowed the horse to a walk, then halted it completely and dismounted. She gazed overhead, noting with curiosity that the sun was now hidden by a majestic line of clouds which had appeared on the horizon. I hope it doesn't rain before I'm finished, she thought. She spied a line of fencing and led the horse along with her as she approached it. She tied the reins loosely to a post, then wandered down the line of fence until she felt she had chosen the right spot for her practice. Then, she turned and strode several yards away and took careful aim the way Tommy had previously shown her. She decided to try shooting at the fence posts to see if she could hit one at all.

She grasped the rifle tightly, closed her left eyelid, and peered down the barrel of the gun. She held the rifle steady, then gently squeezed the trigger.

Oh, drat! she complained silently. I missed it completely. If only Tommy were here to help her with it a bit more. But, no, she wanted to waste no time in waiting until he was free again to give her another lesson; she wanted to surprise Samuel as soon as possible with a fairly accurate aim.

Thinking of her father once more, she lowered the gun for an instant. The events and feelings he had revealed to her yesterday evening had been difficult to hear, even more difficult to understand. Yet, she was already fond of him and she would endeavor to see his side of the entire situation. At least he no longer resents me, she thought.

She took careful aim once again and fired the rifle several times more, finally succeeding in hitting the fence post, shooting away several splinters of weathered wood from its top. She paused and looked overhead, sensing that something was about to happen, noting that the sky had become quite darkened while she had been occupied with her shooting practice. Her satisfied smile faded as she observed the thickening clouds, the stillness of the morning air now beginning to become stirred about by a sudden, strengthening wind. A storm is coming, she told herself. I had better return to the ranch before I'm caught out here in the middle of nowhere.

A sudden flash of lightning brightened the sky, quickly followed by a loud roar of thunder. Amanda now ran to the spot where she had tied up her horse, but was startled and dismayed to discover that the horse had pulled the reins loose and was now galloping away back toward the comfort of the barn, apparently frightened by the thunder and lightning.

What on earth shall I do now? her mind

frantically searched for a way back to the ranch, her heart beginning to race with anxiety as she peered overhead at the swirling clouds.

"What the hell are you doing out here all alone?" she heard a voice whip through the strong wind. She whirled about to face Luke Cameron once again.

"My horse was frightened away by the approaching storm," she informed him defiantly, after recovering from the shock of hearing his voice. "I'm afraid that I have no way back to the ranch." She stood facing him proudly, refusing to back down in the face of his infuriating commanding tone.

"Well, how did you get all the way out here in the first place? You mean to tell me that you came all this way by yourself? Don't you have a bit of sense at all? Does your father or anyone else know where you are?" he interrogated her ruthlessly, dismounting now and striding up to face her, scowling down into her stormy countenance.

"That is really none of your business, Mr. Cameron! I might ask you the same thing; what in the world are you doing out here in the middle of the range by yourself?" she threw at him sarcastically.

"For your information, Miss Lawrence, I heard some shots and came to investigate. But, that is beside the point. You haven't answered any of my questions yet!" he insisted adamantly.

"And, as I told you, that isn't any of your business! I merely wish to return to my father's ranch now, if you would be so kind as to take me there!" she stormed at him, losing her temper at the sound of his scolding voice.

"All right, then! Come on, we better get going before the storm hits us full force!" he shouted at her, raising his voice to be heard above the roar of the blowing wind. Dust was now flying every-where, stinging their exposed skin with the force of its fierce contact.

Amanda and Luke bent their heads against the dust. He pulled off his jacket and placed it over her head. He started to toss her up onto his horse's back, but suddenly halted. He tightly grabbed hold of her arm, clutched the reins in his other hand, then led both her and the horse to a narrow gulley several feet away.

"What on earth do you think you're doing now, you lunatic?" she exclaimed furiously.

Instead of answering her, Luke pushed her roughly down into the gulley, then forced his horse to lie upon the ground nearby, maintaining his hold on the reins to keep the animal steady. He then jumped in the gulley beside Amanda, trying to block most of the wind and dust from her body.

Amanda, however, misinterpreted his actions and struggled wildly to rise and escape. She attempted to beat at him with her fists, but he easily captured her wrists in his free hand and forced her to lie still.

"Don't you dare lay a hand on me! If you harm me in any way, I'll inform my father and he will most assuredly kill you! I am warning you, I will not submit to such an outrage as rape!" she screamed at him, still seeking to free herself from his bruising grasp.

"Rape? What are you talking about?" he shouted in confusion, then began to laugh in pure amusement as it dawned on him what she had believed him to be doing.

"I'm not trying to rape you, you little idiot!" he told her, his lips close to her ear.

"Then, what is going on?" she demanded, still not certain whether to believe him or not.

"Cyclone!" he stated the one word, then pointed.

Amanda jerked her head up to view the now visible curse of nature. She saw the funnel-shaped cloud, then the swirling, twisting black object that swooped down to the ground, dipping with a terrific roar. There was dust, dirt, rocks, and other debris flying everywhere in its turbulent wake.

"Oh, dear Lord!" she whispered in fear.

"Just stay down and lie still!" ordered Luke, now placing his body into position on top of her, seeking to protect her.

After what seemed an eternity to Amanda, but which was actually only a few minutes, the roar began to recede, the dust settle, the ferocious winds die down. She raised her head above the edge of the gulley and peered out at the aftereffects of the cyclone. She observed for the first time a small part of the terrible destruction of which a cyclone is capable.

The fence she had earlier been using as a target was nowhere to be seen. There were trees, tumbleweeds, and rocks scattered about in total confusion. Fortunately, there was nothing within her line of vision which denoted anything either human or animal.

"You may please get up off of me now, Mr. Cameron," she told him shakily, her nerves on end because of the terrifying experience.

"Sure thing, Miss Lawrence," he replied mockingly. He slowly removed his muscular arms from about her body, then rose to his feet. She was afforded her first glimpse of his face since the storm. His features were covered with dust, the creases at the corners of his eyes and mouth accentuated by its caking. His clothes were also extremely dusty, and Amanda looked down swiftly to see that her own attire was equally filthy. She also became aware that her riding skirt had become bunched up well above her knees, and she hurriedly pulled it back down around her ankles, ignoring Luke's amused, admiring smile.

"It seems to me that you are making a habit of rescuing me in such an abusive manner, sir! However, I suppose that I do owe you a word of gratitude for saving me once again," she grudgingly admitted.

"That won't be necessary. Now, what were you doing out here all by yourself? Don't you know how dangerous it is for a woman to wander about this country alone? Aren't you even aware that there are such hazards as renegade Indians, poisonous snakes, and other wild things that could harm you?" he scolded her once again.

"Very well, if you insist upon badgering me for an answer. I was out here practicing with the rifle. You see, I thought to surprise my father with learning to shoot a gun."

"So, I'm right in assuming that he doesn't know where you are. Sam Lawrence is going to be mighty riled at your going off by yourself like that, you know. It's going to take a heap of explaining on your part. I guess I better get you on home now. I only hope the cyclone didn't do any damage to my ranch, your father's, or anyone else's around here."

He clasped her tightly and unexpectedly about her waist and lightly tossed her into the saddle, then, climbing up behind her, he encircled her with his strong arms and grasped the reins.

"I've never seen a cyclone before, Mr. Cameron," she stated conversationally, extremely ill-at-ease at the position she was forced to endure during the ride. She felt his broad, muscular chest and the warmth of his body, felt his arms pressing against her. She tried inching forward a bit to escape the uncomfortable contact.

"Well, you've certainly seen one now, haven't you? Actually, you were damn lucky that you were out here, in a way. It could have been much worse if you'd been inside a building when one hit. They've got a mighty peculiar habit of ripping up everything in their path, including horses, barns, houses, and wagons. Why, folks out here have seen them bend huge trees, drain the water from a creek, lots of other strange things like that. And there isn't any way in the world to know when one's going to drop down out of the clouds. You just have to watch real careful whenever the clouds start boiling and racing like they were. Sometimes it just signals a dust storm. And a dust storm can last for days at a time."

"Oh, I see. Well, I've never before encountered such a fierce wind, either. I don't believe I will ever be able to wash all of this dust out of my hair and skin!" she remarked, wrinkling her nose in distaste.

Changing the subject a few moments later, Luke said, "I was serious when I mentioned renegade Indians. Seems that some folks a few miles north of here in the next county took a few shots at about a half-dozen of them just last week. They'd escaped from one of the reservations, most likely, and they'll steal all they can. I just want to warn you not to go out riding alone any more. And, furthermore, I'll have to talk to your father about those Indians. Yes sir, if I was Sam Lawrence, I'd be sure to give you a good hiding," he commented with a grin, teasing her once again.

"Well, I am most certainly glad that you are not Sam Lawrence," she replied frostily, drawing herself upright. "And, for your information, Mr. Cameron, I am no longer a child, and I am absolutely certain that my father will not treat me as such!"

"Yes, ma'am, Miss Lawrence," he responded seriously, though his blue eyes were glinting with amusement, "I know you're not a child. Seems that I don't have to knock you down twice in a row to be able to tell that."

Amanda drew in her breath sharply and tightly clamped her mouth shut. Oh, the arrogance of this hateful, insolent man! she thought belligerently.

Six

Amanda refused to speak to Luke for the remainder of the ride, and they were soon back at the Circle L. She could see Samuel and the hands scurrying about the grounds, apparently soothing livestock and repairing minor damage done by the cyclone. She immediately jumped down from the horse and hurried over to her father.

"Samuel—" she began, only to be interrupted by the fierce scowl her father turned upon her.

"Amanda! Don't you know I've been worried sick about you? I only discovered a moment ago that you weren't up in your room. Where the hell have you been?" he stormed at her, his large, calloused hands closing on her shoulders, and administering several sound shakes.

"Samuel, please allow me to explain," she insisted, somewhat taken aback by his fury. "You see, I was out riding, well, I was actually out on the range practicing my aim, when my horse was frightened away by the approaching storm. Mr. Cameron brought me home."

"So, you were out riding all by yourself? Damn it, you must have known that I would never allow you to do such a foolhardy thing! I can't believe

97

you did such a damned stupid thing, young lady! You will go inside the house at once, do you understand? I'll talk to you about the matter later, after I've spoken to Cameron here," he sternly ordered her.

Amanda started to defy him, but she became conscious of the curious, amused stares of the ranchhands, and, most of all, of Luke Cameron. She whirled away from her father, flounced up the front steps, and held back angry tears as she slammed the door forcefully behind her.

How dare he treat me like a child, especially in front of all those men? she lamented furiously, her whole being the picture of outraged dignity.

Meanwhile, Samuel and Luke waited until Amanda had disappeared inside the house and until the hands had resumed their various activities. Then Samuel asked the younger man, his voice considerably calmer now, "Cameron, how'd you come to find her?"

"She was having shooting practice at one of my fence posts. Me and some of my hands were out this morning, checking on some stock, and I heard the shots. I rode over to see what all the shooting was about, and found your little daughter in a heap of trouble. The cyclone was about to hit and her horse had been scared away, just like she told you. We waited for the storm to blow over, then I brought her on home," he reiterated.

"Well, I'm much obliged to you for bringing her home. I guess I'll have to have a long talk with her about riding out alone and all. If that's all you have to say, you might as well be getting on along now, Cameron." Samuel had already turned his back on Luke and was striding away toward the corral.

"Wait a minute, Mr. Lawrence. I already told your daughter about this, but I think you ought to be warned. In fact, all the ranchers in these parts are being warned. There's some renegade Indians, looked like Comanches, maybe headed this way. They were seen a ways north of here last week. You'd better tell that daughter of yours exactly how dangerous it would be if she was caught out riding alone by any Comanches."

"I appreciate the information, but what I tell my daughter is none of your damned affair! Now, I'd like it if you'd be on about your business." He turned his back once again and continued on his way.

Luke bit back a comment about how it sure as hell was his business what Samuel told his daughter, seeing as how he had been obliged to rescue her a couple of times now. It seemed she was the type that was forever getting into some kind of mischief. He reined his horse about and galloped away.

Trouble Miss Lawrence might be, he mused as he rode, but she was certainly one beautiful, desirable little bundle of it! Yes sir, Luke, he told himself, most cowpokes around here would be willing to ride many a mile to catch a glimpse of such a pretty lady's face, and here you are, favored with her presence even when you aren't actively seeking it. Perhaps it was fate or something, but she was forever turning up when he least expected it.

Remembering the feel of her soft, womanly curves beneath his hard, muscular body, he smiled wickedly. If only she weren't the daughter of his adversary, though the adversary was not of his choosing, he might be even more tempted to pursue an acquaintance with the high and mighty Boston miss. Yes sir, she could sure enough use a bit of taming, he thought, and I would relish the opportunity to be the one to do it.

Amanda threw herself onto her bed, taking out a small measure of her fury and intense humiliation on the soft pillow beneath her tightly clenched fists. She was unprepared when she heard the loud knock upon her door. Without waiting for his daughter to answer that knock, Samuel walked into her room and shut the door softly behind him.

"Amanda, it's time we discuss what you've done."

"Samuel, I had no idea anything would happen. How could I have known about a cyclone dipping down from the sky? I didn't know my horse would run away," she defiantly informed him, sitting up now, her face turned upward to his.

"I realize that you couldn't know such things would occur. That is not what I'm angry about. You should never have gone riding alone, particularly without telling anyone that you were doing so, and I believe that you know it. I appreciate your desire to surprise me, but I cannot allow you to do such willful, headstrong things! This is my ranch, and I am master here, whether you like that fact or not. Also, I am your father, even if I am a rather late one. Do I make myself clear?"

"Perfectly clear," she replied stiffly. "However, as I have already informed you, I am no longer a child! I resent being treated as one, Samuel Lawrence, and I will not tolerate it! How could you do such a thing, especially in front of all those men out there?" she demanded angrily.

"I apologize for making your chastisement so public. I suppose I don't know too much about being a father, Amanda, but I only know that I was half out of my mind when I discovered you missing this morning. The cyclone was spotted by one of the hands and I hurried up here to get you out of danger," he explained, trying to make her understand his feelings in the matter.

Amanda sat in silence a moment longer, contemplating her father's words and subsequent actions. She was torn between anger and fairness, but fairness eventually won out. She finally said, "Samuel, you have every right to be angry, I suppose. And I can understand that you were very concerned for my safety, not knowing where I had gone. I just cannot tolerate being spoken to as a child! Throughout all of my life, Aunt Martha and Uncle David have dictated my very thoughts and emotions. Can't you see, I am ready to behave as a grown woman? You, of all people, should understand that I possess an independent spirit, though it has been hidden deep within me, not allowed to surface for all these years. Well, I intend to allow it to surface now. With you, Samuel, I can possibly,

101

finally be myself. Please say that you understand," she implored, not at all sure that she had made him understand.

"I understand, Amanda," he told her gently. "I will truly endeavor to desist from either thinking of or treating you like a child ever again. And, the next time you want to go out riding, whatever the reason, will you please promise me that you will take someone with you?"

"Yes, Samuel, I promise." She stood and hugged him suddenly, catching him off-guard. He hesitated for only a brief moment, then returned her unexpected show of affection. The two of them returned downstairs together.

Four days after the events surrounding the morning of the cyclone, Amanda was once again practicing her aim. However, she was now relegated to practicing near the corral. Tommy approached her that afternoon, his face alight with a boyish smile.

"Miss Amanda! Miss Amanda, there's going to be a dance in town tonight. Please say you'll come. You see, there ain't too many single women hereabouts, especially young and pretty ones, and all the men from miles around will be fighting for a dance with you. Do you think your father will let you come?" he asked, his words tumbling over one another in his haste.

"A dance? Why, that sounds as if it would be very enjoyable, Tommy. I haven't had much of an opportunity to meet many people since I've been here. My goodness, I've already been here three weeks, too. I'll speak to my father. I'm sure that he will agree to take me. What time is the dance to begin, and where is it to be held?"

"It's set for seven o'clock, and it's going to be in the courthouse, ma'am. Everyone from a long ways off will come. And, Miss Amanda," he said, his face growing a trifle redder, "well, that is, could you save me a dance, ma'am?"

Amanda gazed into his boyish, attractive face and smiled with pleasure at his obvious admiration.

"I'll save you the first and last dances, Mr. Evans," she replied graciously, rewarded by his delighted expression.

As Tommy returned to his chores, she returned to her practice. She had become quite adept with a rifle now. She aimed at a line of tin cans along a fence, successfully blowing each and every one of them off its post. She reflected once again that she would be glad of an opportunity to display her knowledge and skills to Mr. Cameron. For some reason, she told herself, he always made her feel like a naughty child. And that is certainly not what I am, she thought, recalling the discussion between herself and her father four days ago.

Samuel did agree to escort his daughter to the dance. Amanda dressed with great care that evening, taking extra pains with her appearance. She donned a freshly ironed dress, a green silk frock with an enormous, ruffled bow at the back to serve as a bustle. The neckline was rather low, exposing the tops of her full, creamy breasts, but Aunt Martha had never approved of the dress for other reasons as well. It definitely showed off her

103

figure to the best advantage, fitting snugly in all the right places. She smoothed down the skirt and then faced her reflection in the mirror.

Mrs. Chambers had helped her to arrange her auburn curls atop her head, allowing a few tendrils to curl naturally about her face and neck. Amanda drew on her gloves, selected an evening cape, and descended the stairs to find her father and show him what a stylish daughter he would be escorting to the dance.

However, when Amanda finally located him in the parlor, it was she who drew in her breath at his appearance. Never had she seen her father looking so very attractive, so distinguished. His clothes were a trifle old-fashioned, yet they were still appropriate. The black suit and white shirt accentuated his tanned features, his red, neatly trimmed moustache. Amanda crossed the room slowly and sank down into a deep curtsy before him.

"Mr. Lawrence, I am indeed honored that you will be my escort to the dance tonight. Shall we go?"

"You look very beautiful, Amanda. So very much like your mother, you know," he murmured, his eyes taking in her fashionable appearance and shining eyes.

"And, you have never looked more handsome! Now, come on, Samuel, or we may be late." He offered his arm and the two of them stepped out into the cool October evening air.

"Are the ranchhands riding along with us?" she asked him, glancing around the deserted yard.

"No, those that are going have already gone. Tonight, it's just this fortunate fellow escorting the most beautiful girl he knows," he replied whimsically. He handed her up into the wagon, then climbed up beside her, flicking the reins gently and guiding the horses in the direction of Big Prairie.

As they arrived near the outskirts of town, Amanda heard the faint strains of music coming from the direction of the center of town. Samuel finally pulled up before the "courthouse," a large, wooden building badly in need of a coat of paint. It was certainly not the sort of courthouse Amanda had expected, but she said nothing about it and allowed her father to lift her down from the wagon. She noted that there were quite a number of horses and wagons tied up outside along the street. Her heart began to quicken at the thought of meeting so many strangers, but she lifted her head proudly and shook out her skirts. She took her father's arm and glided smoothly through the doorway of the building.

Inside, the orchestra consisted of an energetic fiddler and other equally lively musicians, all playing a melodious tune. There were several couples engaged in a form of dancing Amanda did not recognize. Her father glanced at her puzzled expression and said, "Amanda, this isn't exactly a society dance like you're used to, you know. There's going to be a lot of square dancing, polkas, and waltzing. There will mainly be folk tunes played. Anyway, I'm sure you have a more than adequate education when it comes to dancing, so you'll do just fine."

Amanda smiled gratefully at his reassuring words and allowed him to lead her out on to the dance floor, which consisted entirely of rough wooden planks nailed together.

"Samuel," she protested, remembering her promise to Tommy, "I told Tommy Evans that I would save the first and last dances for him."

"Well, I think that a father will take first priority over another man any day," he told her as he swung her around and around. She laughed gaily in response and whirled about the room, catching fleeting glimpses of the other men and few women crowded inside the room.

Soon, Amanda became aware that the other couples who had been vigorously dancing when she had first entered with her father had now ceased and had joined the lines of people surrounding the dance area, their eyes riveted on the lone couple now left in the center. Amanda twisted her head about to see the faces of some of the people. She sensed by the look in the womens' eyes that they were envious, possibly jealous, of this new, fashionable young beauty now attracting the attention of everyone present. All of the men she observed, however, were openly admiring and already arguing amongst themselves as to who would claim the mysterious and beautiful young woman for the next dance.

The waltz finally ending, Samuel led Amanda over to the impatiently waiting young men and relinquished her into their care.

"Amanda, it seems to me that these young

gentlemen want to have a dance with you. I recommend that you use extreme caution when making your choice," he told her lightheartedly, obviously enjoying his daughter's success, enjoying his role of the proud father.

The crowd of eager young men nearly toppled over one another in an attempt to petition Amanda for a dance. Within the space of a few moments, her dance card was completely filled. She did, however, manage to save the last dance for Tommy, feeling somewhat guilty as she viewed his disappointed face at the edge of the crowd.

Meanwhile, as Amanda was passed from one enthusiastic partner to another, the women were discussing her amongst themselves. They resented the fact that her stylish dress made their own homemade ginghams and calicoes seem dowdy in comparison. They also resented the fact that she drew all the male attention. True, none of them lacked for dancing partners, but they were envious nonetheless.

Amanda danced to the tune of "The Arkansas Traveler," then was swept away to the strains of "Turkey in the Straw," "The Buffalo Gals," and other folk tunes familiar to the townspeople. She quickly learned the steps to the various square dances and polkas, and her face was becomingly flushed and happy, her feet never still.

Finally, an intermission was declared by the fiddler, who professed to having developed a powerful thirst for some punch. Everyone broke away from the dance floor and flocked to the refreshment tables, then began to drift outside for some cool, fresh air.

Amanda, who was animatedly carrying on a conversation with five or six young men at one time, suddenly felt the pressure of a strong hand on her elbow. She turned a smiling face to its owner, but her gracious smile faded when she saw Luke Cameron's face mischievously smiling down into hers.

"Miss Lawrence," he said, bowing slightly. She noted that he did not wear the same attire as the majority of the men, the freshly laundered cotton shirts and denim trousers. Instead, he wore a well-fitted jacket and matching trousers of new buckskin, as well as polished leather boots.

"Mr. Cameron," she answered coolly, turning abruptly away from him to continue her discussion with the other young men.

"I would like the pleasure of your company outside for a few moments, if you please. I'm sure these gentlemen can spare you for that long," he stated authoritatively, ignoring her polite, but firm, protests. She yielded to the pressure of his hand, not wishing to cause a scene before so many curious eyes.

"Mr. Cameron, what is the meaning of this? Couldn't you see that I was occupied with those other gentlemen?" she demanded angrily, her voice low and furious.

"Sorry, ma'am, but I wanted to talk to you. I've been watching you all evening. It seems that you've made quite an impression on all the men. And, as for the women, I've overheard the comments about the beautiful, haughty Miss

Lawrence," he told her mockingly as he led her firmly outside and around to the side of the building. The full moon was illuminating their path, and Amanda saw that the other couples were returning inside as the music began once again.

"Just what are they saying?" she asked, momentarily forgetting her anger, curious to know precisely how the other women viewed her, yet knowing already that they would not have been saying complimentary things.

"Oh, the usual things women say, I guess. By the way," he said, changing the subject, "what in heaven's name is that thing on the back of your dress there? Don't tell me you're really shaped that way back there. That is one thing I remember the women talking about."

She quickly glanced behind her back, realizing that the odious man was teasing her about her bustle. She drew herself rigidly upright and replied in frigid tones, "That is what is known as a bustle, Mr. Cameron. And, if this were not such a wilderness, you and all the rest of these uncouth people would realize that it is very fashionable! You see, I know that you don't approve of me, and I know that the women here tonight don't approve of me, either. But, I do not care what any of you choose to think of me! They are merely envious, whereas you, Mr. Cameron, you are rude and insufferable!" she informed him, growing quite angry now, completely disgusted with his overbearing attitude. What she told him, however, was not completely true; she did care what others thought of her, particularly the women. It had been much the same way back in Boston. The women there had been jealous also, and she had never acquired more than a very few female friends.

Luke Cameron's blue eyes glinted with a strange, intense light at her words and Amanda immediately regretted her childish outburst. He suddenly grasped her shoulders with his large, bruising hands and shook her forcefully, saying, "Miss Lawrence, I've had just about enough of your high and mighty ways. So has everyone else here tonight. You know, you haven't really given anyone a chance to know you. Hell no, you've been much too busy playing the belle of the ball to so much as even be introduced to any of the other folks. And, for your information, this place isn't any more of a wilderness than that place you come from! No, out here at least, we try to teach our children good manners!"

"Good manners!" she exclaimed, losing her temper altogether now. "Don't you dare to speak to me of good manners, you savage, you! I haven't seen any indication of such a thing as good manners since I left Boston!" With that, she attempted to pull away from him. He released her aching shoulders, only to grab her by the wrist and pull her roughly along with him to a spot near the back of the building, well out of the moonlight's glow, hidden by the shadows created by the overhang of the roof.

"What do you think you're doing now?" she demanded furiously as she tried to wrench her wrist from his grasp.

"I think it's about time you found out you aren't so different from anyone else, Miss Lawrence! I think it's about time I taught you better manners!" he ground out. She flinched involuntarily as it appeared that he was about to strike her, but she opened her eyes wide when he released her wrist and encircled her with his powerful arms. She felt as if she were surrounded by bands of iron, and she increased her frantic struggles to escape him.

"Let go of me!" she spat at him, ceasing to care now whether she acted like a proper lady or not.

Luke stared down into her stormy, luminous eyes for a brief moment, then brought his hard, demanding lips down upon her own, searing her with the brutal intensity of the action. She continued to struggle wildly against him, but was suddenly halted by the peculiar, unfamiliar sensations she was experiencing. As his lips now moved sensuously upon her own, she felt a rising flame building deep within her very being.

Luke whispered her name as he removed his lips, then allowed his warm mouth to travel downward to the curve of her graceful neck, to her white shoulders, then to her bosom. He exposed even more of her full breasts as he pulled the bodice of her gown gently down. Amanda gasped in surprise and shock, her legs beginning to feel weak as his lips continued their tender assault on her unsuspecting body.

She finally awoke from her trancelike state and pushed ineffectually against him, then raised her foot and kicked him as hard as she possibly could,

111

striking him upon the shin of his left leg. He released her with a muttered oath.

"How dare you? How dare you?" was all she could manage to utter at that moment. She whirled away from him and hurried back around the corner of the building, furiously scrubbing away at her bruised lips and hastily rearranging her bodice.

Tommy Evans saw her come through the doorway, her beautiful face flushed, her green eyes sparkling dangerously. He rushed to her side and inquired what on earth had happened to cause such a reaction.

Amanda was unable to hear him at first, so absorbed was her mind with the encounter with Luke Cameron. Tommy again repeated, "Miss Amanda? Are you all right, ma'am? What happened?"

She turned toward him then and forced herself to bestow upon him a bright, frivolous smile.

"Of course I'm all right. I just walked outside for some fresh air. Now, I realize that I've missed a dance or two, but I think that I shall dance this particular dance with you." She held up her arms and allowed him to guide her onto the dance floor. She glanced toward the doorway, but did not see Luke Cameron enter. She forced her thoughts away from him and gave her full attention to the dancing and the several partners who claimed her.

During another well-timed intermission, Samuel spied his daughter and approached her, escorting another woman with him.

"Amanda, this is Mrs. Powell. She sort of helps

run the town, you might say. Her husband is the mayor."

Amanda politely greeted the middle-aged, slightly rotund woman with the graying blonde hair. Her dress, Amanda silently took note, was a bit more fashionable than the others.

"My dear, your father has been speaking of you to me. What he tells me is very interesting. It seems that you have been fortunate to have had a rather extensive education, am I not right?"

"Well, I didn't have precisely what you would call an extensive education, but I was educated in Boston. I did attend the ladies' finishing school for two years," she admitted.

"Nevertheless, child, you seem to be very intelligent and resourceful. We can really use someone like you right now. You see, our schoolteacher got married last week, and we desperately need a temporary replacement for her. The new teacher won't arrive until sometime next month, at least another two or three weeks. Well, I was wondering if you might be interested in the job? Oh, I know you don't need the money, but I thought you might enjoy the experience."

Amanda was surprised at the woman's request. Teach school? Why, that was certainly something she had never before considered doing. Yes, perhaps it might be enjoyable at that. It would give her something with which to occupy her time for a while. She was finding it a bit tedious lately, what with her father and the hands busy elsewhere and Mrs. Chambers seeing to all of the cooking and housework. Amanda considered it briefly, then turned to her father for his approval.

"Samuel, will this be agreeable to you? After all, I am your guest. Do you approve?" she asked him.

"Well, I don't see as how it will do any harm. Mrs. Powell is right; you might have fun at it. I can let one of the hands escort you into town in the mornings and come to ride back with you in the afternoons. Things aren't that hectic right now. If you're sure you'd like to do this, then it's all right with me."

"Mrs. Powell," Amanda said, turning back to the woman, "I accept. I must tell you, though, that I haven't the slightest idea how to teach school, but I will endeavor to do my very best."

"Oh, dear child," she replied, very pleased with this polite young woman whom she had at first judged too harshly, "I will be glad to help you in any way I possibly can. Now, just come on into town the first thing Monday morning and I'll be at the schoolhouse to help you get started."

She strolled away from them and Amanda remarked to her father, "Samuel, I'm not feeling very well. Do you suppose we could go home now? It is getting rather late, you know."

"Oh, of course, Amanda. I'm sure you're very tired after all this dancing and attention. Come on, I'll get you your wrap."

He led her to the doorway and retrieved her evening cape from a peg on the wall. Several of the young men flocked to her side, entreating her to stay, but she firmly announced that she would have to complete her dances some other time.

As she and her father climbed up onto the

wagon seat, she saw the outline of someone's form silhouetted near the side of the building, standing in the shadows. She knew that it was Luke Cameron, watching her, and she turned her head away with a vengeance.

"What is it, Amanda?" Samuel inquired, feeling her stiffen beside him.

"Oh, it's nothing, really. I'm rather exhausted, that's all. Thank you for bringing me tonight, Samuel. You are certain that you approve of my teaching school for a while?" she asked him again.

"I think it might be just the thing for you. It will give you a chance to meet and know some of the other people around here. Once you're teaching their kids, you can't help but get to know them!"

Amanda lapsed into thoughtful silence as they drove homeward in the bright moonlight. She burned with shame and outraged dignity as she recalled the humiliating encounter between herself and Luke Cameron. Oh, that beast of a man! she exclaimed inwardly, still seething with fury as she recalled his insulting words and barbaric actions.

She had never been so thoroughly, passionately kissed or manhandled in such a way before. Peter had bestowed upon her several quick, chaste kisses when bidding her goodnight, as well as a few longer embraces upon occasion, but the majority of his kisses had caused little response. True, she had felt a certain awakening deep within when he had held her in her arms, but certainly nothing to compare with the violent response deep within her this evening! I have never before been treated in such a disgraceful manner as I have been tonight by Luke Cameron! she thought, nearly shaking with the intensity of her emotions.

Why was that terrible man able to affect her in such a way? She still could not fathom the searing, confusing sensations that had assailed her body when he had taken her into his powerful arms and kissed her in such an expert, masterful way. No, I will not think of it again, I must not, she vowed silently.

She fled upstairs to her bedroom as soon as they reached the ranch. She breathlessly shut the door behind her, then began to undress, recalling once more the obvious admiration of the men at the dance. She forced her thoughts away from Luke Cameron as she inspected herself before the full-length mirror. Tonight, she had felt like a woman, no longer a pretty girl, but truly a full-grown woman. She knew that she certainly looked like one, and she turned to pick up the white lawn nightgown that was lying upon the bed. She quickly drew it down over her head.

Her body still tingled with the unfamiliar sensations that dreadful, impossible man had evoked. She uttered an extremely unladylike curse and climbed into bed. She slid between the cool sheets and turned out the lamp.

Somehow, I shall have my revenge on Mr. Cameron for the shameful way he has treated me, she vowed. Thank goodness no one else witnessed her humiliation at his hands tonight!

At the same moment, Luke Cameron was riding slowly back to his own ranch, his thoughts wholly occupied with Amanda. She had the power to infuriate him the way no other woman had ever done before, stirring in him uncontrollable emotions. He regretted losing his temper the way he had, yet he knew full well that he did not regret the passionate embrace they had shared.

Oh yes, Miss Lawrence, he thought, you enjoyed it nearly as much as I did, even though it is far beneath your dignity to admit to such human feelings. He suddenly realized that he had been wanting to kiss her from the first time he had faced her, a rifle aimed tremulously at his heart. Could it be that she was more than a mere challenge to him? Could it possibly be that he was beginning to feel something for the beautiful, willful, headstrong Amanda Lawrence?

"Damn!" he muttered viciously to himself, then dismounted as he became aware that he had reached his ranch.

Seven

Monday morning came and Amanda lazily stretched before rising from her bed. She was aware of an increasing sense of excitement for the adventure ahead that day. She viewed the prospect of teaching school with a touch of anxiety and unaccustomed nervousness. After dressing in a simple but pretty frock of sprigged muslin, she hurried downstairs to breakfast with her father, as was their custom.

"Good morning, Samuel," she said as she took her seat across from him at the table.

"Morning, Amanda. Well, I guess you're all set to start teaching today. I'll have young Evans take you into town, seeing as how you two are such good friends and all," he remarked wryly.

"Now, Samuel, you needn't use that tone of voice with me. You know perfectly well that 'friends' is all that Tommy and I will ever be."

"Well, I want you to be careful today. Be sure to take your rifle with you, all right?" he cautioned.

"Why on earth should I do that? Oh, I suppose you've heard something more concerning those renegade Indians?" she probed.

"No, but I do want you to be prepared, just in

case. There are many things that could happen, and it doesn't hurt to have your gun along with you," he replied casually.

"Very well. You have no cause to worry, though. Everything is going to work out splendidly, isn't it, Mrs. Chambers?" she brightly asked the woman serving them eggs and bacon.

"That's right, honey. Everything's going to be just fine. The only thing is, I'm sure going to miss you being here all day long. I've gotten used to having you around," she said with a resigned sigh.

"Oh, now, I'll still be here for your delicious breakfasts and dinners. And, after school, I'm still planning to help you with those new dresses. I wouldn't break my promise to you."

"Oh, I know it, child. Now, you eat your breakfast and be on your way. It won't do to keep them kids waiting on the first day you're going to take over. Those little rascals are sure enough going to be a handful as it is."

Amanda and Tommy rode away from the ranch on horseback, Amanda having previously persuaded her reluctant father to allow them to use this particular mode of traveling. She had argued that it would be much quicker and perhaps safer than taking the wagon.

"Tommy, I'm glad that my father has given us this chance to speak to one another privately. I haven't seen very much of you since the dance last Friday night," she said.

"Well, I guess I've had an awful lot of extra chores to do, ma'am. You can bet that I haven't been avoiding you or nothing. But, when I have seen you, Miss Amanda, you've been kind of different."

"Different? In what way do you mean?"

"Well, it's hard to say, exactly. You sure ain't been talking much, and your face appears to take on a serious, real thoughtful expression every now and then, like your mind is in a different place than the rest of you. Do you understand what I'm trying to say?"

"I think I do. I've had a great deal on my mind, lately, that's all. It has nothing whatsoever to do with you, and I am sorry if I have been rude to you or to the others," she apologized earnestly, not wishing to reveal the true, secret reasons for her attitude of late. Luke Cameron had crept unbidden into her thoughts more often than she cared to admit.

"Miss Amanda, you could never be rude!" he replied emphatically. "In fact, ma'am, you couldn't ever be nothing but what you are—beautiful, kind, gentle, and a true lady."

"Why, that is very sweet of you, Tommy," she thanked him airily, purposely turning her attention to the countryside on this crisp autumn morning. She knew that what she had inwardly feared about her relationship with Tommy had come to pass; he was falling in love with her. Oh, it was more than likely a simple case of boyish infatuation, but she was at a loss as to how to deal with the difficult problem. She knew that she should discourage him in some manner, but she valued his friendship very highly and was hesitant to hurt him in any way. He was so good and so

120

young, she thought, although he was much the same age as herself.

After Tommy bid her goodbye, Amanda watched as he led her horse over to the livery stable. Then, she turned and faced the schoolhouse, a small, rough structure located near the farthest edge of town. She unconsciously squared her shoulders and lifted her head proudly as she marched resolutely inside. She saw Mrs. Powell at the opposite end of the building, absorbed in leafing through several papers which were scattered about on the surface of a large desk.

"Mrs. Powell?" she said hesitantly, reluctant to draw attention to herself, aware that nearly thirty young faces now turned to scrutinize their new teacher.

"Amanda, my dear. Please come up here and let the children have a good look at you. Children," she announced as Amanda obediently approached the front, "this is your teacher, for the time being, Miss Lawrence."

"Good morning, Miss Lawrence," they responded dutifully at a signal from Mrs. Powell.

"I am very pleased to meet you, children," Amanda replied with composure, striving not to laugh aloud at their curious expressions.

"I'll leave you with them now, Amanda. I'm sure you'll do just fine. I've left a few of their lessons on the desk there, the ones they were working on when their teacher up and got herself married. Well, I'll see you later. Good day, everyone," she said as she hurried from the building.

Amanda turned about and carefully took her seat behind the desk, grateful for the small measure of protection it afforded. She straightened the papers on the desk for a brief moment to gather courage, then politely told the students, "Well, it seems that all of you are now aware of my name, but I still do not know any of yours. Now, beginning at the left, there in the front, you will please stand, one at a time, and state both your name and your age."

The first child, an attractive little girl of perhaps seven years of age, peered about at the others around her, then shyly stood upright to follow the new teacher's instruction. Soon, the others were following suit and becoming increasingly bolder in their pronouncements.

Amanda smiled politely, pleased with the children's cooperation on this first day. Well, now, this doesn't appear that it will be all that difficult, she admitted to herself with relief. Finally, only one pupil remained to speak, and Amanda turned her attention to the tall, lanky blond-haired boy now standing near the back of the room.

"My name is Jake Cameron. I'm fourteen years old. And, I don't need to be in school at all!" he finished, his manner perfectly correct but his tone of voice very defiant.

"Well, Jake Cameron, I am truly sorry that you feel that way, but I promise to try and make school as painless as possible for you," she remarked calmly. The other students laughed delightedly at her rejoinder and Jake's expression grew increasingly stubborn.

Amanda gazed down at the papers in her hands as a startling realization suddenly dawned on her. Of course, he must be Luke Cameron's younger brother! Certainly, she could now see that he resembled him. Oh dear, this will most definitely not make things any easier for me, she told herself. However, she soothed herself with the thought that she need never come into contact with Luke. Simply because she was teaching his brother for a few short weeks did not signify that there would be any further encounters with that terrible man!

Throughout that first day, she copied several problems on the chalkboard and had the children read aloud from their primers. The last problem on the board remained to be solved and it was nearly time for school to be dismissed. She waited patiently for someone to raise their hand and repeat the correct solution. Jake Cameron's hand shot up.

"Yes, Jake? You have the answer?" she inquired coolly, reflecting that she should take care not to become defensive toward the youngster, merely because of his brother.

"Why, hell, yes, I've got the answer! Why else do you suppose I'd be poking my arm up in the air?" he informed her, his words accompanied by an immediate outburst of raucous laughter.

"Jake Cameron," she demanded angrily, "you will remain after school. Children, the rest of you are dismissed for the day!"

As the room emptied, Jake remained passively seated at the opposite end of the room.

"Jake, you will come up here and stand before

123

me at once," she ordered him sternly, then watched as he slowly drew himself upright and approached her where she still sat behind the large oak desk. Good heavens, she mused silently, he's several inches taller than I am!

"Yes, ma'am," he murmured, standing sheepishly before her now.

"Why did you use such language, Jake? I'm sure you have been taught better manners than that." She suddenly recalled the dance and her discussion with Jake's brother concerning manners. No, she firmly resolved, I won't think of his brother!

"Well, I don't know. It just sort of slipped out, I reckon," he replied innocently.

"Well, you will never use such language in this classroom ever again, is that understood?"

"Yes, ma'am."

"You may go now, Jake. And, Jake," she added, just as he was about to go through the doorway, "please tell your brother that I was forced to speak to you about your manners."

"Yes, ma'am." He strode outside then, puzzled as to the reason this new teacher would mention his brother. She sure was a pretty one. Maybe she was sweet on his brother or something.

Amanda immediately regretted her words concerning Luke. Why couldn't she just forget him? she chided herself furiously. She sighed heavily and prepared to leave, gathering up the lessons for the next day.

As she walked outside and began to search the streets with a sweeping glance, she observed Buck Jones leaning against the hitching post, their horses saddled and waiting.

"Howdy, Miss Amanda," he said lazily.

"Mr. Jones, what are you doing here?" she asked, trying to hide the revulsion she felt toward him. He appeared to be waiting for her. Where on earth was Tommy?

"Why, ma'am, I've come to escort you home this afternoon, just like your pa told me to," he replied sarcastically, his eyes boldly appraising her as they always seemed to do.

"Where, may I ask, is Mr. Evans?"

"That young pup had other things to do. Your pa said I was to fetch you home today. Well, now, you ready to go?" he asked, coming toward her now.

Amanda, perceiving his intentions to assist her in mounting, quickly mounted without warning, then kicked her horse into a swift canter.

Buck ground out a vicious curse and jumped on his own horse to follow. He finally succeeded in catching up with her near the outermost edge of town.

"Miss Amanda, that wasn't a very friendly thing for you to go and do. You know, you ain't said two words to me in quite a while now. You know that I already told you I'd be real willing to be your friend, your very good friend. You ain't got no call to act this way to old Buck here," he complained, his eyes shifting repeatedly to the face and form riding beside him.

"Mr. Jones, I have already informed you that I have no particular desire for your company. I may be forced to endure your presence for the remainder of this ride, but I will not be forced to endure it at any other time in the future," she remarked coldly, guiding her horse a few inches farther away from his as his leg made contact with her own beneath her muslin skirts.

"Well, now, ma'am, that's a real shame. Yeah, a real shame. You're willing to waste your time on a young, half-baked kid like Evans, but not with a real, honest-to-God man like me. I just can't understand the sense in your choice, ma'am. It don't make any sense, Amanda, honey," he sneered.

"I am not asking you to understand, sir! I gave you no permission to use my Christian name, either! I must inform you that I find your company extremely distasteful and your manner thoroughly revolting!" she exclaimed haughtily, unaware of the dangerous, menacing glare he now directed toward her.

"What you want to go and act so high and mighty for? You ain't no better than me! You know, you're going to be mighty sorry for the way you treated Buck Jones! You'll come crawling to me some day, little lady. Yes sir, you ain't nothing but a fancy, dolled-up bitch! You ain't any different from any other woman, you know! Underneath them fancy duds and put-on airs, you're made the same way any other one is!" he raged at her.

Amanda recoiled for a moment at his threatening, insulting tone, then stiffened her back and replied stonily, "How dare you! I don't want you to ever so much as speak to me again, do you understand? If you come near me again, I will inform my father of your disgraceful conduct and he will see to it that you are without a job or a reference! Now, get away from me, you foul, distasteful creature!" she hissed at him, kicking her horse into a frenzied gallop and leaving an astonished Buck in her dusty wake. He cursed loud and long, then cruelly spurred his horse to give chase.

Amanda reached the safety of the ranch mere seconds before Buck could overtake her. She quickly jumped down and fled inside the confines of the house. She collapsed into the large wing chair in the parlor and tried to catch her gasping breath.

I should have told my father about Buck Jones the first day he approached me in such an impertinent, insulting manner, she thought. I will most certainly inform Samuel if that disgusting swine ever accosts me again! She shuddered involuntarily.

Attempting to shake off such dismal thoughts, she rose from the chair and climbed the stairs to her room, reflecting once again how very ironic it was that she was the teacher to Luke Cameron's brother. Jake was already showing signs of resembling his older brother in more ways than appearance, she thought. She only hoped that he wouldn't mature to be as overbearing and arrogant as Luke!

Although she tried constantly to forget, she still could not erase the memory of Luke's fiery embrace on the night of the dance. She could still recall the feel of his powerful, muscular arms about her, her own weakening resistance, and then her momentary surrender. She had dreamt of that savage kiss more than once, had found herself yearning for a repeat of the performance. At such times, she would soundly berate herself for her foolishness and vehemently deny to herself that she felt anything other than utmost annoyance and contempt for the ruggedly handsome, infuriating Mr. Cameron.

She quickly settled into her new routine, her teaching responsibilities now uppermost in her mind during the week. The children slowly grew to accept her authority, and only Jake Cameron continued to give her a small degree of difficulty now and then. She fought a constant battle to forget all about Luke Cameron, yet she was daily reminded of his existence by the presence of his brother in her classroom! She had tried not to allow her feelings to influence her attitude in teaching Jake, and she was satisfied that she was succeeding. She was forced to admit that Jake was extremely intelligent and knowledgeable, though he was inclined to be a bit boisterous and somewhat overconfident. Amanda, however, could not bring herself to dislike the youngster.

She thoroughly enjoyed her teaching experience, confident that she was learning something from the children as well as contributing to their education. She learned that most of them had been born in Texas, although many of their parents had not. She had finally become acquainted with a number of their parents now and knew that the women had wholeheartedly accepted her, forgetting their former envy and jealousy of her, willing to admit to themselves that their first opinion of the young lady was in error. After all, she was Samuel Lawrence's daughter. And, he might be a Yankee by birth, but he was, like them, a Texan by choice!

Samuel had begun riding along with Amanda each morning, sending Tommy Evans to do the honors in the afternoons. She had never mentioned Buck Jones to her father, yet he was no longer provided as her escort. She did not question Samuel about the matter, not wishing to reveal her true feelings about his employee. She surmised that Buck had been sufficiently warned away from her that day she had threatened to go to her father.

On one overcast, cloudy day in early November, after Amanda had been teaching school for nearly two weeks, there was an outbreak of measles among the children at school. One little girl had first contracted the disease, which had quickly spread to three others. Amanda knew that it could rapidly develop into a deadly epidemic, and she was strongly advised by the town's physician to recess school until the danger was past. So, on the next afternoon, she announced her decision to the students.

"Children, as you all know, there has been an outbreak of measles among us. Therefore, school will not be held until further notice. I want you all to go home and inform your parents of this latest development, and if any of you begin to exhibit any of the symptoms we have previously discussed, please have your family contact the doctor. I don't know if you are aware of the fact, but measles can be quite serious. Now, are there any questions?"

When no one responded, she informed them that school was recessed. The children happily and quickly fled outside and went their separate ways. Amanda gathered up her cloak and bonnet and strolled outside. She suddenly realized that it was at least two hours earlier than the usual time she ended school.

Oh, dear, she thought, Tommy won't be here for quite a while yet. I don't know whether to wait, or whether to ride on back to the ranch by myself. Recalling that day of the cyclone and Samuel's subsequent scolding, she hesitated to ride without Tommy. But, after all, she was now very skillful in handling the rifle, and she had brought the gun with her. She made the decision to ride to the ranch without further delay.

She flung the warm woolen cloak about her shoulders and tied her bonnet securely upon her head. The weather was becoming quite cool now, though it was considerably warmer than Boston this time of year. She mounted and started for home, waving to several acquaintances as she left town, hoping that her father wouldn't be too angry with her when she arrived.

She had traveled more than three miles from town at a leisurely pace when she sensed the presence of others, other eyes watching her. She glanced about, her head twisting to peer back the way she had come, then to her left and right. There, still some distance away from her to her right, she spied six riders. She was afforded a closer inspection of them as they urged their mounts nearer. She gasped in mingled shock and paralyzing fear, striving to maintain her composure and common sense. She halted momentarily and drew the rifle from its scabbard at the side of her saddle. Her hands were shaking, but she frantically kicked her horse into a gallop, racing like the wind away from the others now pursuing her, gaining on her swiftly.

Indians! She had never before seen an Indian in all her young life, yet she knew with a certainty when she spotted the long, streaming black hair and wild, painted bronze faces, the unfamiliar buckskin breeches and buffalo hides. Dear Lord, she prayed fervently as she urged her horse onward, nearly hysterical now, please help me!

She quickly glanced back, dismayed to see that the Indians were easily closing the gap. Comanches were natural-born horsemen, but she did not know this and still hoped that she could somehow outrun them. When she saw them nearing, a mere few lengths behind her now, she nearly cried aloud in fear and hopeless desperation. She brought the rifle up to her shoulder with her one free hand, then released her frantic grip on the saddlehorn. She accidentally dropped the reins, but had no time to stop and think about what she was doing, merely obeying some natural instinct for survival. She twisted about and aimed the gun as best she could and fired.

The first bullet narrowly missed one of the Indians by a fraction of an inch, and he brought his own stolen rifle up to return her fire in retaliation. But he was sharply commanded to desist by the leader of the small band. Their leader wanted the white woman captured alive.

Amanda was now attempting to fire again, and she managed to shoot once more before the man in the lead reached her side and easily plucked her from the saddle, even though they were traveling at a breakneck speed. She kicked and squirmed and struggled wildly to escape, yet his arms seemed to be made of iron. He finally slowed his horse to a walk and called for a halt. Amanda's frightened horse was pursued and captured by one of the other Indians, and she realized with a growing sense of despair and terrible reality that she had been taken captive by the treacherous savages she had known only by the gruesome tales she had heard of them. She could have wept in frustration when she saw that she had been unable to wound any of them, but she knew that her aim could not have been good, forced as she was to fire upon the back of a fleeing horse. She reflected briefly that these men must be the renegades, the reservation escapees Luke had warned her about so many days ago.

Amanda recovered from her momentary shock and screamed at her captor, striving to claw at his face with her nails. "Let me go, you animal!" She had not yet looked into his face, and as she now did so, she was startled to discover that he appeared to be part white, his features definitely bespeaking his mixed parentage. He laughed brusquely at her

132

futile efforts to free herself, and suddenly relaxed his ruthless hold on her, allowing her to tumble to the ground below.

"How dare you? My father will come searching for me at any moment! You cannot do this thing, you must not! I have nothing of value on my person, so I cannot see what you could possibly want with me!" she cried with as much bravado as she could muster in such a frightening situation. She did not know if they could understand her words, but she knew that they would be able to read her expression and defiant pose. She stumbled to her feet and proudly faced their leader, telling herself that she would not back down, that she would not reveal to them the wrenching fear she felt in the pit of her stomach.

The leader coldly scrutinized this strange, courageous woman with the fiery hair, pleased with what he observed. "You have something we need, woman. You will bring us rifles and horses," he stated in a harsh, guttural voice. Amanda was surprised at his knowledge of her language, and she approached him where he still sat astride his magnificent horse. She noted that his face was almost handsome, though it was much too hawkish and sinister-looking. His eyes were a curious shade of blue and brown.

She gazed at the others, who were staring at her, motionless, noted their coal-black hair and dark eyes, their straight and noble features, their proud bearing. Turning back to their leader, she observed his lighter skin and hair. But, there was nothing more about him which gave any other indication that he was anything more than a savage, a bloodthirsty beast, a horse thief, and now a kidnapper. She reflected that there was no way of knowing what other dreadful, unspeakable crimes this bold man had committed. She met his answering gaze unflinchingly, holding her head proudly erect and her green eyes steady.

"Rifles and horses? Do you mean that you intend to hold me for ransom?" she inquired coolly. Oh, Tommy, she thought, I hope that you will decide to ride to town early today. She knew that he would be riding this very way when he started to town to escort her home from school. She cursed her own foolishness in not waiting for him, but realized that it was too late for that.

"Enough talk now. Get on your horse, woman," the half-breed commanded, his tone indicating that he would brook no further resistance from this prisoner. Amanda, however, tried desperately to stall for time in hopes that someone would come that way.

"I will not! I demand that you release me at once! I can see that you are not like the others, sir. You at least speak my language. If you will only allow me to return to my father's ranch, I will see to it that he does not come after you. I will see that you get food and water for yourselves and for your horses, if that is what you want," she reasoned with him. Surely this man, being part white, would perhaps at least consider her sound advice?

"I speak your language, woman. But, we go

134

now." He signaled then to one of his men, who grabbed Amanda tightly about her waist and threw her unceremoniously upon her horse once again, ignoring her outraged screams and struggles. He drew out a leather thong and brutally tied her hands together, then mounted and led her horse along behind his.

"Where are you taking me?" she demanded imperiously. She noticed that the filthy man had also stolen her rifle. Oh, Samuel, she thought, I only hope you can find me soon.

"It is not your place to ask questions, woman. But, I will tell you. We go to make camp for the night. Tomorrow, we trade you for rifles and horses." He motioned his followers onward and the small band, along with the captive Amanda, rose swiftly toward the south.

Amanda shivered uncontrollably as she grasped the saddlehorn with her tied hands. She didn't know what in heaven's name had possessed her to defy their leader that way, yet she was not sorry. If they were going to kill her, she surmised that they would have already done so. She had heard such horrible things about Indians, but this half-breed seemed different. And yet, those who rode with him appeared to be the embodiment of all the previous descriptions she had heard of the savages.

Would they really allow her to remain unharmed? And, would they keep their word and ransom her tomorrow, allow her to return safely to her father? Her mind was assailed by an increasing fear and doubt. She slowly slumped forward in the saddle, emotionally drained and exhausted from the ordeal. But, she knew that what had just occurred would not tax her courage and strength nearly as much as the hours ahead, when she would be alone, unprotected and virtually defenseless, with these wild creatures who surrounded her.

Eight

Tommy Evans feverishly spurred his horse back toward the Circle L Ranch, inexorably urging the animal faster. He had been to town in order to collect Amanda for the routine afternoon's ride homeward, yet she was nowhere to be found when he arrived. He had anxiously inquired about her, puzzled by her absence, and had been informed by several of the people about the town that the schoolteacher had ridden, alone, away from Big Prairie nearly two hours before. Tommy's first inclination was to conduct a search for her by himself, but he knew that it would be virtually useless to do so, given the vastness of the land surrounding the town. So, he headed back to her father's ranch, hoping that he had somehow missed her and that she would be safely within the boundaries of the ranch when he returned. Deep within his mind, however, Tommy realized that Amanda would not be there, that something must surely have happened to her.

He finally arrived at the ranch, leaped from his horse, and strode inside the ranchhouse without waiting to knock. He found Samuel sitting at the desk in the parlor, apparently absorbed in

137

various books spread randomly before him.

"Mr. Lawrence! Mr. Lawrence, is Miss Amanda back here yet?" he asked the older man in a breathless rush.

"No. Why? What's happened? I thought you had gone to escort her home. What is the trouble?" Samuel demanded, experiencing a terrible sense of dread and foreboding as he rose from his seat.

"I just got back from town, and Miss Amanda had already ridden out. She left, alone, more than two hours ago! I didn't see her anywhere, and I'm sure enough afraid that something might have happened to her! She should have been home long before now!" Tommy replied, nervously twisting his hat in his hands.

"You're sure she left town?" Samuel asked, his features reflecting his worry and increasing fear at the meaning of Tommy's news.

"Yes, sir, she's gone all right. I talked to some of the folks there who said they saw her ride out. What are we going to do now, Mr. Lawrence?"

"Evans, get back outside and tell John to round up all the hands! We're organizing a search party here and now. You ride over to some of the neighboring ranches around here and tell them my daughter's missing. Tell them we'll all meet at the north edge of town. Damn it, don't stand there gawking, move!" Samuel bellowed. He rushed out of the parlor just behind Tommy and threw on his jacket, then strode quickly from the house.

Dear Lord, he thought as he hurried to mount up with the others who were now assembling, what could have happened to her? He recalled

Luke Cameron's warning of the renegade Comanches. No! he told himself furiously.

Damn it, she's probably just wandered off somehow. Maybe she decided to go out and have a look around out on the range, practice her shooting some more. But he realized that he was unable to deceive himself with such false hopes. He knew with a growing certainty that she would have ridden straight back to the ranch. He suddenly couldn't bear the thought of something happening to his daughter, the daughter he had been given the opportunity to finally know, and yes, to love. For now, he realized that he had come to care for Amanda very deeply, that he had come to love her as a father should. He clenched his teeth and vowed silently that he would kill anyone or anything that sought to do her harm!

Samuel curtly issued the orders for his men to split up into pairs and search in various directions, thereby combing more territory in less time on their way to the edge of town. They would then plan to meet back at the ranch when it became good and dark, and, if no one had discovered a trace of Amanda by then, they would all prepare for a more thorough search. The hands rode out with a grimly determined Samuel in the lead.

Luke Cameron carelessly wiped the sweat from his brow with his kerchief and pulled his hat firmly down onto his head once more. He'd been out repairing another line of fence and was now preparing to return to his ranch for the evening meal. Normally, he would have brought a couple of his men along for help, but he felt the need to be alone for a while. He savored the privacy he was afforded out on the range by himself. Now, the sun was rapidly setting, sinking below the majestic white clouds, suffusing the landscape with an orange-pink glow.

He straightened from his labor and gathered up his tools. As he turned to his saddlebags, he was momentarily halted by the sight of several riders on the horizon. Though they were quite a distance from him, he was able to recognize them. Indians! What were they doing out here? He'd heard only yesterday that they had supposedly passed through this part of the country on their way to the south only last week.

His attention was suddenly drawn to one of the riders, obviously not an Indian, and quite obviously not a man. He perceived her ridiculous bonnet flapping about her shoulders, her long, flowing skirts, and her bright, coppery tresses where they had been blown out of their pins by the force of the cool evening wind against her face.

Amanda Lawrence! Hell, that had to be her! No other woman looked like her, that was for sure. Luke caught his breath, then resolved to remain calm and to think fast. It was apparently an abduction, and he swiftly prayed that she had been unharmed, at least thus far. Come on, Luke, he resolutely told himself, make your plans and make them fast.

He knew that he had to rescue her, yet he was aware of the overwhelming odds against him, one lone man against six savage Comanches. Surely Amanda's father and his men would be out searching for her. Unless the Comanches had raided the Circle L and managed to kill or wound them. He decided that this was unlikely and wondered if they even realized that Amanda had been captured. He made the decision to ride alone and then waited, motionless and calculating, until the group of riders began to fade farther into the distance.

It had taken all his strength and willpower to restrain himself from leaping onto his horse and riding down upon Amanda's captors in a vengeful fury. Yet, he forced himself to follow his own plans, to wait and then follow them, remaining well behind until dark, when he would then make his move. It had to work, he told himself encouragingly, he couldn't chance anything happening to Amanda.

Luke, at this particular point in time, refused to dwell upon the true extent of his feelings for Amanda, preferring to push such matters to the back of his mind for the time being and remain single-minded. He couldn't allow his feelings to interfere with his thinking right now. There would be time enough to think through these newly realized feelings after he had rescued her. He did reflect briefly, however, that his insides had been virtually frozen when he spotted Amanda being spirited away by the Comanches.

Damn, if they harmed one hair on her beautiful head, he'd kill every hateful, stinking savage in cold blood. It was enough that he still remembered the horror of his parents' death at the hands of these animals.

As the sun completely sank and the sky was turned to a glorious panorama of dark blue hues and white glittering lights, Luke rode toward the spot the Indians had chosen to make camp for the night. He'd been following far behind all evening and now into the night, utilizing the various tricks and knowledge he had long ago acquired in order to survive in a land where civilized men had to coexist with hostile Indians. So far, he judged he had been unobserved. Finally, he dismounted quietly and tied his horse to a tree. Then, withdrawing his knife, he stealthily crept toward the grove of trees surrounding the stream that flowed through their midst. One of the Indians had been posted several yards out from the camp as a lookout, while another had taken his stand at the edge of the small forest in order to give any warning passed on by the first. The remaining Indians, along with the captive Amanda, were in the center of this small hideaway.

Amanda had been untied and allowed to dismount in order to stretch her cramped, aching muscles alongside the swiftly flowing water. The horses had been led away and tied together near the edge of the clearing, and the Indians began their preparations for the fire and subsequent meal.

"Woman, you will cook," commanded their leader as Amanda straightened from kneeling to drink thirstily at the stream. She dampened her handkerchief and bathed her dusty, sunburned face.

"I most certainly will not!" she answered him defiantly, her inborn strength and courage begin-

142

ning to return to her as she continued to bathe her face and hands. She wouldn't give in to this heathen, no matter what he threatened, she resolved to herself bravely. Her resolutions vanished with his next words and actions.

Brutally grasping a handful of her shining hair in one of his grimy hands, he twisted it cruelly, causing Amanda to wince with the sudden, sharp pain. She fought back rising tears and kicked out at him with her booted feet, struggling to free her hair with her clawing hands and clenched fists. The half-breed merely laughed at her frantic struggles, then administered a shove which sent her sprawling headlong into the dust.

"You will cook. If not, woman, I will kill you," he stated calmly. He turned his back on her and cupped his hands to drink from the stream, leaving a bruised and humiliated Amanda to stagger to her feet and shake the dust from her skirts. She noted that the other Indians were staring at her again, apparently wishing they could indeed kill her and keep the prize of her long, golden red curls. Amanda shuddered violently, then turned about to approach the fire that had been started.

Meanwhile, Luke had successfully surprised the outermost sentry and attacked him swiftly and skillfully, silencing his cries of alarm with the sharp blade of a knife cunningly drawn across his throat. The Comanche slumped forward, dead, and Luke left him without further ado, creeping through the brush toward the second guard, who was standing with a rifle in his hands at the edge of

143

the forest. Luke knew that he had to remain perfectly immobile and quiet until the Indian glanced away from his hiding place, when he would then make his next move.

When the Indian turned his head around to peer in the opposite direction from where Luke tensely waited, Luke sprang up and crept quietly through the brush, halting a few feet behind him. The Indian, hearing a slight noise, whirled about, at which time Luke hurled himself at him, effectively knocking him to the ground and attempting to slit his throat as easily as he had the first one's.

However, the Comanche broke Luke's hold and scrambled to his feet, clutching his long knife and springing toward Luke in an attempt to plunge the blade into his heart. Luke tripped him with his knee and grabbed one of the rifles on the ground, then jumped to his feet and clubbed his opponent's head, breaking his neck with a single crack.

Breathing heavily from the intense struggle, Luke paused a moment to catch his breath and plan his strategy for the next move. He would need to have all his strength and cunning for it, knowing full well that there were still four Comanches to be disposed of. He replaced the knife in his belt, picked up his own rifle, then waited for the space of a minute, listening intently in order to ascertain if anyone had heard the sounds of his combat with the dead Comanche. Satisfied that no one had, he crouched down and crept slowly closer toward the glow of the fire, which was discernible through the trees ahead.

Amanda stirred the beans and bacon, which she

surmised had been stolen from some unsuspecting, or possibly dead, settler. Her face was flushed and hot from being forced to sit so near to the heat of the fire. She glanced at her captors from the corner of her eye.

The three followers of the half-breed were laughing and joking with one another, apparently uttering several lewd and suggestive remarks about their white captive, judging from the manner in which they frequently turned their lustful gazes on her and accentuated their conversation with adequate gestures. The leader, Amanda noted, was staring at her in much the same manner, and she shifted uncomfortably beneath his gaze.

"Your father will pay much for you," he commented brusquely. His eyes were focused on her hair again, which was still refusing to remain in the few pins she had managed to salvage.

"My father will pay whatever you ask, of course, but he does not possess an immense wealth as you seem to believe. If you return me to him, unharmed, however, he will see to it that you get whatever it is you need," she replied, lifting her head proudly.

"Why is it you have no husband?" the half-breed suddenly demanded, curious to know why such a woman as this had no man.

"That is none of your business!" Amanda snapped irritably, then drew in her breath sharply as she realized that she might have angered him once again. Oh, my unruly tongue! she chastised herself. She sought to change the subject and announced loudly, "The food is ready!" She stood and walked away from the fire, plopping wearily down upon a large rock near the stream. The leader apparently allowed the matter to drop for the moment, she saw, as he and the others began to fill their mouths with the hot food. She glanced away from them in disgust.

"Woman, you will eat," the leader commanded, in between huge bites, shoveling the beans and bacon into his mouth with his greasy fingers.

"I am not hungry," Amanda replied coolly, hoping that her refusal would not serve to further antagonize him, yet realizing that, under circumstances such as this, she would be unable to swallow a single bite. He appeared to accept her answer and turned once more to his food with a shrug of his naked shoulders.

Amanda removed her boots and plunged her feet into the cold depths of the stream. Her feet ached so, as she was totally unaccustomed to wearing her riding boots for such an extended length of time. She removed the remaining pins from her hair and combed through its many tangles with her fingers, unaware of the admiring glances of the savages who had now finished eating.

"We go to sleep now, woman," the half-breed directed toward her. Amanda jerked her head about in alarm, not entirely sure of his exact meaning. She widened her eyes in fear as he stood and slowly came toward her.

"I will not sleep with you! Couldn't you perhaps allow me to bed down in a more secluded area, by myself? I must be afforded some privacy," she pleaded with him as he moved closer.

Without answering her, he yanked her up by the arm and dragged her, protesting loudly and trying to free herself from his ruthless grasp, to a spot several feet away from the fire, where he had spread his buffalo robe for a bed. The other three men now lay sprawled on the opposite side of the fire, their eyes closed, their rifles close at hand in case the need should arise.

The half-breed forced Amanda down upon the buffalo robe, then lay down beside her, placing one of his powerful arms across her waist to hold her captive. She attempted to edge a bit farther away from such close contact with the vile savage, but he relentlessly pulled her back tightly against his warm, rank-smelling body.

"Woman, if you try to escape, my men will hear you, and I cannot protect you if they catch you."

"I refuse to lie here quietly and submit to you, you animal!" Amanda hissed, renewing her frantic struggles. She bit into his hand as he clamped it across her mouth. Uttering a sharp curse, he raised his hand and cruelly backhanded her across her face.

"Bah! You are like all white women! Indian women do not give so much trouble! My father beat my mother many times, yet she did not speak to him in such a manner!" he told her, growing angrier by the moment at this captive woman's stubborn resistance. He admitted to himself that the woman intrigued him, that she was much more courageous than he would have expected.

"I am not an Indian woman, and I would not

remain with any man who beat me! In my world, women are treated as human beings, not as chattel! How is it that you can ride and plunder and murder as a savage, when your own father was a white man?" she demanded recklessly, seeking to draw his attention away from herself, stalling for precious time, hoping that she could somehow postpone what seemed to be inevitable.

The half-breed temporarily released her and rose to a sitting position beside her, his interest channelled into another direction for the moment. "My father was white, yes. But, my mother is Comanche. Comanche are my people. When my father deserted us, we would have starved if not for my people. We were free and proud for many years. But now, your people seek to enslave us. Comanche are slaves to no man! We will once more be free! That is why we ride south. We will plan and wait. We will free our people!" he spoke through tightly clenched teeth, his eyes glinting dangerously with a smouldering light.

"But, you are free now. I realize that your people are living on reservations, but the government has given you that land. It is yours, isn't it? No one is seeking to enslave you," she reasoned, hoping that she could keep his attention drawn away from his initial intention. She suddenly realized that this man sitting beside her was capable of any kind of atrocity, that he could kill her as easily as talk to her. She shivered involuntarily.

"We are not free! You do not know of which you speak. But, you are brave, woman. You do not back down from Comanche. Maybe I will keep you with me, make you my squaw. You have no other man. Maybe you would like to have Brave Bear as your husband?" he demanded, his fierce gaze turning upon her once again.

"Certainly not! I could never be your woman! Why, you are nothing more than a savage beast!" she responded without thinking, then cried out harshly as his bruising hands gripped her soft shoulders.

"Brave Bear is not good enough for you? I am not man enough for white woman?" he shot at her furiously as he shook her violently, causing her head to snap forward and then back.

"Let me go! Let go of me! Get your hands off of me!" she now shouted at him, not caring whether she angered him further, only wanting to be free of his grasp and his vile suggestions.

"You will be my woman! I will not send you back to your father! You will ride south with me tomorrow, and you will learn what an honor it is to be the squaw of Brave Bear! Now, I will show you that Brave Bear is plenty man enough for you, white squaw!" he countered furiously.

"No! You said that you would ransom me! I will not be your squaw!" Amanda screamed as he forced her back to the ground, savagely ripping her dress and trying to grab her flailing wrists in one of his large hands. Amanda screamed again, realizing that it was entirely futile, as none of the other Indians would attempt to help her. She knew that she was helpless, yet she fought him like a wildcat, scratching a deep furrow into his bronzed cheek with her sharp fingernails. She screamed again as he slapped her viciously and sought to imprison her legs with his own.

To the half-breed, this defiant woman now represented all of the white race. He would make her subservient to his wishes. She would pay for the desertion of his white father, for the betrayal of her white government, for his own people's imprisonment on the reservations. He would force her to submit, he would punish her for what her people had done to the Comanche.

Amanda quailed before his crazed expression. Why, the man was insane! He had murder in his eyes now, and she fought all the harder, resolving to use the very last of her strength against him. She would rather die than suffer rape at his hands.

"Dear God!" she screamed piercingly as he jammed a knee ruthlessly between her legs. Suddenly, her cries and screams were silenced by the sound of a gunshot.

One of the Comanches pitched backward, having scrambled to his feet and grabbed his rifle to investigate a sudden noise in the trees. Luke shot him, then turned his rifle on another Indian who had risen to his feet, the force of the second bullet knocking him to the ground. The last one rose from the ground, only to pitch backward as the bullet tore through his body.

It all happened so quickly, Amanda had scarcely blinked when she realized that three of her captors now lay dead on the other side of the fire. Her own would-be rapist now jumped to his feet, having been momentarily stunned by the surprise of Luke's attack. Releasing Amanda and twisting about to grab his own gun, he didn't see Luke, who had now entered Amanda's line of vision.

"Luke!" Amanda screamed, both in relief and alarm as she realized his danger. Brave Bear, unable to reach his rifle in time, lifted his knife. Luke's rifle suddenly jammed, and he leaped toward the Comanche, swinging the rifle butt into the Indian's ribs, but not swiftly enough to escape the knife's plunging blade.

Amanda watched in stunned horror as the half-breed was knocked sideways by the force of the blow, and Luke winced from the terrible pain of the knife's blade buried in his shoulder.

"Luke! Luke, he's got a gun!" Amanda shouted as she realized that Brave Bear had crawled to his gun and was in the process of aiming it at Luke. At her warning, Luke drew out his own knife and threw it at the half-breed, its blade embedding itself in the Indian's chest. As he staggered backward, his face contorted with both rage and pain, the discharged rifle narrowly missed Luke's head. The Comanche turned toward Amanda, who gazed at him in shock, then fell forward onto his face and died.

Luke remained standing in the same position, his shoulder now beginning to bleed profusely as he slowly and excruciatingly pulled the blade out of his flesh. He then looked at Amanda, who was still staring at the hideous figure of the dead half-breed. She finally raised her terror-stricken eyes to Luke's face.

"You're hurt," she stated simply, her senses still dulled by the shock of the preceding events.

"Are you all right, Amanda? I mean, they didn't hurt you any, did they? Was I in time?" Luke asked her with concern, holding his wound with his other hand.

"I'm all right. Yes, you were in time," she responded calmly. Luke realized that it was only a matter of time until the numbing shock wore off, until she finally broke under the terrible strain she had been under for the past few hours. She rose slowly and approached him, stopping to tear a strip from her petticoat in order to bind his wound.

"We must get you to a physician at once, Mr. Cameron. But," she paused, glancing around in horror at the bodies of the four men, "what are we to do with these men? Shouldn't we bury them or something?"

"Bury them? Are you out of your mind? We're getting the hell out of here as quickly as possible! Come on, make a bandage for this cut here and let's get going. The vultures can have their carcasses, for all I care," he commented. Amanda did as he suggested and wrapped his shoulder carefully with the strip of petticoat.

"There. That will have to do until we can reach the doctor. At least the bleeding has been halted for a while," she told him as she finished. He gazed at her as she turned away, noting her tangled hair, her sunburned, dirty face, her torn and rumpled clothing. Thank the Lord no real harm had been done to her!

"Well, it'll have to do. Come on, let's get going." He took her arm with his good hand and propelled her toward the spot where her horse

152

remained tied. She mounted and then asked, "What about their horses? And their guns?"

"Don't worry about the horses, they'll either be rounded up by someone or they'll return to wherever those thieving bastards stole them from. As for the guns, I'll see to it that another bunch like this one doesn't find them." He picked up the guns one by one and threw them into the still-smouldering fire. They had no way to carry them, he told the astonished Amanda. Then, he took the reins of her horse and led it out of the clearing, back through the forest to where his own horse was waiting.

"Where will we go now? I just realized that I have no idea which direction to travel," Amanda said as he mounted and they began to ride away.

"Well, we'll go on back to my ranch for tonight. Your father's ranch is too far, so you'll have to wait until morning to get home. Besides, you said yourself that my shoulder needs immediate attention," he insisted as he perceived the signs of rebellion returning to her strained features.

"I am most grateful to you for rescuing me, Mr. Cameron," she told him stiffly. "Yet, I wish to return to my father's ranch immediately. I will ride with you as far as your ranch, then you may have one of your hands escort me to the Circle L."

"I'm afraid your father won't be there at least till morning, Amanda. He and his men will be out scouring the countryside for you by now. It's nearly midnight already. I'll send Jake over there to tell them you're safe as soon as we get to my ranch. For now, though, Miss Lawrence," he commanded in a low, level tone, "I damn sure don't feel like arguing with you about it anymore. You and I both have been through enough tonight already!"

"Well, I suppose I can let the matter drop for the time being, Mr. Cameron. I will handle it when we reach your ranch," she stated rebelliously, then turned away from him.

After traveling several miles, Luke felt his shoulder begin to stiffen. He grimaced with the pain as he adjusted the bandage more comfortably. Turning to Amanda, he asked, "Miss Lawrence, how come you were captured by those Comanches in the first place? You want to tell me how it happened?"

"I had to dismiss school early because of an outbreak of measles. I was simply returning home when they overtook me."

"You mean to tell me that you were riding alone again?" he shot at her, angry that she had once again placed herself in such a dangerous situation.

"Yes, but that is certainly none of your business, Mr. Cameron! I've had quite enough of your authoritative manner, of your insolent, insulting, overbearing ways! I do not have to answer to you, sir, nor will I! I am indeed grateful to you for your assistance tonight, but that still doesn't give you any right to behave this way! I did not ask for you to appoint yourself as my protector! No, I did not ask for your help or your protection at all!" she stormed at him. She began to cry then, deep wrenching sobs. All of her pent-up emotions finally surfaced. She urged her horse away from

Luke's and drew out her handkerchief.

Luke's anger disappeared at the sight and sound of her weeping. He knew that she needed this release, that after this torrent had passed, she would be herself once again. He allowed her to ride behind him for the remainder of the way, losing himself in his own thoughts. Yep, he told himself, you sure enough got some thinking to do.

Nine

Finally riding to within sight of Luke's ranch, Amanda raised her weary head a bit higher and peered ahead at the outline of the ranch buildings so clearly illuminated by the bright moonlight.

"This is my ranch," Luke remarked, much weakened now from loss of blood. They rode up to the main house and he slid painfully from his horse. Amanda jumped down and hurried to offer him the support of her arms.

"Here, please let me help you inside," she offered politely. She noted that the ranchhouse was quite different from her father's. It was a large, two-storied, double log house, with a hallway between, and it appeared to be quite spacious, though its exterior was rather rough-looking.

"No, thanks. I can still walk. Jake!" he suddenly shouted toward the house.

Jake Cameron, fully clothed and wide awake, bounded out of the front door and down the steps of the porch.

"Luke! Luke, where the hell have you been? Have you heard about Sam Lawrence's daughter? The schoolteacher, you know. They say she's maybe been captured by Indians and scalped or something! Ain't it awful? Luke? Luke—" his excited voice trailed off as he spotted the bedraggled Amanda.

"Jake, your brother has most graciously and heroically rescued me. And, as you can plainly see, I have certainly not been scalped. Now, your brother has a serious knife wound in his shoulder and we need you or one of your hands to ride immediately for the doctor," she ordered.

Jake looked from Amanda to his older brother in confusion. Then, recovering his speech, he said, "Luke, all the hands are out helping to look for Miss Lawrence. Do you want me to ride for the doctor like she says?" he asked, apparently questioning Amanda's authority to issue orders on his own home ground.

"Yeah. Do as she says. But, Jake, first, I want you to ride on over to the Circle L and tell whoever happens to be there that Miss Lawrence is here and that she's safe. Go on now, get going," Luke insisted.

"Mr. Cameron, I must insist that I accompany your brother to my father's ranch. I'm sure that your housekeeper can see to your wound until the doctor arrives. I do not wish to appear callous or ungrateful, but I wish to return home as soon as possible. I would gladly remain here to help, but I'm certain that my father is half out of his mind with worry. I think it would be best if I were to ride along with Jake," she protested.

"I don't have a housekeeper, Miss Lawrence, and I already told you that—" he began, only to be halted by a sudden attack of dizziness as he slumped forward. He would have fallen to the ground if Amanda had not rushed to his side and quickly motioned Jake to help her get him inside. The two of them managed to get him up the steps and into the house, where they then placed him on a sofa in the first room to the left of the entrance-way.

"Jake, please hurry and ride for the doctor. Your brother is apparently in much worse condition than I had previously believed. It seems that his shoulder has been bleeding for some time now, but he did not see fit to inform me of that fact."

"Yes, ma'am. It'll probably be quite a spell till I return with Doc Stephens, though," Jake muttered as he ran out of the room and outside to mount up.

Luke had momentarily lapsed into uncon-sciousness, and Amanda experienced no small twinge of guilt as she viewed his bleeding wound. She had no idea that he and his brother lived out here alone with no housekeeper, or she most certainly would not have thought of suggesting that she leave him. Oh, drat! she exclaimed inwardly. His opinion of her would be much worsened after this. She reflected irritably that she did not know why she should be so concerned about Luke Cameron's opinion.

"Oh, my head is spinning," Luke mumbled as he regained consciousness.

"You just lie still," Amanda commanded deci-sively. "Jake has gone for the doctor, and I will do whatever I can for you until he arrives. Now, where may I find some clean bandages?"

"Bandages? We don't have any bandages!" he answered irascibly, considerably embarrassed by his weakened state. Damn, he'd gone and fainted like a woman!

"Very well, I'll just have to use some more strips from my petticoat." She stood and hurried out into the hallway, where she lifted her skirts and tore several more pieces of her fine muslin petticoat, then returned to Luke's side.

"Now, this will probably hurt a bit. Even though you have been bleeding, the blood around the bandage has apparently dried and it will tend to stick to the wound," she cautioned him.

"Just get it over with!" he snapped.

"You needn't be so disagreeable to me!" she retaliated, goaded into losing her temper once again. Bending over him, she gently placed both of her hands on his shoulder and slowly, painstakingly began to pull away the soiled bandage. Watching his face closely, she noticed that his eyes were now tightly shut and his mouth set in a grim line. Taking a deep breath, she pulled the bandage completely away from the wound.

"It is fairly deep, I'm afraid. I am certainly relieved that your brother has gone for the doctor. I'll simply replace this bandage with another for the time being, but this will definitely require medical attention as soon as possible. Now, this will hurt when I place the bandage on there," she warned him again. He made no response and she continued, finally drawing back, pleased that she had been able to staunch the flow of blood once more.

"Are you finished now?" Luke demanded quietly, pale and shaken from loss of blood and the severity of the pain.

"Yes, I believe so. Now, you must be famished. It will do you good to have something to eat, I'm sure. Where is the kitchen?" she inquired, rising to stand beside his prone body.

"Down the hall to your left. But, I don't think I could eat anything just yet."

"Nonsense. I'll prepare some coffee and anything else I can find. May I ask you something?" At his nod, she said, "Why don't you have a housekeeper? Who takes care of this house and sees to your meals and clothing?"

"Jake and I do all right by ourselves. It's been this way ever since my aunt died. She came out here after my folks were killed. Anyway, we all share the household chores. When my brother Boyd is home he helps out, too. What's the matter, Miss Lawrence? Is your feminine pride ruffled because a bachelor is able to get along without a woman's help?" he teased. Inwardly, he was smiling at her curiosity. Maybe she did care about him, after all. Maybe she was hiding beneath that icy aloofness she displayed all too often.

He'd done an awful lot of thinking during that ride homeward, and he was more or less certain now about how he felt. The problem was, how did she feel? Did she really dislike him as much as she pretended to?

No, Luke, he told himself, the time isn't right just yet. He'd better wait a while longer before pursuing any answers from her. He could bide his time for as long as it took. Besides, he needed to think things through for himself before he spoke to her of his feelings.

"Well, I must say, this place certainly looks as if there are only two bachelors inhabiting it!" she commented, looking around at the dirty wooden floors and dusty furniture. "I'll go and make the coffee now." She exited the room gracefully, leaving Luke alone with his thoughts.

Returning several minutes later with two mugs of steaming hot, aromatic coffee, Amanda handed one of them to Luke, who was able to sit up a bit now, his strength gradually returning. Amanda took a seat in a well-worn chair opposite him.

"My father's housekeeper told me that your parents were killed by Comanches. After my own experience, I can see more clearly why so many people fear them," she remarked with a shudder, recalling the horrible, feverish light in the half-breed's eyes.

"They're sure like nothing else you ever saw. My folks came out here to this country a couple of years before I was born. Before that, they'd lived down near San Antonio. My father was a blacksmith by trade," he told her, anxious to share with her the story of his beginnings, the story of his brave parents and the land they loved so dearly. He noted the interest apparent on her face, and so he continued.

"Anyway, he and my mother decided they wanted to move on west. They came out here, intent on going to California, but I guess they sort of fell in love with this part of Texas and so here

161

they stayed. My father was one of the original founders of Big Prairie. He was the only blacksmith they had for years. He and my mother finally decided to try their hands at ranching. Together, along with some help from a few of their friends and neighbors, they managed to round up a few hundred head of longhorn. For years, they made a pretty good go of things. Then, when the war came, there simply weren't enough men left around her to keep the Indians in line. It was terrible; people were butchered left and right by the marauding savages. Most folks moved into the forts and stockades, leaving their ranches and cattle to the dust and Indians. My father left to fight in the war, and my mother and us boys moved into Fort Jameson, which was abandoned some years ago, a few months after my father had gone."

"You mean that you had to leave your ranch, after all the hard work your parents had done to make it flourish?" Amanda asked at this point, completely absorbed in his story, content to listen to his deep, resonant voice.

"Well, leaving the ranch was the last thing my mother wanted, but the Indian problem was out of control by then. We stayed at the fort until after the war. My mother made a living there by doing laundry and taking in sewing, while me and my brother Boyd did odd jobs to help out. Hundreds of settlers ended up leaving this part of Texas altogether, but many of us refused to leave, refused to be driven from our lands. Anyway, after the war, the men started returning and the government even sent troops out to help for a while. My father returned to us and we moved back out here to the ranch. Soon, we'd rounded up another few hundred head and started all over again. The house was miraculously still standing, but we had to rebuild the corral and barn. We added the bunkhouse some time later, when my parents were finally able to afford to pay some extra help. Then, we simply settled down to ranching, even though the problems with the Indians weren't over by a long shot."

"But then, when were your parents killed? Were you and your brothers away at the time?" she asked.

"I was down in Waco. Boyd and Jake were here, though. The hands were all out on the range, leaving just my father here with them. When he spotted the Comanches riding this way, he made my brothers run out back of the house and hide in a deep gulley, out of sight of the Indians. Boyd argued with him about it, but my father wouldn't listen. My mother and he grabbed their guns and bolted themselves inside the house. I think they must have known that it was useless, but they fought to the death. My brothers heard nearly everything. The Comanches, they said it was like they were all over the place, set fire to everything afterward. They broke into the house and scalped and mutilated my folks. They didn't wait around after that. They just took some horses and rode away. Anyway, some of the hands returned shortly after that and found my brothers here. They managed to save the house, but the barn and other buildings were burned to the ground. They buried my parents. I don't guess I'll ever forgive myself for not being here when they needed me most. My brother Jake still wakes up with nightmares about it all every now and then. Boyd's never mentioned it after telling me about it."

"Oh, but there wouldn't have been anything you could have done! I'm sure your parents were glad you weren't here, glad that you would still be alive to take care of your younger brothers," Amanda protested feelingly.

Luke glanced at her face, observing her tear-filled eyes and look of genuine concern on her features. He was about to speak again when she asked, "Where is your other brother now?"

"Oh, he's away at school. It's what my folks wanted, for us all to be well educated. He's down at Waco in college, the same school I attended several years back. Like I said, that's where I was when my folks were killed."

"You attended college?" she asked in surprise.

"I can see that it certainly isn't what you would have expected," he commented wryly. "You thought all cowpokes and ranchers were ignorant, is that it? You thought we were all some kind of barbarians, if I remember your words correctly?"

Amanda flushed uncomfortably as she recalled the night of the dance and her disagreeable encounter with him. Why must he always remind her of that humiliating evening? She gently cleared her throat and stood to gather the coffee cups and return them to the kitchen.

"I need to prepare you something to eat now,

164

Mr. Cameron," she said as she leaned toward him to take his cup. He suddenly grabbed her arm gently, but firmly, and told her, "Amanda, there's something I have to say to you. Yesterday, when I saw that it was you with those Comanches, I was ready to kill. I couldn't bear the thought of what they might do to you. I've been thinking about it ever since. I could have beat you when I found out that you'd been riding alone again! Amanda—"

"No!" she broke in, pulling her arm free, afraid to allow him to continue any further. "Mr. Cameron, you are in a much weakened condition at this moment. Now, I'd best return to the kitchen and see if I can find something nourishing for you to eat." Ignoring the silent entreaty in his blue eyes, she took the cups and scurried from the room.

Luke cursed to himself as she left the room. He knew that she was afraid to hear what he'd been about to tell her. Damn it! He'd never been in a situation like this one before. He knew that he was falling in love with the beautiful, stubborn, proud, willful Amanda Lawrence, and he didn't know precisely what to do about it! It had taken an event like her capture by the Comanches to finally make him admit to himself what he felt for her. You saw it coming long before this, Luke, he told himself. You've known that something was going on ever since you first faced her across the barrel of her father's gun. The only problem now is, what are you going to do about all this? He wasn't at all certain that Amanda would admit to any similar feelings for him, even if his hunch was true. He hoped that she cared for him in some way, even if it were not to the same degree as what he felt for her.

Twenty minutes later, Amanda returned to the room, bearing a plate of eggs and thinly sliced bacon.

"This is all I could find to cook, Mr. Cameron. It would perhaps be more beneficial to you to eat something a bit easier to digest, but you need to get your strength back. I've brought you another cup of coffee, also." She glanced about the room for some sort of table on which to set the plate and mug, then picked up a rough, small end table next to one of the chairs and moved it near the sofa, within easy reach of Luke's good hand.

Luke quickly devoured the food, his appetite returning to him as soon as he smelled the delicious aroma of the bacon and eggs. Finally laying aside his napkin and cup, he settled back against the cushions of the sofa with a satisfied sigh.

"That was very good, Amanda. I didn't realize that you even knew how to cook," he teased her mischievously.

"Of course I know how to cook! I may have been raised in a proper household in Boston, but my aunt saw to it that we knew how to cook, sew, paint, dance, and other such accomplishments. But," she said, changing the subject, "I simply must insist that you continue to address me as Miss Lawrence. You see, I do not believe that my father would approve of your using my first name with such familiarity. I realize, of course, that we are no longer strangers, but I think it would be for the best," she announced coolly, drawing the small table aside and gathering up the dishes.

"You're damn right we're not strangers! And, like hell will I call you Miss Lawrence!" he bellowed at her, losing his temper at her chilly, impersonal tone and manner. Suddenly snaking out his good arm and grasping her firmly about her waist, he caused her to drop the dishes with a loud clatter on the table, and she opened her mouth in outrage and astonishment.

"How dare you use such a tone and language with me!"

"There will be no politeness between us, Amanda! No more social barriers from here on out," he commanded fiercely as he pulled her irrevocably down onto his lap. She struggled to rise, but she was considerably hampered by the fact that he was injured and she did not want to cause his wound to begin bleeding again.

"Let go of me! Your shoulder will start bleeding again if you are not careful!" she warned him as she pushed ineffectually against his broad chest with her hands.

"Then, let it! Amanda Lawrence, be still, because I am going to kiss you whether you like it or not! But I think you will!" he declared as he hugged her tighter against his masculine body and brought his head down to hers.

"No! Luke, don't . . ." she started to say, then was silenced by the pressure of his warm, demanding lips against her own. She squirmed and sought to escape, both from him and her own traitorous emotions, but she could not. Finally surrendering, she relaxed against him and gave herself up to the

167

tingling, delightful sensations as his lips moved sensuously on hers. He lifted his head and whispered in her ear, "Amanda. Amanda, don't fight it. You know it's right between us. Don't deny it to yourself or to me." She closed her eyes in response, thoroughly confused. What do I feel? she asked herself as he continued his tender assault on her lips and emotions.

The warm, exciting sensations strengthened as his lips traveled slowly from her lips to her ears, then to her slender neck, and once again to her parted lips. Amanda gasped in delicious shock as he took her mouth with his own once again.

She leaned close against him in languid surrender as his mouth returned to her ear and he muttered, "Amanda. Amanda, I think I'm in love with you."

She suddenly stiffened in his arms. Love? What was he talking about? Of course he couldn't mean it, he certainly didn't mean such a thing. He only wanted to kiss her like this again, just as he had done the night of the dance. Oh, he surely only wanted to take advantage of her, she could hear her Aunt Martha saying. Love? No, she wouldn't, couldn't believe such nonsense!

"Let me go!" she demanded shrilly as she raised her head and once more resumed her struggles. Startled by her unexpected outburst, Luke released her and she pushed herself up and out of his lap and stood, breathing heavily, her bosom rising and falling rapidly as she glared angrily down into his puzzled expression.

"You are no better than that half-breed! You

would most certainly say anything to get what you want, wouldn't you? Well, I refuse to be taken in by your words, by your deceit!"

"What the hell are you talking about? Didn't you hear me, Amanda? I said that I'm in love with you, woman!" he countered angrily, totally bewildered at her sudden change of attitude.

"Well, I do not believe you! I do not believe that you love me! I'm not at all sure that I believe in such a thing at all! I don't want any part of it, do you hear? Just leave me alone!" she cried as she rushed from the room in tears. How could she have allowed such a thing to happen again? she berated herself furiously. She felt humiliated, degraded. She didn't even want to consider the possibility that Luke had been speaking the truth. She never wanted to see him again! She never again wanted to experience such conflicting, turbulent emotions! She would not allow herself to become vulnerable to any man! Hadn't Aunt Martha always taught her to maintain strict control? She hurried back to the safety of the kitchen and sat down at the table, burying her face in her arms.

Shortly thereafter, Jake returned with the town's doctor. He and the older man entered the house and strode into the room where a totally confused, flabbergasted, and brooding Luke lay reflecting upon what a complex, impossible-to-understand woman he had chosen to fall in love with.

"Luke, are you all right?" Jake asked as he approached his solemn older brother.

"Yeah. Just fine," Luke responded with a scowl.

"Well, let's have a look at that shoulder there,"

said Doctor Stephens.

Some time later, as dawn was nearly breaking, Doc Stephens and Amanda took their leave of the Cameron brothers and headed for the Circle L. Amanda had murmured a stiff goodbye to Luke, merely thanking him once again for his rescue and then hurrying out of the house. Luke hadn't said a word, just sat there gazing at her intensely, making her extremely uncomfortable. Oh, why had she ever met the man? she lamented silently as she and the doctor rode toward her father's ranch.

Arriving home at long last, the kindly doctor politely declined Amanda's offer to come inside for a bite to eat and continued on his way back to the comfort of his own bed. Amanda wearily dismounted and entered the house in search of her father or anyone else who might be about.

"Samuel? Is anyone here?" she called, mustering the last of her strength as she stood in the entranceway.

"Amanda! Child, I been praying for you to come home safe all night long!" Mrs. Chambers exclaimed. "Your pa and all the others are still out looking for you right now. I could scarce believe it when that young Jake Cameron rode by to say you was all right! Come on into the kitchen with me at once! You look like you could do with a strong cup of coffee!" She propelled Amanda back to the kitchen and pushed her down into a chair, chattering all the while.

Amanda related to her the story of her capture, and then of her rescue by Luke. She tactfully omitted any mention of her brutal treatment at the hands of the half-breed leader, and instead focused on Luke's condition and her subsequent ride back with Doctor Stephens.

"Oh, child! I just can't bear the thought of you being captured by those terrible savages! Here now, I see that your dress is all torn, and you certainly do look a sight. You been through enough to last a long time. Your pa and the others ought to be riding in pretty soon. They said they'd be coming back here with the dawn unless they had word of you before then. I just thank the good Lord for returning you to us. Now, I've been selfish long enough, making you sit here and talk to me when it's plain to see that you're plumb tuckered out. I wanted you to see your pa before you went up to bed, but I think maybe you better go on upstairs now, honey." She stood and put her comforting arms about Amanda and helped her up from the table, then turned her toward the door and the entrance foyer.

They paused at the foot of the stairs as the door suddenly swung open. Samuel Lawrence entered the house with his head nearly bowed with defeat, his eyes bloodshot and red-rimmed. He raised his head and blinked twice when he realized that his daughter, the beloved daughter he had prayed and searched for all night long, was standing there before him.

"Amanda! Dear God, you're safe!" he whispered as she broke free from Mrs. Chambers's grasp and hurled herself into his outstretched arms.

"Oh, Samuel. I'm all right now. I was captured by renegade Comanches, but Luke Cameron rescued me. I just rode over from his ranch with the doctor a few minutes ago," she haltingly explained through her tears. It felt so safe and secure to rest within her father's embrace after her ordeal. She reflected that he evidently cared even more for her than she had believed.

"Enough about that now. I'm sure you've told Mrs. Chambers here the gist of everything. I'll have it all from her. You go on up to bed now and get some rest. We'll ride on over to the Cameron ranch when you're feeling better and thank Luke personally for what he's done for us."

"Very well. I don't think I can keep my eyes open for another minute. Oh, it is so very good to be home!" she said as she slipped out of his arms and climbed the stairs with the aid of Mrs. Chambers.

Comanches? Yes, it was just as he had feared. But, how in the world did Luke Cameron come to rescue her? How did he know where to search? All that doesn't really matter, he thought, all that matters is that Amanda is home, safe and unharmed. He hoped that all of the murdering, thieving savages were dead, for if not, he'd go back out and find every last one of them and kill them himself! he vowed irrationally, only visualizing in his mind the terrible scene of Amanda's capture and the time she had spent with the Indians.

Tomorrow, tomorrow he'd tell her that he loved her, that he finally truly felt like her father. It was very nearly daylight now. As he waited for Mrs. Chambers to return downstairs, he thought of

Luke Cameron. He had meant what he'd said about riding over there and offering thanks in person. It would gall him mightily, yet he was a proud man and would always pay his debts. And, he surely owed Luke Cameron a debt for saving his Amanda, a debt he could never fully repay.

Ten

It was two days before Amanda fully recovered from her harrowing ordeal. She had fervently hoped that Samuel would forget his earlier announced intentions to ride with her to the Cameron ranch to thank Luke in person, but she was disappointed in this when she descended the stairs on the third day for breakfast.

"Amanda," Samuel said as she entered the dining room, "we'll ride on over to see Luke Cameron right after breakfast. That is, if you are feeling well enough? It looks like most of your sunburn has faded by now."

She hesitated for a few moments, quickly debating whether or not to feign illness in order to escape from such a disagreeable task, but then she replied, "Very well. Yes, I am feeling much better. After we have spoken to Mr. Cameron, could we perhaps ride into town? I realize that you must have quite a bit of work to do, but I would so enjoy going to town with you today," she commented wistfully.

"All right. I don't suppose it'll hurt any to take part of the day off. Well, let's finish eating and then get going."

Amanda smiled at him in response. She had experienced an increasing closeness with her father, ever since the afternoon following her capture and rescue, when she had come downstairs for something to eat, not wishing to trouble to ring for Mrs. Chambers, who she knew would be busy. Samuel had spied her and asked her to come into the parlor for a word with him. She had done so, taking a seat on her favorite sofa.

"Amanda, I want to tell you something that's been on my mind since I first discovered that you were missing yesterday. It was suddenly revealed to me very clearly. It made me realize something that had been close to the surface of my mind for some time now."

"Yes?" Amanda prompted, anxious for her father to come to the point. He was obviously a bit uncomfortable at what he was going to say to her.

"I just wanted to say that I love you. I truly feel like your father, Amanda, at long last. I don't expect you to feel the same, but I had to tell you of my own feelings. I never really believed it possible, you see, I never believed that this could happen to me after all these years of neglecting you. But, it has," he finished, slightly embarrassed by such an enormous admission.

Amanda remained sitting in silence for a few thoughtful seconds. This was what she had wanted for the entirety of her life—to be loved and wanted by her own father. She stood slowly and approached him where he stood at the fireplace, the skirts of her dressing gown softly rustling as she walked.

"Thank you. Thank you so very much for telling me. And, you're quite wrong, you know. I feel the same way about you. Father, I love you, too," she told him softly, then anxiously awaited his reaction.

At her words, Samuel reached out for her and hugged her tightly to him, silently giving thanks to God for this beautiful, loving daughter. His life had been changed forever, and he would be eternally grateful.

Since that time, Amanda had practiced calling him father and found that she much preferred this form of address to the old one. Samuel appeared quite delighted by it, and the two of them were continually growing toward a closer understanding of one another every day. She no longer yearned for the time she would leave her father and his Texas. Instead, she penned a letter to her Aunt Martha, informing her that she would be remaining with her father a bit longer than originally planned, at least until after Christmas. Beyond that time, Amanda hesitated to make any plans, not knowing precisely what the future would bring.

After finishing their hearty breakfast, Samuel helped his daughter to mount up and the two of them cantered toward Luke's ranch.

"Father, do you really believe this is necessary?" she asked, not at all anxious to face Luke Cameron again.

"Yes, I believe it is. We Lawrences always pay our debts, you know. I'm sure that you've already thanked him most graciously, but I need to do so now, and I thought it would be best if you came along with me. I don't always agree with the young fool, but I respect him in a way. I know you must find that hard to believe, but it's true. Luke Cameron is basically a fine young man, but he's got some damned fool notions. He refuses to listen to anyone else, particularly in the matter of fencing."

"But, if you respect him, why can't you allow him to fence his land the way he believes he should?" she asked in confusion.

"Because, it has nothing to do with him personally. He's doing something that's harmful to all the ranchers around, and we can't allow him to keep on doing it. You don't understand the full implications of fencing yet, do you?"

"No, I suppose I don't. However, I heard that several other ranchers in this immediate area are also considering fencing their land now. It seems to me that such a thing is here to stay, that it could be considered progress," she remarked thoughtfully.

"It won't be here to stay if I can help it!" he vowed grimly. Amanda judged it wiser to drop the matter for the moment, which she did. The remainder of the leisurely ride was spent in conversing amiably about the land and the town. She tactfully avoided any further mention of fences.

They arrived at the Cameron ranch while it was still rather early in the morning. Luke, Jake, and a few of their ranchhands were engaged in breaking several horses at the corral. Luke noted their approach and left his work to greet them.

"Howdy, Mr. Lawrence. Miss Lawrence," he said politely as they halted before him and dismounted.

"Luke, my daughter and I are here for one reason only. And, that's to thank you for what you did, rescuing Amanda and all. I wanted to thank you personally, and if there's any way at all that I can repay you, you've only to say the word," Samuel declared solemnly.

Luke took the outstretched hand in a firm grip and shook it. He turned to Amanda, who was then gently nudged by her father, Samuel having observed her obvious reluctance to speak.

"Mr. Cameron, I too wish to offer my gratitude to you once again," she pronounced stiffly.

"Why, that's mighty nice of you, ma'am. And you too, Mr. Lawrence. I'm sure, though, that you would have done the same for me if the positions had been reversed. As for repaying me, well, let's see," he said, appearing to consider the matter quite carefully. "I know of one way you can repay me, Sam Lawrence. You can stop having your men and the others tear down my fences. That's about the only thing I can think of."

Amanda quickly glanced at her father's face, which she observed was now beginning to show signs of anger. Oh, why had the idiot mentioned the very subject her father wanted to avoid?

"Cameron, you know how I feel about that. You'll just have to think of some other way I can pay my debt to you, for it won't be that way!" he replied, striving to maintain control

178

over his temper.

"Well, then, I guess I'll just have to think of something else. Maybe Miss Lawrence can think of some way," Luke commented seriously, though his eyes twinkled mischievously as he gazed at her.

"I'm afraid not," she answered tartly, then turned abruptly away from him to focus her attention on the activity at the corral.

"Why don't you two come on over to the corral and watch for a while? We're having a bit of trouble with a couple of those ornery creatures. I guess they're just too spirited to want to be broken, but we'll get them tamed eventually. All it takes is a little persistence," Luke remarked casually, though the last bit was directed meaningfully toward Amanda. She coolly drew herself erect in chilly response.

"No, thank you. I promised my daughter to ride into town with her today. We'd best be getting on our way. Good day, Cameron," Samuel said as he touched his hat briefly and turned to help Amanda on her horse.

"Yes, thank you, Mr. Cameron. But I'm afraid that what you said does not always hold true. You see, persistence may not always achieve the results you may want," she told him crisply as she allowed her father to assist her up into the saddle. Samuel nodded curtly toward Luke once more before riding away beside his daughter. Luke stood still, gazing resolutely after them.

You're wrong, Miss Lawrence, he thought as he watched her ride out of sight. I'm going to get exactly what I want. I've never loved a woman before, and I damn sure don't intend to give you up. I usually get what I set my mind on, too. He smiled to himself in determination and turned back to the corral.

The days were becoming quite nippy now, and Amanda shivered slightly as she pulled her warmly lined cloak more closely about her body. The sun had not shown its face yet, preferring to remain hidden behind the thick blanket of grayish-white clouds. Samuel noticed her movements and said, "Are you cold?"

"No, I'm all right now."

"Amanda, I couldn't help noticing that you don't seem to like Luke Cameron too much. Mind if I ask why?"

"No, I don't mind. Well, it's simply that I think he's much too sure of himself, that he acts too superior. He can be very infuriating, you know," she declared emphatically.

"Yes, I know. Well, you won't have to see much of him from here on out."

"Father, I want you to know that I've written a letter to Aunt Martha," she suddenly confessed. "I told her that I'm going to remain here with you longer than we had originally planned. I hope that this meets with your approval?" she asked anxiously.

"Meets with my approval? I want you to stay out here with me from now on! I didn't want to push you, but I'd like for you to stay here with me more than anything in the world."

"I'd like nothing more than that, too, but I don't know what Aunt Martha will say. You see, I do feel that I owe her a certain duty. I can honestly admit, however, that I certainly don't love her the way I love you."

"You can think it over for a while first. There's no hurry about the matter. I want you to know, though, that you're more than welcome to stay with me and consider my home yours."

Arriving in Big Prairie, they were randomly greeted by several of the townspeople milling about the streets. Word had rapidly spread of Amanda's capture by the Comanches, as well as the news that it was none other than Luke Cameron who had rescued her so heroically. Many tongues were set to wagging over the possibility of a romance between the two, but Amanda was happily ignorant of such rumors when she rode into town that day.

She posted the letter to her Aunt Martha, then she and her father strolled down the street to shop. After purchasing several items, they paid a visit to Dr. Stephens.

"Doc, how's the measles epidemic coming along?" Samuel inquired as they stepped inside the small frame house near the edge of town.

"Oh, it's not near as bad as we all thought it might be. In fact, Miss Amanda," he said, turning to her, "you can resume school anytime you want to. We've got everything under control now. Seems that the disease was only in a few isolated cases, thank the Lord. And, speaking of school, I heard an interesting bit of news just yesterday. It seems that the new schoolteacher is due to arrive within the week. What with all the excitement about you,

Miss Amanda, I expect no one remembered to tell you."

"No. I didn't know she would be coming so soon. I haven't had an opportunity to speak with Mrs. Powell since the first of the week when I dismissed school. I'll go to see her immediately. Thank you for the information. I'll spread the news that school will begin again on Monday," she told him.

In all actuality, Amanda was rather sorry that the new teacher would arrive so soon. She had honestly enjoyed her teaching experience, and she would sorely miss the children. Oh well, she sighed to herself, I knew it was only temporary. She would now have to manage to occupy her time about the ranch. If only she could persuade her father to allow her to help out more with some of the various duties about the household. She would speak to him about that later.

After paying a brief visit to Mrs. Powell, Samuel and Amanda left town and rode homeward. Samuel resumed his work, while Amanda decided to walk a bit in the cool air of the afternoon. Riding did not tire her near as easily as when she had first come to Texas, yet she was still not entirely accustomed to riding for several hours on end. She would simply take a short walk about the grounds, and she would have an opportunity to be alone with her thoughts. She hadn't done all that much serious thinking since her rescue, preferring instead to occupy her mind with either reading or conversation. Now, she wanted to contemplate several matters.

"Why, if it ain't the high and mighty Miss Lawrence," she heard a lazy, contemptuous voice utter as she rounded the corner of the bunkhouse.

"Mr. Jones. I have already informed you that I never want you to speak to me again. I warned you what would happen if you ever insulted me in such a manner as the last time," she cautioned him coldly, ill at ease in his presence. She comforted herself with the knowledge that she was well within earshot of any of the other hands.

"Well, now, there ain't no need to be so mean to old Buck here. I just been wanting to know about your capture by them Indians ma'am. Why, if I'd been them, I wouldn't have let no one take you from me. No, I'd have ridden away with you and made you my squaw," he sneered at her.

"You are utterly disgusting!" Amanda cried, then attempted to sweep past him and continue her walk. However, he suddenly blocked her way with his body and said, "Now, Miss Amanda, you don't want to leave just yet. I told you that last time, when you was so unfriendly to me, that you'd be mighty sorry for it. I ain't forgot, honey. I ain't forgot at all. Why don't you just get down off your high horse and let me show you what a real man is like? I can promise you I'm a hell of a lot better than any of those Comanche that might have had their way with you!"

"Get out of my way!" she hissed furiously at him, then gasped as he clamped a dirty, calloused hand over her mouth and squeezed cruelly, bruising her soft skin.

"Ain't nobody going to miss you for a while,

honey. Ain't nobody around here but you and me. The others are all too busy to come looking around, so we'll be all alone for a while. The time has come, honey. I'm going to show you that you ain't no different from any other woman of your kind! Yes sir, underneath them fancy skirts, you're all the same!" he muttered viciously as he forced her to the hard ground below and chuckled evilly at her frantic struggles. She attempted to bite his hand, but it was clamped too tightly over her mouth. She screamed deep in her throat, vainly trying to be heard by someone.

Amanda glowered at her attacker murderously as he tore at her skirts in his frenzy. Her eyes widened suddenly as she perceived the presence of another man who had now come up behind Buck.

"You filthy dog! I'll kill you for this!" shouted Tommy Evans as he grabbed Buck and threw him off Amanda. Amanda pulled down her skirts and staggered to her feet, leaning against the wall of the bunkhouse for support.

"Why, you young pup! You been asking for this for a long time. I'm sure enough going to give it to you now!" growled Buck as he drew out his sharp, gleaming knife.

Amanda gasped in alarm and finally recovered enough of her voice to scream, "Help! Someone help, please!"

Frank, Roy, Slim, and Steve all came running around the corner and abruptly halted as they observed Buck's threatening stance and the knife he flourished in their direction.

"Get back, all of you! This fight is between me

and Evans here! It don't concern none of you, damn it!" he bellowed, then suddenly lunged toward Tommy, catching him off-guard and managing to slash him across the chest. Tommy jerked sideways in time to avoid being killed, and the other hands took this opportunity to close in on Buck. They finally subdued him just as Samuel came bounding around the corner.

"What the hell's going on here?" he demanded, then noted the presence of his daughter, her dress torn and her face scratched and dirty.

"Amanda? What are you doing back here? What's happened?"

"Oh, Father, it's Buck. He tried to rape me, but Tommy came to help. Buck pulled a knife on him and would have killed him if the others hadn't arrived in time," she related breathlessly, moving to Tommy's side.

"Tommy, come on inside the house and let me see to that cut. It doesn't look too serious," she told him gently, then moved along with him back to the house.

"Buck, you're lucky you didn't kill him. If you had, I'd have seen that you were hanged for it. I should kill you myself for what you tried to do to my daughter, and I would, if it weren't for the trouble it might cause for her in the long run. Instead, you better consider yourself damned lucky that I've decided to let you live. However, I'm going to make you pay for what you did to her before I kick you off my land! Tie him to a post!" he commanded the other hands harshly. Samuel was at his most dangerous now, his eyes glinting

185

with a strange light, his mouth set tightly as he strode to the barn and then returned to where they had tied the violently cursing Buck at the corral. Samuel brandished a long bullwhip in his hand.

"This is for daring to lay a hand on my daughter, Buck Jones!" he ground out, then drew back his arm and prepared to strike the man's naked back with the whip.

"I'll kill you, Sam Lawrence! You mark my words, I'll kill you and see to it that your bitch of a daughter pays, too!" Buck threatened. His words quickly changed to bellows of pain as the whip descended on his back. Again and again, Samuel struck him with the punishing whip. Finally, the howls of pain ceased as the man slumped against the post, mercifully unconscious.

"All right. Cut him down. Revive him, then put him and his gear on his horse and get him out of my sight," Samuel curtly ordered. He stalked to the barn, replaced the whip on the wall, then went inside the house to see to his daughter and young Evans.

Amanda had heard Buck's screams of pain, but she had tried to ignore them and turned back to tending Tommy's cut.

"I don't think we'll need to send for the doctor," she assured him. "It's not too very deep, although I'm certain that it will become very sore in a short time. Tommy," her voice altered at this point, "I can't thank you enough for risking your life to help me. I think you are one of the most courageous young men I have ever known." In the back of her mind, she suddenly saw Luke

Cameron's face. She turned aside from thoughts of him and listened to Tommy.

"Oh, it wasn't nothing, Miss Amanda. I'm only sorry I didn't get a chance to fight him fair and square. I felt like killing him when I saw what he was trying to do to you!"

"Well, thank goodness you arrived in time. Buck has been insulting me for some time now, and I suppose it had to come to a head sooner or later. I should have told my father about him in the beginning, yet I didn't wish to cause any trouble. Thank you again, Tommy. I'll never forget your bravery," she repeated, then leaned down to brush his cheek with her lips. He flushed at her light kiss, and would have spoken if her father had not entered the kitchen at that point.

"Amanda, I'm sorry for what happened. Are you all right?"

"Yes, I'm fine," she assured him.

"Evans, we owe you a debt of gratitude. Thank you, son. How are you feeling?" Samuel asked with concern.

"I reckon I'll be just fine, sir. Well, I'd best be getting on back outside and back to work. Thanks for doctoring me up, Miss Amanda," he said as he hurried from the room, embarrassed by so much attention.

"Father, I suppose I ought to tell you something about Buck Jones. You see, he has been insulting me and insinuating vile things to me for some time now. I didn't tell you before now because I didn't wish to be the source of any further trouble for you. I'm sorry now that I didn't tell you. I can see that I made the wrong decision," she admitted.

"Yes, you did. But, it doesn't matter now. He won't be back, and I don't think he'll ever bother you again. Men like that are born cowards, honey. They prey on women and young boys like Tommy. It makes them feel more important to themselves, I guess. Anyway, I hope that you've learned to be more open with me about everything in the future," he cautioned her.

"Yes, yes, I certainly have," she agreed. "What did you do to him?" she asked, fearful that he might have killed the man in his fury.

"I bullwhipped him. Maybe I should have gone ahead and killed him, but I didn't think that would be for your best interest. There would have been a lot of trouble and talk. I never did like him much, but he was a good hand, so I tolerated him. I'll simply have to be more careful in the future. The rest of the hands are different from him, I can assure you. Are you sure you're all right?" he inquired again with fatherly concern. So much had happened to his Amanda in the past few weeks. But he knew she was strong. She was a Lawrence, and she was his daughter. She would always survive, of that he was certain. She possessed a rare sort of courage he had seldom found among the women of his acquaintance.

"Yes, I'm fine. Just a bit bruised and dirty. I'll go on upstairs now and clean up. You have work to do, so you had better get on with it. Why don't we just try and forget what happened? I have to begin teaching on Monday and I have a lot to do before then."

Samuel smiled in admiration as she left the room. Yes, she was gentle and feminine on the outside, but she had courage and stamina underneath, he thought to himself as he returned outside.

Tommy resumed the routine honor of escorting her home from school each afternoon. Her father continued to ride with her in the mornings, as had been their custom before all of the startling events of the past week. Amanda looked forward to teaching once again, and she warmly welcomed the children back to school.

"Children, I am very happy to see all of you once more. I have some interesting news for you. Your new teacher will be here within the next few days. I know that you all look forward to her arrival. Naturally, I will be very sorry not to be teaching you any longer, and I will miss each and every one of you. But that's enough of that for now. Students in grades one through three, please open your primers to page 38. Grades three through six will work on their arithmetic, while you older students will begin writing the themes you were earlier assigned."

The children nearly groaned aloud at the thought of yet another teacher to be broken in. Just when they had gotten used to Miss Lawrence, too. After all, there weren't too many schools that could boast of having their teacher captured by renegade Comanches and then rescued by one of their own neighbors. Why, Jake Cameron had told them all the details.

The new teacher arrived at the end of the week,

riding in on the afternoon stage. Amanda had already dismissed school for the day, and she thronged along with the other people in town to catch a glimpse of this new teacher.

The driver hopped down and opened the door of the stagecoach. He extended a hand in order to assist the lone passenger from the coach. A small, slim hand took his, and the curious onlookers were afforded a brief glimpse of a shapely ankle as the new teacher stepped down, carefully holding her skirts to keep from trailing them in the dust.

Several people gasped aloud at the sight which greeted their eyes. Surely this couldn't be the new schoolteacher! She wasn't at all what one would normally assume a teacher to look like. Barely over five feet tall, she was a dainty and graceful young woman of somewhere in the vicinity of twenty years of age. Her shining blonde curls were piled atop her head, topped by a fashionable, feathered bonnet. Her heart-shaped, sweetly smiling face glanced about at the townspeople and she spoke softly, "I thank you all for extending such a warm welcome to me. My name is Carolyn Tompkins, and I am your new schoolteacher. I am very pleased to be here in Big Prairie at long last."

Amanda watched as the surprising young woman dimpled delightedly at such obvious admiration from the surrounding men. This new teacher was certainly not the shy, rather frumpy creature she had been expecting! She experienced a small twinge of jealousy, along with the other women present, as Miss Tompkins was besieged by offers of assistance from the men who followed her inside the town's boarding house.

Why in the world had such a young woman come all the way out to this wilderness to teach school? Amanda asked herself. Perhaps she was running from an unhappy love affair, perhaps she was simply looking for a husband out here in the untamed west. Well, whatever the reason, she thought, everyone in Big Prairie—the male inhabitants anyway—would be well pleased with the new schoolteacher's presence.

Amanda returned to the schoolhouse, where she set about cleaning the chalkboards as she waited for Tommy to arrive and accompany her home. She was interrupted by a soft, melodious voice from the back of the room.

"Hello. Are you the temporary teacher?" the new teacher inquired politely, her voice giving evidence that she was from the South.

"Yes. How do you do?" Amanda responded as she dusted the chalk from her hands. "My name is Amanda Lawrence."

"I am Miss Carolyn Tompkins. I simply had to rush on over here and see where I would be teaching. The schoolhouse is even larger than I thought. By the way, I will be taking over tomorrow, so if you have any of your personal things in the desk, I suggest that you remove them," she commented a bit coolly.

"I will most certainly make sure of that, Miss Tompkins," Amanda replied mildly, then asked, "Where are you from, Miss Tompkins?"

"Oh, why, I've come all the way from Georgia, Miss Lawrence. I must say, it seemed like I would never get here!" she declared, wrinkling her small nose as she recalled the long and dirty trip.

"I know what you mean. I am out here to visit my father for a while. I came here from Boston, you see," Amanda told her, striving to be friendly. For some unknown reason, she didn't quite like this petite beauty standing in the doorway.

"Yes, I can tell that you're a Yankee," Carolyn remarked with an edge to her voice. "I suppose you might even say that you're one of the reasons I have come to Texas," she declared disdainfully, making it all too apparent what she thought of people from the North.

"I? I'm afraid I don't understand. I had nothing whatsoever to do with your coming out here, Miss Tompkins," Amanda denied frostily, then fetched her cloak and bonnet from the peg on the wall. She started to go outside to see if Tommy had arrived yet, when the new teacher suddenly blocked her way.

"You're a Yankee, aren't you? Well, my family's rather prosperous business was destroyed in the war. We all had to earn a living some way. I taught for four years back home, until I decided to try my luck out here. But then, I'm sure you don't know what I'm talking about, do you? Are you even aware that there was a war, Amanda Lawrence?" she inquired sarcastically.

"Yes, I am aware of it. As a matter of fact, my father fought in the war, Miss Tompkins. For the Confederacy," she delivered this parting shot and then gently, but firmly, pushed past the open-mouthed young woman.

She could see Tommy riding from the livery stable toward her, leading her horse. Without waiting for him to come any nearer to the schoolhouse, she hurried to meet him.

Yes, she thought as she rode home beside him, the townspeople of Big Prairie are in for a big surprise. Beneath that dignified Southern lady exterior, there beats the heart of a coldly calculating vixen, Amanda told herself. She wasn't sure precisely how or why she knew this to be true, but she knew it all the same. She experienced a feeling of regret that her pupils would now be left to the mercy of Miss Carolyn Tompkins. Heaven help them!

Eleven

Now that Amanda was no longer teaching school, she spent more time than ever assisting Mrs. Chambers with the housework, and even setting herself the goal of learning to cook as well as the jolly housekeeper. True, she had indeed received instruction in the culinary arts back in Boston, but the methods of food preparation, as well as the food itself, were quite different in Texas.

She also spent an increasing amount of time with her father, riding out with him on several occasions to check on stock. At other times she would simply watch as he and the hands conducted their business about the ranch. There was always much work to be done, especially with winter approaching. Christmas was a mere three weeks away now, and the majority of the hands would be wintering at line camps out on the range in order to keep an eye on the herd. Already the days were becoming quite cold, and the nights were nearly as chilly as those Amanda had experienced back home in Boston.

Amanda sorely missed the children and teaching. She often found her thoughts straying to Miss

Carolyn Tompkins and her students. Although she was quite occupied about the ranch, she grew more and more curious to discover exactly how the new teacher was getting along with the children.

Actually, Amanda thought to herself, she didn't like the Southern beauty one bit, and she was secretly hoping that Miss Tompkins would tire of the harsh and primitive country and return to her native state. Finally, after the space of more than a week, she persuaded Mrs. Chambers to drive with her into Big Prairie. While the housekeeper purchased several necessary provisions at the store, Amanda would pay a short visit to the schoolhouse.

During the drive to town, Amanda was dismayed when she discovered the turn her thoughts had taken as she sat in silence. Luke Cameron had crept unbidden into her mind once again, as he had quite frequently. Oh, why can't I forget that man? she complained to herself. She found herself recalling their last encounter, that day she had accompanied her father to his ranch. He was so very infuriating, speaking his lies in order to take advantage of her. He was everything Aunt Martha had warned her against.

She suddenly realized that she hadn't yet received a reply to the letter she had mailed to her aunt some time ago. It should have arrived by now. It's just as well, she sighed inwardly. Aunt Martha would probably be angry that she was planning to remain out here with her father through Christmas. Not that Aunt Martha would miss her niece's presence all that much. No, it would simply be a matter of principle with her. Aunt Martha had always possessed such staunch principles concerning any matter.

Amanda finally pushed thoughts of Aunt Martha and Luke aside and proceeded to engage Mrs. Chambers in conversation once more. The two of them had grown quite close in the months Amanda had visited. Amanda viewed the older woman more as a good friend than as an employee of her father's. Mrs. Chambers's good sense and warm manner frequently broke through any social barriers that crept to the surface.

Arriving in Big Prairie, Mrs. Chambers expertly pulled the horses to a smooth halt before the general store.

"Honey, you go on and do what you need to do. I'll go on in the store and see about getting those things I need. I'll meet you back here in a little while," she suggested to Amanda.

"That's fine. I simply want to pay a visit to the school, then I will return here and help you," she replied as she gathered her woolen skirts and jumped down from the wagon seat, her boots striking the hard ground below with noisy impact. There had been a freeze the night before, and a few signs of the frost still remained in evidence in the areas shaded by the buildings.

Amanda again drew the hood of her warm cloak up over her head and settled it in place upon her curls. She then briskly approached the schoolhouse. She paused outside as she experienced a sudden impulse to observe the new teacher without her awareness. Creeping around to the far side of the schoolhouse, she slowly raised herself on tiptoe to peer inside the window. The children's backs were luckily turned to the window, and she looked to the front of the room, where she spied Miss Tompkins.

"I am sick and tired of your mealy-mouthed excuses! Now, you will either do as I tell you, or I am warning you, you will pay dearly for your laziness! And, if I ever catch any of you making such disgusting faces at me or drawing such terrible pictures of me again, I will be forced to take drastic measures!" she announced ringingly.

Amanda couldn't help but hear the angry young woman, her voice carrying loudly and clearly to the back of the room. So, Amanda thought to herself with a small degree of satisfaction, the new teacher and her pupils do not get along very well at all. Why, she had certainly never been forced to raise her voice to the children in such a manner! No, and she had never caught any of the students making faces at her or drawing unflattering portraits of her upon the chalkboard.

Well, I must confess that this is precisely what I might have expected, she told herself as she stood squarely on the ground once more. She resisted the urge to burst into the schoolroom and confront the haughty, dainty little schoolteacher and inquire if she needed any assistance with the children. As she rounded the front of the building, the doors swung open and the students bounded outside into the cool air, happy to escape the confines of the school and the tyranny of their new teacher. Several of them greeted Amanda with happy smiles when they saw her standing at the front of the school-house.

Amanda stood aside and watched smilingly as the children all emptied the building, then observed as Carolyn Tompkins descended the front steps in their wake. Her pretty face was drawn up into a scowl, and she appeared anything but pleased when she spotted Amanda.

"What are you doing here?" she demanded petulantly, flinging her cloak about her shoulders as she reached the bottom step. She viewed Amanda with a chilly, decidedly unfriendly expression marring the features of her childishly attractive face.

"I was in town and simply thought I would stop by and see how you were doing, Miss Tompkins. Are you experiencing any difficulty with the students, by any chance?" Amanda responded, probing with a raised eyebrow.

"Difficulty? Why, I don't know what on earth would make you think that, Miss Lawrence. Quite the contrary. The little darlings all appear to just love their new teacher. I think I have most definitely made a positive contribution to their education already. They were so desperately in need of a firm hand, you see," Carolyn replied sweetly, her eyes silently challenging.

"I see. Well, in that case, I am certainly relieved that they have you to provide them with what they need. I also—" here she was interrupted by the sudden appearance of Jake Cameron.

"Miss Lawrence! We all sure do miss you, ma'am," he blurted out boyishly. "When are you

198

coming back out to the ranch?"

"Jake, how nice to see you again. I miss all of you, also. I don't really know when I will be riding that way again with my father. However, you are more than welcome to come by the Circle L any time you wish," Amanda told him, somewhat taken aback at his friendliness. True, Jake had treated her with a new respect since her capture by the Comanches, yet his words today were marked by a new enthusiasm. Yes, Amanda thought, I can see right now that Miss Tompkins is not at all what the people, or the children, expected.

Carolyn remained silent as the other two continued to converse amiably, both ignoring her presence beside them. Her face suddenly brightened with a new interest as Luke Cameron rode toward the schoolhouse.

"Miss Lawrence. Ma'am," Luke said, tipping his hat politely to both young ladies as he dismounted and clapped his younger brother playfully on the back.

"Luke, what are you doing in town this time of day?" Jake asked.

"I had to ride into town to see a man on some business. Thought I'd stop by and ride home with you today." His eyes strayed to Amanda's slightly flushed face as he spoke.

"Jake, won't you please introduce me to your friend?" Carolyn suggested coquettishly, observing Luke's handsome features with increasing curiosity and interest.

"Yes, ma'am. Luke, this is the new teacher, Miss Tompkins. Ma'am, this is my brother, Luke,"

Jake said politely, although it was obvious that he was performing the task with reluctance.

"I'm very pleased to make your acquaintance, Mr. Luke Cameron," Carolyn replied in her most Southern drawl, her small mouth forming a pretty smile, her eyes sparkling. She drew herself more erect and tossed her head, causing the hood of her cloak to fall to her shoulders, exposing even more of her face and bright curls.

"Pleased to meet you, ma'am. I heard that there was a new teacher in town. Where'd you come here from, Miss Tompkins?" Luke inquired casually, his eyes still glancing toward Amanda. Carolyn mentally noted the direction of his gaze and answered him in her most feminine manner.

"Why, I'm from Georgia, sir. I do declare, I just love Texas, though. I'm loving it more and more each minute, too. Are you a native of Big Prairie, Mr. Cameron?"

"Yes, ma'am. Born and raised here. We've got a ranch a few miles outside of town. Miss Lawrence," he said, virtually turning his back on Carolyn and addressing his remarks to Amanda, "now that you're no longer teaching, just how are you spending all of your spare time?"

Amanda noticed out of the corner of her eye that Carolyn bristled considerably at the loss of attention. She answered Luke coolly, "Why, there is always more than enough to do on a ranch, as I'm sure you know. My father and I remain quite busy." Her gaze remained riveted to her fingers which were now anxiously tying her cloak strings. "If you'll excuse me, I have to hurry and meet someone. Good day, everyone." She was beginning to stroll away from the group, when she heard Carolyn's honey-sweet voice.

"Mr. Cameron, your brother here is one of my brightest pupils. Jake, why don't you go escort Miss Lawrence? I want your brother here to tell me a little bit about your ranch."

"Yes, ma'am," muttered Jake, glad of the opportunity to escape. He caught up with Amanda and walked with her to the other side of the street.

"Miss Tompkins, I don't mean to be rude, but I really do need to be getting on back out to our ranch. Perhaps I can tell you about the ranch some other time. Or better yet, get Jake to tell you about it tomorrow at school," Luke said as he prepared to mount up once again.

"Oh, please sir, don't go just yet. Why, you're one of the very first real cowboys I've met so far. Most of the men here in town run businesses. Why, you're the first real rancher I've talked to. I came all the way out here from Georgia, just hoping to see those cowboys and Indians we all heard about back home," she told him, flirting outrageously with her dimpled cheeks and fluttering eyelashes.

"I see. Well, you'll most likely see a lot of cowboys, ma'am, but I doubt if you'll see any Indians here in town," he replied politely, though his blue eyes twinkled mischievously. "Of course, you should ask Miss Lawrence about Indians. She was once captured by a band of renegade Comanches. Why, the whole town is still talking about her great adventure. If you ever want to come on out and take a look at a real Texas ranch for yourself, her pa has a mighty fine one. Now, good day, Miss Tompkins," he insisted firmly as he mounted and proceeded to turn his horse toward where Amanda was standing across the street with Jake.

Oh! fumed Carolyn in silence as she glared at his retreating back. The man was most certainly rude, and yet she found herself fascinated by him. He had to be one of the most attractive young men she had ever seen, as well as one of the most totally masculine. It was quite obvious that Amanda Lawrence held some sort of interest for him at the moment, but she, Carolyn Tompkins, could most certainly change all of that in the very near future. Yes sir, Mr. Luke Cameron, she vowed, your interest will most certainly be transferred from that Yankee hussy to me, or my name isn't Tompkins!

"Ma'am, if you don't mind, I need to go on down the street and see someone real quick. I'll see you later," Jake said as Amanda smiled in agreement. She was preparing to enter the general store and go in search of Mrs. Chambers, when a deep, familiar voice detained her.

"Amanda. Amanda, aren't you even going to speak to me?" Luke demanded, somewhat irked by her frosty behavior, though he told himself that he should be used to it by now. I might have expected it, he told himself. She's still fuming, still refusing to face the truth. And, that little Southern witch back there didn't help matters any. He found his anger giving way to amusement as he realized the possible source of Amanda's chilly reception.

That was it, he told himself exultantly, Amanda was jealous! She was actually jealous of that little flirt!

"I have nothing whatsoever to say to you, sir. Why don't you go back and instruct Miss Tompkins in the ways of the West?" she replied with biting sarcasm, then silently chided herself for exposing her inner feelings about the new teacher.

"What's the matter, Amanda? Don't tell me you're jealous!" Luke responded with a crooked grin. He had by now dismounted again and sauntered over to stand directly before her.

"Jealous? You must be insane! I don't have to remain here and be insulted by you, Luke Cameron!" she exclaimed angrily, whirling about to enter the store. She was halted by the firm pressure of his strong hand closing upon her elbow.

"Wait just a minute! If you aren't jealous, then how come you're acting so all-fired mad about her?" he demanded, gazing down into her stormy eyes.

"I happen to dislike the young woman! She has made it very clear from the first time we met that she regards me as a distasteful Yankee. Now, are you satisfied? If so, will you kindly release my arm? People are beginning to stare at us," she hissed in a low, seething tone as she glanced about to ascertain if anyone was a witness to their humiliating conversation.

Luke, however, did not give in to her demands. Instead he pulled her tightly against him, then placed one of his powerful arms beneath her knees and lifted her off the ground. Amanda opened her mouth in astonishment, while Luke tossed her up onto his saddle and quickly mounted behind her.

Mrs. Chambers, emerging from the general store at that moment, observed Amanda's position upon Luke's horse. Luke called to her, "Mrs. Chambers, ma'am, I'm going to see Amanda home today. Jake's just down the street there; get him to ride home with you. Please tell him for me that I'll see him at the ranch later."

"Sure enough, Luke," replied Mrs. Chambers with an answering smile.

"Mrs. Chambers, I am being held against my will! Please—" she began, only to be silenced by Luke's voice in her ear.

"Amanda Lawrence, if you don't shut up right this minute, I'll turn you across my knee right in front of all these good people in town here! Now, be quiet and settle back!" he commanded in a low, even tone, then spurred his horse and tightened his hold about Amanda's squirming body as they rode away from the town.

Amanda reddened uncomfortably beneath the gaze of several of the curious onlookers. As if they hadn't been gossiping enough about the pretty daughter of Sam Lawrence and the handsome, eligible Luke Cameron, now they had more fuel to add to the fire! Several of them turned to one another and commented on the likelihood of a Christmas wedding between the two.

Mrs. Chambers chuckled good-naturedly as she saw Luke ride away with her charge. Yes sir, there was something between those two. She'd known it for a spell now, even though Amanda acted as if she disliked the young man. Well, she'd better find that young scamp, Jake, and get him to ride back with her.

Amanda refused to acquiesce to Luke's commands and she continued to struggle as they galloped out of town. When they were out of sight of Big Prairie, Luke slowed his horse and relaxed his hold on her a bit.

"Now, I've got some talking to do to you, young lady. First off, I've been wanting to talk to you about that day at my ranch for some time now. I meant what I said, Amanda. I'm in love with you. I no longer just suspect it, I know it. You don't have to believe me just yet, I'll be patient a bit longer," he teased her unmercifully as she whirled about to face him in angry defiance.

"I don't believe a word of what you are saying! You know good and well that you don't mean it! You only wish to try and take advantage of me again, and you darn well know it!" she cried in frustrated anger.

"Such languge from my proper Boston miss!" Luke replied teasingly, then continued, "I mean every word of it. You just won't see the truth of it. You little idiot! You're just too proud and uppity to admit that you feel something for a Texas cowpoke, is that it? What kind of fool notions did that monster of an aunt of yours put into that head of yours?" he demanded roughly, adminstering a couple of shakes to her shoulders. He spurred his horse into a canter, slowing it to a halt as they eventually came to a formation of large rocks.

"What in heaven's name are you doing?" Amanda exclaimed as Luke halted his mount and jumped down. Without bothering to answer her, he reached up and lifted her to the ground beside him.

"If you think I'm going to stay here and talk to you, you are indeed out of your mind!" she raged, struggling and holding back as he strode with her to the rocks and forced her to sit down upon the largest one.

"Sit there and be quiet, woman!" he yelled, startling her into momentary silence. He plopped down beside her and frowned menacingly as he observed her attempts to inch further away from any contact with his body.

"I love you, damn it! Furthermore, you love me! Yes, you do," he insisted as she opened her mouth to deny it. "I don't know when you'll have enough gumption to admit it, Amanda, but, like I said before, you will admit it eventually and I'll damn sure be around to hear you. Now, hold on a minute," he ordered as she started to rise. "That isn't all I wanted to say to you. There's something else, and it concerns your father."

Amanda turned back toward him in surprise. Her father? What on earth could he possibly have to say about Samuel? Why, he and Samuel no longer even liked one another.

"I'm sure I do not wish to hear anything you have to say regarding my father," she responded frostily, turning her head away from him.

Luke suddenly snaked out an arm and yanked Amanda closer to him. She cried out in furious

206

protest, but he relentlessly continued, his face close to hers, "You sure will listen to me, nonetheless. There are times when it becomes necessary to get a little rough with you, Amanda. Your father and his men have caused enough trouble in these parts to last for quite a spell. I'm referring to the matter of the fences. He and his so-called friends have taken to having my fence lines cut and torn down again. That is something I will not tolerate, and you may tell Sam that I said so!"

"Why are you telling me this? Aren't you man enough to speak directly to my father?" she replied tauntingly.

"Yes, I'm man enough. I just thought that you'd want me to avoid another confrontation with your father. If you'll tell him that I aim to fight back, well, then, maybe he'll listen to sense from you. You know deep in your heart that it isn't right, what he and the others are doing. I happen to think that you understand a lot of things you won't admit to."

"I'll certainly inform him of what you said, Mr. Cameron," she replied haughtily, then rose from her seat on the rock and faced him, feeling a small degree safer by the added height. "Will you please take me home now? I think you have said enough for one day. Mrs. Chambers will begin to worry if I do not appear back at the ranch fairly soon."

"She won't worry. She knows good and well that you're safe with me. And, no, I haven't said all I wanted to say yet. I want to know when you're planning on going back to Boston," he demanded, his commanding tone brooking no defiance.

"That is really none of your concern!" she countered, then decided that it might be best to give him the information he sought and therefore end this disturbing discussion. "I wrote to my aunt and informed her that I would remain here through Christmas. Beyond that, I really hadn't made any plans as of yet, though I suppose I will have to return a short time after the holidays," she told him, feeling uncomfortable beneath his searching gaze.

"Good. Then that gives me a little bit more time, doesn't it? You see, you won't be returning to Boston at all. In fact, you'll probably never see Boston again, unless we decide to pay a visit to that family of yours there sometime in the far future. I don't want you under the influence of that old goat of an aunt of yours ever again!' he declared, then watched as the flush on her face mounted once more and she stormed at him.

"What? How dare you presume to tell me my own plans! How dare you speak as if you have any control over my future at all! For the last time, I do not believe a word of what you said! In fact, I don't believe in love at all! I'm tired of being ordered about by other people, tired of being treated like a mindless idiot! I want to enjoy my independence. I very well may not return to Boston, but it will be my own decision, not yours!" She stood clenching her fists, her eyes virtually shooting sparks in her fury.

"You can rail and scream about it all you want to, but that's the way it's going to be. You're going to marry me one of these days, and it won't be all that far in the future. There'll come a time when my patience will run out, and that's the time I'll marry you, even if I have to drag you to the church! I'm a mighty determined man, Amanda, and I won't give you up. That's the way things are going to be. The only thing is, you sure are making it one hell of a fight, aren't you?" he asked her with an amused grin. "Now, I suppose we've talked enough about this for one day. Don't worry, though, you'll be seeing a lot more of me in the future. The only way to tame a little filly is to spend a lot of time and effort on her! Of course, if you really find my company all that distasteful, I'm sure Miss Tompkins would be glad to substitute for you," he teased her, then laughed aloud in utter delight as she drew herself stiffly erect and narrowed her beautiful eyes threateningly. Luke stood and faced her.

"Amanda, you're quite a woman, did you know that? Yep, you're exactly the woman for me. Why, between the two of us, we'll certainly never have a dull moment!" he spoke softly down at her, then caught her face between his two large hands and slowly brought his mouth down to hers. Amanda found herself being lifted off the ground by his muscular arms and her face level with his as he continued his searching kiss.

Once again, she found her first, initial desire to struggle against him fading away into oblivion as she experienced the warm, wonderful, tingling sensations just the nearness of this infuriating man seemed to produce in her. Once again, she found a small voice in the very back recesses of her mind surfacing to question whether or not he might be speaking the truth about his love for her, as well as if she really felt the same for him. She cursed her own weakness and pushed such thoughts aside and could only concentrate on the passionate embrace they were now sharing.

Amanda was amazed at her own daring when she found her arms creeping up to surround his neck. She pressed herself even closer against his hard body and parted her lips in breathless surrender. She was becoming so very engulfed by the flames of desire rising within her that she could simply stand and stare with open mouth when she found her feet once more touching solid ground and her arms now empty.

"That's enough for now, Amanda. Damn it, woman, I'm only flesh and blood, after all! I can't stand around kissing and holding you all day like this and expect nothing more to happen! Come on now, I'm taking you home." He strode away from her and began gathering up the reins of his grazing horse.

Amanda glared after him in humiliation. She was totally embarrassed by the fact that he had realized her increasing response. How could she have been so disgustingly weak? She flounced toward him and stiffly allowed him to place her upon the horse.

The two of them rode in silence for the remainder of the trip, arriving at the Circle L in the late afternoon. Amanda's cheeks were a becoming bright red, due to the cold air biting at her face throughout the ride. Luke told himself that she had never looked more beautiful. He helped her dismount without a word, then delivered this parting speech: "Amanda, don't forget anything of what I told you today. I'll bide my time, but there'll come a time when my patience runs out. And, when that happens, you'd better watch out, because I'll be coming to get you. Also, be sure and tell your father that there's going to be a whole lot more trouble if he and his cohorts don't quit tearing down my fences. Remember," he cautioned her as he mounted once more, "you won't be able to avoid me much anymore. If you try, you'll just end up making things a lot harder on yourself in the long run. Good afternoon, Miss Lawrence,' he teased as he tipped his hat politely and galloped away and out of sight.

Amanda whirled about and climbed the porch steps, entering the house with a frustrated air. She found Mrs. Chambers already back in the kitchen, just beginning her preparations for the evening meal.

"Oh, there you are, Amanda. Did you and Luke have a nice ride?" she inquired innocently, keeping her attention fixed on the dough she was rolling out for the evening meal's biscuits.

"You know very well that I did not wish to go with him! Why didn't you say something to him?" Amanda complained indignantly.

"It wouldn't have done any good, honey. Why, that there young man is as bullheaded as they come. Yes sir, he sure is crazy about you. Why, it was all over town today about you two. Folks ain't blind, Amanda, even if you are," she remarked knowingly, then observed the telltale flush rising on the younger woman's frowning face.

"That is quite enough, thank you! He is an overbearing, conceited, barbaric cowboy! I don't want to see him ever again!" she declared, then turned away and hurried from the room and up the stairs.

Mrs. Chambers heaved a sigh and thought, you sure are trying to fight it, honey, but you can't win. Nobody ever wins against fate, and it's sure enough fate for you two to be together. I can see it coming, for sure.

An hour later, Amanda returned downstairs for the evening meal with her father. He waited until she had seated herself at the table, then he took his own place opposite her.

"Did you have a good day today, Amanda?" he queried.

"Oh, I suppose so, Father. Mrs. Chambers and I finished a bit of sewing, then went into town. I looked in on the new schoolteacher while I was there. It appears that she is having a bit of difficulty in handling the children."

"Oh, really? Well, I don't know anything about her just yet, but I suppose we'll see her at the Christmas social," he replied casually as he cut into his thick beef steak.

"Christmas social? What is that?" Amanda asked with interest.

"Oh, all the folks around here get together in town and have a big holiday celebration. There'll be dancing, games, singing, just about everything. Didn't anyone in town today tell you about it?"

"No, no, I didn't remain in town for very long," she responded quickly, then fixed her gaze on her plate.

"Well, the social will be next Friday night. I guess you and Mrs. Chambers will want to cook up a batch of food to take. Do you have an appropriate dress for Christmas, honey?" he asked her. "If not, I'd be more than happy if you'd buy some material and make yourself something. I want you to have whatever you want, you know that."

"Yes, Father, thank you. I know you are more than generous. I have something very suitable already, a red velvet that Aunt Martha allowed me to have made up last year. Speaking of Aunt Martha," she suddenly remembered, "I haven't received a reply to my letter yet. Do you suppose it was lost along the way?"

"Could be. Maybe she didn't want to reply at all. I wouldn't worry about it. She simply might not approve of your staying here with me so long, you know. Besides, I don't give a damn what she thinks," he commented decisively.

"Father! How can you say that? After all, she did raise me, you know."

"Yes, that's true. And, I am most sincerely grateful to her for that, for you've turned out to be a fine young woman. But, she doesn't own you, Amanda. You're my daughter, after all, even if I am a little late in acknowledging that fact. I want you to remain out here with me from now on."

"I know that. And I truly believe that I want to remain out here. It's just that I feel a certain obligation to Aunt Martha and Uncle David. Oh well, let's not discuss it anymore for right now. I need to consider the possibility that she may have written me off for good," she said with a resigned sigh.

After a few moments of silence, Samuel looked up from his food and said, "Amanda, one of the hands told me that Luke Cameron brought you home on his horse today. Why didn't you tell me?"

Amanda nearly choked on the mouthful of potatoes she was chewing at the time. She swallowed and took a quick drink of water before answering him.

"I didn't think about it. Well, at least I didn't want to think about it. Mr. Cameron has made quite a nuisance of himself with me, you see," she told him, frowning slightly at the recollection of her earlier discussion with Luke.

"Well, what did he say to make you so upset?" Samuel demanded, growing angry.

"Oh, nothing, really. He did give me a message for you, however. He informed me that you and your accomplices have once again been tearing down and destroying his fences. He told me that if you continue to do so, he will be forced to retaliate in some manner. I think that was the gist of his little speech."

"Who the hell does he think he is, giving me such a message, hiding behind the skirts of a woman?" Samuel bellowed.

"He wasn't hiding behind my skirts, Father," Amanda countered, then found herself wondering why in the world she felt compelled to defend the man to her own father. "He simply didn't wish to fight with you anymore about it, that's all. He wanted me to tell you in order to avoid any further confrontation between the two of you. And, frankly, though I hate to admit it, I think he did the right thing. You see, I can't help but agree with him to some extent. I don't think you and the others should destroy another man's property," she insisted stubbornly, refusing to back down.

"You don't understand the whole issue here, Amanda!" Samuel argued angrily.

"Yes, I think I do!" she replied. "I think I understand all I have to. I understand that you don't wish to see the end of the open range, but that is going to happen whether you try to stop it or not. All that Luke and the others like him are doing is going along with the natural flow of progress, Father. Soon, all of the ranchers will probably be fencing their lands. You, yourself, will someday be forced to acknowledge that. Why don't you try to stop fighting it? Why don't you realize that you cannot fight the changing times?" she demanded, steadfastly refusing to keep her silence in the face of his unreasonable anger.

Samuel peered across the table at the animated, concerned features of his beloved daughter. He knew, deep within his very being, that what she was saying was right, that he was facing an undefeatable foe. Progress would always win, he was painfully aware. But, he couldn't knuckle under yet, he couldn't allow his dream of an open range to die just yet.

"I see the sense in what you are saying, but I cannot give in. I love this country, and I can't just sit back and watch it go the way of so-called civilization. I want it to remain the way it is now. Is that so very awful? There are plenty of others who see things my way, and I realize that it's probably true that we'll have to give way to progress in the long run. But, until that day comes, we will fight it. The next time Luke Cameron has a message for me, you can tell him that he can damn well deliver it in person!" With these last angry words, he rose from the table and stalked out to the hallway, then outside, slamming the door behind him.

Amanda remained seated at the table for some time afterward, feeling her heart nearly break for her father. He believed in what he was trying to do. She knew that he would be defeated, yet she couldn't help admiring him for his courageous struggle. She found herself growing even more furious and resentful toward Luke Cameron. As if he weren't already the source of enough confusion and upheaval in her own life, he and the other young, farsighted ranchers would ruin her father's hopes, would destroy his dream. For that, she didn't believe she could ever forgive him.

Twelve

The afternoon of the Christmas social arrived, and Amanda was carefully completing the finishing touches of her painstaking toilette. She turned about to face the mirror in her room and critically surveyed her image.

Yes, she thought to herself in satisfaction, I suppose this will do very nicely. The rich, luxurious folds of the deep red velvet only served to further enhance her flawless, creamy complexion. She recalled that Aunt Martha had always maintained that redheads should most definitely never wear such a color, but Amanda could see for herself that the effect of such an unusual combination was positively stunning. It had taken much effort and determination to persuade her aunt to allow her to have the dress made up, Aunt Martha finally capitulating under persistent pressure. However, Amanda had never yet worn the dress.

As she faced herself in the mirror now, she decided that her arguments had been well worth it. The heart-shaped bodice, cut lower than usual across her swelling bosom, the full, graceful sleeves, the cinched-in waist, and the gathered, flowing skirt of the frock were all total perfection.

She clasped a strand of creamy white pearls about her slender neck, having earlier arranged her shining hair in a loose mass of curls cascading about her neck and shoulders. She only hoped that her father would be proud of her appearance this night. She realized that his opinion meant more to her than anyone's ever had.

Crossing the room to her dressing table, she carefully took a seat upon the satin-upholstered chair, taking special pains not to crease or wrinkle the precious velvet of the dress. As it was still several minutes early, she busied herself with straightening the various items scattered about on the surface of the table. As she occupied herself with this task, she allowed her thoughts to wander.

Although Luke Cameron had masterfully vowed that she would see a good deal more of him after their last disturbing encounter, she had not. She had severely chided herself whenever she found herself wondering when she would see him again. It was quite true that the unbelievable, impossible man had aroused her innate curiosity. Why, she had even caught herself looking about for him when she had again driven into town with Mrs. Chambers, and also whenever she accompanied her father out riding on the range. However, there had been no further sign of him since that unforgettable day when he had calmly and infuriatingly informed her that she would some-day marry him.

Imagine! she fumed anew as she recalled his startling words. The absolute gall of the man! Still, his alarming speech had remained fixed in her mind and she had been unable to completely shake the uneasy feeling she experienced whenever she thought of him. That feeling, coupled with the unfathomable emotions and sensations she experienced whenever she remembered his passionate kisses and warm embraces, only served to further confuse and distract her. Just what in the world would he say or do next? she thought. Her rather sheltered upbringing in Boston had left her completely unprepared for anyone such as he.

"Amanda! Aren't you ready to leave yet?" her father's deep voice rumbled up from downstairs.

"Yes! I'm coming right away!" She stood and hastily shook out the folds of the dress, then hurried downstairs to join Samuel in the front hallway.

"My dear, you look absolutely beautiful!" Samuel declared proudly as she gracefully descended the last few steps and came to stand at his side.

"Thank you, sir. I must say that you look quite elegant yourself. Where are the Chambers?" she inquired as she glanced about.

"Oh, John's outside hitching up the team and Sally's out there with him. Let's get going, honey. The weather's a mite nippy this late in the afternoon. Could be there's a storm on the way for later tonight," he commented as he escorted her out the front door, assisting her with her cloak as they went.

"You mean that it might even snow?" she inquired.

"It sure might. We do get snow out here, you

know. Why, sometimes we get a regular blizzard. The winters out here can be every bit as harsh and unrelenting as those you're accustomed to back in Boston. There's a very popular saying among the folks out here—the weather in Texas is as changeable as a woman's mind," he teased.

"How very ungallant of you, sir!" she gaily retorted as she stepped down into the cold air of the December afternoon. She peered upward at the sky, only to notice the dark, ominous cloud covering which blocked the sun's rays from her sight.

Mrs. Chambers slid a bit farther over on the wagon seat as Amanda was lifted up by her father.

"I just can't wait to see what you got on under that cloak. Why, I bet it's so all-fired pretty, you'll make all the rest of us feel plumb dowdy," Mrs. Chambers remarked good-naturedly as Amanda settled herself upon the seat.

"No, really, it's just a dress I had made up for last Christmas. Although, I must confess that it might perhaps be a bit extravagant for tonight. But, I wanted this to be an extra special celebration. I don't know if I will be here for any future Christmas socials," she replied wistfully.

John took his place beside his wife and gathered up the reins. Amanda saw her father mounting his horse beside the wagon.

"Father, aren't you going to ride in the wagon with us?" she asked.

"No, I'd just as soon ride, Amanda. Besides, there really isn't enough room for all four of us on that wagon seat," he replied casually.

"Well, I suppose you and I could ride in the back," she responded helpfully.

"No, honey, we'll just go on like this. You just bundle up real good there. I'm quite used to riding in weather like this," he insisted.

Amanda declined further argument, assisting Mrs. Chambers in drawing a warm, woolen blanket up over their laps. John gently flicked the reins and softly urged the horses onward.

As the wintry conditions were not too conducive to much conversation, they rode in silence, finally arriving in Big Prairie just before dusk. Amanda gratefully allowed her father to lift her down from the wagon. She and Mrs. Chambers hurried into the warm confines of the building, with the two men following a few minutes later.

Amanda eased out of her cloak. then bent to remove the warm boots she had slipped on over her red dancing slippers. She straightened up and deftly tucked a few wayward strands of hair back into place, then turned to her father, who now stood beside her.

"You go on in," he told her as he slipped off his own coat, then placed all of their outerwear over pegs on the wall. "I have to speak with some folks. I'm sure there are quite a number of young men who will be only too happy to have the honor of the first dance with my beautiful daughter," he remarked as he gestured toward the crowded room. Amanda nodded with a smile and complied with his request, noting that there were indeed a large number of people present, certainly quite a few more than at the last dance she had attended here.

Of course, this was not merely a dance, but a family celebration of Christmas.

The strategically placed wood-burning stoves gave off a comforting warmth, and the groups of people milled about, some beginning to dance to the lively strains of the fiddle, others standing and chatting. Children were happily scampering about in the opposite corner of the large room, obviously enjoying the many foods and home-made treats arrayed upon a long, gaily decorated table. There was a rather scraggly Christmas tree in the center of the room, brightly adorned with colorful bits of calico, ribbon, popcorn, and other similar ornaments, with gifts for the children to be exchanged later in the evening.

Amanda remained in the doorway, not wishing to enter just yet, preferring to gaze about the room for a moment or two first. Her wandering glance alighted upon Carolyn Tompkins, who was seated across the room, almost completely engulfed by her surrounding admirers.

The pretty, petite schoolteacher's blonde hair was elaborately arranged atop her head. Her low-cut dress was of deep blue satin, shimmering brilliantly in the bright light. Her features were quite animated, her face illuminated by a most becoming glow of self-confidence and satisfaction, and it was quite apparent that she was pleased with the eager attentions of the young men around her. Amanda could not refrain from experiencing a small twinge of jealousy at such a scene.

Tommy Evans glanced up from Carolyn's side at that moment and spotted Amanda standing in the doorway. Several other of the young men managed to tear their admiring gazes away from the blonde Southern belle, and soon Amanda was also besieged with a score of requests for dances. Feeling that she should perhaps honor Tommy with the first dance of the evening, she turned graciously toward him, only to be greeted by his astonishing words.

"Miss Amanda, it's right nice to see you looking so pretty and all. Have you by any chance met Miss Tompkins yet? I'll be sure to introduce you two later on if you haven't. Right now, I got to get on back over there and claim that dance she promised me before all them others take advantage of my absence! I had to fight my way to her side just to ask her for the first dance. Ain't she something, ma'am? Save me a dance for later, Miss Amanda!" he cheerfully called in a breathtaking rush. He muscled his way back through the crowd to the side of the newest object of his exuberant admiration.

Amanda's beautiful features froze in shock and indignation. How utterly humiliating! she seethed inwardly. Tommy Evans actually, in a sense, deserting her for that little vixen! Well, she wouldn't waste another moment's thought on the pair of them! She whirled back to face the throng of young men and began rapidly filling up her dance card. She managed to save a dance for her father, but she deliberately omitted Tommy's name from her list. She couldn't help feeling that she had somehow been betrayed, and that Miss Carolyn Tompkins was the direct source!

Amanda scanned the room for her father's face as she danced, but he was nowhere to be seen. She relaxed and smiled brightly at her young partner, causing him to flush with embarrassment at such an honor. She noticed that Carolyn was constantly whisked from one partner to another.

Well, I do not care, she told herself sternly. I refuse to be envious of that particular young woman! Besides, I have more than enough partners, she thought with rather smug satisfaction.

After what she judged to be either her sixth or seventh dance, she begged to be allowed to sit and rest for a few minutes. Her present partner was soon dispatched to fetch refreshments, and she leaned back against the wall to watch the merriment of the celebration.

The many children running about at the other end of the room were laughing and singing. Mothers were busily admonishing several of the joyful youngsters to desist from their efforts to topple the Christmas tree. Most of the young people were dancing, while the older or married ones were engaged in lively conversation with their friends and families. Socials such as this one provided an excellent opportunity to visit with folks that one might not otherwise get to see for quite some time.

A most disturbing thought suddenly lodged itself in Amanda's mind as she glanced about the room. Where was Luke Cameron? She hadn't noticed Jake present this evening, either. Surely those two would wish to come to such an event.

She rose from her seat and searched among the celebrants for any sign of him, taking care to appear as if she were merely viewing the crowd in general. It isn't that I wish to either see or speak with him, she firmly assured herself. It was simply that she was curious as to the reason he hadn't come.

Just as she was about to abandon her secretive visual search and take her seat once again, she spotted the face of Carolyn. Though she had certainly appeared quite gay and flirtatious before, she was now beaming, her eyes suffused with an even brighter smile. Amanda quickly glanced at her partner, whose face was momentarily hidden by another couple. As the couple moved away, she drew in her breath quite sharply as the identity of Carolyn's partner was revealed to her eyes.

Luke Cameron! Why, he was here and hadn't even bothered to come in search of her. He hadn't even approached her long enough to make his presence known to her. Amanda grew rigid, unconsciously drawing herself to her full height.

Well, if that odious man thought he could treat her in this manner, he was most definitely in for a surprise! The audacity of him, informing her that he loved her and would soon marry her one week, transferring his attentions to another woman the very next! She had only to look at his handsome features to ascertain that he was enjoying the companionship of the pretty new schoolteacher.

Amanda silently schooled herself to take hold of her tumultuous emotions. Why in heaven's name was she becoming so upset about such a thing?

What did it even matter to her if he were dancing with Miss Tompkins, or if he had indeed transferred his fickle affections? She had positively no right, nor wish, to view him as some sort of possession of her own, did she? No, and what was more, she definitely didn't wish him to be her possession, ever! I don't care in the least, she thought. I want nothing more than to be rid of that man, and what better solution than if he becomes totally infatuated with the Southern flirt? Then why do you feel so cold inside? she heard a tiny voice within her ask.

She firmly endeavored at that moment to shut off any further thought of him, and even managed a warmly welcoming smile for her returning partner. She accepted the proffered glass of punch and proceeded to drink it rather hastily. She immediately began to cough and splutter, not having been aware of the fact, that at functions such as this one, the punch was regularly spiked with more potent ingredients by mischievous young pranksters.

"Miss Lawrence, ma'am, are you all right? You shouldn't ought to have drunk it down so all-fired fast. You want me to go fetch you some water or something?" her young admirer inquired with genuine concern.

"No, thank you, I'm fine now," she managed to gasp out, finally regaining control of her breathing. She quickly handed the empty glass to her partner.

"If you don't mind, I would like to go look for my father now. Thank you very much for the punch." She dismissed him with this polite little speech and walked away, her face still somewhat flushed from the powerful effect of the quickly downed punch.

She finally located Samuel near the front doorway, where he was engaged in conversation with several other men.

"Oh, Amanda, honey. Are you enjoying yourself?" he asked as he acknowledged her presence. He took her arm and introduced her to the gentlemen she had not met.

She then drew him away from the group and said, "Father, why in the world are you spending the entire evening talking to those men? This is supposed to be a Christmas celebration, remember? You men look as if you're discussing something other than Christmas!"

"It's just a business matter, Amanda. I don't get much of an opportunity to speak with them too often. Besides, don't tell me that you've actually had time to miss your old father?" he teased with a twinkle in his eye.

"I have had more than sufficient partners, if that's what you mean," she retorted, then added, "I wanted to have a dance with the handsomest man in the room. If you believe you can spare me the time, sir, will you please do me the honor of this next dance?" She smiled bewitchingly and sank into a small curtsy.

"Certainly, my dear. I would be very proud indeed to partner the most beautiful young lady in the room." He led her over to the dance area and whirled her about into the circular movements of the dance.

Later that evening, after Amanda had danced with quite a score of various young men, the musicians announced that they would have to take a break. The tiring dancers drifted off to the refreshments table and to sit and rest. Amanda's present partner, the same one who had brought her the punch earlier, left her again to fetch more punch. Amanda glanced up from her seat near the center of the room to observe Mr. Powell take a pose on the musicians' stand.

"Folks, it's mighty nice to see all you people gathered here tonight. I just want to say welcome to all of you, especially to any visitors or newcomers amongst us. Speaking of newcomers, we all want to give a warm welcome to our pretty little schoolmarm, who's come all the way from Georgia! Welcome, Miss Carolyn Tompkins," he announced, nodding with a big smile toward that lady.

Carolyn stood from where she was sitting beside Luke and acknowledged Mr. Powell's speech with a sweetly voiced rejoinder.

"Why, thank you, sir. Thank all of you for making me feel so much at home here in your sweet little town of Big Prairie. I do look forward to a happy life here," she drawled. She blushed becomingly and once more took her seat, dimpling quite prettily at something Luke leaned over to whisper in her ear.

Amanda viewed the two of them with a cold stare, reflecting bitterly that it was indeed quite a talent for the schoolteacher to be able to blush on cue! She is a more than adequate actress, Amanda thought wryly, noticing the way Carolyn responded to Luke's comments.

Luke happened to look up at that moment and his piercing gaze swept across the room to fix upon Amanda. She immediately averted her eyes and fixed her own gaze in another direction. Luke smiled sardonically, obviously pleased with her reaction.

Of all the nerve, Amanda fumed as she felt his eyes still upon her. To treat me in such an offhanded, sarcastic manner. It must be as I have believed all along, that he was simply lying to me about his undying love and devotion, his supposed honorable intentions! And why in heaven's name did he have to choose that calculating belle as his companion for the evening? He knows good and well how I feel about her, yet he appears to be flaunting his attentions to her before my face, and probably for my benefit, too. Well, I refuse to give him the satisfaction of another glance. I knew everything he said to me was untrue, she repeated to herself.

Deciding not to wait for her partner to return with the punch, Amanda left her seat and went in search of her father once again. At least there was one man's love she could be sure of! She recalled that she hadn't seen Samuel again since their last dance. Why has he made himself so scarce all evening? she asked herself. She finally located John and Sally Chambers and inquired if they knew the whereabouts of her wayward father.

"Well, Miss Amanda, ma'am, he—uh, that

229

is—" John began in some confusion, only to be silenced by a sharp nudge by his wife's elbow in his side.

"He had some business to take care of, honey. He said for us to go on home without him, that he'll meet us there later on," she explained to Amanda, warning her husband with her eyes to remain silent.

"I don't understand," answered Amanda, thoroughly confused by her father's puzzling behavior. "What sort of business would be so important that he would leave the celebration, particularly without notifying me first?"

"Now, don't you worry none about it. He'll more than likely be home before we are," Mrs. Chambers assured her, stealing a glance at her husband to make sure that he wouldn't say anything further.

Amanda sensed that they weren't telling her all they knew about her father's absence, yet she couldn't understand why they would feel it necessary. So, she merely thanked them for the information and wandered across the room to the front entrance of the courthouse, intending to peek outside and see if her father's earlier predictions of snow would be upheld.

She nudged the heavy door open and peered outside. It was indeed snowing, though the accumulation so far was barely enough to coat the cold ground. *My father had to ride out in this weather for business reasons?* she wondered silently. It didn't make much sense to her. She would be certain to question Samuel most completely about his activities when they all returned to the ranch tonight!

Closing the door securely against the blowing north wind, she turned back toward the inner doorway and sharply bumped into someone, someone whose hard, muscular arms reached out to steady her as she composed herself.

"What's the weather like out there?" Luke Cameron inquired lazily, his large hands still closed upon the softness of her upper arms.

"Take your hands off me!" Amanda whispered furiously, then nearly stumbled backward as he complied with her demand more quickly than she had anticipated.

"You wouldn't by any chance be looking for your father, would you, Amanda? I'd kind of like to find him myself."

"That is certainly none of your business, Mr. Cameron! Besides, I haven't the slightest idea where you may find my father!" she retorted. She shot him one last smouldering look, then flounced back into the main room, ignoring his amused chuckle.

Strolling down to the far end of the room where the children were playing, Amanda took a seat and decided to observe them for a while. Suddenly, she heard her father's name mentioned. She looked about, only to discover a small group of women clustered together a few feet away, their backs turned toward her. She knew that she shouldn't eavesdrop, yet she began to listen more intently as they spoke.

"Yes, and my Zeb says that they all know exactly

what they're doing, so, I tell you, there weren't no talking to that man of mine!" one woman declared in a loud whisper to the accompaniment of knowing, sympathetic clucks of agreement from the others.

"I know just what you mean, Mary. I hope to goodness they don't all get stranded out in this weather somewheres. My boy just told me a while ago that it's started to snow. My Fred told me to take the kids on home before too late, since he kind of doubted that they'd be able to make it back to town tonight," another woman said.

"Well, I just hope that there ain't any more trouble that comes of this thing," the first woman replied.

"Shhhh!" cautioned a third woman as she suddenly discovered the presence of Amanda within earshot. "You want her to hear you?"

"Well, it don't matter none if she does, Lucy. After all, her pa's the one who organized the whole thing to begin with," retorted the first woman. Nonetheless, the group of women stood and wandered away, several of its members glancing back now and then toward Amanda as they walked.

So, that was where her father, and apparently the husbands of those women, had disappeared to. Their business involved some kind of mysterious plan. It suddenly dawned upon Amanda what they must have been talking about, what her father's "business" must entail. They were riding out to tear down fences, to destroy other men's property. Yes, that must be it, she told herself. She shivered involuntarily, aware those, if that were indeed their plans, it could become quite dangerous.

She recalled the reactions of the Chambers when she had inquired if they knew where her father was. It all made sense. They could plan to ride out, tear down the fences, and ride home while everyone else for miles around was occupied at the social. Afterward, the dismayed fence owners would be furious, yet they would be unable to prove a single charge, since there would be no actual witnesses.

Amanda's mind continued to work feverishly, and she could not refrain from scanning the room for Luke. She knew with a certainty that his would be among the fences destroyed this night. Perhaps that was why he wanted to speak with her father, she thought as a sudden suspicion lodged itself in her mind. Perhaps he too overheard something tonight. That could be the reason he appeared so anxious to find Samuel. She only hoped and prayed that others would not become suspicious as well. She hoped that other wives or friends would not be so careless with their speech.

Thinking of Luke, she realized that no amount of effort to keep such plans secret would work with him. No, his mind worked differently from the other men's, his steely blue eyes seemed to probe deeper than any others. She wouldn't put it past him to do anything he thought necessary to protect his fence lines, either.

As her thoughts continued to search for possible solutions, Amanda was oblivious to the fact that Luke was taking his leave of Carolyn Tompkins at that moment.

"But, Luke, I don't understand why you have to leave so early. Why, the party's still going strong!" Carolyn insisted, her small mouth forming into a childish pout which she hoped would cause him to reconsider.

"I'm sorry, but something else has come up. Thanks, though, for a delightful evening, Miss Tompkins," Luke replied politely, then turned on his heel and strode away from her without a backward glance.

It's all the fault of that Lawrence witch, I know, Carolyn told herself with malicious anger. She'd seen the two of them speaking together a few minutes ago near the doorway. She couldn't hear what was being said, but she had noticed the way Luke had smiled, the way Amanda had whirled away from him in anger.

There is something between those two, she reflected, but I personally intend to change all that as soon as possible! Carolyn wanted Luke Cameron for herself. She had never met such a magnetically virile, handsome, masterful man before. He was so very masculine, and she wasn't about to let that Yankee female have him! No, she resolved to herself, I'll see to it that I have other occasions to work my most feminine wiles on him. I'll show that Lawrence hussy!

Amanda had hurried into the front hallway and was pondering what to do as she again peered outside at the thickening snow. Maybe she could find some way to dissuade her father. But no, she had no idea where to find him.

"I saw you heading this way, Amanda," she heard Luke's voice drawl behind her.

"Really?" she responded coolly, then watched as he began drawing on his heavy coat and gloves.

"Surely you aren't leaving so soon, Mr. Cameron?" she inquired a bit too politely, feeling a sinking sensation in the pit of her stomach as she realized that her fears were justified. Luke must suspect something.

"Yes, I am," he answered her unsmilingly, his mind racing to figure out why she was even speaking to him after their last encounter. A plan had already taken shape in his mind, and she seemed to be falling right in with that plan.

Amanda searched frantically for some way to detain him, finally reaching out to place her hand upon his arm and say, "Well, I, that is—I thought you might wish to dance with me just once this evening." Then, swallowing her pride, she continued, "I'm afraid I behaved quite rudely to you before. I now simply wish to make amends." She utterly deplored having to behave to him in such a demeaning manner, yet she knew that the humiliating thing she was doing might perhaps be beneficial to her own father's welfare. She bitterly reflected that Luke would probably believe that he was beginning to win his little game, that she was weakening. I will keep him occupied. I will play my part for this evening, then I will never speak to him again! she resolved inwardly, clenching her teeth.

"I see," Luke replied, still unsmiling. So, she does know where her father is, or at least she suspects, he thought. It's a good thing young Evans let that little bit of information slip out.

Tommy had grown increasingly jealous as he watched Carolyn lavish all her attentions upon Luke. He had finally confronted Luke near the refreshment table, demanding to know why Luke had all of a sudden attached himself to the schoolteacher. Luke had tried explaining to Tommy that things weren't as they seemed, that he could rest assured that nothing would come of it, at which point Tommy angrily replied, "Well, if it ain't what it seems, then how come you ain't left her side the whole time you've been here? Besides that, I thought you had fixed your interest on Miss Amanda. Just wait till I tell her pa about this when he and the others get back tonight!" He had stormed away, not realizing that he had told Luke the very thing needed to confirm his growing suspicions. Tommy was a goodhearted young man, but he was given to a small measure of hot-headedness whenever he felt as deeply about something as he did tonight.

"I know of a perfect way to make your amends," Luke suddenly suggested, a strange glint now appearing in his blue eyes. "You're going to come with me." That had been his plan all along, to take her with him, but he wouldn't let her know that.

"Come with you?" she demanded in astonishment, glancing about to assure herself that no one else could hear them. "What on earth are you talking about? I have no wish to leave here for some time yet!"

"I think it's about time you changed your mind

then, Amanda," he replied seriously. "You see, your little game isn't going to work with me. You aren't going to detain me here any longer. You haven't fooled me one little bit, you know. You know as well as I do that something's going on, something that concerns your father and his friends, the very ones who consistently agree with him on the matter of fencing."

"I'm sure I don't know what you mean," she told him stiffly, schooling her features to remain passive beneath his searching gaze.

"Yes, you damn sure do know what I'm talking about! Now, are you going to come with me peacefully, or do I have to carry you off with me by force?" he threatened, his tone low and commanding.

Amanda knew only too well that he was perfectly capable of carrying out such a threat, even if it were done in front of everyone in the crowded room. She certainly had no wish to go with him, yet she knew that she might be able to help in some way if she did. She certainly didn't want there to be another fight between her father and this man again, nor did she want to see anyone else get hurt.

Amanda turned a rather flushed face up toward him and replied, "Very well. But, first, please allow me to inform the Chambers that you will be escorting me home." She turned her back on him and hurried across the room to find her friends.

"Mrs. Chambers, Luke Cameron will be escorting me home tonight. If my father gets home before I do," she said, closely observing their reactions, "please tell him that I hope his business went very well tonight." She observed their surprised expressions before she left them without another word, catching a glimpse of Carolyn's face as she once more approached Luke.

Well, I will at least receive some measure of satisfaction from going with him, she told herself, unable to avoid a tiny smirk in the teacher's direction as she allowed Luke to help her with her cloak and boots.

She only hoped that she and Luke didn't find any trace of her father and his friends, that they might have decided to abandon their plans because of the weather. If all went as she hoped, Luke Cameron would have to admit to looking foolish and would have to escort her back to the Circle L and face the wrath of her father. Her mouth turned up into a slight smile at such a thought.

"Let's get going before the weather gets any worse. I guess it's too much to hope that this snow will keep them from carrying out their plans," he commented grimly as he escorted her out the front door. He hurried across the street with her, the two of them grateful to reach the livery stable and get out of the bitter wind.

"Looks like we'll have to ride double, seeing as how you don't have a horse with you. I'd borrow one of these others, but there's no telling when I'd be able to get it back," Luke remarked as he saddled his horse.

"You mean that you actually expect me to ride all the way to your ranch, assuming that's where we're going, of course, with you on your horse?"

she asked.

"You really don't have any choice, do you? Now, come on," he said as he lifted her onto his horse, then lithely swung up behind her. "It's not going to be too warm of a ride in this weather. We'll have to snuggle up real close to keep from freezing," his voice spoke softly against her ear.

"I think you are insane to insist that I accompany you! I don't know what purpose you think having me along will serve," she remarked petulantly as he kicked his horse gently and they rode outside into the cold night air and snow.

"Well, I thought your father might come to his senses if he sees you with me at my ranch. I think you were maybe thinking along those same lines, seeing as you came with me without putting up your usual fight," he replied mockingly.

Amanda refused to answer him, instead drawing the warmly lined hood of her cloak more securely about her head. The snow was still continuing to fall steadily, though it still had not become too heavy.

I must have been insane myself to agree to come with him! she silently chided herself as they rode. She wondered if she had done the right thing, if she might have been a bit too impulsive about this whole matter. Why, her father and the others might have already abandoned their plans by now, her father might be back at the ranch waiting for her to return with the Chambers.

She tried inching away from such close contact with Luke, but his arm across her waist only pulled her back tightly against him. She could feel the heat of his body through his heavy coat and her cloak. His muscular thighs were pressing against her legs and hips. His face was close to her own, his arm clamped securely about her waist. She realized that she was always disturbed by this man's nearness, though she could not conceive why he should have such an effect upon her.

"We're going to go on out to my ranch, just like you thought. If they haven't hit there yet, we'll wait," he informed her after they were a few miles outside of town.

"What makes you think they will be coming to your ranch?" she inquired, striving to make her voice sound casual and disinterested.

"Let's just say I have a feeling that they will. You really don't know what all's been going on lately, Amanda, do you? On raids such as this one, they usually ride right up to a man's ranchhouse and tear down his corral, besides cutting and tearing down his fences out on the range."

"My father wouldn't do such a thing!" she protested adamantly.

"I just got through saying that you don't know very much about it. It's happened in the past, and it'll happen again, till they're caught in the act. Until that time, a man has got to defend his property as he sees fit," he replied grimly.

"You wouldn't shoot at them, would you? You surely wouldn't want to kill anyone over this!"

"No, I don't want to kill anyone at all. But a man has to do what he thinks is right. And, tearing down other men's fences and destroying their property just isn't right, and you know it. I must say that they took me by surprise tonight," he admitted. "I really wasn't expecting them to ride out tonight, which is exactly why they planned it this way. It will catch everyone unawares."

"Except you," she reminded him bitterly. "What made you decide to ride out by yourself? Why didn't you alert the other fence owners and organize?"

"Amanda, I want to avoid the sort of trouble you're afraid of happening," he explained patiently. "I needed you to come along because your father is their leader. I figured he might be swayed much more by the sight of you beside me. I think you feel the same. He might listen to reason from you."

"You mean that you planned to make me come with you?" she asked in surprise. At his nod, she said, "I could have refused to come with you, you know."

"It wouldn't have done you a bit of good, and you know it. You could have made all the fuss you'd wanted to back there, but I'd still have made you come with me, even if I had to draw a gun on some of my friends. 'Course, I wouldn't have shot anyone. I wouldn't have had to," he commented with an amused smile.

"Don't you have any scruples whatsoever? You are completely unprincipled!" she declared angrily.

"Yeah, I guess I am at that," he replied with an unabashed grin.

241

Amanda jerked her head back around to the front and tried to concentrate on what she would do if they did indeed discover the riders at the Cameron ranch. She resolved not to waste any more time in trying to talk to the infuriating man who rode behind her, his hard-muscled and masculine body pressed so closely against her own.

Thirteen

Luke and Amanda arrived at his ranch just as the snowfall was becoming thicker, the wind increasing in velocity. Luke guided the horse to the front steps of the house and placed Amanda on the top step without dismounting.

"You go on inside and get warm. I'll see to my horse and then join you," he shouted to be heard above the wind's fury.

Amanda nodded her agreement as he rode away toward the barn. She felt half frozen as she stumbled across the porch and into the shelter of the dark house. She paused momentarily to allow her eyes to become accustomed to the darkness, then removed her cloak and hung it in the front hallway, noticing with dismay the soddenness of its outer folds.

She hurried into the parlor, grateful to see that there was wood already stacked neatly in the huge fireplace. She soon had a fire started, having been taught how by her father. He had said that knowing how to build a good, lasting fire could mean the difference between life and death someday.

Luke finally stepped inside the house, tightly shutting the door against the strong gusts of wind which now pounded the house. Amanda could hear his movements as he drew off his wet coat, hat, and gloves. She rose from her task at the fireplace and faced him across the darkness of the room as he stood in the doorway.

"I see that you know how to build a fire. It's a good thing we beat the worst of the storm in getting here," he remarked as he strode across the room to stand beside her, extending his cold hands to warm them before the growing flames.

"Do you still believe they will come?" she asked him anxiously, her concern for her father increasing.

"You know, that's the first time you've admitted that you know what's going on," he stated mockingly, then sobered. "Yes, I honestly do think they'll come. Those men are bound and determined to carry out their plans and they won't be suspecting anyone to be looking for them on a night like this." He spoke grimly, a determined set to his mouth. "I guess they've got sense enough to take shelter if a blizzard blows in, though. It sure looks as if that's what we're in for."

Amanda's features relaxed a bit at his slight reassurance, and she peered downward at her red velvet dress, now thoroughly wet and crusted with ice about the hem. The snow and ice had even managed to creep into the tops of her boots.

Luke observed her scrutiny of her clothing and said, "You'd better be getting out of those wet things right away. We don't want you catching your death of cold."

"I have absolutely no intention of removing one

article of my clothing!" she snapped, growing nervous at being in the room alone with him. At a sudden thought, she asked, "Where is your brother? I noticed that he didn't come to the social. Is he ill?"

"Who, Jake? No, he's down in Waco visiting with Boyd until sometime after Christmas."

"You mean that we're actually alone in this house?" she demanded, aghast at such a thought.

"Yep, sure are," he replied nonchalantly.

"But, where are all of your hands? Surely they didn't all go into town tonight?"

"Nope, the ones that didn't go to the social are out in the line camps," he told her.

"Then why in heaven's name did you bring me here with you? You know that this is entirely improper! Why, I cannot stay here with you, alone, all evening until my father comes, if he does indeed come!" she insisted angrily.

"Why not?" he retorted, his eyes beginning to come alive with amusement at her indignation. He was thinking how pretty she was when she was so riled up like that.

"You know very well why not! You are being extremely difficult, as usual. What am I going to do if my father doesn't come here at all?" she demanded, suddenly beginning to question the wisdom in coming with him.

"You should have thought about that before you agreed to come along with me," Luke said, almost as if he could read her mind.

"You gave me no choice! Besides, I thought that perhaps I could talk to my father and the others, that I could persuade them to abandon this scheme of theirs. If they don't come here, then I suppose I will simply have to borrow one of your horses and ride home by myself," she declared stubbornly.

"Oh no you won't!" he commanded imperiously, the smile in his eyes fading as he realized that she just might attempt such a foolhardy thing. "You won't leave this house until I say so, is that clear?"

"I will leave any time I choose to do so, sir! You have no right to keep me here against my will!" she exclaimed, flushing in her anger.

"All right," he said in a low, even tone, "I warn you, Amanda, that if you try anything like that, I'll personally tan your pretty little hide!"

She gasped aloud at his threat, realizing that he was deadly serious, knowing that he would do just as he threatened. Oh, why did I ever come with him? she lamented silently. Now, she'd have to wait until either her father came or Luke decided to take her home. Why, she wouldn't put it past the deplorable man to force her to remain here with him all night. She had placed herself in the unfortunate position of remaining his captive if he so chose!

She now realized that she must have correctly judged him from the beginning; he only cared about her for one thing and one thing only. She supposed that everything Aunt Martha had told her must indeed be the truth. Men were simply not to be trusted, and a young woman should definitely not consent to be alone with one until they were legally and properly married!

"Very well," she capitulated with an ill grace, "I will wait, for now. However, I resent your treating me like a child!"

"Then quit acting like one. I'm warning you, you'd better not try anything like that," he sternly reminded her, then relented enough to say, "Look, it's not what you seem to think. You know, I don't particularly want you staying here with me alone all night either, for very good reasons of my own. But, you can't go off riding alone in a snowstorm, you little idiot! Just how far do you think you'd get in weather like this?"

Amanda refused to acknowledge his question, turning back instead to face the fire as she lifted the wet hemline of her skirts slightly to expose her boots. She would dearly love to remove them, yet she certainly didn't wish to do so with him standing there watching her every move. No, she would have to keep them on for the moment. As for her dress, she realized sadly that it was probably ruined.

"You still need to get out of those wet things and into some dry ones. You go on upstairs to Jake's room, the first one on the left, and put on some of his things," Luke ordered her, then frowned rather ominously as she opened her mouth to rebel once more.

"If you don't get upstairs right now and do as I tell you, I'll have to undress you myself!" he teased.

Amanda glared at him and whirled about, throwing him one last glance of defiance as she flounced from the room and up the stairs. She entered the room Luke had indicated, noticing that it definitely had the look of belonging to a fourteen-year-old boy.

Hurrying across the bare wooden floor, she opened the large oak wardrobe and drew out several articles of clothing. She went to the large poster bed and drew off her once beautiful red dress, now heavy with moisture, and draped it over the footboard. Next came her petticoats and corset, then her boots and slippers. She quickly donned one of Jake's flannel shirts, which comically reached almost to her shapely knees. She drew on a pair of his trousers, securing them about her waist with a belt she discovered in one of the drawers. They would have fallen off if not for the belt, and she nearly laughed aloud as she caught a glimpse of herself in the mirror hanging above the washstand in the corner. She found a pair of thick woolen socks and put them on her feet.

Well, I'm certainly not fashionable, but I am much warmer. Her anger cooled somewhat as she realized that she should be grateful to Luke for forcing her to change out of her wet things. She quickly gathered up her clothing and hurried back downstairs to be near the warm fire once more.

"Those clothes don't exactly look like what a fine Boston lady should be wearing, but you'd look mighty pretty in anything," Luke commented with a grin as he watched her enter the room, her head held high. He too had changed into dry clothes and was on one knee before the fire, poking it with a vengeance to stir up more flames. He replaced the poker on a nail beside the mantel and stood up to offer Amanda a comfortable chair which he had just drawn closer to the fire's warmth.

"Do you think that they have already been to some of the other ranches? That is, do you believe that they are actually carrying out their plans?" she asked hesitantly as she sank into the cushiony softness of the chair.

"Well, that's hard to say. Could be they decided to give up the whole idea for tonight and go on home when all this started blowing real bad," he replied, his nod indicating the howling wind outside. "It's hard to tell what that father of yours is thinking at any one time. I know that he's a good, decent man down deep, Amanda, but he's bullheaded and damn hotheaded most of the time."

"You are most certainly not qualified to judge him on those faults, Mr. Cameron!" she cried, feeling that his comments were entirely unjust when he himself had displayed the most stubborn, unreasonable, impossible manner she had ever before encountered!

"Hush!" he suddenly commanded, his tone sharpening as he said, "I think I hear them coming."

Amanda didn't have time to take umbrage at his rude tone of voice, instead jumping to her feet and drawing on her boots, then following Luke as he hurried out of the room and into the front hallway.

"I'm coming outside with you," she told him as she flung her cloak about her shoulders.

"All right, but you keep quiet and let me talk

first," he insisted, then caught up his gun.

"Surely there is no need for you to be armed?" she asked in surprise as she saw the gun.

"You don't think I'm going to face those men out there without some way to defend myself or my property?" he demanded.

"But, you agreed that I could try and persuade them to leave peacefully, to abandon their plans. You surely wouldn't wish to shoot any of them!"

"I'll give you a chance to talk, but I'd be crazy as hell if I took a chance on being out there without my gun, even if you are standing by my side." He turned his back on her without another word and wrenched open the front door, then strode outside and took a stance on the front porch. Amanda followed closely behind him, praying silently that there would be no need for violence to settle this matter tonight.

Samuel Lawrence rode at the head of the group, his hat and coat covered with the snow, his face stern and forbidding as he and his followers rode toward the corral. He had just issued the order to begin the destruction, when he was halted by a shout from the direction of the house.

"I wouldn't do that if I was you, Lawrence!" Luke yelled.

The riders turned in surprise, then slowly rode toward the house. Amanda stood huddled beneath her cloak beside Luke, her face only partially exposed behind the warm hood.

"Amanda!" Samuel exclaimed in astonishment at her presence. "Damnation, girl, what are you doing here?" he thundered, his face suffused with

250

anger and disapproval.

"Father, please don't do this thing. It doesn't matter how or why I'm here. Mr. Cameron knows all about your plans. I had hoped to persuade you to abandon your plans, for all of you to return to your homes and families without any further incident," she said in a rush as she moved closer to her father.

"Not another word, do you understand, young lady?" Samuel commanded, then turned to Luke. "You must have been crazy to bring her here with you, Cameron! I ought to drag you off that porch and horsewhip you for letting her ride all the way out here on a night like this!"

"Seems to me that there's an awful lot of folks out riding on a night like this, ain't there?" Luke drawled in response, the corners of his mouth turning up into a sardonic grin. "We can settle all of this like grown men, some other time. Now, why don't you all go on home like the lady says?" he suggested, lowering his gun to bring it level with the eight riders.

"Come on, Sam. We still got work to do. We ain't got time to wait around out here, freezing our tails off in this snow and listen to you argue polite-like with Cameron. Now, are you coming with us or not?" one of the men asked.

"Yeah, there ain't no other way for us to settle this, Cameron," another one spoke. "We're gonna settle things the only way we think it'll ever do any good. It don't make a damn whether Lawrence's little gal tries to talk us out of it or not."

"Lawrence, this little organization of yours is

just about finished, anyway. There doesn't have to be any more fighting between us, because you're fighting a losing battle, and you know it. Me and the other fencers aren't about to let you get away with things like this any longer. Now, all of you get your carcasses off my land! I don't reckon I want to have to shoot any of you, but I damn sure might if you don't get going!" Luke threatened evenly.

Amanda felt a shiver travel down her spine at his words. She knew that he was perfectly capable of pulling the trigger. She had once seen him shoot down several Indians in her defense.

"Please, Father, tell your men to return to their homes," Amanda implored, fearful as she observed the signs of serious trouble.

"Hell, are you gonna play nursemaid to your little Yankee daughter all night, Sam?" the first man spoke again, his tone insulting as he glared at Amanda.

"That's enough," Luke spoke mildly, though the steely light in his blue eyes revealed his anger at the man's words. "I don't want to hear another word about Miss Lawrence. If I do, you'll have me to reckon with." He tightened his grip on his gun almost imperceptibly and the man backed down.

Samuel clenched his teeth and glowered toward his daughter. After a few more moments of hesitation, he said, "You had better be home before I am, young lady! I'll speak to you about this then! I hope you know that you've succeeded in humiliating me, in shaming me before these men!" he hissed.

"As for you, Cameron, we will indeed settle our personal matter at another, more convenient time! I expect you to see to it that my daughter gets home safely tonight, or you'll pay out of your hide for it!" Samuel threatened, then whirled his mount and rode away at a determined pace through the thickening snow, his friends muttering their agreement as they followed.

Amanda stood stock-still upon the porch, numb with the cold and shock. She had never witnessed her father in such a temper before, and it frightened her. She was quite aware that he took the matter of fencing seriously, yet she realized now that it must mean even more to him than she had believed possible. She honestly couldn't blame him entirely for his reaction to her presence here, however. She had expected him to be angry, yet she had truly hoped that she would be able to reason with him, that he would at least pay some heed to his own daughter. Now, she stood white-faced as she recalled his terrible fury and her own sense of complete disappointment.

"Let's get back inside," Luke said, drawing her along with him through the front door.

"He refused to listen to me. He wouldn't even allow me the opportunity to talk," she reflected aloud, tears beginning to form in her eyes.

"Yeah, I know. I'm sorry he took it so bad. I was kind of hoping he'd listen to you, too. That's the only reason I thought of bringing you with me in the first place. I swear, I could have put my fist in his face for the way he spoke to you!" Luke declared angrily.

"How dare you say such a thing! No matter what he said to me, or the way he said it, he is still my father, and I love him! He had every right to be angry with me, just as he and the others have every right to believe the way they do. What makes you so certain that they aren't the ones who are right about this entire matter?" she suddenly stormed at him, not caring that she was being unreasonable and unfair, only seeking to lash out at him, to hurt him in some way.

"What the hell do you mean?" he furiously demanded, losing his temper now. "You know damn well that it isn't right for anyone to force their beliefs on another man! Just because I, and other men who realize that fencing is inevitable, choose to fence our own, legally owned, lands, what right do your father and the others have to tear those fences down, to destroy what is rightfully mine? Answer me that!"

She gazed at him in surprise, amazed at his violent outburst. She opened her mouth to speak, but he interrupted her.

"I know very well that he's your father and that you love him. That's the one and only reason I didn't round up the other fencers and take out after your father and his men. Don't you talk to me about what is right and what isn't! Damn it, woman, you're the reason I'm in such a hell of a mess now! I can't very well go shooting at the father of the woman I love now, can I? No, but if things weren't the way they are, if I didn't feel about you the way I do, I would have handled things the way I've always handled them. I'd have fought fire with fire!'' he raged at her, his deep and resonant voice booming in the quiet of the house.

"How dare you speak to me in such a manner!'' she responded, refusing to back down in the face of his anger. "I think it's time you took me home now. I will be very happy to leave this house and your company and never see either again!''

"I know why you're so all-fired angry, Amanda. It isn't just this thing with your father. No, it's much more than that. It's because you're jealous, isn't it?'' he probed, barring her way with his body, forcing her to hear him out.

"Jealous? You are out of your mind!''

"No. I know I'm right. You're mad at me because I didn't pay any attention to you tonight, because you've already come to take me for granted. You're mad because I spent all evening with Carolyn Tompkins, aren't you? Come on, you little minx, admit it! You swear up and down that you don't want me, but you certainly don't want any other woman to have me, either!''

"I refuse to hear another word of such insulting talk. If you won't see me home right this instant, I will have no other recourse but to go on my own,'' she informed him stiffly, her face proud and defiant. She heard a tiny voice at the back of her mind insisting that what he had just said might possibly be the truth, that she might actually be jealous. No! She refused to listen.

"I've already warned you what I'd do to you if you tried it. I'll take you home when I'm good and ready, not one minute before. I think it's time you and I got some things straight between us.''

"Oh, I hate you, Luke Cameron!" she declared tempermentally, losing all control now. She was aware that she was behaving quite childishly and unladylike, but her good breeding and sheltered upbringing were all put aside now. He had pushed her beyond her limit!

"No, you don't hate me. You feel something very strong for me, Amanda, but it certainly isn't hate. I guess it's about time I showed you the difference," he told her, his voice low and calm now.

He suddenly swept her against him, his strong arms crushing her softly curved form tight in his embrace. She struggled violently, yet her efforts were futile. He easily lifted her in his arms, ignoring her outraged cries of protest, and strode with his squirming burden into the parlor. There, he dropped her unceremoniously upon the well-worn sofa, taking a seat beside her before she could escape.

"What do you think you're doing? Let go of me!" she demanded, becoming panicky as she viewed the intent in his smouldering eyes.

Luke ignored her protests and swiftly brought his warm lips crashing down upon her own, effectively silencing her furious, sputtering words. She tried to jerk her head away, but he clamped an iron hand on the back of her head, forcing her to remain rigidly in his embrace. His bruising lips soon became gentle as Amanda felt herself melting against him, her lips finally parting beneath his.

"Amanda, you know you don't hate me. What you feel is the exact opposite, and you only feel it because you're a full-grown, passionate woman, and because you know in your heart that you care for me," he whispered softly against her ear when he finally released her lips.

"No," she whispered in reply, a small whimper escaping her as she realized that there must be some truth to his words. I don't care about you at all, and I wasn't jealous tonight, she told herself sternly. But, she knew deep within her heart that she was merely trying to convince herself that it wasn't so. She remembered feeling the urge to pull the schoolteacher's blonde curls out by their roots tonight when she had seen her laughing and flirting with Luke! But surely that was only because she disliked the young woman, not because she was jealous.

"Please let me up," she implored him, renewing her struggles to rise. She thought at first that he would defy her, but he finally stood and looked down into her flushed face. She couldn't help feeling a slight disappointment that he had complied so easily, yet she stood too and faced him squarely, determined to end this disturbing situation.

Luke had released her because he had suddenly realized that he was on the verge of losing his self-control and taking her there on the sofa. But he didn't want it to happen that way, he wanted the time to be right. It wasn't the time yet.

"I must be getting home right away," she reminded him crisply, straightening her clothing. "I will have one of the hands return your brother's clothing, since it appears that my things are beyond repair and will only become further soaked if I wear them on the ride home."

"All right. I already told you that I didn't want you staying here all night with me. I'm afraid that certain things might happen if you did," Luke said, then left the room.

Amanda was embarrassed by her response to him when he had kissed her, and she wanted only to be safely home once again, to avoid thinking of this night ever again.

She gathered up her clothing, bundling them together, then walked into the front hallway to get her cloak. The front door suddenly swung open and Luke entered, tightly shutting it once more.

"I'm sorry, but we'd be fools to try and ride out on a night like this. It's a regular blizzard now. It's hard to see even three feet in front of you. I guess you'll have to stay the night after all."

"But I can't! I must get home!" she insisted stubbornly.

"I must have been crazy as hell to even think of taking you home in this! Your father will just have to come gunning for me, I guess, because I'm not about to risk our lives riding to the Circle L in a blizzard," he asserted. He was just as uneasy as she was about the whole situation. He wanted her all right, wanted her so badly it hurt. But, he wanted her permanently, he wanted her to be his wife and the mother of his children. The trouble was, how to convince her that they were made for each other? He'd only paid attention to that Tompkins vixen tonight to make Amanda jealous. It appeared that it had worked, too. He knew his Amanda, though.

She'd most likely be stubborn to the very end, fighting him all the way to the altar!

"What am I going to do? My father will be half out of his mind with worry if I don't get home tonight," she contended anxiously.

"I doubt it. I don't think he'll make it home himself. He and the others probably had to take shelter somewhere else for the night. Anyway, maybe we can get you home in the morning. Meanwhile, we might as well make ourselves comfortable in front of the fire. I'll go on out to the kitchen and make us some coffee." He hated to see that despairing look on her face, but there wasn't a whole lot he could do about it. They'd just have to make the best of things for tonight.

Amanda sullenly glared at his retreating back. Why, oh why, had she placed herself in this compromising situation? Her father may not have been able to make it home tonight, but that wasn't the most immediate problem facing her this minute. She was alone with Luke Cameron in his house for the entire night.

Several minutes later, Luke returned to the room with the steaming cups of coffee. He and Amanda drank it in silence, both absorbed in watching the colorful flames of the fire, both completely lost in their own thoughts. Amanda finally broke the spell by rising to her feet and announcing, "I think I will go to bed now. I assume that I am to sleep in Jake's room?"

"Yes. If you need anything, just holler. I'll be sleeping right next door."

"Thank you," she murmured politely, slightly

on edge as he smiled at her before she left the room.

Once upstairs, she removed the shirt and pants, folding them neatly and placing them at the foot of the bed. Wearing only her chemise, she hurried to snuggle beneath the warm covers of the huge bed. At a sudden thought, she threw back the covers and quickly tiptoed across the cold wooden floors to lock the door. Finding that there was no lock, she picked up the only chair in the room and placed it in front of the door, wedging it tightly beneath the doorknob. There, she thought as she viewed it with satisfaction, that will at least awaken me if anyone tries to enter this room. She knew that she was being a trifle silly, yet she still didn't trust Luke.

She lay back down on the bed and again drew the several quilted covers over her shivering body. The events of the night had been utterly exhausting. She heard the sounds of Luke preparing for bed in the room next to hers. The thought of him just next door was less than comforting.

Schooling her mind to avoid any further thoughts of either Luke or her father, she was soon fast asleep, too tired to worry any longer about being alone in the house with Luke. She was unaware that he lay wide awake in the next room, unable to sleep, only able to think about the woman he loved sleeping so peacefully next door.

Much later that night, Amanda began dreaming. Aunt Martha and her two cousins were laughing and jeering at her. Dressed in Jake's flannel shirt and trousers, her hair hanging down her back, she was slowly walking up the aisle of a church in what appeared to be a wedding ceremony. As she neared the altar, she saw that it was Buck Jones who stood waiting for her there, his face ugly and sneering. She screamed again and again as his hands reached for her, his fingers viciously clawing at her clothing.

Luke burst into the room at that point, knocking aside the chair with a crash, having been awakened from a troubled sleep by her first piercing scream. Amanda heard the loud crash as he charged into the room, and she jerked upright in the bed, the covers falling away from her body as Luke glanced quickly about the room, then stalked toward the bed.

"What in tarnation's going on?" he thundered, clad only in his long underwear, a gun clasped menacingly in his large hands.

"I—I must have been having a nightmare," Amanda sleepily replied, then came fully awake as she felt his gaze on her rounded bosom, now almost totally revealed beneath the thin chemise. She sharply pulled the covers up all the way to her chin, then paused to stare at the sight of his muscular body, the shape of which was alarmingly revealed to her eyes beneath the clinging material of his underwear.

"You sure you're all right?" he asked, relaxing now and allowing the gun to slip to his side.

"Yes. I'm fine. Thank you for your concern," she answered stiffly, flushing as she tore her eyes away from his thoroughly male form.

"I thought something might have happened to you. I swear I didn't bust in here with any other intentions," he assured her mockingly.

"Will you please leave this room now? I have had quite enough of your company for one evening," she replied frostily.

Luke's lips tightenend in a thin line of anger before he swooped down upon her and lifted her in his arms, startling her with the intensity of his gaze.

"That's all the thanks I get for nearly busting my head to make sure you were all right? That old goat of an aunt of yours has sure drummed into your head that there's only one thing men want from women, is that it? Well, I'm telling you once and for all that it isn't the only thing I want from you, although that is a big part of it. I love you, damn it, woman!" He dropped her back upon the bed, then placed his own body over hers to still her struggles.

His lips seared her own, his hands roamed freely over her womanly curves protected only by the thin material of her chemise. His hands seemed to burn her with their caresses, and she moaned beneath his lips as his tongue drove into her mouth.

Yanking the straps of her chemise down past her shoulders, he bared her bosom to his fiery gaze. His lips traveled downward to her neck, to her soft shoulders, then to her full breasts. His mouth gently fastened on one of them, teasing the nipple with his lips and tongue, then moving to do the same to the other one. Amanda gasped and squirmed at the rapturous, burning sensations she was experiencing, trying ineffectually to push against him, her arms pinned at her sides.

Luke continued his tender assault on her breasts, then brought one of his hands down to the hem of her chemise, slowly lifting it and caressing the lower half of her body. His hand roamed across her smooth belly, over her rounded bottom, then gently stroked the downy softness between her thighs, her cries of protest drowned beneath his passionate kisses. She tried to escape his questing fingers, then couldn't refrain from arching her back as his touch began to catapult her toward complete arousal.

"Luke," she whispered between kisses, her breath becoming more uneven and gasping as his caresses became more inflaming.

Luke suddenly removed his hands and his lips, pushing himself away from her with a savage oath, climbing out of the bed and standing beside the still-prone Amanda.

"No, I don't want it to be this way. Not like this," he breathed, gazing down at her beautiful form, at her shocked features. "I'm sorry, Amanda, I didn't mean for this to happen. When I do finally take you, I want it because you want it, too. I want you to admit that you love me, too. I want you to be my wife. Good night, my love," he whispered, then turned and left the room, shutting the door softly behind him.

Amanda lay where he had left her, still striving

to catch her breath. She was shocked by his sudden withdrawal. Why hadn't he finished what he had begun? You ought to be grateful that he didn't rape you, she told herself. You ought to be grateful that he left. Yet, she had been unable to remain passive and unaffected by his caresses, by the delicious sensations burning within her. She still felt a deep yearning within her very being.

I'm so ashamed, she thought in humiliation then. That I could actually allow him to do those things to me. True, she had resisted in the very beginning, but after that, she had been unable to resist any longer. No, she was partly to blame for what had transpired between them.

She didn't want to think about his parting words, about love and marriage. She didn't want to think of him at all anymore for tonight. She knew that she couldn't bear to face him in the morning, either, not after what had just transpired between them.

She climbed out of the bed and hurried to the window. Drawing the curtains aside, she saw that the storm had nearly stopped, that there were only a few snowflakes floating to the ground now. Everything was a blinding white outside, but she knew that she had to find her way home.

She would wait until she thought Luke would be asleep once again, then she would creep downstairs and out to the barn. Luke would be furious when he discovered that she had ridden off alone, but she didn't care. She only wanted to escape him, to escape the confusing emotions he had aroused in her. Her life had seemed so peaceful and orderly until she had met that man. Now, every thought of him only served to further confuse or provoke her. She had to get away, she had to reach the safety and security of her father's ranch.

Fourteen

Amanda carefully guided the plodding horse through the deep drifts of snow, congratulating herself on managing to steal away from the house without Luke's knowledge. She could mentally picture him when he discovered she was gone. Well, I do not care, she reminded herself briskly. She was still feeling ashamed and mortified as a result of her unladylike abandon. To think that she had actually allowed a man, a man she supposedly detested, to do the things he had done with her body!

She judged that it might take hours for her to reach her father's ranch, but at least the snowfall had ceased. She only hoped that she could reach the ranch before her father did, if he were not already there. She didn't feel capable of facing his wrath again just yet; she had enough on her mind at the moment. She was beginning to think that she should never have come to Texas in the first place, that she should have remained in the security and safety of her dull and orderly life in Boston.

She rode with a preoccupied manner all the distance to the Circle L, finally reaching its boundaries well after sunup. She had been relatively warm throughout the ride, still bundled up in Jake's clothing and her own boots and cloak. She turned the weary horse toward the barn, hoping that none of the hands would detect her arrival. She quickly unsaddled the poor creature and led him to a stall with a generous supply of hay, pausing to vigorously rub him down with a bit of the straw. Then, she waded through the snow to the house, completely unaware of the lone rider watching her progress.

Well, I might as well start on back now, Luke thought as he turned his horse back the way he had come, his path clearly outlined in the wet snow. He had been following Amanda almost ever since she had left his ranch. Unable to fall asleep once again, he had heard her leaving his house and had guessed her intent.

At first, he'd been mad as fire when he observed her riding away, but then he had justly realized that she must be experiencing a terrible emotional conflict after what had occurred that night between them. He had momentarily lost his head when he had burst into her room and seen her lying there in that bed, her luminous eyes wide, her flaming hair cascading about her creamy shoulders, her enticing curves so aptly revealed beneath that thin thing she was wearing. It had taken all his resolve to leave her. He still felt a small twinge of remorse when he remembered the way he had pounced on her. And yet, he knew that it might be the very thing to shake her out of her confusion and stubbornness once and for all. For now, she couldn't help but think about him, no matter how hard she tried not to. He'd still be praying that she would come to her senses, and soon. It was becoming nearly impossible to remain patient any longer.

Come on now, Luke, he told himself, you've got to get on back and see to things at your own ranch. That young woman is disrupting your whole way of life, he mused with a grin, and you know you wouldn't have it any other way!

Amanda entered the house quietly and drew off her cloak and boots, careful not to track in any of the snow which clung to her things. She headed toward the kitchen, where she hoped to find Mrs. Chambers. There was no sign of her father anywhere, and his coat was not hanging in its usual place in the front hallway.

"Amanda! Child, where on earth have you been?" Mrs. Chambers demanded with relief as Amanda appeared in the doorway of the kitchen.

"Is my father home?" Amanda countered, ignoring her question for the moment.

"No. He didn't make it home last night. I expect he'll be along anytime, now, though. Answer me, honey, where have you been all night? How come Luke didn't bring you on home?" she insisted.

"The weather turned too severe. I was forced to spend most of the night with Mr. Cameron at his ranch," she answered in a monotone, embarrassed as she realized what the woman must be thinking.

"I see. Well, I guess it's sure enough a good thing that your pa don't know about that."

"Oh, but he does. At least part of it. You see, he

268

and the others rode out to Luke's ranch last night. I was there to try and speak to my father, to try and persuade them to change their plans. He ordered Luke to escort me home afterward, but by then it was simply impossible. I was so fearful he would be waiting for me when I returned home, that there would be further trouble between him and Luke."

"You're right there. But we won't tell your pa the rest of what happened. We can just let him think you got home last night like you planned. Are you sure no one saw you riding in just now?"

"I don't think so. I didn't see anyone. Mrs. Chambers," she said, her tone changing. "I—that is, nothing occurred last night. Mr. Cameron and I were alone in his house, but we spent the night in separate bedrooms. I hope you believe me."

"Why, of course I do! Amanda, honey, I know you better than you think, and you don't got to tell me that nothing happened! As for Luke, well, he's a right honorable young man, no matter what your pa thinks of him. It's plain to see that he's plumb crazy about you," she assured Amanda.

Amanda was close to tears as she observed the kindly woman's concerned features. She felt compelled to tell her the entire story, to relate to her everything that had happened the previous night, no matter how humiliating. It was the first time she had ever revealed her innermost feelings to another human being, that she had completely confided in another woman. She felt as if a huge load had been lifted off her shoulders when she had finished. She sat perfectly still, waiting for the older woman to comment on what she had told her, particularly on the encounter between herself and Luke in the bedroom last night.

"Well, now," the older woman said, taking a deep breath as Amanda finished, "I truly appreciate your telling me all of this, Amanda. It makes me feel real honored. Now," she remarked, squaring her shoulders a bit, "I think it's time you faced up to a few things. Luke Cameron is in love with you, gal, and you can't help but know it. I kind of think you feel the same way about him, but you haven't figured that out for yourself just yet. I know you got a lot of fool notions from that aunt of yours, meaning no disrespect, but they ain't the whole problem. You act as though you ain't real sure about love at all. Well, you'll just have to find out that it is real, and that it is completely different from what your aunt led you to believe. All I can tell you straight out is that you got a whole lot of thinking to do. Just be honest with yourself, honey, that's all it'll take. You gotta make sure. There ain't nobody else can do your thinking for you."

Amanda pondered what her friend advised. It was so good to be able to share the burden of her confusion with someone else. She stood and leaned toward the woman, hugging her as she said, "Thank you. I still don't know how I feel or what I am going to do, but you have helped me immensely, I assure you. Now, I had best hurry upstairs and change before my father comes home and sees me wearing these ridiculous clothes!" She smiled as she left the room.

Yes sir, Mrs. Chambers reflected, that gal is

made of strong stuff all right. She certainly don't belong back in Boston where they'll most likely treat her like some fragile little doll the rest of her life. It's plain to see that she's meant for better stuff than that.

Later, Amanda returned to the kitchen to assist Mrs. Chambers in baking the bread. Samuel finally stomped inside the front door just as they were popping the dough into the oven.

"Sounds like he's home. You'd best go on out and talk to him, act like nothing's happened," Mrs. Chambers suggested.

Amanda nodded a bit nervously and did as her friend advised, entering the front hallway with a fixed smile upon her face. She greeted her father casually.

"Good morning, Father."

Samuel looked up from his efforts to draw off his boots and frowned. "You and I had better have a serious little discussion right away. Please go into the parlor and wait for me there." His manner was cool, but Amanda was grateful that he was no longer in such a terrible fury.

She entered the room and took a seat on the sofa, clasping her hands together and sitting with her back rigid. I feel like a naughty schoolgirl who's been discovered in the middle of a prank, she thought. Well, she was no longer a schoolgirl, and she'd be darned if she'd allow him to treat her like one.

"Amanda, first things first," Samuel said as he took a seat in the chair opposite her. "I'm sorry I spoke to you in such a disgraceful manner last night. I was so surprised at seeing you there with Luke Cameron, the very man who opposes me in this matter. I hope you'll try and understand my feelings."

"Yes, sir," she dutifully replied. "I do understand that you were a bit surprised, hurt, angry, and whatever else I don't know. However, I accept your apology. You had no right to speak to me that way in front of all those other men."

"I know," he answered wearily, a sigh escaping him as he glanced at her face, an imploring look in his bloodshot eyes. "I really am sorry, you know. I let my temper get the best of me. It's just that I was caught off-guard. But, now, let's discuss other matters. Why in heaven's name did you consent to go with him last night?" he demanded.

"Because I actually believed that you would listen to me. I had overheard some talk about what you and some of the other men were planning to do, and it seemed that Luke had already suspected something. So, I agreed to go with him in an attempt to help. He really isn't the terrible young man you believe him to be," she remarked, then reflected that she was actually defending the man to her own father once again.

"Well, I can't say that I approve of your decision, as you are well aware of by now. However, I suppose it took a lot of courage to do something like that. I suppose your intentions were good, anyway," he conceded.

"Yes, they were. I can't sit idly by any longer, pretending that I don't know what is going on between you and your organization and the

272

fencers. Why, nearly everyone at the Christmas social knew about this matter, didn't they? I discovered last night that you actually destroy the corrals of those men, as well as their fence lines. What else do you do that I'm not yet aware of?" she inquired bitterly.

"Amanda," he explained, beginning to sound weary, "I'm sorry you had to find out about those things. We just do what we feel we must in order to win this fight. Can't you see that? They won't listen to us any other way. Hell, we aren't the ogres you seem to think! We're good, honest men who are fighting against something that seems to overwhelm us every way we turn. We believe very deeply in our cause, honey. Maybe we are a bit unorthodox in our methods, but we have to try to do something to stop this thing that threatens us."

"I know that, Father. I do understand your feelings in this matter, I truly do. But surely you can see now that you are waging a losing battle, that Luke Cameron was right about that? I don't want to see you get hurt. I don't really have any solutions for you, and yet I can't condone the destruction of other men's property. Surely there is some other way to settle this. Why can't you allow them the right to fence their own lands, while you have the right not to fence yours?" she asked with feeling.

"Because it won't work that way. If part of this range is fenced, the rest of it will eventually have to be fenced, too. I don't want to see that happen. I want things the way they used to be, the way they were before those men started putting up those damned wires." He sank back into the comforting softness of the chair and closed his eyes. Amanda noticed that his face was paler than usual, despite the fact that he had just come in from the cold air outside.

"Father, what is it? What's the matter?" she demanded anxiously.

"Something happened after we left Cameron's ranch last night. It began snowing very heavily, but we all decided to try and pay a visit to one more place. We didn't have any idea that some of the hands would still be there. We thought everyone would be in town, or at least out in the line camps. We figured wrong, though," he said, his face grim. "We rode toward the corral. We were just beginning to throw our ropes around the posts when some shots rang out. Before we all knew what had happened, it seemed that two of our men were shot. We rode out of there as fast as we could, leading the wounded men's horses along with us. Anyway, we made it to Joe Walsh's ranch. We got everyone inside and found that both Joe and Henry Taylor had been shot, Joe in the right shoulder and Henry right square in the chest. Joe's going to be all right, but we don't know if Henry's going to make it. Joe's wife patched him up as best she could, but it was snowing too hard to get through to the doctor. I rode to town first thing this morning and fetched him, then came on home. He couldn't tell us whether Henry will live or not, said it's still too soon to tell." He sighed heavily at the end of his story.

"Oh, Father, I'm sorry," Amanda murmured,

tears spilling over her lashes.

"They didn't even give us any warning when they started shooting. That's what gets me. No matter what else we've done, we never shot anyone over this. Now, I'm afraid things are going to get even worse. I'm afraid there may be a full-scale war after this," he told her tersely.

"But surely you won't retaliate? You won't seek revenge, will you? Hasn't there been enough harm done already? Don't you think that things have gone far enough? I should think that this whole incident would only serve to convince you that your methods are futile," she insisted as she clasped his large hands between her two small ones, kneeling on the rug before him now. She gazed into his eyes, hoping to discover some sign of capitulation, some sign of compromise.

"I don't know yet. Right now, we don't have anything planned. I don't want to make any plans till we see how Henry does. If he dies . . ." His voice trailed away. He passed a hand over his face, trying to erase some of the weariness therein.

"Have you had your breakfast yet? How about having some with your old father here? That is, if you think you can forgive me for the way I behaved toward you last night," he said, his voice a trifle unsteady, his expression earnest.

"Of course I forgive you. And, I love you, no matter what," she assured him, giving him a tight hug as they both stood.

In the next couple of days, Amanda and her father seemed closer than ever, despite the incident at Luke's ranch. She despised having to keep the secret of her night spent in Luke's house from her father, but she knew that it was absolutely necessary. They finally received the good news that Henry Taylor would indeed live, and Amanda now hoped that any plans of revenge would be put aside.

She had so far not heeded Mrs. Chambers's advice about searching her heart for answers about her feelings for Luke; instead, she had again sought to avoid all thought of him. She would awaken at night, tossing restlessly, vividly recalling the way he had kissed her, the masterful way he had caressed her body. She would berate herself for her shameless behavior, then resolutely punch the pillow and turn over on her side. Maybe Mrs. Chambers was right; maybe she should do some serious considering of his love and her own feelings, but she didn't feel she was ready to do that just yet. It was much easier to postpone it, for there was so much for her to decide.

For instance, she still had not received any reply from her Aunt Martha. Christmas was only a few days away, and she was sore at heart that her family in Boston had sent her no holiday greetings. Perhaps they were angry that she had not returned when originally planned. Whatever the reason, Amanda felt that they could have at least answered her letter.

And then there was still the matter of the fencing. Samuel and his group had not organized again just yet, but she knew that they would eventually do so. She was afraid that there would be worse trouble than they had previously encountered, for, next time, someone might actually be killed.

Now, as she descended the stairs with a heavy sigh, wearing one of her oldest and most faded dresses, she turned at the sound of a loud, insistent knock upon the door. She hurried to respond, wondering briefly where her father and Mrs. Chambers were. She opened the door to reveal a young man standing there patiently, hat in hand, smiling across at her.

"Peter!" she exclaimed in complete astonishment.

"Amanda, my dear! How very good to see you once again," he responded, stepping across the threshold and taking her stiff body in his arms.

"But, what on earth are you doing here?" she demanded, still in shock at his sudden appearance at her father's ranch here in Texas, so very far from Boston. She disengaged herself from his embrace and stared up into his face.

"I came to see you. What else? Now, are you going to invite me in properly?" he asked with a friendly smile.

"Of course. How silly of me. Won't you please come in?" She motioned for him to enter the house and then led him into the parlor.

"Won't you please have a seat and tell me what brings you here?" she said.

"Oh, dearest Amanda, I'm so very glad to see you. I've had quite a journey, you know. I just couldn't bear to be away from you any longer. When your aunt told me that you were not coming home before Christmas, I decided to visit you, to see for myself what sort of life you were living out here in this wilderness. Your aunt and uncle assured me that you would be coming home before too much longer, but I was impatient. I thought that I would come and escort you home myself."

"Home?" she repeated. "I—I don't know how I'm going to tell you this, Peter. Or my aunt and uncle. I haven't decided for sure just yet. But, you see, I may not be coming back to Boston at all."

"Not coming back to Boston?" he demanded crisply, the smile on his face disappearing.

"Well, I just told you that the matter had not yet been decided. But, there is that possibility," she murmured, uneasy as he frowned sternly across at her.

"Well, then, if you haven't decided yet. You haven't completely lost your wits. Don't worry, my dear. I'll soon help you to see things in their proper perspective. Now, aren't you going to tell me how very pleased you are that I have traveled all this way here just to see you?" he prompted.

"Of course. I really do appreciate this, Peter. It was really too kind of you," she responded mechanically. "I am quite flattered. Why, after our quarrel, I hardly expected to see you again."

"Let's forget about that for now. What's past is in the past, right? Now, how about a welcoming kiss for your fiance?"

"Fiance?" she repeated in confusion.

"Yes. Don't tell me you don't remember that we are unofficially engaged to one another?" he demanded.

"But, you haven't so much as written me in all

278

these months! And, you didn't even come to see me off at the train station last September!" she retorted, becoming angry at his taking so much for granted.

"I told you, Amanda, let's put all of that behind us. Perhaps I did behave a bit foolishly," he admitted stiffly, "but, so did you. That's not important now. All that matters is that I've come all this way to see you, to reassure you of my affection," he said, his aristocratic face smiling charmingly once again. His clothes were rumpled, his hair a trifle mussed, but he was nonetheless the epitome of the latest fashion. Peter always did have impeccable taste in clothing, Amanda mused as she glanced at him.

"Peter, this is all too much to discuss on such short notice. I suggest that we wait until a later time. Now, would you like to go upstairs and wash up a bit? Dinner will be in about an hour. I'll be happy to show you to your room," she suggested, turning her back on him and going to the doorway without waiting for his response. All she could think of at this moment was to sort out her thoughts. Too much had happened too fast and her mind was in a whirl.

Peter started to say something, but changed his mind and followed her out of the room and up the stairs. So, this was obviously going to be a bit more difficult than he had believed. Her aunt had warned him that it might be, particularly since she had stayed longer than the original two months they had decided upon. Well, I won't allow this to go on much longer, he resolved to himself. I'll force her to see where her duty lies. She agreed to become my wife, and I intend to see that she does. Why, she's already dressing like one of the common folk he had seen in town, if you could call it a town. And her behavior was not at all proper. As soon as they were married, he'd see to it that she remembered her position in life.

Amanda left Peter in his room and hurried back downstairs to appraise Mrs. Chambers of the visitor's presence.

"Mrs. Chambers, an old friend of mine from Boston has come for a visit. Please set another place for dinner. I just hope my father doesn't mind," she thought out loud.

"A friend of yours came all the way from Boston just to visit you?"

"Yes. Well, he isn't exactly a mere friend. You see, we were once engaged. Unofficially, of course. Although he still believes I intend to marry him," she told her with a preoccupied air.

"I see. Well, how long's he gonna stay?" Mrs. Chambers asked, her features reflecting her disapproval of this old friend and supposed fiance.

"I don't really know. I don't believe it will be for more than a few days, however. You see, he believes that I am going back to Boston with him. Oh, I don't know what to do about him!" she lamented.

"Now, now, don't you worry none. You'll end up handling this the right way. I only hope you realize that the right thing to do is to stay here where you belong, with us!" she declared decisively.

Amanda smiled gratefully and scurried out of the kitchen as she heard her father entering the house. She approached him just as he closed the front door.

"Father, a friend of mine from Boston has come to visit us. I hope you don't mind. I put him upstairs in the spare bedroom on the right. I don't think he'll be staying very long," she told him in a rush, anxious that he not disapprove.

"Sure, honey. Who is this Boston friend of yours?" he casually inquired as he hung his coat in the hallway.

"Peter Norman. You remember the Normans, don't you, Father? I believe there were some Normans in Boston when you lived there."

"Yeah. I remember some Normans," he murmured with a frown.

"Well, he'll be down to join us for supper in a few minutes. Oh, and Father, he seems to think that I am prepared to return with him to Boston," she informed him, wanting him to be aware of the situation.

"What! So, that's the reason he came all this way! Well, we'll just see about that!" he exclaimed ominously.

"Please, Father, don't become upset. I'll handle things in my own way. Now, shall we go upstairs and get ready for dinner?" she suggested sweetly.

Dinner that evening was a silent affair. Samuel barely spoke a word to Peter, who felt extremely uncomfortable with the gruff older man. Amanda endeavored to keep the conversation from lagging, but soon abandoned her efforts. After dinner, she led Peter into the parlor as Samuel brusquely excused himself to go elsewhere.

"I suppose your father disapproves of my coming here," Peter sullenly remarked, taking a seat before the fire.

"Well, he doesn't want me to leave, Peter. He and I have come to care for each other a great deal," she patiently explained.

"I find that very hard to understand, considering the shabby way he has treated you all of these years! Why, the man has ignored his duties as a father for most of your life, Amanda!"

"Peter," she informed him, striving to control her temper, "please refrain from speaking that way about my father. I will not tolerate it!"

"Very well. But, your father is beside the point. You belong in Boston, you belong with me as my wife. I've followed you all this way to prove it, haven't I?" he insisted, a bit too sure of himself in Amanda's opinion.

She suddenly wondered how she could ever have believed herself to have cared for this young man. For, now, she saw him through enlightened eyes, and she was grateful that she could look at him without feeling any hurt or disappointment.

"Perhaps you're right, Peter, about my belonging in Boston. I honestly don't know the answer to that yet. But, as for my belonging with you, I'm afraid you're wrong there. I have come to realize that I don't want to be your wife, that I never really did," she informed him calmly, not wishing to hurt him, only wanting to be honest.

"That can't be the truth!" he protested, much insulted.

"It is the truth. I was suspicious of it when I left Boston, but I am absolutely sure of it now. You see, I've also come to realize that I want more out of life than being a dutiful wife to a successful, socially prominent man in Boston. I don't want to end up like so many of the other wives, who are mere ornaments for their husbands to show off. I'm much too independent for you, Peter, and I really believe that you've always been aware of that. I'm sorry if what I'm saying hurts you, but it is the truth. If I ever do return to Boston, it cannot be as your wife."

"You don't know what you are saying! Why, I came out here to remind you of your duty, of your sense of honor! We were affianced, we still are, as far as I am concerned!" he insisted stubbornly.

"I'm sorry, Peter," she repeated. "I don't suppose you will want to stay here much longer now. I'm sorry you traveled such a great distance for nothing. But, you see, it wasn't for nothing at all. I am positively certain now that we would not suit, and I think that you have discovered the same. At least we have things finally settled between us. I hope we can be friends. You see, I don't really believe that you love me, that you ever did," she said.

Peter was stung by her words. She had deeply wounded his vanity, his masculine pride in refusing his offer of marriage. She had no sense of duty any longer. And yet, if he were truly honest with himself, he would be able to see the truth of her words.

Peter hadn't come all this way because he loved her; no, he had come because he had been prompted by his family and by her aunt to do so, to return her where she belonged. He had always taken it for granted that they would eventually marry, even after they had quarrelled and she had left to come to what he judged to be a totally godforsaken wilderness! Now, he saw all of his plans destroyed.

Peter resolved that he would not, could not give in without a fight. He was an honorable young man, and a determined one. Maybe he didn't love her as passionately as she wished, but he still believed they would suit one another very well. Why, it might take him months, even years, to find another young woman with as much beauty, intelligence, and breeding as Amanda. He simply couldn't allow her to slip from his grasp, not after spending the past few years cultivating her, preparing her for the day she would grace his table, raise his children.

"Amanda, I would prefer to forget all of this nonsense you have just uttered. I intend to take you back with me, and I refuse to give in. Now, I'll say goodnight," he announced stiffly, still too angry to bestow a kiss upon her cheek, bowing politely instead and marching from the room.

Oh, Peter! she thought as she stared deep into the dancing flames of the fire. I wish I could love you. You're what I'm accustomed to, what I've always thought I wanted.

She thought of Luke Cameron as she sat there, unable to keep from comparing him to Peter. The two of them were entirely different. Luke was so totally masculine, demanding, masterful, passionate! Peter was controlled, honorable, stiffly correct. She had felt absolutely nothing when he had embraced her earlier, and yet she couldn't forget the times when Luke Cameron had encircled her body with his strong, muscular arms. She couldn't erase the memory of his rugged, handsome face, of his hard body pressed against her softness.

Stop this! she commanded herself sternly. You cannot compare the two of them, it isn't fair. They're from two different worlds. Peter can't help what he is, any more than Luke can. She knew that she didn't love Peter, though. And yet, how did she feel about Luke? She didn't want to love him!

Dear Lord, she entreated silently, please help me! please help me decide what to do with my life.

Fifteen

Even though Amanda repeatedly assured Peter that she would not change her mind, he insisted on remaining a few days longer. Samuel avoided the young man as much as possible, and even the good-natured Mrs. Chambers couldn't quite bring herself to be more than barely polite to him. It was apparent that no one at the Circle L approved of his coming, more especially of his unceasing efforts to try and persuade their Amanda to leave and return to Boston with him. The ranchhands had also made their disapproval known, by referring to Peter as a "greenhorn Yankee who didn't have a lick of sense."

Tommy Evans, meanwhile, endeavored to patch up his friendship with Amanda, who had still behaved rather coolly toward him whenever they encountered one another. He and the other hands were kept very busy with their various winter chores, though Tommy did manage to slip into town now and then to visit his new ladylove, Carolyn Tompkins. Amanda never doubted for even a moment that the pretty schoolteacher was merely using Tommy for some reason, perhaps only to flatter herself with his boyish attentions.

Amanda thoroughly disapproved of his infatuation with the flirtatious young woman, but he refused to heed a single word of her good advice and warnings. Amanda grew even angrier with him when he murmured that, to him, Carolyn was absolutely perfect.

Christmas Day was a joyful time for Amanda, the first Christmas she had ever spent with her father. Everyone gathered in the dining room to partake of the delicious, rather elaborate meal which Mrs. Chambers and Amanda had prepared. It was a festive occasion, and it was quite clear from the outset that Peter did not, as Mrs. Chambers said, "fit in." He was barely civil to the ranchhands, considering them far beneath him socially, and he was jealous whenever he observed Amanda gaily chattering with the other men. He grew uneasy whenever Amanda's father glanced his way; that fierce and forbidding scowl was enough to bother anyone. But then, he reminded himself with rather smug satisfaction, I'll have Amanda away from here and the influence of these common, uncouth folk.

Amanda received numerous gifts from her father and friends, her favorite being a split riding skirt, fashioned out of soft buckskin, given to her by Samuel. Peter had presented her with a beautiful, though quite impractical, frilly parasol. She received his gift with gracious thanks, and he seemed pleased.

She had also received a gift from Luke. Mrs. Chambers had given it to her later that evening, telling her that Luke had asked it be kept a secret from anyone else. Amanda had taken it up to her room and opened it in private. There had been a card, which simply said "I love you," accompanied by a beautiful turquoise necklace. Amanda had gasped aloud at its exquisite beauty, but then had resolutely returned it to the box and stashed both the card and the necklace in one of her dressing table drawers. She didn't want to think about the significance of such a gift.

Two days following Christmas, Amanda and Mrs. Chambers were discussing their plans to travel into town, when Peter strolled into the kitchen and overheard their conversation. He smiled and said, "My dear, why don't you allow me to escort you into town? That way, Mrs. Chambers will be able to remain here and see to her duties, won't she? I would so enjoy the ride with you, and I also need to post a letter."

Mrs. Chambers visibly bristled at his condescending manner, and Amanda rushed in to reply, "Peter, that's very kind of you. But, Mrs. Chambers and I look forward to our visits into town together. Perhaps some other time," she gently declined.

"No, I must insist. I will be leaving here in a few days, and I would like to have a word with you, alone. Besides, you might wish to show me about your little town before I go."

Amanda glanced helplessly at Mrs. Chambers, who responded, "That's all right, honey. You and I will be going to town tomorrow afternoon for that quilting bee, anyhow. This young feller is right; he won't be here that much longer. You two go on now and have a good time. I'll just stay right here and do my chores like he says." She had turned her back on Peter while she was speaking, so that now only Amanda could see her face. She winked broadly and Amanda was forced to stifle a giggle at her comical gesture. Controlling her mirth, she left the kitchen with Peter.

Peter allowed Amanda to handle the reins of the wagon as they drove toward town. He professed a complete ignorance of such conveyances, viewing the wagon with a visible amount of disdain as he climbed up beside Amanda. She couldn't help thinking that he seemed rather helpless away from the sophistication of his own world. That's strange, she thought as she flicked the reins and gently called out to the horses. His world is my world also, at least it once was. And yet, I can't think of it that way now. It all seems to be growing increasingly foreign to me.

Peter renewed his efforts of persuasion as they jostled along over the rough road, the fierce north wind whipping against their faces. There had been no further snowstorms since the one last week, but Amanda judged that there was a possibility of snow before nightfall. Oh no, she groaned inwardly, the last thing I want is to be forced to stay in town for a while alone with Peter!

As Peter talked on and on, Amanda allowed her thoughts to wander. After all, she had heard everything he was lecturing on now. How well he believed they would suit one another, what a nice and prosperous life they would have in Boston, what dutiful children they would raise, the wonderful parties and social events they would attend together.

She recalled the time she had first left Boston and journeyed to Texas. How very different she had viewed everything then as opposed to now. She had become accustomed to the people, to their customs, to the town, to the countryside, and even to the ever-changing weather. She would sorely miss all of it if she left, especially her father.

She had actually found herself becoming tempted to return to Boston with Peter. Perhaps his words had penetrated the back recesses of her mind, perhaps it was something else. But no, she told herself, you can't run away by going back to Boston. For she realized that she was wanting to do just that; to run away. But, run away from what? she asked herself as Peter continued speaking, apparently oblivious to the fact that she wasn't even listening.

Are you perhaps trying to run away from your feelings? she probed deep within her mind. Is it Luke Cameron who is influencing you to either remain or leave? Could it possibly be that Mrs. Chambers was right, that you do feel something for him, something very strong, something you cannot control any longer, and won't admit?

She had found herself thinking more and more of Luke ever since Peter had arrived. She couldn't help dwelling on the differences between the two, the different worlds in which they belonged. Since she was certain that a man such as Peter would not suit her, could it possibly be true that it was a man such as Luke Cameron she wanted?

"Amanda! You are not paying attention to me!" snapped Peter irritably, jolting her out of her reverie.

"Oh, Peter, I'm sorry," she apologized a bit absentmindedly.

"Well, I must say, you certainly never used to behave this way when we were together. I don't believe that I care for the strange effect this savage country is having upon you at all!"

"I know perfectly well what you were saying, even if I wasn't listening very closely for a few moments. I know that I cannot marry you, Peter. Can't we just drop the subject for a while and enjoy our visit into Big Prairie?" she suggested, still preoccupied and bothered by the turn her thoughts were taking before he had interrupted them.

"Very well," he stiffly complied, "but we will discuss it later."

Amanda sighed heavily and guided the horses into town. She finally pulled them to a halt before the general store. "I need to make a few purchases in the store here. Would you like to come with me, or would you rather look about the town until I am finished?" she asked him.

"I suppose I may as well remain outside. I'd like to observe some of these people. They'll never believe me back in Boston, however, when I relate the things I have observed about the people and their clothing, their methods of transportation, and other such outmoded things," he remarked critically, eyeing the various men and women who were walking along the street.

"All right," she readily agreed, glad of the brief respite to escape his droning lectures. She jumped down from the wagon without waiting for his assistance, and ignored the look of stern disapproval on his features as she escaped inside the general store.

This simply will not do at all, he thought as he watched her disappear inside the store. She had apparently forgotten all the feminine graces she received instruction in at the ladies' seminary. Well, I will most certainly remedy that as soon as we return to Boston.

It appeared that she was going to remain quite obstinate about her refusal to marry him, but he still believed that he could eventually persuade her in that respect as soon as she was safely back in the environment where she belonged. This wild place known as Texas had evidently affected her judgment.

Climbing down from the wagon, he leaned against it and peered about the street. Seeing nothing worthy of his interest, he started to turn toward the store and go inside to find Amanda, when his actions were suddenly arrested by the sight of a petite feminine figure coming out of what apparently was the schoolhouse near the end of the street.

Carolyn shook out her full skirts and gracefully descended the steps of the schoolhouse, tying the ribbons of her pert bonnet as she walked. She turned in the direction of the general store, where she intended to buy a few necessities before returning to her room in the boarding house. She was expecting several callers this evening, and she wanted to purchase a length of blue satin ribbon to match her new dress.

If only Luke Cameron was to be one of her callers, she thought as she heaved a dissatisfied sigh. He hadn't even come near her since the night of the Christmas social, when he had deliberately snubbed her by leaving early with that Lawrence female. And, after having paid such delightful attention to her for the entire evening, too! She couldn't fathom what in the world could have come over him to make him behave so rudely all of a sudden, but she knew that it surely must have something to do with Amanda.

I've been trying my very best to lure him away from her, she thought, but there had so far been no apparent results. Why, she'd even seen him in town yesterday, and all he'd done was respond politely to her greeting and then ride on.

Oh, but you haven't heard the last of me, Luke Cameron, she vowed silently as she crossed the street. I have a particular plan in mind. I intend to fix it so that Miss Amanda Lawrence will no longer be on her high and mighty pedestal! We Tompkins never give up without a good fight.

Peter watched as Carolyn approached the general store, thoroughly enchanted and captivated by the beautiful little creature. He had most certainly never seen the likes of her in this wilderness yet! He wondered curiously where she could have come from, what she was doing in such a hovel as Big Prairie. He tipped his hat politely and bowed slightly in her direction as she stepped around the wagon in order to enter the store.

Carolyn stopped in surprise. A Yankee gentleman for sure! Here in Big Prairie! What on earth would a stylish man such as he be doing here? She started to sweep past him with a frigid look. After all, no matter how attractive and polished, he was still a Yankee. She observed Amanda coming their way at that moment.

"Peter, I see that you've met our schoolteacher, Miss Tompkins," Amanda remarked coolly as she came to stand beside him.

"I haven't had the pleasure just yet," Peter replied, smiling down into Carolyn's surprised countenance.

"Miss Carolyn Tompkins, may I present a good friend of mine from Boston? This is Mr. Peter Norman," Amanda politely made the introductions. She would have dearly loved to ignore the Southern minx, but it was obvious that Peter was interested. Wouldn't that be something? she thought to herself in amusement. Peter interested in someone like Carolyn.

Carolyn's slight frown turned into a dimpled smile. Well, he was obviously an admirer of Amanda's. She'd have to be extra nice to him because of that, wouldn't she? she thought mischievously.

"Oh, but Amanda and I are more than good friends, Miss Tompkins," Peter amended. "You see, we are engaged."

"Peter!" Amanda cried in annoyance. Of all the people he had to say that to, it had to be the troublesome schoolteacher!

"That isn't quite true, Miss Tompkins," she tried to correct, only to be interrupted by Carolyn's sugary voice.

"Engaged? Why, that's simply marvelous, Amanda!" she simpered as she dimpled again beneath Peter's avid gaze. "I didn't know you were engaged to be married. Why, I do declare, you have most certainly gone and got yourself engaged to a delightfully attractive young gentleman!" she said in her most exaggerated Southern drawl. She smiled winningly up at Peter.

"Thank you, Miss Tompkins. I must say that it is refreshing to meet someone who actually approves of my marrying Amanda," Peter replied.

"You don't understand." Amanda spoke through clenched teeth. "Peter Norman and I were once engaged, but no longer. Mr. Norman apparently seems to have forgotten that fact. Now, if you'll please excuse us, we really must be going. I promised to show Mr. Norman the town before he returns to Boston."

Just as Amanda uttered these words, the three of them heard another voice speak.

"Why, if it isn't Miss Lawrence and Miss Tompkins. Good morning, ladies," Luke said with a mocking grin as he advanced upon them. He led his horse beside the wagon and tied the reins securely to the hitching post.

"Who's your friend here?" he asked lightly, unable to miss the special look Peter directed toward Amanda as he approached.

"A friend of mine from Boston," she managed to say, flushing beneath his scrutiny. She hadn't seen him since the night she had spent alone with him at his ranch, the night he had burst into her bedroom, clad only in his underwear, and had proceeded to treat her in a shameless, humiliating manner.

"Well, now, you came all the way out here from Boston?" Luke asked with increasing interest as he observed Peter's slight frown.

"Yes, I did, though I must say that it's no concern of yours. Who are you, sir?" he demanded haughtily.

"Name's Luke Cameron. What do you go by?" he answered, completely unabashed.

"I am Mr. Peter Norman," he replied stiffly, then turned to Amanda to remark, "Amanda, is this young man an acquaintance of yours?"

"Why, he most certainly is," Carolyn piped up in her singing voice, jealous of Luke's attention to Amanda, and also jealous that both men seemed to be ignoring her completely. "Luke Cameron is a very dear friend of your fiancee, Mr. Norman," she commented with a flutter of her eyelashes, the corners of her mouth turned up into a deceptively sweet smile.

Amanda glared at her, secretly wishing she could hurl herself at the malicious little vixen and rip her frilly dress to shreds! She didn't know how to explain all of this to Luke now. But why on earth should I have to? she reminded herself staunchly. After all, it's none of his business!

"You never told me you were engaged to someone back in Boston," Luke uttered, his mouth set in a tight line. There was no humor lurking in his steely-blue eyes now. Amanda bristled beneath his gaze.

"I am not engaged! Peter and I used to have a childish understanding, that is all! He will be returning to Boston in a few days, alone," she insisted, growing thoroughly disgusted with the entire conversation. This is getting totally absurd! she thought. She turned to Peter and firmly gripped his arm, saying, "We must be going, Peter. I don't believe we'll have time to look around the town today, after all."

"Of course. Well, I was very honored indeed to make your acquaintance, Miss Tompkins," he told Carolyn, taking her hand and gallantly raising it to his lips.

She smiled her delight at his action and replied, "Thank you, kind sir. I hope that your fiancee will bring you into town before you return to your home." She bestowed a knowing look on Amanda and slipped her arm through Luke's.

"Good day, Mr. Cameron," Peter murmured toward Luke, then turned to help Amanda up onto the wagon seat. He hurried around to take a seat beside her.

Luke had still not uttered another word, and Amanda quickly glanced back before snapping up the reins and urging the horses onward. What she had seen in Luke's face and eyes boded ill for both herself and Peter Norman. She knew that he was merely jealous, and she grew even angrier as she told herself that he had no right to be jealous of her! She did not belong to him, or to any other man!

Luke tightly crossed his arms across his broad, muscular chest and watched as Amanda and Peter rode away in the wagon. Why, he could have killed that fancy Yankee! He knew that Amanda was telling the truth, that she and that Norman character were no longer engaged, but it didn't ease his jealous feelings much at all. It was obvious that Norman hadn't given her up yet, that he still wanted her for his wife. Over my dead body! Luke fumed silently. Or, better yet, over Norman's dead body!

"Luke?" he heard Carolyn pronounce. He glanced down at her, standing beside him with an imploring look on her pretty little face, one of her dainty hands placed appealingly on his forearm. "Wasn't Amanda's young gentleman nice? I mean, to think that he actually came all the way out here from Boston just to renew their engagement!" she remarked wickedly, delighting in the mischief she was creating. Now, maybe Luke would pay more attention to her. Now, maybe he'd realize that Amanda Lawrence was not for him, that she was a fickle and totally unsuitable female for the likes of a real man such as he. Of course, she herself was precisely what he needed in a woman!

"Yeah, right nice," he murmured tightly, then stepped abruptly away from her, ignoring her outraged protest. He flung himself up into his saddle and trotted away without a backward glance.

He had done it to her again! Carolyn fumed. Why was he forever chasing after that Lawrence hussy? Well, she had had all she was going to take of his rude treatment, as well as the superior manner of Amanda Lawrence! She would put her plan into action at the first available opportunity, and then she would see who would eventually win the prize of Luke Cameron!

Amanda and Peter rode back toward the ranch in virtual silence, broken only by an occasional comment by Peter, who attempted to engage her in conversation several times. Amanda, however, was much too enraged to carry on a conversation with him at the moment. He had purposefully gone against her wishes and told Carolyn that they were engaged. She could still slap his well-bred face for that!

And the way that troublesome mischief-maker of a schoolteacher had enjoyed herself when Luke had entered the scene. Oh! she thought furiously. It hadn't helped one bit, either, to see Luke's murderous looks directed toward Peter. He had no right to look that way! she told herself. She didn't know which of the three deserved her anger the most, and she didn't care. She only wanted to get home and escape to the peaceful solitude of her room for several hours!

When he saw that Amanda would not speak to him at all, Peter began thinking of Carolyn Tompkins. What a charming young woman, and that Southern accent was perfectly delightful. Her classical features had been almost perfection, too. It was obvious that Amanda disliked her for some reason. He mused that it was probably nothing more than jealousy. After all, with two such beautiful young women in the same small town, men such as that Luke Cameron must be having a difficult decision deciding which one to pursue. Thinking of Luke Cameron briefly, he frowned. That particular cowboy had been much too bold, behaved much too familiarly toward Amanda. He couldn't wait to get her safely away from such creatures. But, time was growing short. He only had a few days in which to finally persuade her to see the sense of his arguments.

Amanda continued to behave coolly toward Peter at dinner that evening. She retired early, professing that she had developed a nagging headache. She actually wanted to avoid any further confrontation between the two of them. She was growing so weary of his persistent arguments, of his persuasive tactics. She would honestly be relieved when he departed for Boston.

As for Luke, she fumed anew over the way he had behaved in town that day. Just when I was beginning to overcome some of my anger and resentment toward him, she thought, he behaves like a jealous, possessive husband! That's precisely what he wants to be, she heard a tiny voice at the back of her mind utter. She sank down on her bed and attempted to shut off all thoughts of him. She would instead think of ways in which to repay Miss Carolyn Tompkins for her disgraceful behavior.

She realized that she had actually already made the decision not to return to Boston with Peter when he left. She didn't want to decide precisely how long she would remain with her father in Texas, so she was simply going to inform Peter that it would be for an indefinite period of time. He would then relay her message to Aunt Martha. It was the only decision she felt qualified to make at the moment. She didn't feel quite prepared just yet to make a permanent decision about anything.

As she started to fall asleep, she reflected that she would hate to leave her father and Texas just yet. In fact, she thought just as she slipped into unconsciousness, I would hate to ever leave.

Amanda and Mrs. Chambers prepared to journey into town the next afternoon for the quilting bee, which was being held in honor of one of the local rancher's daughters, engaged to be married in a few weeks. All of the ladies for miles around would gather at the home of one of them and ply their needles all evening to sew a quilt for the prospective bride and her intended. The event would also be used to provide a social occasion for the ladies to gather and talk, to drink tea or coffee and visit for a few hours, away from their homes and families. Most of them anxiously looked forward to such a prospect, an evening of female conversation.

It had indeed snowed a bit the night before, but the ground was coated with only a few inches of snow as they prepared to leave. Samuel had given his permission for them to go, warning them that the wintry conditions could always worsen in a matter of minutes. However, he trusted Mrs. Chambers's good sense if severe weather arose.

Amanda had purposely avoided Peter for the entire day, informing him briskly of her plans for the afternoon. He reminded her that he would be

301

leaving the morning after next. She said good day to him before she left, still furious with him for the shabby trick he had played on her in town. She was still fuming as she thought of the attitudes of both Carolyn and Luke. She knew that she could somehow manage to handle the troublesome schoolteacher, but Luke Cameron was another matter entirely.

The large room in Mrs. Powell's house was already crowded when Amanda and Mrs. Chambers crossed the threshold. Several women called out their greetings, and they were shown to a seat where they began conversing with the other ladies. Amanda noticed that Carolyn was seated directly across the room, wearing a mysterious, but triumphant, expression as she stared at Amanda. Amanda ignored her and the quilting bee began shortly thereafter.

After the women had talked and sewed for nearly an hour, Carolyn suddenly smiled and turned to a group of ladies around her, announcing in a clear voice which could be heard about the room, "Did you hear the news? I mean, about Amanda Lawrence and that big, handsome Luke Cameron? Well, I heard from a very reliable source that the two of them were snowbound together last week, and for a whole night, as a matter of fact. Yes, and the two of them were all alone out at his ranch. Isn't that terribly exciting?" She smiled her satisfaction at the surprised and curious faces around her and continued, "I can't imagine what her father must have thought about her spending the night all alone with a young man as good-looking as that Luke, can you? I mean, after all, I heard only yesterday that Amanda Lawrence is already engaged to a young man back home, who just so happens to be visiting her right now. Won't he be furious when he finds out about his intended bride? I can imagine that the two of them didn't just talk all night when they were out there alone, if you get my meaning." She turned a gloriously triumphant face upon Amanda, who had been shocked into momentary speechlessness by the scheming young woman's catty words.

Amanda finally recovered her senses enough to reply, in an equally clear voice, "How dare you, Carolyn Tompkins! I don't know where you got your information, but what you are insinuating is certainly not true!"

"You ought to be downright ashamed of yourself for spreading such vicious gossip," Mrs. Chambers rebuked her loudly. The other ladies in the room remained silent, eyes widened, curious about what was taking place. They couldn't imagine why Carolyn Tompkins would announce such startling gossip to the whole assembly, especially in front of Amanda.

"Oh, but I believe that it is true, Miss Lawrence. You and Luke Cameron spent a night alone together in his house, didn't you? Well, you're the one who ought to be ashamed, ashamed to even show your face in the company of decent women-folk!" she insisted vigorously, glancing about the room in smug satisfaction as several of the women were now beginning to whisper amongst themselves, and seeing that Amanda's face was flushing uncomfortably beneath their interested gazes.

Amanda stood upright and straightened her back, totally humiliated but unwilling to show it. She lifted her head and bestowed a smouldering look of fury upon Carolyn, who visibly backed down as she observed the raw anger in Amanda's flashing eyes.

"Luke Cameron and I were indeed forced to spend a night alone together at his ranch, due to the severe weather. However, nothing untoward happened, Miss Tompkins. You have allowed your evil-minded, jealous thoughts to run rampant far too long. Good evening, ladies," she announced briskly as she swept from the room, leaving an astonished group of women in her wake.

Mrs. Chambers, too, stood and spoke to Carolyn. "I never heard such disgraceful gossip in all my born days! You ain't no lady, Carolyn Tompkins, and I darn well think you showed us all that tonight. You got some nerve spreading such tales about Amanda, and you're going to be mighty sorry someday for what you just did to her." She paused and her glance swept the entire assembly. "And you all, you know Amanda Lawrence. You know what a good and kind and real decent young lady she is. If you want to believe what this jealous little hussy says, well, you're not the women I think you are. I've had my say now, I guess. I'll be saying good night, too." She followed Amanda out of the room. The two of them quickly donned their cloaks and stepped outside into the cold, brisk wind of the December evening.

"How could she do such a thing?" Amanda murmured in humiliation as they drove away from town. She was well aware that such gossip could tarnish her reputation beyond repair. And, a woman's good name in this day and time was extremely important, her honor essential.

"Honey, you shouldn't pay no mind to her at all. She don't deserve any more notice from anyone! You can take my word for it, there ain't anyone ever going to want to have a gossip like that around at any more quilting bees! Now, don't you worry none. Most of them women back there won't believe what she wants them to," she said, trying to comfort the stricken Amanda.

"Oh, but some of them undoubtedly will. They'll be perfectly willing to believe that something happened between Luke and myself. Something did happen, but not the way Carolyn wants them to believe. Oh, why did she have to do this to me? What am I going to do now? How am I ever going to hold my head up in town again?" she lamented, beginning to shed a few tears of anger and humiliation now.

"You told the truth tonight, Amanda, and I believe that the truth eventually wins out every time. It don't matter what the others want to believe. After all, the people who really know you will believe you." She knew, however, that it did matter, and mattered very much. Such juicy gossip as this would spread like wildfire all over the countryside in no time at all.

"I've already seen how very fast news travels around here. What about Father? He doesn't know about that night. He'll want to kill Luke when he hears about this! I'm afraid he won't pause to question before he does something drastic!"

"I'm afraid you're right there, honey," her friend agreed grimly. "But, maybe it'd be best if you talked to him about it first, before he hears about it from someone else."

"Oh, I simply can't tell him! He'd be so angry and hurt and disappointed that I didn't tell him in the very beginning, don't you see? I'm so humiliated whenever I think about what people are going to believe. Samuel will be furious!" She began crying in earnest now, and Mrs. Chambers placed a comforting arm about her shoulders as they drove home in the darkening twilight.

Amanda went straight up to her room when they arrived home. Mrs. Chambers watched the dejected figure climb the stairs, shaking her head sympathetically. At least Amanda wouldn't have to face either her father or that Norman feller tonight. Poor child, she thought, but maybe this will finally make her see that she's fighting against something that it won't do no good to fight against. When news of tonight reaches the ears of both her father and Luke Cameron, well, things will really start happening mighty fast then.

Amanda wearily climbed beneath the covers of her bed, burrowing deep into the softness of her pillow, wanting to erase the memory of Carolyn's taunting words and the whispers of the other women. She cried a bit more at the humiliation of it all, realizing that she would probably be branded by some as a shameless, dishonored woman. She finally fell asleep, exhausted by the torrent of her weeping.

She saw Luke's face swimming before her as she began to dream. He was smiling his beguiling smile, his blue eyes were twinkling, and he was telling her again that he loved her and wanted to marry her. Then, she saw Carolyn's face, and then Aunt Martha's. The two of them were staring at her in disdain and disgust. Peter's face appeared, his features angry and hurt and disapproving. Last of all, she saw her father's face. He was telling her that he was ashamed of her, that he would be forced to avenge her honor, that she had made him the laughing stock of the whole territory. Amanda tossed and turned the entire night, unable to forget the original reason for the embarrassing incident, that night spent alone with Luke Cameron.

Sixteen

Amanda's worst fears began to be realized the next afternoon as she was helping Mrs. Chambers with some of the housework. Peter suddenly stalked into the parlor, where she was engaged in dusting the mantel above the fireplace. She turned round in surprise as he burst out rudely, "I should have known that it was something like this! I knew that there had to be some sort of explanation for your refusal of my honorable proposal of marriage, your hesitation to return to Boston. And to think that I actually intended to make you my wife, to bestow upon you my good name!"

"What on earth are you talking about?" Amanda countered, then experienced a terrible feeling of dread as she realized that he must have somehow heard about yesterday's incident.

"I can see by the guilty expression on your beautiful, deceitful face that you know perfectly well what I'm talking about. I've heard about your wicked little affair with that uncouth Cameron fellow. It's no use trying to hide it any longer, Amanda, for the entire town apparently knows all about it by now," he declared with a sneer.

"How did you hear about it?" she inquired

calmly, not even bothering to deny what he believed to be true.

"That doesn't really matter, does it? But, simply for your information, I happened to hear it from Miss Tompkins when I rode into town this morning. It seems that she heard it from one of your father's own employees. I was in town to make the arrangements for the two of us to take the stagecoach out of Texas and back to Boston. I don't need to tell you how shocked and humiliated I was to hear the news of your indiscretions!" he stormed indignantly.

"Your humiliation!" she exclaimed. "How dare you speak to me of your humiliation! How on earth do you think I felt when that vengeful hussy announced the whole ugly gossip last evening? And that's all it is, Peter, gossip. You didn't even bother to question if it were the truth or not, did you? No, you simply took that Southern vixen's word for it!"

"You certainly do not have the right to say one word against that gallant lady. I don't for one minute believe that she started the 'gossip' as you call it. Why, she was very distraught over the news. You should have had the decency to tell me about your involvement with Cameron when I first arrived. I feel like a complete and utter fool now! Here I've been trying to convince you to marry me, to persuade you to return to Boston where I believed that you belonged, and all the time you knew that I would eventually discover the truth about what's been going on between the two of you! It is thoroughly disgraceful!" he accused her angrily, not even noticing the stricken look on her face as he continued to accuse her unjustly.

"Don't you dare to speak to me in that insulting manner!" she hissed, absolutely furious at his injustice, at his refusal to listen to her explanation. "I have told you what that jealous, spiteful woman told you is entirely untrue. Very well, since you refuse to listen to me, I'm sorry that we have to part this way. I was still hoping that we could at least remain friends, but I see now that it is impossible. You simply cannot trust me, can you? You've known me a good many years, and yet you dare to stand there and accuse me of something which you should know I am incapable of."

"Trust you?" he repeated sarcastically. "I can recall the intense way you and Cameron looked at one another when we were in town. Don't bother trying to deny it any longer. Why, it is perfectly clear for anyone to see. And to think that I thought you would be returning to Boston with me! I can see now why you refused. Oh no, you wanted to stay here with your lover. Besides, such indecent, disgraceful behavior would simply not be tolerated in Boston!" he taunted her cruelly.

Amanda's palm literally itched to slap his cruel, derisive face, but she controlled the powerful urge and instead whirled about to present her back to him, refusing to acknowledge his heartless words. He coldly informed her that he was leaving and would spend the night at the hotel in town before taking the stagecoach back to a world where people were not common ruffians and where women knew how to behave properly. He turned about and slammed the door with a resounding noise after him.

Well, she thought as she sank down into a chair, that certainly takes care of Peter, doesn't it? She bitterly reflected that Miss Carolyn Tompkins would have been very satisfied indeed if she had been a witness to the previous scene. She hates me, Amanda thought, and she's hated me even before her jealousy concerning Luke surfaced. Well, she certainly ought to be happy now. Peter had stated that the whole town would know about it by now. Many would refuse to believe the malicious tale, but many wouldn't.

Oh no, she thought, jerking herself upright. Samuel was in town at this very moment! The dread she already felt deepened. She had already planned to explain everything to him tonight, but it seemed that it was too late now. By now, he would certainly have been apprised of the gossip in town. Oh, why did I put it off? she chided herself.

She heard the front door slam a few minutes later, and then the hoofbeats of a galloping horse as Peter rode away from the ranch in great haste. Now, she would have to face her father. Peter would be nothing in comparison to what it would be like with Samuel.

Not more than an hour later, Samuel stomped into the house and found Amanda still sitting where Peter had left her, her eyes closed and her features relaxed in sleep. He hesitated to wake her for a brief moment, but then called her name.

"Oh, it's you, Father. I suppose I must have

dozed off for a few moments," she explained as she sat upright in the chair and watched as he strode over to the mantel and leaned against it.

"Amanda, I've just come from town. I heard something there and I need to talk to you about it before I make my final decision about how to handle it," he said sternly.

"Yes, Father, what is it?" she asked innocently, as if she didn't already know the terrible things he must have heard.

"There's a rumor going about that you and Luke Cameron spent a night alone in his house. Is that true?" he demanded sharply.

"Well, yes, it is true."

"What!" he thundered. "You mean to sit there and tell me that Cameron didn't bring you on home like I told him to? Did he keep you there all night against your will?" he demanded with a murderous gleam in his eye.

"No, it wasn't like that at all. Please, Father, let me explain before you lose your temper completely. You see, we meant to ride over here as soon as you and your men left, but the blizzard worsened. You yourself were unable to make it home until the next morning, remember? Well, the same thing happened to me. I wanted to come home, but it was simply impossible. So, I was forced to spend the night there in Luke's house. We slept in separate bedrooms, and I awakened early the next morning and rode home by myself," she told him, then watched his face closely for any sign that he would settle for her explanation.

"Are you telling me the truth, Amanda? Nothing happened between you two?" he urged.

"Yes, I am telling you the truth, Father. Nothing occurred that night. I didn't want to tell you about it for just this very reason. I knew that you would be upset about it if you knew, that you would lose your temper," she explained.

"All right, I believe you when you say that nothing happened. But, all the same, Luke Cameron must be the one who's spreading those lies. After all, if you two were the only ones who knew about that night, there was no one else to start the rumors!"

"Mrs. Chambers knows, also. But, no one else. Or at least that's what I believed before Carolyn Tompkins confronted me with this yesterday at the quilting bee. She's the one who provoked the gossip."

"Yeah, but she had to find out from someone, didn't she?" he insisted stubbornly, his fury rising once again. "And who else could have told her but Luke Cameron himself?"

"No, you're mistaken," Amanda declared, fearful that he would still attempt to retaliate against Luke.

"It has to be him, Amanda. Why, I myself saw how he paid close attention to that little school-teacher all night at the Christmas social. Everyone there talked about those two. He's done this in order to get back at me," he muttered grimly. "He's using you in order to have his revenge on me for my opposition of his damn fences! Well, he sure as hell won't get away with an underhanded trick like this!" he stormed, then strode out of the room and toward the front door.

"No, Father! What are you planning to do? You can't go confront Luke with this, you simply can't! I know it isn't his fault that this gossip was started. Wait—now I remember. Peter said that Carolyn got the news from one of your employees. That's it, Father, it was probably Tommy who told her! He's completely infatuated with her right now, and he must have seen me riding in that morning. He must have let it slip to her when they were together," she reasoned, trying to hold him back.

"I don't believe that, Amanda. Young Evans wouldn't do a thing like that. No, it was Luke Cameron. It's his way of exacting his revenge!" He shook off her restraining arm and stalked outside to his waiting horse, his fury building each moment.

"No, Father, please don't ride over there!" she implored him.

"Amanda, this is between Cameron and me. It's got to be settled, and settled now. A man's about as low-down as he can get when he attacks the good name of another man's daughter. I could kill him for dragging your name through the mud like this!" he pronounced furiously, then kicked his horse and quickly rode away, unsure of his exact intent toward Luke, but wanting to have it out with him once and for all.

"Father!" Amanda shouted after him. She quickly glanced about to see if anyone else was in sight, but the hands were apparently working elsewhere, and Mrs. Chambers was still occupied

314

back in the kitchen. Making a rapid decision, she grabbed her cloak and boots and hurried out to the barn to saddle her horse.

I can't let him do this, she thought as she feverishly saddled her horse. It isn't Luke's fault and I know it. It must have been Tommy who told Carolyn, it must have been. None of the other hands would have told her. Tommy wouldn't have done it intentionally, but he could easily have let it slip all the same. He still believed that Carolyn was perfect, and he would have trusted her with the information.

She swung up into the saddle and kicked the horse, urging him on to follow in the wake of her father. She had to reach Luke's ranch when he did, she couldn't allow him to do anything foolish. Oh, if only he'd listened to her! But then, he was already itching for some way to get back at Luke for that night, for being forced to ride away from Luke's ranch with his own daughter standing there as witness. Now, this was simply one more thing to be accounted for. Dear Lord, she prayed, please don't let anything happen before I can get there and make them both see reason!

She knew that Luke was hesitant to quarrel with her father. He had already told her that when they had talked that night. He had told her that he didn't want to shoot the father of the woman he loved. Loved. If he truly loved her, she hoped that he would refuse to fight with Samuel at all. She knew that a fight between the two of them would only make matters worse, that it would only cause further gossip, only serve to inflame the vicious story making the rounds of the countryside.

Samuel reached Luke's ranch and rode up to the steps of the front porch of the house. He shouted toward the door, "Cameron! Luke Cameron! You get your dirty, low-down carcass out here!"

Luke happened to be inside the house at that moment. He casually opened the front door and stepped out onto the porch, leaning negligently against a post.

"What is it, Lawrence?" he inquired nonchalantly. Samuel noted that he was unarmed.

"Get your gun, you bastard!" Samuel spoke through tightly clenched teeth.

"Why?" Luke responded good-naturedly.

"Because, I'd sure as hell hate to have to shoot an unarmed man, that's why!"

"Now, I can't say as I know what brought this on, Sam Lawrence, and I don't suppose you're in any mood to enlighten me, are you?"

"This is a personal matter. I told you that I'd settle it with you some other time, didn't I? Well, this is the time. Now, I'm going to take it out of your hide for bringing my daughter here with you that night, and for damn well keeping her here all night!"

"Did she tell you about that?" Luke asked, standing erect now, his features becoming serious.

"She didn't have to. I happened to hear about it in town today. I happen to think that you're the one that spread it about, too. I think you did it to get back at me, and that's what burns me up the most. You damned coward, you didn't even have the guts to confront me with it face to face, did you?'' Samuel spat in disgust.

"I don't know what the hell you're talking about. You're telling me that there's some gossip going around town about Amanda and me?'' Luke demanded to know.

"That's right. Don't act like you don't know all about it! It's all over the place about you two spending a night alone out here last week during that blizzard! But, that isn't all that's being said. They're saying that it wasn't quite as innocent a night as it should have been!''

"I don't know what the hell makes you think I'd ever say anything about Amanda in the first place,'' Luke insisted, growing angrier by the moment. "I happen to be in love with your daughter. Damn it, man, I wouldn't hurt her for the world!''

"I've had enough of this talk. We're just wasting time. Now, are you going to get your gun, or do I have to take you on with my bare hands?'' Samuel ground out.

"I tell you, Sam, I didn't have anything to do with that story getting round. Nothing happened between Amanda and me that night, I swear. I ain't in the habit of lying, either,'' he stated, his expression deadly serious, his eyes narrowed dangerously.

"All right,'' Samuel said as he dismounted, "if that's the way you want it!'' He brought his fist up toward Luke, who effectively dodged it and jumped down from the porch.

"Sam, I don't want to hurt you none. I already told Amanda that I didn't want to have to hurt

317

you. She knows why. I love her, Sam, and I want to marry her."

"Shut up about my daughter!" Samuel bellowed. "How dare you even speak her name, you dirty bastard! You don't fool me one little bit! All you want to do is dishonor my daughter's name in order to get back at me!" He lunged for Luke and knocked him to the ground with the force of his attack.

"All right, if you won't listen to me, then I guess I'll have to make you, damn it!" Luke muttered, bringing his fist up into contact with Samuel's left jaw. Samuel staggered backward, then recovered and countered with a quick right to Luke's chin. The two of them continued to exchange blows, and neither heard when Amanda finally arrived.

Amanda gazed in fascinated horror at the two men locked in combat as she reined in her horse a few feet away from them. She knew that she had to do something to make them stop, but she didn't know exactly what to do.

As she watched her father bring his bloody fist into brutal contact with Luke's jaw, she experienced an overwhelming sensation, an emotion she could not define. She only knew that it distressed her considerably to see the strong, overbearing, proud young man being hurt by her father. She couldn't put a name to it, but she felt a powerful desire to protect him, to fly to him and soothe away his wounds.

She gazed at Luke in wonder, almost as if she were seeing him for the first time. All her thoughts, all her memories of him jumbled

318

together as she sat astride her horse, watching as her father and the man who was having such a startling effect on her emotions fought against each other in such fury.

"Father! Luke! Please, stop this at once!" she commanded.

The two of them abruptly jerked their heads about to observe her presence. Samuel's bruised and bloodied face grew even redder.

"Amanda, get the hell out of here!" he shouted. "This is none of your concern!"

"Oh, but it is, Father! The gossip was about me, remember? It most certainly is my concern. Now, I think it's time you two stopped behaving like children and tried to work things out in a more mature, civilized fashion. I'm so darn sick and tired of every man out here believing that brute force is the only thing that will work!" she stormed with feeling.

Luke, breathing heavily from his exertion, gazed at her in love and admiration, though he too echoed her father's concern.

"Your father's right about that, Amanda. This is something we have to settle between ourselves."

"You keep quiet, Luke Cameron!" she snapped, though in the back of her mind she was still marveling at the turbulent emotion she had experienced as she rode up. "I refuse to stay out of this quarrel, for this particular quarrel is supposedly about some silly gossip concerning my good name, isn't it? Well, you two aren't fighting about that at all. No, you're actually fighting about fences, and down deep you both know it," she informed them, dismounting now and striding toward them, her hands on her hips.

"You don't know what you're talking about," Samuel gruffly denied.

"Oh, yes I do. You're angry and vengeful toward Luke because he chooses to fence his lands, not because of the gossip concerning him and me. And you, Luke Cameron," she said, turning to him, finding it extremely difficult to control her breathing as she tried to look him squarely in the eye, "You're fighting because my father and the others choose to oppose your views. Both of you need to admit it and cease this ridiculous brawling." She stood with her flashing eyes challenging them to deny her words.

Samuel gazed down at the ground, a bit unsteady on his feet as he pondered her speech. His face was puffy and bruised, his hands bloody and broken. Luke stared at Amanda, his bloodied mouth turned up into a disarming smile. Amanda fought down the overwhelming urge to cry as she looked at his purpled bruises, his split lip.

"I guess you're right," her father finally admitted, grudgingly. "I guess we are all riled up over this fencing matter, but I swear it was because of you, too."

"I told you, Lawrence, I didn't say anything to anyone about Amanda's spending that night here alone with me," Luke repeated, striving to catch his breath after his struggle with Samuel.

"That's right, Father. I'm almost positive that Carolyn received her information from Tommy, unintentionally, of course. But, I'll speak with him about that later. For now, I suggest the two of you cease this fighting and at least declare some sort of truce. I know that the two of you used to be friends, and I fail to see why you can't at least behave civilly toward one another, even if you do hold opposing viewpoints about fencing," she told them decisively.

The two of them appeared to concentrate on all that she had said. Samuel was finally able to see the sense of his daughter's insistence that Luke hadn't been the one to start the gossip, that it wasn't like him to spread malicious tales about a lady. He looked at Luke and said, "Cameron, I guess she's right about that, too. I guess you wouldn't have done a thing like that after all," he admitted.

"No, Sam, you know good and well I wouldn't. I'm just as angry about it as you are, and you already know the reason why. I meant what I said about your daughter earlier. Don't worry, I'll take care of that rumor," he vowed purposefully.

"If you don't, I will," Samuel remarked. He helped Amanda up into the saddle, then painfully mounted his own horse. As they turned away, Amanda stole a quick glance back at Luke, who still stood breathing heavily, his face bruised and swollen, his cut mouth grinning nevertheless. She smiled inwardly as she rode away beside her father.

Why on earth did I feel that way when I saw him earlier? she asked herself as they rode away in silence. Mrs. Chambers must have been right; there was certainly something very powerful between herself and Luke Cameron. She wondered if it were perhaps his physical attraction, or if it were even more. She wanted to analyze the startling, tumultuous feeling she had experienced a short while ago. She had never felt this way before. She had never before actually felt protective toward any man except her own father. Why did it bother her so much to see that proud young man being humbled by her father's blows?

As they neared the Circle L, Samuel finally spoke. "I'm sorry I lost my temper and tore out of there the way I did. I've been doing an awful lot of thinking all the way home. My temper seems to get me in more trouble than I can handle sometimes."

"That's all right, Father. But, please, don't be upset about this matter any longer. If Luke said that he would take care of the gossip, you can be assured that he will. It seems that particular young man always gets what he goes after, doesn't it?" she remarked.

"Yes, he always has. He was that way when he was a lot younger, too."

"Father," she tentatively began, "what did he mean about saying something about me to you earlier?"

Samuel's mouth tightened again in a thin line before he replied. "It doesn't matter what he meant, honey. He wants something he can't ever have."

"What do you mean by that?" she demanded.

"Amanda, has Luke ever asked you to marry him?" he countered with another question. He watched as her face colored beneath his gaze.

"Yes, he has. But, I most certainly have not accepted!" she assured him.

"I see. Well, that's what he meant. He told me that he loves you and wants to marry you. Do you feel the same way about him?" he asked, then waited anxiously for her answer.

"Certainly not!" she retorted, a bit too emphatically.

"I just wanted to make sure, that's all. He shouldn't ever have said a word to you about marriage without coming to me first. But, since you've apparently made it clear to him that you won't have anything to do with him, I guess it turned out all right after all."

"Yes, it turned out all right after all," she repeated. Her father had made it clear that he would disapprove of such a match between his daughter and his adversary, she was thinking as they rode toward the barn. Then, why in heaven's name did it bother her that he felt that way about Luke?

Samuel offered to take care of the horses, and Amanda went in search of Tommy. She found him on the far edge of the corral, mending a bridle.

"Tommy, may I have a word with you?"

"Yes, ma'am. I ain't seen you for a spell," he told her with a friendly smile.

"I don't suppose you've been in town, have you? I mean, you haven't heard the rumors circulating about myself and Luke Cameron, have you?"

"No, ma'am, what rumors are you talking about?" he asked in puzzlement.

"Carolyn Tompkins informed all of the ladies present at the quilting bee yesterday that I had spent a night alone with Luke Cameron at his ranch. She further implied that something—well, that something improper took place between us. I informed her, of course, that she was wrong about what she thinks took place. I heard, however, that she received the information from one of my father's own employees. Tommy, I believe that you were the one who told her."

He blushed to the roots of his hair and answered, "Yes, ma'am. I guess it was me. But, Miss Amanda, I didn't mean to tell her about it. I let it slip out about seeing you ride up that morning after the blizzard!" he assured her eagerly, ashamed that he had been so careless.

"I'm sure you didn't do it deliberately. However, she is spreading this malicious gossip about me all over the town. I thought that you should be aware of it. I want you to know that I can't blame you for it, Tommy. You see, it isn't the fact that I was forced to spend a night alone with Mr. Cameron due to the bad weather that is the bulk of the gossip. Oh no, it's the extra little 'embellishments' she's giving the story," Amanda remarked bitterly.

"I'm sorry, ma'am. I wouldn't have had this happen for the world," he told her, totally mortified by what had occurred. He suddenly realized that Carolyn had broken her word to him; she had promised never to tell another soul of what he had let slip out. She's betrayed my trust, he thought to himself. Maybe Miss Amanda's been right about her all along. Why, if she's spreading that tale all over town, it's got to be for no other reason than to hurt Miss Amanda.

"You want me to ride into town right now and

talk to Carolyn about it, ma'am?" he offered, his disenchantment with the flirtatious schoolteacher nearing completion now.

"No, that won't be necessary. But, thank you all the same. Luke Cameron is going to take care of the matter." She walked away from him, pleased that his eyes had finally been opened as to the true character of his ladylove. Mrs. Chambers was always saying that good came out of everything, no matter what.

She entered the house and immediately ran up the stairs and into her room, closing the door securely behind her. She removed her boots and plopped down upon the softness of the bed, not caring that she was rumpling her dress and the bedcovers quite terribly.

Why had Luke Cameron declared his love and intentions to her father today? Was it merely because of the gossip? To placate Samuel's fatherly indignation?

And why had she felt the impulse to go to Luke today, to protect him? He was overbearing, stubborn, mocking, infuriating. Why should she care if he were humbled a bit? Shouldn't she be pleased if he didn't get his way for a change? Wasn't she always hoping that he would be taken down a peg or two by someone?

No, she thought. I don't want him to be hurt. For some reason, I don't ever want to see his pride damaged, his strong, masterful spirit broken. But, why? she continued to ask herself. Why does he matter so much to me all of a sudden?

She had no answers to her questions just yet, but

she intended to have them soon. For now, she would try and think things through for herself. She wanted to discover why her heart had softened toward him, when she had ceased resenting him. She didn't feel antagonistic toward him any longer. All of these thoughts and feelings left her completely bewildered.

One thing was for certain; Luke Cameron was imprinted on her mind. Even if she were to leave Texas and return to Boston tomorrow, she would find it impossible to forget him, whatever the reason.

Seventeen

Luke was true to his word when he declared that he would take care of the matter of the gossip. He decided to ride into town that very afternoon, as soon as he got himself cleaned up a bit, of course, and head straight for the source of the rumors, Miss Carolyn Tompkins. He did just that, calling for her at the boarding house. He was told by the proprietor that the young lady would be down shortly, so he took a seat in the parlor to wait.

He couldn't get over the way Amanda had looked at him today, he thought in puzzlement. It was as if she were surprised at something about him all of a sudden. He only hoped it meant one thing; that she was finally discovering that she was in love with him. He still believed that she was, no matter how hard she tried to fight against it. If he hadn't believed that she returned his love, well, he told himself, it would have been a lot tougher to keep from getting depressed by her antagonism. But, for some reason, today she hadn't looked at him in either anger or resentment. No, it had looked as if she felt the sudden urge to approach him, to speak to him about something serious. Whatever it was, it greatly puzzled him. He'd have to see that the two of them got a chance to speak together alone real soon.

He was sorry that he and Samuel had fought one another, but it had kind of served to clear the air a bit. Now, maybe Lawrence would listen to his daughter, who possessed an intelligence and spirit that was difficult to resist. Damned if Amanda wasn't the most beautiful and stubborn female he'd ever before encountered!

As for Carolyn, well, he'd tell her a thing or two just as soon as she quit stalling and came on down to face him. It made him boiling mad all over again whenever he thought of the terrible insinuations she'd made about Amanda and him. That young woman needed a good talking to, and he was going to administer it.

"Why, if it isn't Luke Cameron," Carolyn spoke sweetly as she glided through the doorway of the parlor.

"Howdy, ma'am. I'd kind of like to have a little talk with you if you don't mind," he said as he stood and politely waited for her to take a seat beside him on the sofa.

"Whatever do you have to talk to little old me about?" she simpered, spreading her full skirts gracefully about her as she sat down.

"Well, I expect that it'd be for the best if I was to come straight to the point. You see, there's a story going about town right now, a rumor that concerns me and Amanda Lawrence. The gossip goes that we spent a night alone together last week out at my ranch, and that we did something that wasn't quite honorable, if you get my meaning?"

he asked, pausing in order to gauge her reaction. The little idiot didn't fool him one bit when she pretended ignorance.

"Why, that's simply terrible!" she stated innocently, widening her blue eyes.

"Yeah, it sure enough is. The only thing is, I heard tell that you were the one who started this story to begin with."

"Me? Why on earth would anyone accuse me of such a thing? I would never do a thing like that!" she protested indignantly, her small mouth pouting effectively.

"Well, now, I guess I know why you'd be the one to do such a thing. Because you're a jealous, blue-eyed, blonde-haired little flirt who thought that by damaging the good reputation of another woman you could hope to gain something you never had a chance at in the first place!" he informed her savagely, the smile on his face replaced now by a threatening scowl.

Carolyn realized that it would do her no good to pretend ignorance any longer, and she responded angrily, "You have no right to speak to me in such an insulting manner, Luke Cameron!"

"Oh, but I do. You see, Miss Tompkins, I happen to be in love with Amanda Lawrence. And, what's more, I intend to marry her," he told her coldly.

"Marry her!" Carolyn repeated dumbly.

"That's right. And I'm not about to allow you to go about spreading tales about the woman who's going to be my wife!"

"There's nothing you can do about it!" she

retorted, recovering her composure. No, it can't be true, she thought. He can't be in love with her, he can't be planning to marry that Yankee vixen!

"There sure as hell is something I can do about it," he responded ruthlessly, shocking her into silence. "You aren't the only one who knows how to spread vicious little tales. How'd you like to be run out of this town by the good ladies who hear that the teacher of their innocent little children is nothing more than a no-account little whore?" he threatened with a menacing frown.

"You wouldn't dare spread such a lie about me!"

"Yes I would. I'd do anything to protect the good name of the woman I love. Now, are you going to retract the gossip you've been spreading about? Are you going to let it be known that you made a little mistake, that your information was wrong?"

"You have your nerve! You led me on, Luke Cameron!" she spat at him, rising to her feet and facing him with the light of battle in her eyes: "You led me to believe that you were interested in me! Everyone saw us together at the Christmas social! I can tell everyone that you broke your promise to me, that you led me on and are planning to do the same to Amanda Lawrence!"

"I only paid attention to you that night to make Amanda jealous!" he told her. "I'll warn you right now, Carolyn," he said, standing beside her now. "If you want a fight on your hands, you go ahead and keep spreading the lies. But, let me warn you right here and now, you've never faced an opponent like me before, young lady. You see, no matter what you try, I'm going to win if you declare war. I'll see to it that you'll never be able to hold your little scheming head up anywhere again!''

"You are no gentleman, sir!" she raged at him, furious now, frustrated that she was helpless against his threats.

"I sure ain't no gentleman when I'm doing battle with someone who sure enough ain't no lady," he responded mockingly.

"Oh! Get out of here! Get out of here and never show your face to me again! Get out of here before I scratch your hateful face for you!" she stormed.

"Yes, ma'am. I reckon I said all I came to say. I don't figure I'll be hearing any more about Amanda being a dishonored woman, now, will I? I also don't reckon I'll be seeing you again," he taunted before he strode from the room.

Carolyn flounced out of the room and up the stairs in a most unladylike manner, slamming the door to her room with a vengeance. She threw herself down on her bed and beat viciously at her pillow, envisioning it as Luke Cameron's head.

Luke left the boarding house, satisfied that he had accomplished his purpose. If he knew women, and he could usually predict them when it came to the ones like Carolyn, he knew that she'd never dare to say another word about Amanda. He smiled to himself as he mounted his horse. He still had a lot of work to do that day, and he still wanted to make some plans.

Carolyn cried out her frustration for nearly an

hour, finally rising and washing her face. She sniffed in self-pity as she proceeded to rearrange her curls and straighten her crumpled skirts. She purposefully left the room and strolled down the stairs and outside, taking up her parasol on her way out of the boarding house. She needed a diversion, she told herself, something to take her mind off the disturbing encounter with Luke Cameron. She spotted Peter Norman a few yards away and called out to him in a sweetly cheerful voice.

"Why, it's Mr. Norman, isn't it? But, what on earth are you doing in town today, and by yourself? I thought for sure you'd be out at the Lawrence ranch with your Amanda."

"Hello, Miss Tompkins," Peter responded politely, striding over to offer his arm as an escort. "No, I've left the Lawrence ranch for good. She isn't my Amanda any longer. I'm staying in the hotel for tonight. My stage is scheduled to leave tomorrow morning," he informed her somberly.

"Oh, I see. Well, in that case, I don't suppose that Amanda will be going back to Boston with you?" she probed in a delicate manner.

"No. She's no longer my fiancee. I am extremely grateful to you for opening my eyes as to her true character, Miss Tompkins. It seems that she certainly isn't the young lady I remembered her to be." He hesitated for a moment, then said, "Would you possibly consider having dinner with me this evening? We could dine at the hotel's restaurant. I'm sure it isn't too elegant, but I would very much enjoy spending the evening in your company."

"Why, thank you, sir. I'd be utterly delighted."
She smiled warmly at him and continued down
the street on his arm. Oh well, she thought as they
strolled along the street, if I can't have a man like
Luke Cameron, maybe a rich young Yankee will
do just as well. My family would naturally
disapprove, but they aren't the ones who need to
catch a husband! After all, I'm tired of this
backward town, of this wild country, these wild
and savage men. A fine, cultured young man such
as Mr. Norman might be the very thing for me after
all.

She beamed at him once again as he began to
relate to her what he judged to be the fascinating
story of his life, prompted occasionally by her little
words of encouragement.

Amanda avoided going into town for the next
few days. She was still smarting from the humiliating gossip, but she hoped that Luke had been
able to put a stop to it, somehow. Her father and
Mrs. Chambers endeavored to take her mind off
the embarrassing situation, and she was grateful
for their attention.

Luke. Simply thinking of him affected her so
strangely. She hadn't mentioned this latest development to Mrs. Chambers. She knew that her
friend would probably insist that she had fallen in
love with Luke, and that was something she
certainly didn't want to face, at least not yet. Her
feelings had apparently undergone a drastic
change, and she was even more confused. Things
had happened much too swiftly for her ever since
she had come to Texas, she thought with a sigh.

She suddenly wondered if perhaps Luke's feelings had also undergone a change. Why did the possibility of this cause a terrible feeling of loneliness and despair within her? Oh, why should it matter to me whether he still loves me or not! she insisted to herself in exasperation. I don't know that I even believe in love, despite what Mrs. Chambers has told me. Still, the memory of Luke's tender, passionate kisses and violent embraces continued to burn deep within her mind, and in her dreams at night.

Samuel returned from a meeting one evening after the first of the year in a very distracted frame of mind. Amanda knew that he had met with the other ranchers who opposed fencing, but he had never returned from one of the meetings with such a look on his face before. She insisted that he tell her what was preoccupying him so much. He told her that he heard some news that was now spreading throughout the territory, causing a great deal of concern and consternation.

"Sheep," he then uttered the one word grimly.

"Sheep? I don't understand," she responded in confusion. "Why should the matter of sheep be of any concern to you or to the other ranchers?" She strolled into the parlor, Samuel following behind her.

"We've heard the news that there's some sheepmen planning to move their flocks into this area before too long. As if we didn't have enough problems hereabouts already," he mumbled with a disgruntled air.

"But why should such a prospect bother you so

much? Surely the range is more than large enough for sheep and cattle alike," she reasoned.

"You don't understand, Amanda. Sheep will ruin the range. Make it unfit for anything else. Why, they smell so damn bad, they'll make the whole country smell the same way! Cattle won't drink where they've watered. Besides that, they crop the grass off so short it takes years to grow back!"

"But, I've heard that sheep and cattle are actually very similar animals, that they are indeed able to coexist alongside each other in harmony."

"The sheepmen try to spread just such talk around. But, it isn't true. And it won't work out here. We don't intend to ever let them come in."

"How can you keep them away? You don't own every square inch of the range. I don't see why you can't allow them to graze their sheep on a section of it."

"Sheep and cattle weren't meant to graze side by side. You'll understand more about it if they ever do come in. But, we don't aim to let that happen. Our organization is making some plans of its own," he stated purposefully.

"Oh, Father, surely you aren't planning to use violence and force as a method of keeping them out?" she asked with concern apparent in her luminous eyes.

"We'll do whatever we have to do. Meanwhile, we've also heard that they've already sent some men calling themselves 'scouts' ahead to sort of clear the way. They ought to be here before too long. 'Hired guns' is a more adequate term for such vermin," he muttered.

"Then, you are anticipating violence?"

"Now, now, there's no reason for you to start worrying just yet. We still intend to see to it that things don't get that far, if we can help it. The trouble is, there aren't enough of us left in the organization to do a whole hell of a lot if things get too rough."

"Father," she suggested, "why don't you and your organization of non-fencers meet with the other ranchers? From what you've been telling me, this particular situation will affect all of you, even the men who choose to fence their lands. Isn't that right? Well, if so, then I propose that your two groups band together in order to combat this newest threat."

"Amanda, I should have known that you would be certain to think of some sort of idea for working things out. You know, you're very much like your mother. I only wish she could have lived to see it for herself. Well," he commented, sighing heavily, "I guess your suggestion is worth a try, anyway. I'll send word to Luke Cameron to come on over and discuss it all with me whenever he gets a chance."

"Luke Cameron? But why should you speak to him?" she demanded in surprise. She didn't want to face that man right now! She wasn't ready to see him again. She still hadn't discovered why he was affecting her so strangely all of a sudden.

"Because," Samuel patiently explained, "he's the leader of the fencers, that's why. Besides, after the other day, I got the idea that you wanted me to patch things up with him."

"I did. I mean, I do. Oh, very well, send word to him if you like. I still have work to do," she said as she rose and briskly marched from the room, her color heightened a bit as she swept past him.

So, he thought as he watched her leave the room, I'm beginning to think that my suspicions are right after all. He'd been able to tell that she felt something for young Cameron, though he didn't know precisely whether it was love or hate! Either way, he wanted to find out. If it was hate, well, then, that would be just fine with him. He admitted to himself that he wasn't prepared to give her up to some other man just yet. But, on the other hand, if she had fallen in love with Luke, that would be a bitter pill to swallow. Either way, he proposed silently, I'm going to find out. Whatever it is she feels for him, it's mighty strong to make her behave the way she does whenever I so much as mention the man's name.

Two days later, Luke rode onto the Circle L, alone. He had received word that Samuel wanted to speak with him, and he could already guess what it was about. He, too, had heard the distressing news about the sheep. He and the other fencers didn't intend to let them move in, either, and he guessed that was what Lawrence wanted to speak to him about. Of course, it could also be that he wanted to talk to him about Amanda, but he doubted that. He didn't think Samuel would want to even think of the possibility of a union between his beloved daughter and the young man who was a constant thorn in his side!

He rode up to the front porch and dismounted, looping the reins over the hitching post. Glancing quickly about, he ascertained that most of the hands must be out on the range checking on the stock, the same as his own. Winter was hard on cattle. He climbed the steps and knocked loudly upon the front door. Mrs. Chambers swung open the door to greet him.

"Why, howdy there, Luke. I expect you'll be wanting to see Amanda?" she inquired innocently, attempting to hide her grin.

"Well, I'd like to, ma'am, but actually I'm here to speak with Mr. Lawrence. He sent word that he wanted to see me."

"Sure, sure, come on in here. He's in the front room there. You go on in, and I'll hang up your coat for you."

"Thanks, Mrs. Chambers," he responded with an answering grin. He slipped out of the heavy leather coat and handed it to her, then removed his hat and carried it at his side as he entered the room. Samuel was engaged in doing some bookwork at his large oak desk, and he glanced up as Luke strode into the room.

"Mr. Lawrence? I got word that you wanted to see me about something?" Luke remarked as he approached the desk.

"Yes. Take a seat," Samuel replied, gesturing toward a large arm chair. He came around the desk and took a seat on the sofa. Clearing his throat, a bit ill at ease at being alone in the room with the young man he had clashed with upon several occasions, he searched for adequate words to begin the discussion.

"Ain't this something, Sam? Me and you sitting down polite-like and carrying on a conversation as if we were just old friends or something?" Luke suddenly remarked with amusement, his mouth turned up into a smile, his blue eyes twinkling.

"Yeah, it is something, isn't it?" Samuel agreed, chuckling in spite of himself and relaxing a bit. When Luke smiled that way, it reminded him of the time when he was just an awkward young boy. It also made him look even more like his late father.

"Well, now to get down to why I asked you to stop by. I'm sure you and your friends have heard about the sheep? I mean, about those sheepmen proposing to bring their stock out here on our range?" he asked.

"We've heard. Had a little meeting to discuss the matter just last night."

"We had a meeting, too. Anyway, I have received an intelligent suggestion from Amanda concerning this problem. It seems that she believes our two organizations should combine, meet together in order to make plans to fight the influx of those damned sheep."

"Amanda thought of that, huh?" Luke commented. "It sounds just like her. And, hell, Samuel, it makes sense, doesn't it? We all used to be friends, you know, before this thing about the fencing came between us all. We still meet socially at social events, and yet we're at each other's throats when it comes to the fences. I'd say your daughter's right. It's time we put our heads together and came up with some solutions."

"This will only be to discuss the matter of the sheep, Luke," Samuel gruffly reminded him. "This won't make any difference whatsoever when it comes to the fences."

"All right. We all know how important this thing about the sheep can be. Why, we've all heard about other places where the critters have ruined the land. I don't want to see them come in here any more than you do, even if my land is fenced."

"It's settled then. We'll all meet to discuss this matter. How does tomorrow night sound to you? You can get word to the others by then?"

"Sure. I'll ride on out today and tell them. You'll see to it that your men are notified?"

"I will. Well, now," Samuel said, rising to his feet. "I guess that's all we had to discuss. Thanks for coming by, Luke."

"My pleasure, Sam. It's too bad things don't always go this easy between us." He extended his hand and shook hands with the older man, then left the room.

Samuel remained very thoughtful after Luke departed. He resumed his seat at the desk, but his pen didn't move for the space of another fifteen minutes.

Luke had wanted to ask where Amanda was, but he thought that might have been pushing things a bit too far with Samuel for one time. He wanted very much to see her right at this moment. He needed to tell her about his interview with Carolyn, and also about the startling news he had received as he had ridden into town yesterday.

340

Following a sudden intuition, he led his horse toward the barn. Sure enough, he spotted Amanda inside, rubbing down and grooming her horse, gently crooning to it as she worked. He knew that she must have seen him ride up, and had escaped out here to the barn in order to avoid him.

"Howdy there, ma'am. Nice day, ain't it?" he drawled lazily as he leaned against a stall to survey her as she worked.

Amanda dropped the curry comb in astonishment and turned an angry face upon Luke.

"What do you mean sneaking up on me like that?" she demanded petulantly.

"Sorry. Didn't mean to get you all riled up, Amanda," he replied mockingly, then edged closer.

"What are you doing out here, anyway? My father is sure to disapprove of your little visit!" she snapped, stooping to retrieve the comb and continuing with her chore.

"No he won't. In fact, you know as well as I do that he invited me to come. He told me the whole thing was your idea."

"It was not! I merely suggested that all of you ranchers combine your efforts to face this problem with the sheep. However, I said nothing whatsoever to my father about inviting you here in order to speak with him on the matter!" she protested a bit too vigorously.

"Well, it was a good idea, anyway. Fact is, we're all going to meet together tomorrow night. I'm glad we've finally got the chance to get together and talk things out."

"Yes," Amanda mumbled in reply. Bending over to gather a clump of hay to offer to the gentle mare, she suddenly found herself clasped tightly against Luke's chest, his powerful arms surrounding her as she straightened up.

"What do you think you're doing! Let go of me this instant!" she demanded in a low, furious tone. She glanced about to make certain they were not being observed by any curious eyes.

"Amanda, it's been too long since I've had an opportunity to speak privately with you. I really only meant to come in here and tell you something, but the temptation was just too great for me. Now, shut up, woman, and kiss me," he commanded huskily, stilling her cries of protest with his demanding lips.

Amanda felt herself melting against him, completely overwhelmed by the searing desire which swept through her at his touch. What am I doing? she asked herself. I know I should resist, but I can't! She lifted her arms to wind them about his neck, pressing herself even closer against his lithe, muscular body. She could feel his heartbeat close against her own.

Luke groaned as she pressed her soft curves against him, molding her body so perfectly to his own. It was more than he could handle. He reluctantly released her and said, breathing a bit heavily, "That's enough, my love! You don't seem to realize what you do to me. I can't keep on this way much longer, Amanda. I'm getting too impatient! I love you in every way, and this is just one of those ways. I could tell when I held you in my arms, I could tell that you must care for me. It isn't mere physical attraction, either, because I saw the way you looked at me the other day. You looked as if you were searching for something as you gazed at me that day. I think the truth is beginning to dawn on you. I only hope you won't fight it too much longer. I still aim to have you for my wife, Amanda Lawrence, and my patience and endurance are running mighty low! Now, I'd best tell you what I came to tell you before I say to hell with patience and endurance and throw you across the back of my horse and take you home with me where you damn well belong!'' he informed her with a strange glint in his blue eyes.

Amanda gasped aloud at his audacity. And yet, she realized fairly, she had asked for it. She had actually been aching for him to take her into his arms and kiss her passionately, hungrily the way he had. I don't know what on earth has come over me, she chided herself furiously. She stepped away from him and waited for him to speak, trying not to reveal the turbulent emotions running rampant throughout her mind and body.

"I was in town yesterday and I heard some news I thought you might be interested in. Seems your former fiance left town. He took the stage out of here a couple of days ago. He stayed in town a mite longer than I think he was planning to."

"I know that he was planning to leave. What's so surprising that he just postponed it for a few days?" she demanded irritably, still angry with herself for behaving the way she had, for feeling the way she did. Dear Lord, she prayed as she gazed up at him, why am I finding it so difficult to breathe whenever he is near me?

"He didn't exactly leave town alone, Amanda. Carolyn Tompkins went with him."

"What!" she exclaimed, incredulous at the news.

"That's right. Seems the two of them thought they'd suit one another real well. I talked to her about that gossip the other day. I guess what I said to her kind of put a scare into her or something. Anyway, I guess she decided it was about time she got out of town. She and Norman told the woman at the boarding house that they were leaving for Boston."

"Well, I never! I never would have expected that the two of them would run away together!"

"Yeah, I think it surprised a lot of folks. The rumor about you and me has almost died down completely now. Seems that folks don't want to believe the word of a Southern belle who runs off with a fancy Yankee gentleman, deserting her post as the town's schoolteacher without giving any notice at all."

"Well, I am certainly relieved that people have stopped believing the lies she told. I was afraid that I would never be able to face anyone around here again, that I might have to return to Boston in order to be treated with respect once again," she murmured thoughtfully.

"Return to Boston! Hell, gal, don't you know that news like that would have reached there quicker than you did, especially judging from that greenhorn ex-fiance of yours! Besides, I'm not about to let you leave Texas. I reckon that, before too much longer, I'm going to have complete say-so in the matter!" he vowed authoritatively.

"You most certainly will not!" she protested with spirit.

"Yes I will. And, from the way you're beginning to weaken, I'd say it won't be too much longer at all. Good day, ma'am," he announced with a mocking grin, then sauntered out of the barn.

"Oh!" Amanda raged as she watched him mount his horse. She could think of nothing appropriate to say to him at the moment. He tipped his hat politely as he cantered away.

She smiled to herself as she watched him ride out of sight. He really was the most impossible, provoking man! Her smile faded as she realized where her thoughts were leading her. No, she reminded herself, I don't want to feel that way about him, about any man just yet. I don't know that I'm ready to become nothing more than a slave to a man's wishes. Surely there is more to love than that!

She recalled the way Mrs. Chambers had described it. As an overpowering sensation, a lasting emotion that you were helpless to resist. And she certainly didn't behave as though she considered herself a slave. No, quite the contrary, Amanda thought with a smile. Her friend was obviously very fond of her husband, and the two of them apparently shared something very special. Her father and mother had also shared something special, something that still affected her father even though his wife had been dead all these years.

And yet, she thought, perhaps it is only that way for a select few. Her Aunt Martha and Uncle David certainly didn't share such an emotion. No, all they shared were their two daughters. They hardly even spoke to one another unless absolutely necessary.

No, Amanda vowed, if I ever do marry, it certainly will not be that way for me! It will have to be different, it will have to be the way it is for Mrs. Chambers and her John, the way it was for my parents.

She finished with the horse and returned to the house, washing her hands at the wash basin on the back porch before she entered. She went into the kitchen, where she found Mrs. Chambers doing the dishes.

"I'll help," she offered as she picked up a towel.

"Thanks. Oh, by the way, you got a letter today."

"A letter? For me? Where is it?"

"Right there on the table. I put it there so I wouldn't forget to tell you about it. Though I can't for the life of me imagine how I could forget a thing like a letter. We don't get too many of them things out here. I could tell from the writing there on the outside that it's from Boston," she told her.

Amanda took a seat at the table and broke the seal, tugging at the envelope's contents. She hastily scanned the brief letter, then carefully read it once more.

"It's from my Aunt Martha. She writes that she hopes I won't be reading this, that I will already be on my way home with Peter. Anyway, she tells me

346

that my cousins are both to be married this month. They are to have a double wedding. I can't say that I ever expected to hear such news!" Amanda remarked sardonically.

"Ain't your cousins anything like you, Amanda? I mean, ain't they pretty?"

"No, you certainly couldn't call either of them pretty. I can't imagine where Aunt Martha finally found them husbands, particularly at the same time! She goes on to say that she expects me to come home for the wedding," she uttered disconsolately.

"Home? But, honey, this is your home now!" her friend protested.

"Yes, I suppose I've begun to consider it home, also. In fact, I suppose I've thought of it that way for a long time now. But, just the same, I don't want to disappoint Aunt Martha any more than I already have. She'll be furious when I don't turn up with Peter. She'll be even more upset when she sees who he brought with him in my place! Anyway, I do owe her something. She was the one who raised me, after all. I feel that I should return for the wedding, if only to please her. Though I must admit that I can't look forward to returning to Boston right now."

"Of course you don't. Why, Amanda, if you could only see how much you've changed in the few short months you've been here! You don't even seem like the same scared, lonely, too-proud little gal that you were when you first came here. No sir, you've changed mightily. You're a woman now. You ain't no green girl any longer, and I don't

347

expect your aunt would approve, not from what you've already told me about her."

"I know what you're saying is true, but I still feel compelled to go all the same," Amanda said with a sigh.

"When do you need to be there?"

"Not until the last of the month."

"Well, then, if you do decide you have to go, you won't have to leave until at least next week or so," Mrs. Chambers suggested.

"Yes, I suppose I could stay at least until then. Don't worry, I fully intend to return," Amanda reassured her friend with an encouraging smile.

"I know you do," she muttered, "but things don't always turn out the way you mean for them to. I'm just afraid that if you go back there now, you'll never come back here."

"Oh, but of course I will. I would certainly have to return to see my father and my friends again," she replied warmly.

"Honey, we want you to live here from now on, not just come back now and then for a visit. You can't go putting off a decision like this forever. You're a grown woman now, and it's about time you decided where it is you're planning to spend the rest of your days. You can't keep shilly-shallying between Boston and Texas. No sir, you need to have roots, honey, just like everyone else. Why, take your father. He's a prime example. He wandered about for years, but I've never seen a man change as much as he did, and all because he got this place here and put down roots, gave his life purpose. You've got to do the same. I'm only telling you all this because I love you dearly, Amanda, I love you as if you was my own daughter," Mrs. Chambers stated, tears spilling over her lashes.

Amanda immediately went to her and gave her a comforting hug. "I feel the same way about you. I've never received as much warmth or affection as you've all shown me here. You and the others have made me feel at home, made me feel safe and secure and loved. I don't think I could ever leave any of you for good. Don't worry, now," she said, "I intend to remain in Boston for the wedding and only a few days longer, that's all. I feel that I must go, can't you see? I owe my aunt so much, even if she was never the mother I needed her to be."

"I understand how you feel, honey. But, you can't spend the rest of your life feeling like you owe your aunt something every time she wants you to do something. After all, honey, you are her dead sister's only child. I feel that she only did what she should have done in taking you in and raising you. I know you feel like you should go, but I can't say that I want you to all the same."

"Well, it's more than a week until I will have to leave. I still need to speak with Father about this. I'm quite sure that he'll feel the same way about it as you, but I'll simply have to persuade him that it's for the best."

Samuel did indeed respond the way Amanda had expected he would, but she finally made him see the sense of her decision. He agreed that she could go, but only for the wedding and a few days afterward. Then, he sternly commanded her, he wanted her to return to him immediately thereafter!

As Amanda climbed into bed that night, she realized that she was viewing the journey ahead with no small amount of trepidation and unease. She knew that she didn't wish to go, that it was something she would do out of duty and nothing else. She suddenly wondered about Luke. What would he think of her returning to Boston for a visit?

Well, I won't tell him! she told herself. He has no hold on me, no right to dictate to me about any part of my life. And yet, she mused as she began to drift into sleep, I don't know how it will be, being away from him for a few weeks. He's been such an integral force in my life ever since I arrived.

Eighteen

Buck Jones cruelly dug the points of his Spanish spurs into the smooth flanks of his horse as he rode toward the town. He and his companions, five other riders wearing equally harsh and forbidding expressions upon their rugged faces, rode through the center of Big Prairie on a cold, drizzly January afternoon. They wanted to show the townspeople that they were not afraid of anyone or anything, that they had simply come to do a job, and that they would do it no matter who or what stood in their way.

Several heads turned to stare curiously at the grim-looking riders, several people whispering amongst themselves, discussing the identity of the men. A few recognized Buck Jones as a former ranchhand of Samuel Lawrence's, and they couldn't understand why he now rode with these men. They were finally enlightened as to the identity and purpose of the six riders when someone was heard saying that these six men were the so-called "scouts" sent ahead by the sheepmen, the hired guns sent to clear the way.

Buck Jones had signed on for this job for one purpose, a personal reason of his own. He intended to exact his revenge on Sam Lawrence and his Yankee bitch of a daughter. He didn't mean to let Lawrence get away with treating him like a dog that day he had brutally whipped him, the day his back had been scarred forever. And, as for Amanda, he meant to show her that she couldn't treat him like dirt under her dainty little feet, that he was a man and she was nothing better than any other common low-life strumpet. Oh yes, he thought to himself with a malicious smile upon his thin lips, I'll have my revenge on the both of them. Taking this job with those sheepmen was merely a means to serve his own purpose.

He's heard about this job by accident when he was in a saloon over in Ft. Worth. He'd made inquiries and then been signed to the job with no questions asked. The sheepmen were hard up for men willing to risk their necks in the heart of cattle country. He personally didn't give a damn about either the men or their fool sheep, he only wanted to do what he had planned and then ride on. But, until the time was right, he'd stick it out with the others and take some pleasure in terrorizing the good folk of Big Prairie. They were nothing but psalm-singing, high and mighty hypocrites, anyway. He didn't give a damn about them or their two-bit town.

He and the other men had received orders to do whatever they thought necessary in a show of force for the benefit of the cattle ranchers. The only restriction that had been placed upon their activities was that they were forbidden to kill anyone. Beyond that, they were given free license.

All six of them were ruthless mercenaries. If they did their job and did it well, they all stood to make quite a bundle of money off this deal. None of them cared one way or the other who won the battle—sheep or cattle—but they did care about making the money they had been promised if they could convince the ranchers that it would be useless to fight against the sheep being brought into the territory.

The news had quickly spread about that the men were working for the dreaded sheepmen. People paused to stare as the six hired guns rode out of town and headed in the direction of the old Swenson homestead, where they intended to make their headquarters for the present.

The next day, Amanda and Mrs. Chambers rode into town to buy their weekly supply of food and other provisions. They were immediately apprised of the situation concerning the six hired mercenaries of the sheepmen. Amanda also happened to overhear that Buck Jones was among the six.

She nearly gasped aloud as she heard the news. So, the foul creature had dared to return. She knew that such news would make her father furious. He had warned Buck never to return, and now he was being openly defied. It would make it even worse when she discovered that Buck was now employed by the sheepmen, the hated opponents in the brewing trouble.

Oh dear, she thought as she frantically searched her mind for any solution to this new problem. Perhaps she should head straight home and tell Samuel of the situation herself. She knew that he and all of the other ranchers were planning a meeting tomorrow night, a large gathering to be held in the town's courthouse. The situation was already an explosive one.

"What's the matter? Your face went awful pale all of a sudden," Mrs. Chambers remarked after they left the general store. "I guess the bad news of those six men is enough to shake anyone up. I can tell now that there's going to be some awful bad trouble."

"Yes, I'm afraid so. You apparently didn't hear another bit of interesting information. It seems that Buck Jones is riding with those men," she told her as she climbed up on the wagon seat.

"Buck? Now, why would he want to go and sign on with a bunch of sheepmen? Well, I don't reckon he ever was any good. Me and John never did think he was a good sort to have around, but your pa needed him at the time he signed on. I'm sure your pa ain't going to like that one bit."

"No. Samuel is sure to become deadly furious," she commented worriedly as they rode out of town.

As they jostled along in the creaking wagon, Amanda felt an ever-growing fear in the pit of her stomach. Buck Jones had returned, and she knew that he might have plans for some sort of revenge, revenge for her father and the way he had treated him, and revenge for herself and her defiance of him. She found herself recalling his savage attack, and she shivered uncontrollably.

"You cold?" Mrs. Chambers asked solicitously.

"No, just a sudden chill, that's all. It looks like we may be in for some more snow, doesn't it?" she said as she glanced upward at the sky, wanting to think of anything other than Buck.

"Yep, sure does. I can see you're getting used to watching for signs of the weather, ain't you? Well, we'll be home shortly, long before it starts snowing, if it decides that's what it's going to do."

Less than two miles from the ranch, Amanda suddenly perceived a lone rider following them along the rutted road. As he began closing the gap, she gasped in shock and horror as she recognized him as Buck. She turned quickly to Mrs. Chambers and said, "Buck Jones is following us! Quick, give me the gun and see if you can't make the horses go any faster!"

"Buck? Tarnation, he sure enough can't be meaning to pay a social call on us! Here, the gun's under my feet here. Get up there!" she shouted to the horses, snapping the reins with a violence. Amanda grabbed the gun and turned back once more to ascertain if he were coming any closer. She noted that he was only a few yards away now.

"It's no use! We can't outrun him. Pull up and let's hear what he has to say!" Amanda shouted to her friend. The wagon slowly eased to a halt. Buck drew up beside Amanda, his horse wheezing heavily from its exertions.

Amanda faced him with cold determination, forcing herself to remain composed as she faced the man who had tried to rape her. She leveled the gun directly at his chest as he spoke.

"Well, now, if it ain't the high and mighty Miss Lawrence and the faithful housekeeper of the Circle L," he sneered as he kept his squinty eyes on

355

Amanda, an evil smile on his face.

"You get away from here and leave us be, Buck Jones!" demanded Mrs. Chambers.

"Shut your trap, woman! My business ain't with you, it's with Miss Lawrence here," he responded savagely. "Now, then, missy, ain't you gonna say how glad you are to see old Buck again?" he taunted maliciously.

"What do you want?" Amanda asked through clenched teeth. She held the gun steady, daring him with her blazing eyes to try something.

"I just want to have a little word with you, ma'am," he replied sarcastically, his mouth turning up into a twisted grin once more. "I got a message for your pa. I want you to tell him that Buck Jones is gonna pay him back for what he done to me."

"He treated you the way you deserved! In fact, I'd say that he was too merciful!" she snapped.

"Would you now?" he responded. "Well, now, you just tell your old pa that I'm aiming to pay him back, no matter what. You tell him that the men I'm working for now are gonna be moving their stock into this here territory, and it don't make no difference at all what he and the other ranchers hereabouts thinks about it. Me and the others aim to see to it that them sheep come in here."

"You're nothing but a coward! If you had any guts at all, you'd be telling this face to face to Sam Lawrence himself!" Mrs. Chambers suddenly retorted.

"I told you to shut up!" Buck threatened her

belligerently. "Now, I guess that's all I got to say to you, Miss Lawrence, honey. Except that I also aim to have you, to make you pay for your bad treatment of Buck here, too."

"I'll kill you before I ever let you touch me again!" Amanda warned him unwaveringly.

"Well, now, you might just have to try that then, ma'am. Because it won't do you no good, anyway. You mark my words. You and me's gonna spend a little time together real soon." He laughed derisively and whirled about, galloping quickly away, leaving a shaken and apprehensive Amanda behind.

"Don't you worry, your pa and the others will see to it that he never comes near you again," Mrs. Chambers spoke decisively as she watched him ride away, her face serious and concerned as she placed an arm about Amanda's shoulders.

"I refuse to be afraid of him!" Amanda vowed aloud. She found herself wishing that he had tried something, tried to attack her again so that she could have shot him!

"We'd best be getting on home, Amanda. You've got to tell your pa about this right away. We've got to warn him about that no-account rattlesnake!" She whipped the reins and drove the wagon homeward, her anxiety for Amanda apparent on her kindly features.

"I wish I could have killed him then," Amanda uttered before lapsing into silence.

She jumped down and went in search of her father as soon as they pulled up in front of the house. She located him out in the barn, busily forking hay into the stalls. She knew that he had been doing most of the work about the ranch himself lately, since winter had set in and most of the hands were kept busy out on the range.

"Father," she said, slowly approaching him.

"Oh, so you're back. What's on your mind, honey?" he asked, continuing with his chore.

"We heard some distressing news while we were in town," she told him hesitantly.

"You mean about those hired guns taking up out at the old Swenson place? I heard about them from one of the hands today. And that isn't all I heard. I heard that they've already begun making threats around here. Last night, several fences were cut and a barn was burned. Damnation, we've got to do something to stop them, and do it fast. That's why we called that meeting in town tomorrow night," he told her as he viciously stabbed another pile of hay.

"You didn't hear anything else about them?"

"No. What are you talking about?"

"Father, Buck Jones is one of those six men hired by the sheepmen."

"Buck Jones!" he exploded. "Hell, I never though he'd dare to show his face around here again! I told him to get out of these parts and never come back!"

"Yes, yes, I know. But, that isn't all. He followed Mrs. Chambers and me out of town today. He told me to give you a message. He said that he is going to have his revenge, that he is going to get even with you for what you did."

"What? You mean to tell me that he actually

confronted you two lone women in order to make threats to me? He's even more of a yellow-bellied skunk than I thought!" he declared angrily.

"Please," Amanda broke in, attempting to calm him down a bit. "Don't do anything rash, Father. He is a coward, and therefore I don't think he has enough courage to try anything. I think he just wants to upset us with his threats."

"Amanda," Samuel demanded at a sudden thought, closely scrutinizing her face, "did he make any threats to you?"

She started to deny it, but she knew that Mrs. Chambers would tell him if she didn't.

"Yes, he did." She grabbed his sleeve as he dropped the pitchfork with a savage oath and began to stalk out of the barn.

"Please, don't do anything! This is what he wants, don't you see? He wants you to come after him so that he can ambush you in some way, so that he can get you out alone and shoot you down in cold blood!"

"I can't let him get away with this! He can't go around issuing threats to a man's daughter and get away with it!"

"But, this isn't the way to do it!" she reasoned, feeling a glimmer of hope as she saw that he had now stopped in order to listen to her. "He's part of the band that was hired by the sheepmen, right? Well, then, he and those other men are intending to terrorize the ranchers, to show them that they won't tolerate any resistance to the sheep coming in, isn't that what you told me? Therefore, you don't need to fight against Buck, you need to fight against them all. You need to organize. The meeting tomorrow night is an excellent way to plan your strategy. You can take care of Buck as you take care of the others, can't you? You told me yourself that you've all been making progress at the other meetings you've held."

"Amanda, if you don't have the most exasperating manner of arguing a man right out of his mind!" he declared ruefully. "I guess you're right, though. I just don't know how I'm going to keep from killing that coyote until that meeting!"

"Please, promise me you won't attempt to go after him, to try and find him by yourself!" she insisted.

"All right. I promise that I won't, at least not until after that meeting. But, if he even so much as dares speak to you again, I swear I'll hunt him down and tear him to pieces!" he vowed ruthlessly.

Amanda heaved a sigh of relief, grateful that a terrible crisis had been averted, at least for the time being. She hugged him tightly, then left the barn and returned to the house. She went straight up to her room, still a bit shaken by the entire incident.

She was still planning to leave and return to Boston for her cousins' wedding at the end of the week. She certainly didn't relish the prospect, but she had decided that it was something she must do. She found herself wanting to inform Luke of her impending departure, but she didn't understand why or how.

After all, she reflected with amusement, I can't very well ride over to his ranch and simply inform him that I'm going back to Boston for a visit, and would he please tell me how he feels about it! If he still professed to love her, well, he would be waiting for her to return. It was only to be for a few weeks, anyway. She wondered if she wanted him to be waiting, and then was intrigued when she realized that the answer was yes. Somehow, and for some reason, the idea was comforting to her.

She recalled Buck Jones's face again as he had threatened her that afternoon. She prayed that the meeting of the ranchers tomorrow night would resolve something. She remembered that her father had said something about those men tearing down fences and burning barns. They were doing such things to innocent men, men who had never done anything to deserve such destructive treatment. Nothing except to make it known that they opposed the sheepmen bringing their flocks into the territory, into cattle country.

That night, another barn was burned to the ground while its owner and his family watched helplessly. No one had been able to see who had put it to the torch, but they knew all the same. Several lines of Luke's fences were cut, along with similar acts of destruction to other ranches. Things were building fast, and it was with a purposeful and grimly determined manner that each and every one of the ranchers attended the meeting in town the next night.

"Please be careful," Amanda had implored her father as he left for town that evening.

"Don't worry. We intend to put a stop to this damned thing right away! When we're all together on something like this, I know there isn't anything that can stand in our way! I'll be home late. Don't wait up for me, I'll tell you all about what took place tomorrow morning. I'm leaving John here at the house with you and his wife.''

She felt compelled to warn him once again as she watched him ride away. She had never felt so much love for him as she did at that particular moment, knowing that he rode into a dangerous, explosive situation. Dear Lord, she prayed silently, please take care of him tonight. And before she fully realized what she was doing, she had also murmured a prayer for Luke's safety as well.

There was a large turnout at the meeting that night. Many of the ranchers had brought along their ranchhands, while a few, like Samuel, had come alone. The meeting was quickly called to order, a serious intent of purpose evident as the ranchers began discussing plans to combat the threat of the hired mercenaries, the threat of the sheep. Enough had already occurred to make them fighting mad.

Samuel stood up at one point in the meeting and announced, ''Men, I think you ought to know that destroying fences and burning barns aren't the only methods they're willing to use. Yesterday afternoon, my daughter and my housekeeper were threatened by one of those men. It just so happens that it was Buck Jones, as some of you probably already know. You all know that he used to work for me, and now he's sworn to some kind of personal vengeance. Well, fine, that's a matter between him and me. But, besides that, he's working for these damned sheepmen. He sent a message through my womenfolk, and I thought you might like to be aware that the others just might try the same thing with your own women and children. I say we do something before this thing goes any farther!"

There were several shouts of agreement with his statement, and the mood of the meeting deepened even more as other ranchers stood to state their views on the situation. The meeting had been in session for nearly an hour when the door to the courthouse suddenly burst open, startling the men inside with the unexpected arrival of the six mercenaries they had been discussing.

"Well, well, looks like there's some kind of meeting going on, don't it?" one of them remarked sarcastically as he took a threatening stance near the doorway.

"Yeah, and I wonder how come we wasn't invited!" another one commented mockingly.

"I suggest you all break up this little meeting of yours, unless you're prepared to face the consequences," another one threatened. They all stood poised for action, hands near their holsters as they surveyed the crowded, smoke-filled room.

"This ain't none of your damned business!" one of the ranchers shouted in anger. "This is a private meeting, and you ain't either invited or welcome!"

"That's right. You'd better get the hell out of here if you know what's good for you," Samuel stood up to insist.

"Oh, we know what's good for us, Lawrence," Buck Jones sneered. "You shouldn't have all gone off and left your womenfolk unprotected tonight.

There might be some more barns that burn down tonight, as well as some other 'accidents.' It wasn't too smart of you all to go off and leave your homes tonight.''

"We've had enough of your threats and destruction!" Samuel declared, his furious eyes blazing directly at Buck. "We won't put up with this any longer. If you don't all get out of town tonight, we're likely to start stringing you up to the nearest tree!"

"Can't do that," one of the other hired men commented lazily. "The law can't do a damn thing about us being here. There ain't no proof that we done anything at all. Ain't likely to be none, either. We're just 'scouts' sent ahead by our bosses to make sure things are nice and settled down before they bring their sheep in here.''

"If you don't break up this little meeting of yours and get on home right away, there might be even more trouble than you bargained for," another of the men insisted.

"I'd suggest all of you get the hell out of here right now, pronto, or we'll have to drag you out of that doorway!" one of the ranchers retaliated.

"No need to get testy, now, is there?" the man beside Buck replied. "Just wanted to tell you that this here meeting ain't going to do you one bit of good. Good night, gentlemen. Hope you still have homes to go home to," he remarked sarcastically. He motioned and the others followed him back out of the courthouse.

They were outside mounting up when Samuel suddenly approached Buck.

"Buck, I'm going to get you for threatening my daughter! If you weren't such a damned coward, you'd have come to me yourself!" Samuel ground out, fists tightly clenched at his sides.

"I aim to get even with you myself, Lawrence!" Buck replied viciously, turning his back on Samuel and preparing to mount up. He'd have liked to kill the bastard right now, but the time wasn't right. Besides, there'd be too many witnesses and he'd get caught and strung up for sure.

"One last thing, Buck," Samuel told him. "I heard some talk about you today. It seems that someone heard tell that you killed a man down in San Antonio a couple of years back. Seems that you may even be wanted for murder."

"You ain't got no proof!" Buck declared, eyes shifting about nervously.

"I could sure as hell get it! Now, you leave me and mine alone, do you understand? I'll kill you if you ever come near my daughter again!"

"You're the one that's going to die, Lawrence! I'm going to kill you for what you done to me!" Buck replied savagely as he swung up into the saddle and then rode quickly away.

Samuel turned back toward the courthouse with a muttered curse. The meeting was breaking up now. Most of the men wanted to get on home and make sure their houses or barns had indeed not burned down. None of them were too worried about their womenfolk. They knew they were sure as hell far from defenseless! Every woman in these parts could shoot most as good as any man.

Luke had followed Samuel and Buck outside.

He had guessed that there was bad trouble brewing between the two. Why, he himself had felt like killing Buck when he'd heard Sam telling about his threatening Amanda. He decided that he'd better keep an eye on things, for Amanda's sake anyway. He watched as Samuel rode away alone into the night, then he mounted up and began to follow, far enough behind to avoid detection, the new-fallen snow on the frozen ground helping to muffle the hoofbeats of his horse.

Amanda saw her father ride past the house. She had waited up for him, anxious to hear how the meeting had progressed, unable to even consider sleeping. John and Mrs. Chambers had retired back to the kitchen, where they too were waiting for her father's return. She flew into the front hallway and threw on her cloak, hurrying outside and across the yard to the barn. She scurried inside and found Samuel unsaddling his horse. She wanted to speak with him alone, before the Chambers began plying him with their questions, also.

"How did the meeting go, Father?" she asked as she came toward him.

"I thought you'd already be in bed by now," he remarked. "The meeting went pretty well, all things considered. Those hired henchmen broke things up for a while, but they left without any further trouble. I spoke to Buck Jones. I don't think he'll be bothering you anymore," he told her grimly.

"I was only concerned for you when it came to him. I'm afraid he actually means to kill you if he gets the chance. Oh, I hope you and the other ranchers will be able to do something about all of this. I'm worried about you, and about the others," she commented, shuddering involuntarily as she recalled Buck's savage expression.

"We mean to do something all right. We've got some plans worked out. We're going to form patrols of our own to catch those cowardly varmints. We can't murder them in cold blood, but we mean to outwit them, to catch them in the act and then call in a United States Marshal. If not, well, we won't worry about that just yet."

"I hope your plans work. In the meantime, why don't you come on inside the house and let me fix you some hot coffee. You look half frozen," she told him.

"He's gonna be stiff as a board before too long, Amanda, honey," came a grating voice from the shadows.

"Buck," Amanda whispered fearfully. She watched as he stepped into the light, his face well illuminated now by the glow of the lamp.

Samuel attempted to go for his gun, which was still on his saddle, but Buck saw his intent and said, "I wouldn't do that, Lawrence! I'm aiming to fill you full of holes soon enough! After I've had my fill of your fancy little gal here." He gazed at Amanda, the lustful intent apparent in his wide eyes.

"Over my dead body!" Samuel roared. He lunged for Buck, but wasn't quick enough. Buck pulled the trigger of his pistol shooting Samuel in the left shoulder. Amanda screamed at the noise of the loud report, and watched in horror as her father slumped to the ground, blood seeping from the ugly wound in his flesh.

"You killed him!" she screamed accusingly at Buck.

"He ain't dead yet, but he soon will be. I'm gonna finish him off just as soon as I finish with you, you little bitch! I'm gonna show you what you fought so hard against. I aim to make you scream and beg for mercy before I get through with you!" he uttered menacingly as he came toward her.

"No! You'll have to kill me first!" she shrieked as he reached her, grabbing her cruelly by her bright hair, forcing her face upward toward his own.

"Now, I'll have a little fun with the high and mighty Yankee bitch! Yes sir, I'm gonna make her beg me for mercy. I'll show her that she ain't any better than any other two-bit whore! If she's real good, well, then, I may keep her alive for a while longer to enjoy her some more!" he jeered, bringing his lips crashing savagely down upon her own.

Amanda screamed deep in her throat, squirming and beating at him with all her strength, but she was powerless to escape his cruel embrace. She again screamed her outrage deep in her throat as his hands roamed ruthlessly over her body. He cruelly pinched her breasts and attempted to rip the clothes from her body as the two of them struggled together. Dear Lord, she prayed, please help me! Please don't let Samuel die! Just when she thought she would faint dead away with the sheer horror of it all, she heard a familiar voice.

"Get your filthy hands off her, you damned, low-down bastard!"

Buck widened his eyes in astonishment, momentarily stunned as he saw Luke in the doorway of the barn, a shotgun pointed directly at him. He maintained his vicious hold upon the still-struggling Amanda, using her unwilling body as a shield.

"Go ahead and shoot, Cameron!" he taunted, making Amanda cry out in pain as he twisted her arm behind her back.

"You stinking coward, let go of her and face me like a man!" Luke ground out, the murderous gleam in his eyes nearly unnerving Buck.

"Get out of my way! Me and the little gal is gonna ride out of here, and you ain't gonna be able to do a damn thing to stop us! Now, either you get your carcass out of the way, or I'll put a bullet in her pretty little head right now!" Buck threatened, the pistol pointing directly at Amanda's temple.

"Shoot him!" Amanda screamed hysterically. "For heaven's sake, shoot him! He's going to kill Samuel if you don't!"

Luke appeared to hesitate for the space of a moment.

"Don't listen to her! Now, get out of the way or she gets it!" Buck repeated. He watched in silent satisfaction as Luke began to lower the shotgun, his face staring straight ahead in what appeared to be resignation.

Damn! he thought as he lowered the gun. He

couldn't shoot a shotgun in the direction of Amanda. Didn't she know that it would kill her, too? He'd have to play along for now, think of some way to overpower Buck without endangering his Amanda.

"That's right. Just let it fall to the ground there. Now, kick it on over here," Buck ordered. Luke did as he said, sliding the gun across the hard-packed dirt of the barn floor.

"You and me are gonna be going away together after all, missy," he hissed in Amanda's ear. "But first, I'm gonna do what I came here to do. I'm gonna kill your pa!"

"No! Dear God, please don't kill him! I'll do anything you say!" she begged him, striving to see her father through her tears.

"Shut up!" Buck commanded. Amanda gazed helplessly across at Luke, who appeared to be concentrating on a spot somewhere past her head. She screamed again as Buck pointed his pistol at Samuel's head where he still lay upon the cold ground, bleeding profusely from his gaping wound.

In the split second when Buck lost reason, when he sought to place revenge above personal safety, Luke made his move. He dropped low to the ground, withdrawing his long, sharp-edged knife from inside his coat, all in one continuous motion. He threw it with an expertise learned many years ago, and it found its target.

Buck gasped in shock and pain as the knife was buried in his chest clear up to the hilt. He attempted to speak once more, staggered, and fell heavily to the ground, his features hideously frozen in death.

Amanda watched in horrible fascination as Buck collapsed to the ground. She then flew to Samuel's side, assuring herself that he was still alive and breathing, though his pulse was very faint.

"You've got to go for the doctor, Luke! I'm afraid he'll die if you don't get the doctor right away!" she declared, still in shock from the terrifying events of the past few minutes.

As she spoke, John and Mrs. Chambers appeared in the doorway. Mrs. Chambers flew to Amanda's side as John assisted Luke in lifting the unconscious Samuel. They gently and carefully carried him inside the house and placed him on the sofa in the parlor.

"Don't you worry none, honey," Mrs. Chambers assured Amanda as they entered the parlor. "He's tough. He'll pull through."

Luke stood and headed for the doorway, detained for a moment by Amanda's words.

"Please ride as swiftly as you can! And, Luke," she said softly as he turned to leave, the tears beginning to spill over her lashes now as the numbness began to wear off, "thank you." She turned back to Samuel as Luke left the house. John and Mrs. Chambers hurried out to the kitchen to fetch water and bandages.

Oh, hurry, Luke, please hurry, she silently entreated him as she knelt on the floor beside her father. She couldn't face losing Samuel, not when she had only just found him, only come to love

371

him such a short time ago.

She had resolutely averted her eyes from the grotesque body of Buck as she had been led from the barn by Mrs. Chambers. She would never forget what had occurred, the events would be forever imprinted on her mind. The memory of Samuel falling as he was shot, of Buck's face as he forced himself upon her, the memory of him as he died. But, most of all, she would remember that it was Luke who had arrived in time to save them. Luke who had saved the life of her father and herself. Luke who had looked ready to murder Buck when he had seen him attacking her.

She recalled that it was Luke who had always seemed to come to her rescue when she needed him the most. When the horses had nearly run her down in town, when the cyclone had struck, when the renegade Comanches had captured her. It was Luke who had taken care of the matter of the gossip about her.

She knew in that instant, she knew what she had been fighting all along, what had always been inevitable between them. She realized that she loved Luke Cameron, that she had for quite a while. She had been a complete fool not to face it sooner. For, what had been so terrible about the thought of loving him? She couldn't understand now why she had run away from it for so long.

It had taken a terrible, drastic incident such as this to finally open her eyes, to finally force her to admit her love for him. Now, she knew that it was indeed the overpowering, consuming emotion she had heard described. She knew that she would have died herself if Buck had killed Luke instead.

And she hugged the security and knowledge of Luke's love for her to herself. She knew that he must surely love her in return. Why else was he always willing to risk his own life for hers? Why else would he have been so patient for so long? Yes, she thought, I love him. I always will. Nothing can ever change that now, I cannot go back. I would be nothing without his love, and I am glad and relieved and hopeful all at the same time.

As she knelt on the floor beside her father, trying to stop the bleeding of his shoulder with a torn strip from her petticoat, she prayed that her love would indeed be returned, that Luke would still want her for his wife. She thought she would die if he did not. She never wanted to be away from him again.

She resolved to keep her startling revelation a personal, cherished secret for the moment. After all, she thought as she gazed lovingly at her father, there will be plenty of time for that later. For now, she would have to spend all her time praying that her father would live, attempting to keep him alive, hoping that Luke would return with the doctor in time.

Nineteen

Amanda awakened to see the bright shafts of sunlight drifting through the calico curtains of her bedroom window. She stretched contentedly, then reluctantly crawled out of the warm bed and began to dress for breakfast.

Samuel's shoulder was healing very nicely now, and she would be leaving for Boston tomorrow morning. She could not have proceeded with her plans for the trip if her father hadn't begun recovering so quickly. She splashed water on her face and dried it with the thick towel hanging beside the washstand.

She reflected once again on the events of that terrible night as she dressed. It had been nearly a week now since Buck Jones had attempted to kill her father and then rape her, since Luke had arrived in time to prevent it.

She had waited anxiously in the parlor with her father and the Chambers, nearly sick with relief when she saw Luke return with the doctor almost two hours later. Dr. Stephens had worked over Samuel in silent concentration for some time, finally extracting the bullet, then pronouncing him weak but out of danger, the bleeding now

374

under control.

Amanda recalled that she had warmly thanked the good doctor again and again, then insisted that he remain for the remainder of the night. He had readily agreed to her suggestion and had been shown upstairs to a room by Mrs. Chambers.

Once her father had been taken care of, Amanda had finally collapsed from the effects of the terrifying ordeal. She still couldn't remember much about what happened after that. Mrs. Chambers had told her that Luke had caught her, lifting her in his strong arms as easily as if she were a child, then carried her upstairs to her bedroom. Mrs. Chambers had followed, had heard Amanda repeatedly murmuring her gratitude to Luke, then had watched as Amanda had dropped off into a sleep of deep exhaustion. After that, she told Amanda it seemed to her that Luke was angry or upset about something, quietly leaving the room and shutting the door gently behind him.

Amanda had listened to this recital with mixed emotions. She only hoped that Luke was not angry with her for some unknown reason. She could think of nothing that would have caused such a troubled look upon his face, save for his concern for herself and her father.

As she now donned her petticoats and dress, she thought once again that it was not like Luke to stay away this past week. She was beginning to think that he had indeed became incensed with her for some reason. She had hoped to see him after that night, to speak with him, to ascertain if he still felt about her the way he had been professing to almost from the first moment she had arrived in Texas. She needed to be reassured of his love for her, of his desire to marry her. But, he had not come.

She was puzzled, angry, hurt, and disappointed by his absence. She had desperately wanted, needed to reveal her love for him, had wanted to share her beloved secret with the object of that love.

And, tomorrow morning, she would be returning to Boston. She certainly did not want to go, but knew it was her duty. She had postponed leaving until the last minute, hoping that Luke would arrive to persuade her that he couldn't bear to be away from her even for a few weeks, that he still loved her and wanted to marry her right away. But then, she reminded herself again, he doesn't even know yet that I love him in return.

Oh, why hadn't he come? She had wanted him to come, had needed for him to come. She didn't know how she would be able to endure leaving tomorrow, how she could return to Boston without speaking to him first. She grew increasingly fearful that he had changed his mind, that perhaps something had occurred the other night which had revealed that he didn't truly love her at all.

She tortured herself with such thoughts for days following the ordeal of that night. Last night had been the first time she had been able to sleep without interruption from nightmares, nightmares in which Luke rode away from her forever. She had fallen asleep exhausted, exhausted from the draining emotions she had experienced this past week.

As she now descended the stairs, she thought again that something else of consequence had come about as a result of that night. The sheepmen would now be forced to look elsewhere for the grazing land they desired. They had been threatened with the charge of being accessories to Buck's attempted murder of Samuel. They would never dare to bring their stock into the area now, for fear of serious reprisal for Buck's actions. The mercenaries had left the territory in great haste.

Amanda entered the parlor, where Samuel was reclining upon the sofa, fidgeting disagreeably in an effort to find a more comfortable position for his wounded shoulder. He glanced up when he saw his daughter enter the room.

"I'm damned sick and tired of being treated like an invalid in my own house!' he grumbled. "I feel all right now, and I can't see the sense in my lying here useless like a sick calf!"

"Father, you know what Dr. Stephens told you. You won't be permitted outside until tomorrow at the very earliest. I'm afraid you'll simply have to tolerate your confinement a little while longer," she replied soothingly.

"Women!" he commented in mock disgust as she took a seat opposite him.

"You men don't know what you'd do without us!" she retorted with a wicked smile.

"Are you all packed yet?" he asked, changing the subject abruptly.

"Almost. I must say, though," she remarked

with a heavy sigh, "I certainly don't look forward to this particular visit. You can be assured that I will return here as soon as I can possibly get away!"

"I hope so. To tell the truth, though, I still don't think you should be making this trip at all."

"Why do you say that? Is it because you're still afraid that I won't return? You know I can't stay away from here, Father. This is my home now. I've come to appreciate it more and more each day. I don't think that I could ever stay away permanently."

"I sure hope not. But, it seems to me that something's been bothering you this week, something other than the prospect of returning to visit your aunt and cousins. I don't know what it is, but I think I have an idea. Could it possibly have anything to do with Luke Cameron?" he probed delicately. He knew that she'd been mooning over that young man all week long! Why else would she have been behaving this way? The problem was, would she admit it to herself? She could be awfully stubborn and willful when she chose to be.

"Whatever gave you such an idea?" she responded casually, hastily averting her eyes from his searching gaze.

"Just the way you've been acting lately. You're certain there's nothing you want to tell me?" he insisted, narrowing his eyes as he scrutinized her expression.

"No. There's nothing wrong," she denied. She suddenly rose to her feet and briskly approached the doorway, turning to say, "I still have some packing to do, remember? And I haven't had my breakfast yet, either. I'll see you later." She quickly escaped from the room.

She's hiding something all right, Samuel thought to himself. Maybe she is in love with Cameron after all. He suddenly realized that he approved. Yes, he decided, that particular young man will make her a fine husband, a fine husband indeed. He's the only one I've ever seen that just might be able to handle a headstrong, spirited girl like Amanda. Sparks would certainly fly when the two of them finally married, but he realized that they would be happy all the same.

At a sudden thought, a slight frown marred his features. If his daughter did marry Cameron, he'd have to stop fighting him about the fencing matter. He couldn't very well carry on a feud with his own son-in-law. But then, he thought with a sigh, things had slowed down considerably since the trouble with the sheepmen. There was no longer so much hostility between the fencers and non-fencers. Because the ranchers had been forced to work together against the threat of the sheep, no one seemed inclined to renew the old trouble now. No, Samuel told himself, you'll just have to get used to the idea.

Not that he still didn't believe in an open range. But, he now realized that Amanda had been right, that fencing was inevitable. He'd hold off giving in until he couldn't put it off any longer, though. He'd been beat and there was nothing left to do about it except to give in gracefully, which was something he'd never learned to do. But, he would try. He'd have to if his own daughter ended up married to a fencer!

Amanda finished her breakfast and carried the dishes back to the kitchen. Mrs. Chambers looked up from the sink where she was cleaning vegetables and remarked, "You didn't have to do that, honey. Seeing as how this is your last day here and all, you ought to be taking it easy. We're sure gonna miss you something fierce!"

"I'm going to miss all of you, too. But, I suppose that this trip is really for the best. It will give me time to think about my life, to view it more objectively than if I remained here," she replied, sinking into a chair at the table, leaning her chin on her hands as she heaved another sigh.

"You ain't looking forward to this trip, are you?" Mrs. Chambers asked as she put aside her work and came to take a seat beside Amanda.

"No, not really. But, I'll do my duty and go anyway. Aunt Martha would be furious with me if I did not come."

"Maybe so, but I can tell that there's something worrying you. What is it? Is there anything I can do to help?" she offered, her features revealing her concern.

"Oh, it's nothing that a few weeks away shouldn't cure. There isn't really anything that anyone can do. My absence should take care of everything, should settle things one way or the other," she commented sadly.

"You mean about you and Luke, don't you?" the older woman probed gently.

"Yes," Amanda answered without thinking,

then straightened up and asked, "How did you know?"

"I ain't blind, honey! Anyone can see that you two are in love! The question is, what are you going to do about it?"

"I don't know if there's anything to be done. I'm not sure that he even loves me any longer," Amanda responded, tears beginning to well in her bright eyes.

"Why, it's as plain as the nose on your face that he loves you!" Mrs. Chambers declared indignantly. "You love him, don't you?"

"Yes, I do. But, he doesn't know it yet. And it doesn't look as if I'll ever have a chance to tell him, at least not until I return from Boston. I'm so afraid he won't be waiting for me when I return!" she cried, a few tears beginning to spill over her lashes now as she briskly dashed them away.

"Then, why don't you send him word to come see you before you leave? Or you could even ride on over there now and talk to him. Tarnation, gal, if you want the man, go and get him!" she suggested decisively.

"Oh, I couldn't do such a thing! I'm not sure he returns my regard, and I would simply die if he responded negatively! Oh, I don't know what I'm going to do, except to go on to Boston and give us both time to think about the whole, confusing situation!" she stated with exasperation.

"Well, there ain't no one that can make up your mind for you, Amanda. You've got to do what you think is best. But, if I was you, I sure as shooting wouldn't go running off to Boston without getting things settled! You're going to be plumb miserable if you don't!'' she declared.

"I know, I know. I don't understand why he hasn't at least stopped by this week, why he's stayed away when I needed for him to come so very much!''

"I suppose he's got his reasons. Knowing Luke, it sure isn't because he's changed his mind about you! Why, he's crazy about you, child! You can be sure he's got good reasons for not coming around right now,'' Mrs. Chambers reasoned.

"I don't know. But, then, it really doesn't matter, does it? I'm still leaving on the morning stage tomorrow for Boston, aren't I? If I don't see him before then, well, it will all just have to wait until I return in a few weeks' time, won't it? Now,'' she said, rising to her feet, "I still have packing to do.'' She smiled pathetically and swept from the room and up the stairs.

Maybe my absence will indeed be for the best, she thought for the hundredth time. Maybe it will reveal to Luke his true feelings for me. She was still hopeful that he would hear of her impending departure, that he would ride over to inform her masterfully that he couldn't tolerate the few weeks without her. It's only for a few short weeks, she told herself again. Why then did she feel as if it would be years?

The next morning, Amanda bade a tearful farewell to her father. She hugged him tightly, careful not to cause him extra pain in his wounded shoulder, then resolutely climbed up on the wagon seat beside John and Mrs. Chambers, who would drive her to town and see her off on the stage. Samuel was still forbidden to do any traveling, so he waved to his daughter until she had finally disappeared from sight.

Things would be mighty lonesome without her for the next few weeks, he told himself. It had been one of the toughest things he'd ever done to bid her goodbye. He was still a bit apprehensive that Martha would find some way to dissuade Amanda from returning to him, a prospect he knew he couldn't face. She was much too dear to him now.

Amanda rode in silence all the way to Big Prairie, her beautiful countenance a study in both despair and misery. She said goodbye to her two friends as she boarded the stage, pausing to clasp Mrs. Chambers to her once more before taking a seat inside the coach. After desperately searching the street for any sign of Luke, she heaved a sigh of heavy melancholy, managing a slight smile as she waved and the stage pulled out of town. She reflected sorrowfully that it was taking her away, away from both the man and the country she had come to love so very much.

Luke rode with silent determination toward the Circle L, thoughts and plans jumbling together in his mind. He had given Amanda plenty of time now to make up her mind once and for all. Hell, he'd only stayed away this week to force her to finally make a decision. He knew that he hadn't been mistaken the other night when he thought he had seen something in her eyes that had nothing to do with either fear or relief or gratitude. Damn it, he didn't want her gratitude! That's what had gotten him so riled up when he'd carried her upstairs that night. He'd been as patient and understanding as any man could be, but now his patience had worn out!

He had it all planned; he would go to her father first, do the honorable thing in asking for his daughter's hand in marriage. Then, with or without Sam's blessing, he'd go find Amanda and demand an answer to his proposal of marriage. If she dared to refuse him, well, he'd have to force her to change her stubborn little mind! He knew that she loved him, whether she was willing to face it or not. The time had come to settle things between them. Damn, she sure enough couldn't claim that he was rushing her any!

Reaching the Lawrence ranch, he slowed his mount to a walk and approached the house. He started to dismount and climb the steps to the porch, when he spotted Samuel standing out near the corral, apparently viewing some new horses. Turning his horse, he purposefully rode toward him.

"Sam," he started, dismounting now, "I've got something to say to you, and I want you to keep quiet and hear me out."

"Luke. What's this all about?" Samuel demanded mildly, gazing once more at the horses in the corral.

"First off, I've come to ask for your daughter's hand in marriage," he announced with determination.

"But, Luke—" Samuel began.

384

"Don't interrupt me! Now, listen, I want to marry your daughter, do you hear? I aim to do so with or without your approval, so you might as well know that right now. I love her, Sam, and I know she loves me. I just wanted to be able to tell her that I did the right thing and came to you first. Now, will you give us your blessing, or are you going to be ornery about it?" he demanded, crossing his arms across his muscular chest.

"Luke, shut your damn trap and give me a chance to talk!" Samuel responded irritably. "I don't disapprove, you young idiot! But, you're too late. Amanda isn't here."

"Not here? What the hell do you mean?" he burst out.

"That's right. She left for Boston on the morning stage."

Twenty

Amanda rode uncomfortably along in the bouncing, rocking stagecoach, endeavoring to staunch the flow of fresh tears as she was taken farther and farther away from the man she loved. She had only recently realized the extent of her feelings for him, and she was loath to leave him, if only for this brief visit to Boston. She felt as if her heart were breaking, still afraid that he no longer loved her, that he would find another woman before she returned. No! she thought fiercely. That simply cannot happen! Why, oh why didn't he come to bid me goodbye? Surely he must have heard about my impending departure? Perhaps Mrs. Chambers was right, perhaps she should have sent him word. But, she couldn't do such a thing, she knew she couldn't bear his refusal of her love.

"Honey, you look plumb awful! There anything I can do to help?" the woman sitting opposite her inquired.

"No, thank you. There's nothing anyone can do." She dabbed at her eyes, sniffed, and raised the window flap in order to gaze disconsolately out at the passing countryside. The air was cold and damp, and she surmised that there would be a storm before too long.

She allowed the flap to drop back into place and stole a glance at her fellow passengers. The other woman was traveling to Ft. Worth with her husband. The two of them had boarded the stage at the town before Big Prairie. She reflected that they were complete opposites; the woman kindly and rather stout, the man somewhat surly and thin as a rail. The woman chattered incessantly about their nice little farm and their seven children back home. Amanda listened politely, answering in occasional monosyllables as the woman continued talking.

Oh, how can I be doing this? she lamented as she clutched the sides of the window for support. How can I be leaving the man I love without first telling him how I feel? How can I be sure I haven't already lost him?

She sat in abject misery, drawing her warmly lined cloak more closely about her body. At this rate, she mused, it will take several days to reach Ft. Worth. Not that she was in any hurry to reach Boston. It was merely that she wished to get the entire ordeal over with and then return to Texas. If only Luke hadn't changed his mind by then.

They must have been traveling for close to three hours when Amanda suddenly realized that the stagecoach was beginning to slow to a gradual halt. She glanced quickly across at the other two passengers, but the two of them had miraculously managed to fall asleep, despite all the swaying and weaving of the coach as it made its way over the rough road.

Before she fully realized what was happening, the door of the coach was wrenched open, and she found herself face to face with none other than Luke Cameron.

"Luke!" she exclaimed in astonishment.

"Damn it, woman, get out of that coach!" he ordered in a commanding tone.

"What on earth do you think you're doing?" she demanded, striving to hide the incredible joy she experienced in seeing him here.

"Shut up and do as I say!" he commanded angrily.

"I will do no such thing when you speak to me in such a manner!" she retorted with spirit, wondering why in heaven's name he appeared to be so furious with her.

"You sure as hell will!" he answered tightly, reaching for her with his powerful arms, plucking her none too gently from her seat and dragging her out of the coach with him.

"Where do you think you're taking that poor young woman?" the woman passenger demanded. She and her husband had been rudely awakened by the sound of Luke's angry resonant voice.

"This here is my wife, ma'am. She's run away once too often, and I aim to see that it doesn't happen again," Luke lied convincingly.

"He's lying!" Amanda protested as Luke threw her up on to his horse's back. He swiftly mounted behind her, imprisoning her struggling body in his iron grip.

"You ought to be downright ashamed of yourself!" the woman spoke with stern disapproval toward Amanda. "Why, I wouldn't blame your poor husband there for taking a switch to you!" Her husband nodded his silent agreement at his wife's indignant words.

"Let me go!" she demanded of Luke, twisting and squirming upon the horse's back.

"See you later, Pete," Luke called to the driver, before turning his horse back along the road. The driver cracked the whip and the stagecoach continued on its way in the opposite direction.

"What do you think you're doing?" Amanda demanded, still struggling futilely to escape his tight grasp on her waist. Smiling secretly to herself, she kept thinking that he had come after her, that he must still love her! "What about my baggage?"

"I told Pete to send it on back when they get to Ft. Worth," he tersely replied, then raged at her, "What in the blue blazes did you think you were doing?" He glared at her with his stormy blue eyes as she turned her head about to face him. "Whatever gave you such a fool notion? You could at least have told me that you were planning to run away!"

"I was not running away!" she informed him. "I was simply returning to Boston for a visit. I had every intention of returning to Texas!"

"Yeah, your father told me about your little 'visit.' But, I knew I damn sure couldn't trust you to come back! I knew I couldn't let you go on back to Boston, because that old goat of an aunt of yours would find some way to put the idea into your head that you should stay there and not come back here at all! Well, I'm telling you here and now that you aren't ever going to get back there if I have anything to do with it!"

"You have no right to tell me what I can or cannot do!" she responded, still secretly delighting at the masterful approach he had used in order to stop her from leaving. She was dangerously close to melting against him, to passionately declaring her love for him. No, she told herself, I want to be sure of how he feels first. I want to make sure of the reason he came after me.

"I damn sure have. I love you, woman, and I'm going to marry you. I know you love me, whether you'll admit it or not. I'm tired of all this waiting! I've given you more than enough time to come to your senses about us, and I'm sure as hell not going to wait any longer! I warned you once that my patience would run out, that I would come and get you and make you marry me. Well, it's happened!"

"Stop shouting at me!" she commanded imperiously, her eyes lighting up with amusement, feeling overwhelming joy at his words.

"I'll shout at you if I want to! Now, are you going to marry me willingly, or do I have to drag you to the altar?"

"You haven't even bothered to ask me how I feel. Oh no, Luke Cameron, you've simply been ordering me about, as usual. Wouldn't you rather have an answer from my own lips?" she insisted, the humor now apparent to him in her shining eyes.

"Well, then, go ahead if it makes you happy," he

agreed, unable to resist grinning now as his anger began to wear off.

"It makes me happy," she responded. "I love you, Luke. I didn't fully realize it until the night you saved my father's life, the night you saved us from Buck. I realized then that I've loved you for a long time. I was simply unwilling to face it. But not any longer. I love you and I want to marry you."

"You're sure? You're sure you don't just feel gratitude toward me, that you're not confusing it with love?" he demanded.

"Now, that's a question coming from you!" she retorted. "You've been telling me for months now that I loved you! Well, I do! It was tearing me apart to even think of returning to Boston. Don't you understand? I've wanted to see you ever since that night, wanted to tell you how I felt. But you didn't come. I didn't know what to do. I decided to go ahead with my visit, knowing that you'd be waiting for me when I returned if you still cared. Why didn't you come to at least say goodbye?"

"I wanted to give you time to make up your mind, once and for all. I didn't even know you were going. I'd have waited, Amanda, but I'd have been ready to wring your little neck when you returned!" he replied with an engaging grin.

"Well, I'm glad it's finally settled. I never knew I could be so happy, Luke. I love you so very much," she told him with bright and happy eyes, then said, "Where are we going?"

"To Big Prairie."

"But, aren't you taking me home?" she asked

in confusion.

"Nope. I'm taking you into town to marry me."

"What! But, Luke, I'm not ready! I don't have a dress, my father and my friends—" she protested.

"Amanda, there's been enough talk for a while," he declared authoritatively as he slowed the horse to a halt, dismounted, then forcibly pulled her down beside him.

"What are we doing?" she asked in puzzlement.

"You and me are going to get 'properly engaged' before we get legally married. Now, shut up and obey me for a change!" he commanded as he grasped her tightly in his arms and proceeded to kiss her most thoroughly, taking her breath away as she melted in his fervent embrace. Finally allowed a moment to speak, she uttered, "Oh, Luke. I just thought of something. What about Aunt Martha? What will she think when I don't arrive for my cousins' wedding?"

"To hell with Aunt Martha! We'll send her word when our first child is born!" he remarked exuberantly, silencing her once again as he hungrily took her lips with his own.

Epilogue

"Oh, Luke," Amanda remarked with a happy sigh as she faced her new husband in the privacy of their bedroom, "I can't believe all of this is happening, that I am now actually a married woman! Everything happened so quickly, you didn't give me any time to think!"

"The hell I didn't!" Luke responded with a mischievous grin and a determined sparkle in his eyes as he slowly approached her where she had turned her back to peer out the window, still attired in the traveling suit which had also served as her wedding gown that day. "I told you all along that you'd be mine, that you were going to marry me sooner or later! I gave you plenty of warning, Mrs. Cameron!" he insisted with a meaningful smile as he turned her about and gathered her up in his strong, muscular arms. He carried her toward the large, four-poster bed, as Amanda laughingly protested.

"Luke! Can't you even have the decency to wait until I have changed into my nightclothes?"

"Nope," he answered blithely, placing his precious burden on the edge of the bed. Kneeling before her, he began to unfasten the buttons of her jacket.

"Luke," Amanda repeated, growing a bit nervous as she realized how very inexperienced and naîve she actually was, "Luke, I—I don't want to disappoint you. I don't want you to ever regret your decision to marry me. I don't want you to be sorry that you love me," she told him in a rather tremulous voice.

"Amanda, darling," Luke replied, continuing with his pleasant task as he gazed up into her concerned face with a sudden intensity, "I love you more than anything in this world, and I swear here and now that you could never disappoint me. Nothing can ever change the fact that I love you, that you're my wife." He tenderly smiled his encouragement as he drew off her jacket and now concentrated his efforts on her blouse.

Amanda put out a rather shaky hand in order to stop him, saying, "Are you certain that you're not regretting anything, Luke? Are you sure you did the right thing in marrying me? How on earth is my poor father going to react when he receives that message we sent him?" she suddenly asked, her beautiful face a study in consternation. "Perhaps we should have waited until we could have arranged a proper church wedding and all."

"Amanda," he said, rising to his feet and drawing her to her feet in front of him, "I wouldn't have waited a moment longer! I've waited long enough, woman! I love you, you love me, and that's all there is to it. We were meant to be together. I didn't marry your father, I married you! Now, will you please stop all this worrying and concentrate on your new husband?'' he commanded good-naturedly.

Amanda couldn't refrain from laughing at his obvious impatience, and she wrapped her arms about his neck and pulled him closer for her kiss.

Soon, the two of them were completely undressed, standing naked before the other's loving, admiring gaze. Amanda blushed profusely as Luke remarked in a soft voice full of something akin to awe, "You're the most beautiful thing I've ever seen." He pulled her down with him upon the bed and lay back upon the pillows, taking her lips with his once more as they reclined together in the spacious bed.

"Oh, Luke," Amanda whispered fervently, thinking how very wonderful it was to be in love, to be loved, to be desired and wanted as much as this. All of her earlier fears and anxieties now seemed to vanish, and she surrendered herself completely to the affections of her new husband. She gasped aloud as Luke's warm lips began traveling tenderly from her lips to her slender neck, then lower to her full breasts. His hands caressed her soft curves with a growing impatience, though he tried to keep his own flaming desires in check in order not to frighten his new wife.

His lips fastened upon one of her taut nipples, and she moaned softly as his tongue lazily circled that delectable point, as his hands now gently parted her trembling thighs and began caressing her intimately at the most private part of her womanhood. She felt her thighs opening further, felt the searing fires deep within her making her yearn toward something still unknown, yearn for some unfamiliar fulfillment. She gasped again as his lips now continued their delightful torment on her other naked breast, and she slowly ran her slender fingers through his thick hair as she began to experience the full throes of a woman's passion, the passion of a true woman and not a young girl.

Luke's loving mouth returned to her parted lips, and he whispered fiery words of love against those lips as he kissed her again and again, as he felt himself about to burst with the overwhelming force of his desire. Able to wait no longer, he positioned himself above her, still kissing her with a fierce demand. He judged that she was indeed ready to receive him, so he carefully plunged into her inviting softness, stilling her first, initial cry with his lips.

Amanda soon felt the sharp pain gradually subsiding, to be replaced by a totally wonderful, rapturous sensation as Luke began to slowly move within her, as he soon brought her with him to a blazing, all-consuming fulfillment.

Afterward, as they lay entwined in the soft afterglow of loving, Amanda said, "Oh, Luke, it was so—so very wonderful! I never dreamt it could be this way, I never knew I could experience such indescribable feelings."

"I know, darling, I know," Luke quietly replied, smoothing the bright strands of hair from her flushed, beautiful face. "It was the same way for me. I promise you that it will only get better, too!" he declared with a soft chuckle.

"I love you so very much," Amanda said, drawing herself upward and leaning upon her elbow as she looked down into his beloved face, noting with immense pleasure that she was indeed married to a handsome, fine man.

"I love you, Amanda," he responded in a deep, husky voice as he gazed intensely into her shining green eyes, then once more pulled her closer for his gentle kiss.

There would be many more such delights shared between them, but none would be quite as precious as this, the first, tender portrayal of their everlasting love.

HISTORICAL ROMANCE AT ITS BEST!
by Carol Finch

MIDNIGHT FIRES (1487, $3.75)

Danielle should have been terrified when the handsome American captain who rescued her told her they were now in the midst of war. Instead, all she could think of was how his tight breeches clung to his thighs, and the way his eyes dwelled on her full red lips!

PASSION'S VIXEN (1402, $3.75)

Mesmerized by his sensuous smile, Melissa melted in the powerful arms of her captor—the awesome woodsman, Jack. Having teased him with her charms, she'd leave him in the morning and pray he wouldn't betray her love . . .

RAPTURE'S DREAM (1037, $3.50)

By day Gabrielle is the insufferable waif who tests Dane Hampton's patience; by night she is the phantom lover who brings him to the heights of ecstasy!

ENDLESS PASSION (1155, $3.50)

Brianna was a sensuous temptress who longed for the fires of everlasting love. But Seth Donovan's heart was as cold as ice . . . until her lips burned his with the flames of desire!

DAWN'S DESIRE (1340, $3.50)

Kathryn never dreamed that the tall handsome stranger was wise to her trickery and would steal her innocence—and her heart. And when he captured her lips in one long, luscious kiss, he knew he'd make her his forever . . . in the light of DAWN'S DESIRE.

Available wherever paperbacks are sold, or order direct from the Publisher. Send cover price plus 50¢ per copy for mailing and handling to Zebra Books, 475 Park Avenue South, New York, N.Y. 10016. DO NOT SEND CASH.

THE BEST IN HISTORICAL ROMANCE
By Elaine Barbieri

AMBER FIRE   (848, $3.50)
Ever since she met the dark and sensual Stephen, Melanie's
senses throbbed with a longing that seared her veins.
Stephen was the one man who could fulfill such desire—
and the one man she vowed never to see again!

AMBER TREASURE   (1201, $3.50)
When Melanie's husband fell ill she had no one to turn to
but the arrogant Captain Randolph. Mesmerized by her
provocative curves and exotic eyes, the bold virile man
promised to help—but only if Melanie would pay his price!

AMBER PASSION   (1501, $3.95)
Awakening from drugged sleep, the auburn-haired beauty
Melanie found herself wrenched from the side of her beloved Captain Randolph—their ship captured. But even as
her cruel jailor's eyes raked hungrily over her voluptuous
curves, she vowed loyalty to her one true love.

SWEET TORMENT   (1385, $3.75)
Though Morgana tried to avoid the arrogant dark-haired
stranger on the long sea voyage to Mexico City, his slow,
contemptuous smile refused to be ignored. With one taunting look he sent her blood rushing, and with one searing kiss
he set her body aflame . . .

LOVE'S FIERY JEWEL   (1128, $3.75)
Lovely Amethyst was on the verge of womanhood, and no
one knew it better than the devilishly handsome Captain
Damien Staith. She ached with passion for him but vowed
never to give her heart.

*Available wherever paperbacks are sold, or order direct
from the Publisher. Send cover price plus 50¢ per copy for
mailing and handling to Zebra Books, 475 Park Avenue
South, New York, N.Y. 10016. DO NOT SEND CASH.*

THE BEST IN HISTORICAL ROMANCE
by Sylvie F. Sommerfield

BETRAY NOT MY PASSION   (1466, $3.95)

The handsome sea captain's hands felt like fire against the raven-haired Elana's flesh. Before giving her heart she wanted his pledge of everlasting love. But as the prisoner of his fierce desire she only prayed . . . BETRAY NOT MY PASSION.

TAME MY WILD HEART   (1351, $3.95)

Fires of love surged through Clay's blood the moment his blue eyes locked with the violet of Sabrina's. He held her bound against him with iron-hard arms, claiming her honeysweet mouth with his own. He had bought her, he would use her, but he'd never love her until she whispered . . . TAME MY WILD HEART!

CHERISH ME, EMBRACE ME   (1199, $3.75)

Lovely, raven-haired Abby vowed she'd never let a Yankee run her plantation or her life. But once she felt the exquisite ecstasy of Alexander's demanding lips, she desired only him!

TAMARA'S ECSTASY   (998, $3.50)

Tamara knew it was foolish to give her heart to a sailor. But she was a victim of her own desire. Lost in a sea of passion, she ached for his magic touch — and would do anything for it!

DEANNA'S DESIRE   (906, $3.50)

Amidst the storm of the American Revolution, Matt and Deanna meet — and fall in love. And bound by passion, they risk everything to keep that love alive!

Available wherever paperbacks are sold, or order direct from the Publisher. Send cover price plus 50¢ per copy for mailing and handling to Zebra Books, 475 Park Avenue South, New York, N.Y. 10016. DO NOT SEND CASH.